III I IIIIIIIII II III II IIIII IIIIIIII III III

✍ **W9-BYZ-144**

A PENGUIN BOOK

The Yellow Eyes of Crocodiles

Katherine Pancol is one of France's best known contemporary authors. *The Yellow Eyes of Crocodiles* was a huge success in France, where it won the Prix de Maison de la Presse for best novel of the year. To date, it has sold some 2.4 million copies in thirty languages. Katherine was born in Morocco, grew up in France, taught school in Switzerland, and worked as a journalist at *Paris-Match*. She lived in New York City from 1980 to 1990 and has published two sequels to *The Yellow Eyes of Crocodiles*: *La Valse lente des tortues* (2008) and *Les Écureuils de Central Park sont tristes le lundi* (2010).

The Yellow Eyes of Crocodiles

KATHERINE PANCOL

Translated by
WILLIAM RODARMOR *and*
HELEN DICKINSON

PENGUIN BOOKS

PENGUIN BOOKS

Published by the Penguin Group
Penguin Group (USA) LLC
375 Hudson Street
New York, New York 10014

USA | Canada | UK | Ireland | Australia | New Zealand | India | South Africa | China
penguin.com
A Penguin Random House Company

First published in Penguin Books 2013

A Pamela Dorman / Penguin Book

Copyright © 2006 by Editions Albin Michel - Paris
Translation copyright © 2013 by William Rodarmor and Helen Dickinson
Penguin supports copyright. Copyright fuels creativity, encourages diverse voices, pro-
motes free speech, and creates a vibrant culture. Thank you for buying an authorized
edition of this book and for complying with copyright laws by not reproducing, scanning,
or distributing any part of it in any form without permission. You are supporting writers
and allowing Penguin to continue to publish books for every reader.

Originally published in France by Editions Albin Michel - Paris in 2006
as *Les yeux jaunes des crocodiles*

This edition is an abridgement of the original French-language work.

LIBRARY OF CONGRESS CATALOGING-IN-PUBLICATION DATA
Pancol, Katherine, 1949–
[Yeux Jaunes des Crocodiles. English]
The Yellow Eyes of Crocodiles / Katherine Pancol ;
translated by William Rodarmor and Helen Dickinson.
pages cm
ISBN 978-0-14-312155-8 (pbk.)
1. French fiction—21st century—Translations into English.
I. Rodarmor, William, translator. II. Dickinson, Helen, 1967– translator. III. Title.
PQ2676.A4684Y4813 2013
843'.914—dc23   2013028077

Printed in the United States of America
1   3   5   7   9   10   8   6   4   2

Set in ITC Galliard   •   Designed by Elke Sigal
Map Illustration by Virginia Norey

This is a work of fiction. Names, characters, places, and incidents either are the product of
the author's imagination or are used fictitiously, and any resemblance to actual persons,
living or dead, businesses, companies, events, or locales is entirely coincidental.

To Charlotte,

To Clément,

My loves . . .

Acknowledgments

♦   ♦   ♦

J am thrilled that *The Yellow Eyes of Crocodiles*, which has been such an unexpected best seller in France and elsewhere, is finally available in English. The book has been translated into twenty-nine other languages, and American readers will now have a chance to sink their teeth in it.

Many wonderful people have helped bring this project to fruition. I particularly want to thank Solène Chabanais, foreign rights director at Albin Michel in Paris, and publisher Pamela Dorman and her associates Kiki Koroshetz and Julie Miesionczek at Penguin Books in New York. Thanks also to Patricia Connelly, who worked tirelessly to generate interest in an American translation of *Crocodiles*. She was the first good fairy to wave her magic wand over the book in the United States.

Finally, a special thank-you goes to translator William Rodarmor, who has been bravely wrestling *Crocodiles* for more than a year. William did more than translate the book. He immersed himself in the French text, characters, and plot, and then re-created them in English. This is the work of a true writer, for which I am enormously grateful.

As always, heartfelt thanks go to my friends and family for their support. To my long-suffering children Charlotte and Clément, I really do love you more than crocodiles.

—*Katherine Pancol*
Paris, 2013

The Yellow Eyes of Crocodiles

♦　♦　♦

Casamia, *
Marcel & Josiane's apartment

Cimetière +
de Montmartre !

Moulin
Rouge

Arc de Triomphe

Gare
St. Lazarre

Parc Monceau

Opéra

Champs - Élysées

Cap

Rue L
de Ri

Hôtel George V *

* Givenchy

Tour Eiffel

Quai d'Orsay
Rue de
l'université

Ave. Bosquet

Musée
d'Orsay

Champ de
Mars

Tour
Montparnasse

Blvd. Ke

* Joséphine Cortès's home
Courbevoie

Palais des
Congrès

*
Quartier
de la Défense

Arc de Triomphe

Bois de
Boulogne

* Dupin
family home

Cimetière
de
Montparnasse

Sacré-Cœur

Funiculaire

Paris

✳ Location in
The Yellow Eyes of Crocodiles

Porte
St-Denis

Rue St-Maur

Ritz Hotel

Palais-Royal

Place de la République

Musée du
Louvre

Conciergerie

Notre-Dame

de
Cité

✳ Bastille

...ermain

Île
St-Louis

Jardin du
Luxembourg

Gare
de Lyon

Panthéon

Jardin des
Plantes

Seine

Rue
Claude-Bernard

Bvd. de Port-Royal

PART I

♦ ♦ ♦

Chapter 1

♦ ♦ ♦

*J*oséphine gasped and dropped the vegetable peeler. The blade had slipped on the potato and cut a long gash into her wrist. There was blood everywhere. She looked at her blue veins, the red streak, the white sink, the yellow plastic colander where the peeled white potatoes lay glistening. Leaning against the sink, she began to cry.

I need to cry, Joséphine thought. *I don't know why. There are plenty of reasons, and this one is as good as any.* She grabbed a dishcloth and pressed it on the cut. *I'm going to turn into a fountain of tears, a fountain of blood, a fountain of sighs. I'm going to let myself die.*

That was one solution. Just die, without a word. Fade away, like a lamp slowly dimming.

I'll die standing here at the sink, she thought, then corrected herself. *No one dies standing up. You die lying down, or with your head in the oven, or in the bathtub.* She'd read in some newspaper that the most common form of suicide for women was jumping out the window. For men it was hanging. Jump out the window?

She could never do that. But to weep as she bled to death, unable to tell whether the liquid streaming out of her was red or white? To fall slowly asleep . . .

Joséphine took a deep breath, adjusted the dish towel on her wrist, choked back her tears, and stared at her reflection in the window.

Get on with it, she told herself, *peel those potatoes. You can think about all that other stuff later.*

It was a late May morning, and the thermometer read 82 degrees in the shade. Out on their fifth-floor balcony, Joséphine's husband was playing chess against himself. Antoine worked hard to make it realistic, switching sides and picking up his pipe as he went. He hunched over the chessboard, blew out some smoke, lifted a piece, sucked on the pipe, put the piece back, exhaled again, picked up the piece again and moved it, shaking his head as he put the pipe down and went to sit in the other chair.

He was of average height, with brown hair and eyes. The crease of his trousers was razor sharp, and his shoes looked as if they had just come out of the box. His rolled-up shirtsleeves revealed slim forearms and wrists, and his nails had the luster of a professional manicure. He looked nicely groomed, the type of man you'd put in a furniture catalog to inspire confidence in the merchandise's quality.

Suddenly Antoine moved a piece, and a smile lit up his face.

"Checkmate!" he announced to his imaginary partner. "Poor guy, you're screwed. Never saw it coming!"

He got up, stretched, and decided to make himself a little drink, even though it wasn't quite that time yet.

He usually had a cocktail around six, while watching his favorite TV quiz show, *Questions pour un champion*. It had become a daily ritual, and he looked forward to it. Missing the show put him in a foul mood. Every evening he would tell himself that he should try out for the show himself, but things never went any further than that. He knew that he'd have to get past the elimination rounds, and something about the words *elimination rounds* chagrined him. He lifted the lid of the ice bucket, carefully dropped a couple of cubes into a glass, and poured himself a Martini Bianco.

Antoine followed the exact same routine every day. Up with the kids at seven, breakfast of whole-wheat toast, apricot jam with salted butter, and freshly squeezed orange juice. Next came a thirty-minute workout: back, stomach, abs, quads. Then the newspapers, which his daughters took turns bringing him before they left for school. This was followed by a careful perusal of the help-wanted ads and mailing his résumé when he saw something interesting. Then a shower and shave, selecting his clothes for the day, and finally, a game of chess.

Choosing what to wear was his morning's most challenging moment. He had lost a sense of how to dress. Relaxed weekend style, or a suit and tie? One day he had thrown on some sweatpants, and his older daughter wasn't pleased when he picked her up at school.

"Aren't you working, Dad?" asked Hortense. "Are you still on vacation? I like it when you're all handsome in an elegant jacket, a nice shirt and tie. Don't ever pick me up from school in sweats again, okay?" Seeing Antoine's face fall, she softened her tone. "I'm saying this for your own good, so you'll always be the world's most handsome dad."

Hortense was right. People looked at him differently when he was well dressed.

The game of chess over, Antoine watered the plants along the edge of the balcony, picked off dead leaves, pruned the older branches, spritzed the new buds with water, turned the soil with a spoon, and added fertilizer. He was quite concerned about the white camellia. He spoke to it, took extra time caring for it, lovingly wiping each leaf.

It had been the same thing every morning for the past year. On this particular morning, however, he'd fallen behind schedule. The chess game had been unusually tough, and he had to be careful not to lose track of time.

"Watch it, Tonio, don't let yourself go," he said aloud. "Get your act together." He'd gotten used to talking to himself, and he frowned at the self-admonition. He decided to let the plants go for the day.

He passed the kitchen where Joséphine was peeling potatoes. Seeing her from behind, he again noted that she was putting on weight. When they first moved to this suburban apartment building just outside Paris, she was tall and slim. Their daughters were so little, barely reached the edge of the sink. Those were the days. He would lift up her sweater, put his hands on her breasts, and whisper things in her ear until she gave in. Jo would bend down over the bed, smoothing the bedspread all the while so it wouldn't get rumpled.

Sundays, she would cook. Pots would be steaming on the stove, dishcloths drying on the oven door handle. Chocolate for a mousse would be melting in a double boiler. The kids shelled nuts or gave themselves mustaches with chocolate-covered fingers, then licked them off with the tips of their tongues.

Tenderly, Antoine and Joséphine had watched the girls grow up. Every couple of months they would measure them, penciling their heights on the wall, which was soon laddered with little lines followed by dates and the girls' names, Hortense and Zoé.

Every time Antoine leaned against the kitchen door frame, he felt overwhelmed by sadness and loss, remembering a time when life had seemed to smile on him. This never happened in the bedroom or the living room; always in the kitchen, which had once held all his joy.

A book by the medievalist Georges Duby lay open on the kitchen table. Antoine bent down to read the title: *The Knight, the Lady, and the Priest.* Joséphine had been working in the kitchen. What used to be a hobby was now paying the bills. She was a historian specializing in twelfth-century women at the Centre National de la Recherche Scientifique, the famed CNRS. Antoine used to make fun of her work, saying, with a laugh, "My wife is passionate about history, but only the twelfth century." Now the twelfth century was putting food on the table.

Antoine cleared his throat to attract Joséphine's attention. Her hair was piled on top of her head, held in place with a pencil.

"I'm going for a walk," he said.

"Are you coming back for lunch?"

"I don't know. Don't wait for me."

"Why didn't you tell me earlier?"

Antoine hated confrontation. He probably should have simply left, shouting, "I'm going out, be back in a bit." That would have been all. He'd be in the stairway and she'd be in the kitchen with her questions stuck in her throat. He'd find some excuse when he came back. Because he always came back.

"Did you read the help-wanted ads?"

"Yeah. Nothing interesting today."

"There's always work for someone who wants to work."

Work, sure, but I'm not about to take just any old job, he thought.

"I know what you're going to say, Jo."

"You know it, but you don't do a thing to make it happen. You could take whatever job you can, to help make ends meet."

He could have continued the conversation on his own. He knew it by heart: lifeguard, groundskeeper at a tennis club, night watchman, gas station attendant. But all he could think was that the phrase "making ends meet" had a funny ring.

"That's right, smile!" she spat, glaring at him. "I must sound like a broken record, always talking about money. Monsieur doesn't want to tire himself out for just any old job. Monsieur wants respect! And right now, all monsieur wants to do is run off to his manicurist!"

"What are you talking about, Joséphine?"

"You know exactly what I'm talking about!"

Now Joséphine was facing him, shoulders back, the dishcloth around her wrist. She was daring him.

"If you mean Mylène . . ."

"Yes, I mean Mylène."

"Jo, stop! This is going to end badly."

Who could have told her? They didn't know many people in the building, but when there's gossip to be had, friends appear out of nowhere. Someone must have seen him going into Mylène's place, two streets away.

Joséphine was still facing him.

"You're going to have lunch together. She'll have made you a quiche and a green salad—a light meal because, afterward, *she* at least has to go back to work." Joséphine ground her teeth as she said "she." "Then you'll have a little nap. She'll draw the curtains, take off her clothes, and drop them on the floor. Then she'll climb under the white cotton lace bedspread with you."

Antonio listened to her in shock. Mylène *did* have a white lace bedspread. How could Joséphine know that?

"Have you been to her apartment?"

Joséphine laughed harshly and tightened the dishcloth with her free hand. "So I was right. White lace goes with everything!"

"Jo, stop it!"

"Stop what?"

"Stop imagining things that aren't true."

"Are you saying she doesn't have a lace bedspread?"

"You really should be writing novels. You've got the imagination for it."

He was suddenly furious. He couldn't stand his wife anymore. He couldn't stand her schoolmarm tone, her slouch, her shapeless, colorless clothes, her bad skin, her limp brown hair. Everything about her reeked of effort and thrift.

"I'm leaving before this conversation gets out of hand."

"So you *are* going to see her? At least have the courage to tell the truth, since you don't have enough balls to look for work, you lazy bastard!"

That last word did it. He felt anger pounding at his temples. He spit out his words so that he wouldn't have to take them back:

"Okay, fine! I meet her at her place every day at twelve thirty. She heats up a pizza and we eat it in her bed under the white lace bedspread. After brushing away the crumbs, I take off her bra, which is also white lace, and I kiss her all over. Happy now? I warned you not to push me."

"If you go to her now, don't bother coming back. Pack your bags. It'll be no great loss."

He stumbled to their bedroom like a sleepwalker. He pulled a big suitcase out from under the bed, lifted it onto the quilt, and piled his T-shirts, socks, and underwear in it. The red wheeled suitcase was from his days at Gunman & Co., the American hunting gun manufacturer. He had been their director of European sales for ten years, taking wealthy clients on hunting trips to Africa, Asia, and South America to the bush, the savannah, or the pampas. In those days he was the white man with the year-round tan who had drinks with his clients, some of the wealthiest people on earth. That was when he started calling himself Tonio. Tonio Cortès. It was more masculine, more accomplished-sounding, than Antoine. He had to be those men's equal. He was proud of being able to hang out with these people without really being one of them.

He earned a big salary and got a generous year-end bonus, a

good retirement plan, and plenty of vacation days. He used to love coming home to Courbevoie. His apartment building had been built in the 1990s for young professionals like himself who couldn't yet afford to live in Paris proper. They lurked just on the other side of the Seine, waiting for their chance to move to the elegant neighborhoods of the capital whose lights they could see at night, glittering like a neon birthday cake.

Antoine never said when he was coming back from a trip. He would just push open the front door and wait a second in the entry before whistling briefly to announce his arrival. Joséphine was always absorbed in her books. The two little girls would be in their bathrobes, one in pink, the other in blue. Hortense, the pretty, sassy one, had him wrapped around her little finger. And then there was soft, chubby Zoé, who loved to eat. He'd sweep them up in his arms, repeating, "My darlings, my little darlings." That was the ritual. Sometimes he'd feel a pang of guilt, recalling the sex he'd had just the night before. Antoine would hug them all the tighter, and the images of the other women faded. Then he'd launch into his hero act. He made up stories about hunting expeditions, including one about a wounded lion he finished off with a knife, an antelope he caught with a lasso, and a crocodile he knocked unconscious.

Then a year ago Gunman & Co. was bought out, and he was fired. That's the way it is with Americans, he explained to Joséphine. One day you're the head of sales with a three-window office, the next you're filing for unemployment. For a while, his generous severance package allowed him to keep up the house payments, pay for school fees, language-immersion trips, the upkeep of the car, and ski vacations. Antoine had been philosophical about it all. He was fine. He wasn't the first person this had happened to, and he wasn't just anybody: he would soon find work.

But after going through his savings, he felt his self-confidence wavering. Especially at night. He would wake at three in the morning, quietly get up, pour himself a whiskey in the living room, and turn on the TV. In the past, he had always felt very strong and insightful. When he first heard about the buyout and possible layoffs, he told himself that his ten years at Gunman & Co. would certainly count for something. He was the first person to be laid off.

Antoine sat on the bed and stared at the tips of his shoes. Looking for work was so depressing. He was just another number on a form. He sometimes thought about this while he was in Mylène's arms. He told her what he would do the day he became his own boss. "With my experience, you know what I'd do?" he would ask her, and Mylène listened. She believed in him. She had some money that her parents had left her, but he hadn't accepted any yet. He hoped to find a more impressive partner to join him on his next adventure.

Antoine first met Mylène Corbier when he took Hortense to the hairdresser on her twelfth birthday. Mylène was so impressed with the girl's composure that she gave her a free manicure. Hortense held out her hands as if she were granting a special privilege. Ever since that day, whenever she had time, Mylène polished Hortense's nails, and the girl would leave the salon admiring her reflection in her shiny nails.

Mylène made Antoine feel good. She was petite, blond, vivacious, and had deliciously creamy skin. Her slight reserve and shyness made him feel at ease and confident.

The red suitcase was soon packed. Yet Antoine dawdled, pretending to look for a pair of cufflinks and cursing loudly in the hope that Joséphine would hear him and come into the bedroom and beg him to stay.

He went into the hallway and stopped at the kitchen door. He waited, still hoping that she would take that step toward him, would try to piece together a reconciliation. But she didn't budge.

"Well, that's it," he said. "I'm leaving."

"Fine. You can keep your keys. You'll probably have forgotten things and you'll need to come back for them. Warn me so I can plan to be out. It's better that way."

"Good idea. I'll keep them. What will you tell the girls?"

"I don't know. I haven't thought about it."

"I'd rather be here when you speak with them."

She turned off the faucet and leaned against the sink.

"I'll tell them the truth, if you don't mind. I don't feel like lying."

"But what will you tell them?"

"The truth. That Daddy doesn't have a job anymore. That Daddy isn't feeling well and needs some time to himself, so he left."

"Time to himself?" Antoine repeated the phrase, comforted by it. "That's good, it's not too final. It's good."

Leaning against the door frame was a mistake. He was suddenly overcome by a wave of nostalgia.

"Just go, Antoine. There's nothing left to say. Please go!"

Joséphine was staring at the floor. He followed her gaze to the suitcase at his feet. He'd completely forgotten about it.

"Okay then. Good-bye. If you need to reach me . . ."

"You can call. Or I'll leave a message for you at Mylène's salon. She'll always know where to find you, won't she?"

"What about the plants?"

"The plants? Who gives a damn about them? Fuck the plants!"

"Jo, please! Don't get so worked up. I can stay if you want."

She gave him a withering look. He shrugged, picked up his bag, and headed for the door. And then he was gone.

Gripping the edge of the sink, Joséphine began to sob so hard that her body shook. First she cried about the void Antoine would be leaving in her life after sixteen years of living together, the first man she ever slept with, the father of her two children. Then she cried thinking about the girls. Never again would they feel completely secure, knowing that they had a mother and a father who loved each other. And finally, there was the fear of being alone. Antoine had always been in charge of the finances, the taxes, and the mortgage. He chose their cars, and he unclogged the sink. She could always count on him. She just looked after the house and the girls' schooling.

The phone rang, jolting her out of her despair.

"Jo, is that you, darling?"

It was Iris, her older sister, whose upbeat, seductive voice got to Joséphine every time.

♦ ♦ ♦

Iris Dupin was a tall, slim forty-four-year-old with long black hair that flowed over her shoulders like a wedding veil. She was named for her intense blue eyes.

In her twenties, Iris had been the kind of woman who set trends while seducing every man she met. Iris didn't live or breathe like other mortals: she reigned.

After college, she left for New York and enrolled in the film program at Columbia University. At the end of each year, the two best graduating students were given the funding to make a thirty-minute short feature. Iris had been one of the two. The other student was her boyfriend, Gabor Minar, a tall, shaggy Hungarian. They kissed backstage at the awards ceremony. Iris's future in movies was as plain to see as the Hollywood sign.

And then out of the blue, she gave it all up. She was thirty years old, had just come back from the Sundance Festival, where she'd won some prize. She was planning a full-length feature that was already getting buzz. She even had a verbal commitment from a producer. And without any explanation—Iris never explained anything—she flew back to France and got married.

It was incredibly traditional: the white veil, the church, and the priest. The place was packed, and everyone was holding their breath, half expecting Iris to whip off her dress and, stark naked, shout, "Just kidding!" Like in a movie.

Nothing of the sort happened.

The groom was a certain Philippe Dupin, who looked quite handsome in his morning suit. Iris said they had met on a flight to Paris, and that it had been love at first sight.

Philippe was an uptight corporate lawyer full of his own convictions. He'd started an international business practice and formed alliances with big law firms in Paris, Milan, New York, and London. He was successful and couldn't understand why everyone else wasn't as well. "Where there's a will there's a way," he liked to say.

At the wedding, he looked at his wife's assembled friends with nonchalance mixed with disdain. His mother and father wore a slightly superior look that suggested they thought their son was marrying beneath him.

The wedding guests left in disgust. Iris was no fun anymore. She was no longer the stuff of dreams. She had become horribly normal, and in Iris, this was in very poor taste. Some of her friends disappeared forever. She was off her pedestal, her crown rolling away.

In time, Iris wound up embracing the same verities Philippe held so dear: a child behaved and did well in school; a husband made money and provided for his family; a wife took care of the household and made her husband proud. Iris didn't work. "There are women who suffer an embarrassment of leisure and those who master it," she said. "Doing nothing is an art."

I must live on another planet, Joséphine thought, listening as her sister's semiautomatic chatter was now coming around to the topic of Antoine's unemployment.

"Tell me, has your husband found anything yet?" was Iris's favorite line, to which Joséphine would always say no.

"Really? So he still hasn't worked that out? How can he afford to be picky, with such modest talent?"

Everything about my sister is phony, Joséphine thought, wedging the phone against her shoulder.

"Is anything wrong?" asked Iris. "You sound odd."

"I have a cold."

"Poor thing. Don't forget, we're having dinner with Mother tomorrow night."

"Tomorrow night?" She had completely forgotten.

Every other Tuesday, Iris had Henriette over for dinner. Antoine tried, with some success, to avoid those dinners. He couldn't stand Philippe, who seemed to need to give Antoine footnotes when he spoke to him. He didn't like Iris either. When she talked to him, she made him feel like a wad of chewing gum stuck to the sole of her stilettos.

"Yes, darling," Iris said. "Are you bringing Antoine, or is he vanishing into thin air again?"

Joséphine smiled sadly. That was one way of putting it. "He's not coming."

"We'll have to make up another excuse for him. You know Mother doesn't like his not being there."

"To be honest, I really don't care."

"You let Antoine get away with way too much. I would have thrown him out ages ago. Anyway, you're never going to change, poor darling."

For as long as she could remember, Joséphine had been the brainy one, the one who spent hours in the library doing research papers along with the other losers and misfits.

She aced exams but couldn't be trusted with eyeliner. She

twisted her ankle going down the stairs because her nose was in a book by Montesquieu. She even plugged in the toaster under running water because she was listening to France Culture on the radio. Jo stayed up till all hours studying while her seductive older sister went out and conquered the world.

When Joséphine passed a prestigious teaching exam, Henriette asked about her plans. "Where is that going to get you, dear? To be target practice for high school kids out in the slums?"

When she finished her dissertation—"France's Economic and Social Development in the Eleventh and Twelfth Centuries"—and got her doctorate, her mother had again reacted with cynicism. "Poor darling, you'd do far better writing about Richard the Lionheart's sex life. That at least would interest people. A film could be made out of it, or a TV series. You could pay me back for all those years I slaved to pay for your studies."

Henriette had been hard on Joséphine from the very beginning. Joséphine's father used to say, affably and even lovingly, "The stork must have picked the wrong house." This feeble joke earned him so many cold looks from his wife that he eventually stopped saying it.

One evening, the night before Bastille Day, he put his hand to his chest, said, "It's a little too soon to set off the fireworks," and died. Joséphine and Iris were ten and fourteen. The funeral was magnificent. Looking tragic and majestic, Henriette orchestrated the whole thing, down to the smallest detail: the big sprays of white flowers strewn on the coffin, the funeral march. She copied Jackie Kennedy's black veil and had the girls kiss the casket before it was lowered into the ground.

How could I have spent nine months in the womb of that woman people claim is my mother? Joséphine wondered.

The day Joséphine was hired by the Centre National de la Recherche Scientifique, she'd raced to the phone to tell her mother and sister. Neither understood what there was to be excited about. Recruited by a research center? Why would she want to work in that black hole?

Joséphine had to face facts: she just didn't interest her family. Marrying Antoine had been the only thing they understood. For once they had reacted positively. She had stopped being a mystery to them and become an ordinary woman, a wife, a mother.

But Henriette and Iris were soon disappointed: Antoine wasn't going to cut it. His hair was too neat (no charm), his socks too short (no style), his paycheck too small (and paid by Americans!), and he sold hunting guns—how degrading! Worst of all, he had a sweating problem. Antoine's in-laws intimidated him, and when he was with them—and only them—he would perspire profusely.

Jo suddenly felt a wave of pity for Antoine. Forgetting that she had resolved not to talk about him, she blurted: "I just kicked him out, Iris. I—"

"You kicked him out? For good?"

"You don't know what it's been like to live with an unemployed husband. I feel so guilty about my job. I've been hiding my work behind pots and pans and potato peelings."

Joséphine looked at the kitchen table. *I should clear it off before the girls get home from school for lunch.* She'd done the math: eating at home was cheaper than in the cafeteria.

"After a year, I would think you'd have gotten used to it," said Iris.

"That's a shitty thing to say!"

"I'm sorry, darling. But you seemed to be coping. So what are you going to do now?"

"I'll keep working, of course, but I need to find something else, too. Give French lessons, grammar, spelling, whatever."

"You know, there's a need for that. There are so many dunces out there these days! Starting with your nephew Alexandre. He came home from school yesterday with a 38 in dictation. A 38! You should have seen Philippe. I thought he was going to have a stroke!"

Jo couldn't help but smile: the highly accomplished Philippe Dupin, father of a dunce.

Alex was ten, the same age as Zoé. At family gatherings the two would hide under the table and talk, looking serious and concentrated, or go off to build models together.

"Do the girls know?"

"Not yet."

"How will you explain it to them?"

Joséphine didn't answer. She picked at the edge of the Formica table with her nail until she'd accumulated a little black ball of grease, then flicked it across the kitchen.

"Jo, darling, I'm here." Iris's voice had turned soothing, and it made Joséphine feel like crying again. "You know I'm always here for you, and I'll never let you down. I love you as much as I love myself, and that's saying something!"

Jo laughed.

The doorbell rang.

"That must be the girls. I have to go, but please, not a word about this tomorrow night. I really don't want to be the main topic of the evening!"

"All right, Jo, I promise. And don't forget: Cric and Croc clobbered the big Cruc creeping up to crunch them."

It was the old tongue twister they used to recite as kids. Joséphine laughed again and hung up. She wiped her hands, took off her apron, pulled the pencil out of her hair, and ran to the door. Hortense breezed in without looking at her mother.

"Is Dad here? I got a terrific grade in creative writing! And I got it from that bitch Madame Ruffon."

"Hortense, please! That's your French teacher you're talking about."

"Well, she *is* a bitch."

Hortense put down her backpack and took off her coat with the studied grace of a debutante removing her wrap before the ball.

"Don't I get a kiss?" asked Joséphine, annoyed at sounding needy.

Hortense offered her soft, peachy cheek, pulling a mass of copper-colored hair away from her neck.

"I can't believe how hot it is! Positively tropical, as Dad would say."

Hortense went to the stove and lifted the lid off one of the pots. At fourteen, she already had the look and manners of a woman. Her pale complexion contrasted with her coppery hair and her large green eyes.

Just then, ten-year-old Zoé burst into the kitchen and wrapped her arms around Joséphine's legs.

"Mommy! Guess what? Max Barthillet invited me over to watch *Peter Pan* at his place! His dad gave him the DVD. Can I go after school? I don't have any homework for tomorrow. Okay, Mommy? Can I?"

Zoé looked at her mother, her face full of trust and love.

"Of course you can, sweetie."

"Max Barthillet?" scoffed Hortense. "You're letting her go to his house? He's my age and he's still in Zoé's class! He keeps being held back. He's probably going to end up being a butcher or a plumber."

"There's no shame in being a butcher or a plumber, Hortense."

"Whatever. There's just something weird about him, with his pants two sizes too large, his studded belts, and his long hair. I don't think we should be seen with him."

"I don't care if he is a plumber," cried Zoé. "I think Max is handsome. You'll let me go, right, Mommy? What's for lunch? I'm starving!"

"Scrambled eggs and potatoes."

"Yum! Can I break the yolk? I can squoosh it all together and add tons of ketchup."

Zoé still had her babyish looks: round cheeks, chubby arms, freckles, and deep dimples in her cheeks. She loved to give people loud kisses, and hug them tight.

"Max is only inviting you over because he wants to get to me," Hortense declared as she nibbled a French fry with her perfect white teeth.

"That's not true. He invited me! Nobody else! So there!"

"Little brat! Max Barthillet. Let him dream. He doesn't stand a chance. I want a big strong man, like Marlon Brando."

"Who's Marion Bardo, Mommy?"

"A famous American actor, sweetie."

"Marlon Brando! He's so handsome. He was in *A Streetcar Named Desire*. Dad took me to see it. He says it's a masterpiece."

"Yum! The fries are great, Mommy."

"Isn't Dad here? Did he have a meeting?" Hortense wiped her mouth.

This was the moment Joséphine was dreading. She met her elder daughter's inquisitive gaze, then looked at Zoé, who was absorbed in dipping her fries in her egg yolk, which was splattered with ketchup.

Antoine had never wanted to speak about money troubles or worries about the future in front of the girls. Hortense's unconditional love for him was all that remained of his past glory. She used to help him unpack when he got back from a trip. She admired his suits, felt the quality of his shirts, smoothed his ties. Joséphine sometimes felt they had their own private world, that their family was divided into two castes: Antoine and Hortense were the nobility, and she and Zoé were the vassals.

Hortense was looking at Joséphine, her question hanging in the air.

"He left."

"When is he coming back?"

"He's not. I mean not here."

Zoé raised her head.

"He left for good?" she asked, her mouth open in shock.

"Yes."

"He won't be my dad anymore?"

"Of course he will. He just won't be living here with us."

Joséphine was terrified. She wished she could turn back the clock to her first days of motherhood, the first vacations the four of them took together, the first fight, the first making-up, the first awkward silence that became more and more silence. When did the charming man she'd married become Tonio Cortès, her tired, irritable, unemployed husband?

Zoé started to cry. Joséphine hugged her, burying her face in Zoé's soft curls. Above all, she knew she couldn't cry. She had to show them that she wasn't afraid. She told them all the things the psychology books suggest parents say to kids in the event of a separation. Daddy loves Mommy. Mommy loves Daddy. Daddy and Mommy love Hortense and Zoé, but they can't live together anymore, so Daddy and Mommy are separating. But Daddy will always love Hortense and Zoé, always be there for them, always. Joséphine felt she was talking about people she'd never met.

"I have a hunch he didn't go very far," Hortense declared in a tight voice.

"He'll come back, right, Mommy?" Zoé asked.

"Don't say such stupid things, Zoé. Daddy left, and he's not coming back. What I don't understand is, why her? Why that *bimbo*?" She'd spat the word out with disgust, and Joséphine realized that Hortense knew about Mylène—had probably known long before she had.

"Problem is, now we're going to be really poor. I hope he'll give us a little money. He has to, doesn't he?"

"Listen, Hortense . . ." Joséphine stopped, realizing that Zoé shouldn't hear the rest.

"Go blow your nose and wash your face, sweetie," she said, gently pushing her younger daughter out of the kitchen.

Zoé sniffled as she trudged off.

When she was out of earshot, Jo turned to Hortense. "How come you know about . . . that woman?"

"Get with it, Mom. The whole neighborhood knows. I was embarrassed for you. I wondered how you could possibly not know."

"Actually, I did know about it. I just turned a blind eye."

That wasn't true. Joséphine had only learned about Mylène the night before. Shirley, her neighbor and friend across the hall, told her.

"How did you find out?" Jo asked Hortense.

Her daughter stared at her coldly.

"Open your eyes, Mom! Look at how you dress. What your hair looks like! You've let yourself go. It's no surprise he went looking elsewhere! You need to leave the Middle Ages and come live in this century."

Hortense was using the same amused disdain as Antoine. Joséphine closed her eyes, covered her ears with her hands, and started to yell.

"Hortense! I forbid you to speak to me with that tone! We've been scraping by because of me, and because of the Middle Ages!

Whether you like it or not. Don't you ever look at me like that! I'm, I'm your mother, and I . . . you have to . . . respect me!"

She was babbling, she felt ridiculous. And now a new fear gripped her: she would never be able to bring up her two daughters. She didn't have any authority, she was in way over her head.

Joséphine opened her eyes, and found Hortense looking at her oddly. She felt ashamed at having lost her temper. *I can't get everything mixed up*, she thought. *They have only me to look to now, and I have to set an example.*

Chapter 2

♦ ♦ ♦

The girls walked back to school after lunch, and Joséphine went over to Shirley's. She already couldn't bear to be alone.

Shirley's son Gary opened the door. He was a year older than Hortense and in the same class, but she refused to walk home with him, claiming he was utterly uncool.

"Why aren't you in school? Hortense already left."

"We don't have the same schedule. On Mondays I get back at two thirty." He paused. "Want to see what I invented? Check this out."

He showed her two Tampax, and somehow was able to make them swing in circles with one hand without their strings getting tangled.

"I've invented environmentally friendly perpetual motion."

Jo watched in amazement. "It reminds me of those Chinese yo-yos," she finally said. "Is your mother here?"

"She's in the kitchen, cleaning up."

"Aren't you helping?"

"She doesn't want me to. She'd rather I invent things."

"Well, good luck with that."

Shirley was at the kitchen sink, rinsing plates and scraping leftovers. The big pots simmering on the stove smelled of rabbit stew and mustard. Shirley was committed to fresh, natural food. Never ate anything canned or frozen. She allowed Gary to eat one artificial ingredient a week "to immunize him against the dangers of modern nutrition," as she put it. She hand-washed the laundry with Marseille soap, hardly ever watched TV, and every afternoon listened to the BBC, which she said was the only intelligent radio station. She was a tall, broad-shouldered woman, with thick blond hair cropped short. From behind, people sometimes mistook her for a man. "Half man, half vamp," Shirley would say, laughing. "I knock them out, then I revive them by batting my eyelashes!" She had a black belt in jujitsu.

Originally from Scotland, Shirley said she'd come to France to attend hotel school and never left. She made her living giving voice lessons at the Courbevoie conservatory, tutoring English, and baking cakes that she sold for 15 euros apiece to a restaurant in Neuilly. She was raising Gary on her own, and never spoke about his father. When the subject came up, she merely grunted, which said what she thought of men in general, and of that man in particular.

"Do you know what your son is playing with, Shirley?"

"No, what?"

"Tampax!"

"He's not putting them in his mouth, I hope?"

"No."

"Well, at least he won't freak out the first time he sees a girl with one."

"Shirley!"

"Joséphine, how come that shocks you? He's fifteen years old; he's not a child. So what's up with you?"

"I've been on a roller coaster all morning. Antoine left. I kicked him out, I mean. I told my sister and I told the girls. Oh, God, Shirley, I think I've made a terrible mistake!"

"You're not the first woman to lose her husband. And I'm going to tell you a secret: we do just fine. It's hard being alone at first, but after a while we wouldn't have it any other way. You'll see. Life alone is sheer bliss! When I'm in the mood, I sometimes cook candlelit dinners, just for me."

"I'm not quite at that point."

"I can tell. But this has been coming for so long. Everyone knew except you. It was obscene."

"That's what Hortense said. Can you believe it? My fourteen-year-old daughter knew more than I did! Not only was I being cheated on, but people must think I'm a moron. But none of that matters now, anyway."

"Do you wish I hadn't told you?"

Joséphine looked at her friend's sweet face, her short and slightly upturned nose covered in tiny freckles, her honey-green eyes. She shook her head.

"You're the nicest person I know, Shirley. And it's not really that woman Mylène's fault. If Antoine had been working, he'd never have gotten involved with her. Being put out to pasture at forty, it's just not right!"

"Stop it! You're giving him too much credit, and you're not seeing straight. It happened now because it was bound to happen sometime. Come on, pull yourself together. Chin up!"

Joséphine shook her head, unable to speak.

"Will you look at this amazing woman? She's about to die of fear because a man left her! Let's have a cup of coffee and some chocolate. You'll see, things will start to look up."

"I don't think so, Shirley. I'm so scared! What's going to become of us? I've never lived alone—ever! I can't do it."

Shirley went over and took her by the shoulders.

"Tell me exactly what it is that frightens you. When you're scared, you have to face your fear. Otherwise it'll eat you alive."

"No, leave me alone. I don't want to think."

"Tell me what scares you."

"How about that coffee and chocolate?"

"Okay, but you're not off the hook," Shirley said with a smile. "Arabica or Mozambique?"

"Whichever. I don't care."

Shirley took out a bag of coffee beans and an old wooden coffee grinder. She sat on a stool, wedged the grinder between her thighs, and began to steadily turn the handle, without taking her eyes off her friend. "It's like my brain. It grinds slowly, but exceedingly fine."

"You look so pretty sitting there in your apron like that. I feel so ugly."

"Don't tell me *that's* what's scaring you!"

"Who taught you to be so direct? Your mother?"

"Life did. It saves time. But you're cheating again; you keep trying to change the subject."

Joséphine looked up at Shirley, squeezed her fists between her knees, and started talking. She began in a rush, then slowed down, stopping and repeating herself.

"I'm afraid. I'm afraid of everything. I'm a great big ball of fear. I want to die right here, right now, and not have any more worries. I'm afraid I'll never find love again. I'm afraid of losing my job. I'm afraid of talking to people I don't know. I'm afraid of losing my mind. I'm afraid of breast cancer. I'm afraid of dying alone."

"Tell me your worst fear, the one that paralyzes you and keeps you from being the brilliant Jo who can speak so wonderfully about the Middle Ages that I sometimes want to go back there. What is it that makes you shrivel up into a ball?"

"I feel ugly. I keep telling myself no man will ever fall in love with me again. I'm fat. I don't know how to dress or fix my hair. And I'm just going to get older."

"That's true of everyone. What is it that you can't face?"

Joséphine looked bewildered.

"You really don't know?" asked Shirley.

Joséphine shook her head. Shirley stared at her for a long time and then sighed.

"That's the fear you have to identify, Jo, the one that's behind all the others. Once you do that, nothing will frighten you ever again, you'll see."

"You sound like a fortune-teller, Shirley."

"Or a witch. In the Middle Ages they would have burned me at the stake!"

✦ ✦ ✦

"What are you doing tonight?" asked Bérengère, pushing the piece of bread away from her plate. "If you're free we could go to Marc's opening together."

"I have a family dinner," said Iris. "Is the opening tonight? I thought it was next week."

Bérengère Clavert and Iris Dupin met at the same restaurant every week. It was a trendy place where you could see politicians whispering; a starlet trying to impress a director; a few titless models with bony hips. At a table for one, a regular waited for a tasty piece of gossip like an old crocodile lurking in a swamp.

Bérengère picked up the bread again, and impatiently flicked it with her index finger. "I feel like I'm surrounded by vultures watching an animal die. They won't say anything, they're way too polite. But it's in their eyes. 'How's the Clavert woman doing, now that she's been dumped again? Thinking of slitting her wrists?' It's humiliating. Marc will be showing off his new girlfriend, and I'll be sick with rage, love, and jealousy."

"I didn't know you had such deep feelings," Iris said.

"How can you say that?"

"Because you're mixing up pride and love, and I'm not buying it. You're irritated, but you're not hurt."

Bérengère wasn't sure whether to cry or counterattack. She'd initially planned not to tell Iris anything, to protect her friend from the rumor going around Paris. But she also loved gossip and backbiting, and she wasn't about to let her own ox be gored without retaliating. She put her elbows on the table and her chin in her hands, and smiled.

"Not everyone can have a smart, rich husband like yours, Iris! If mine were more like Philippe, I'd be faithful and content."

"Contentment doesn't take away desire. You can be content with your husband and wildly passionate with your lover."

"And you know this because you have a lover?"

The question surprised Iris. Bérengère was usually a lot more subtle.

"Why wouldn't I?" she asked without thinking.

Bérengère sat up and leaned close. Iris noticed that the left corner of her friend's mouth went up a little.

"Have you had your lips plumped up?"

"No, I haven't! Tell me about this lover!"

Rather than answer, Iris tapped on the slight bulge at the corner of Bérengère's mouth.

"I swear, something looks weird there, on the left side. Your lip is sticking out. Or maybe curiosity is distorting your mouth. Are you so bored that you have to snap up the smallest bit of gossip and make a big deal of it?"

"You're so nasty!"

"Oh, in that department, I'm not even in your league."

Bérengère sat back in her chair and glanced casually toward the door. There were a lot of people in the restaurant, but no one she knew. She leaned close to Iris again.

"I'd understand perfectly if you needed . . . more. You've been married to Philippe for so long. Desire doesn't weather all that cheek-by-jowl toothbrushing."

"Well, I'm pleased to report that our cheeks and jowls get it on pretty often."

"Oh, come on! Not after all these years." *And not after what I've been hearing!* Bérengère thought.

She hesitated for a moment, and then, in a hoarse voice that caught Iris's attention, she added: "You know what they're saying about Philippe?"

"Yes, and I don't believe a word of it."

"Neither do I. It's absurd!"

Bérengère seemed about to burst with joy.

It must be serious, thought Iris. *Bérengère wouldn't get this worked up over just any old rumor. And to think she calls herself my friend! Whose bed is she going to stick Philippe into this time?*

They'd known one another for a long time, and shared the cruel intimacy of two women in constant competition with each other.

"Do you really want to know?"

"Hurry up, or I'll forget what we were talking about. Then it'll be much less interesting."

"They say Philippe is in a serious relationship, 'something special.' That's what Agnes told me this morning."

"That bitch! Do you still see her?"

"She calls me from time to time." Actually, they spoke every morning.

"And may I know who Philippe is supposed to be fooling around with?"

"Ah, that's where the shoe pinches. Better you should hear it from me than someone else."

Iris folded her arms against her chest. "Check, please," she told a passing waiter.

She would pay the bill, imperial and magnanimous. She felt like the poet André Chénier, coolly marking the page in the book he was reading as he climbed the steps to the guillotine.

By now, Bérengère realized she had said too much, and was squirming with embarrassment. "Oh, Iris, I'm so sorry. I shouldn't have."

"A little late for that, don't you think?" said Iris icily, glancing at her watch. "I'm sorry, but if you're going to beat around the bush much longer, I won't be able to wait."

"All right! They say he's going out with a . . . a . . ."

"Oh, for God's sake, Bérengère, stop stammering! A what?"

"A young guy. A lawyer who works with him."

There was a moment of silence as Iris looked her over.

"Well, that's original," she said, struggling to keep her voice neutral. "I didn't expect that. Thanks for letting me know."

She got up, took her purse, and put on her elegant pink leather gloves, pushing each finger in carefully, as if each one corresponded to a thought. Then she walked out.

Despite her turmoil, Iris remembered the row and number of her parking space in the garage, and slipped into her car. She sat tall and straight, the way she'd been taught, pride making her rigid. After a moment, she felt her nose quiver, her mouth tremble, and two enormous tears form at the corners of her eyes. She brushed them away, sniffled, and started the car.

Marcel Grobz reached across the bed to pull Josiane Lambert closer. But she had slipped out of reach and was ostentatiously turning her back to him.

"Don't pout, sweetie-pie. You know I can't stand that."

"I'm telling you something super important and you're not listening."

"Okay, okay, I'm listening. I promise."

Josiane relaxed and rolled back over till her purple and pink lace negligee was touching Marcel's ample body. His fat stomach hung over his hips, and red hair covered his chest and formed a fuzzy halo around his bald head. Marcel was no prize, but he did have mischievous blue eyes that made him look far younger. "You have the eyes of a twenty-year-old," Josiane would murmur to him after making love.

"Move over, you're taking up all the space," she said now. "You've gotten fatter, Marcel. There's fat everywhere." She pinched his waist.

"Too many business lunches. Go on. I'm listening."

"So here's the thing . . ."

She pulled the sheet up below her large breasts, and Marcel tried not to stare at the two mounds he'd been eagerly sucking minutes before.

"You should promote Chaval. Give him responsibility and a sense of importance."

"Bruno Chaval?"

"Yes."

"Why should I? You have the hots for him?"

Josiane let out that deep, raucous laugh he found so sexy. He joined in the laughter, then tried to grab her again.

"If you don't stop I'm going on strike," she said. "I won't let you touch me for forty days and forty nights! And this time I'll keep my promise, I swear."

To break the last forty-day embargo he'd had to give her a necklace of cultured South Sea pearls, with a platinum clasp set with diamonds.

And because Marcel was crazy for everything about Josiane—her body, her mind, and her earthy common sense—he listened.

"Promote Chaval, or he'll go to the competition."

"There's almost no more competition left. I cut them all off at the knees."

"You may have hurt their business, but they could come back to bite you. Especially if Chaval helps them."

Josiane, who was as serious about business as she was about pleasure, sat up.

"It's simple. Chaval's a great salesman, but he's also an excellent accountant. I'd hate to see you have to compete against a guy with both people and money skills."

Marcel propped himself up on one elbow.

Josiane went on: "Salesmen know how to sell, right? But they usually don't get the finer points of a financial transaction. Payment schedules, due dates, shipping costs, discounts—you know, that stuff."

Now Marcel was also sitting up, his head against the copper bed frame. He took Josiane's logic one step further:

"So you mean that before Chaval can turn against me and become a threat—"

"You promote him."

"What should I do with him?"

"Put him in charge. And while he's growing the business, we diversify, we start new product lines. We'll let him wrestle with the day-to-day while we surf the wave of the future! Not a bad idea, eh?"

This was the first time Josiane had said "we" when speaking about the business. Marcel moved away to get a good look at her: she was intent, flushed, focused, her thick blond eyebrows knitted in thought. He thought of how this woman, who never hesitated at any sexual act, also had all this ambition. What a combination! Generous and insatiable in bed, tough as nails at work.

Marcel had hired Josiane as a secretary fifteen years earlier. Her only diploma was from some rinky-dink school that taught her stenography and very approximate spelling. She came from the slums, same as him, and life had kicked her around. Rough men had felt her up and screwed her whether she liked it or not. When Marcel met her, he understood at a glance that Josiane just wanted a way out of the gutter. He flipped a mental coin and hired her. A few weeks later, he got her into his bed.

Nine months after starting the job, she came to him and said, "My salary is pitiful. Why don't you cheer it up?" He did that and more. He taught her business, made her his executive secretary. And little by little, she displaced the other mistresses consoling him for his loveless marriage. And he didn't regret it. He was never bored with Josiane. The only thing he regretted was that he'd married Henriette in the first place.

"Are you listening to me, Marcel?"

"Yes, sweetie-pie."

"Specializing is over. We need generalists again, people who are good at lots of things. And that's exactly what Chaval is."

Marcel smiled. "I'm a generalist."

"That's why I love you."

"Tell me more about Chaval."

As Josiane talked, Marcel could see his own past before him. Marcel's parents were Jewish immigrants from Poland who'd settled in the Bastille neighborhood of Paris. His father had been a tailor, and his mother took in laundry. With eight kids living in two rooms, there was very little tenderness, many beatings. Very little luxury, lots of stale bread.

Marcel earned a degree in chemistry from a second-rate school, and landed his first job at a candle factory. The boss there didn't have any children and took a liking to him. He loaned him the money to buy out a business that was going under, then another one, and another. That's how Marcel had become a turn-around specialist, a vulture capitalist. He didn't like the phrase, but he loved the work, buying failing companies and building them back up with savvy and sweat.

Maybe because his own home life had been so barren, Marcel decided to launch a company built around the concept of "cozy." Within a few years, his Casamia stores were offering scented candles, table settings, lamps, couches, frames, bathroom fixtures, kitchenware, and so on. Hominess on a budget. Everything was made abroad. One of France's first businessmen to outsource, Marcel opened factories in Poland, Hungary, China, Vietnam, and India.

Then one fateful day, a big supplier said to him, "Look,

Marcel, the stuff you sell is fine, but your stores don't have any style. You should hire a designer. Someone who can give your products that certain something, turn your business into a brand."

Marcel was still mulling this over when he met Henriette Plissonnier, a stylish middle-aged widow.

What class! Marcel thought when she showed up in response to his help-wanted ad. Henriette had just lost her husband and was raising two daughters alone. She didn't have any experience, she admitted. What she had, she said, was a first-class education and an innate sense of elegance, form, and color.

"Would you like me to demonstrate?"

Before he had the chance to answer, Henriette moved two vases, rolled out a rug, pulled a curtain aside, and shifted three knickknacks on his desk. Then she sat down, smiling. His office suddenly looked like something out of an interior design magazine.

He first hired her as an accessories consultant, then promoted her to decorator. She designed his shop windows, and chose the color of the season—blue, tan, white, gold.

And Marcel fell head over heels in love with her.

Henriette represented a world that would forever be out of his reach. At their first kiss, he felt he was touching a star. During their first night together, he snapped a Polaroid picture of her while she was asleep and put it in his wallet. For their first weekend together, he took her to the Hotel Normandy in Deauville. She didn't want to leave the room. He interpreted this as modesty, because they weren't married. Much later, he realized she was ashamed to be seen with him.

A few months later, he asked her to marry him.

"I have to think about it," she said. "It's not just me. I've got two little girls, remember." Six months passed and she never mentioned his proposal, which drove him crazy. Then one day out of the blue she said, "You know that question you asked me? Well, if the offer still stands, the answer is yes."

Henriette was the one who'd christened him "Chief." She thought "Marcel" was common. Now everyone called him Chief—except Josiane, of course.

René had warned him about Henriette. René was his warehouse manager and buddy, and they often had drinks together after work.

"I'll bet she's frigid."

"I admit that my johnson spends a lot of time out in the cold with that woman. Hand jobs? Blow jobs? No dice. She's too uptight."

"So dump her."

As if it were that easy, Marcel thought. Not only was he married to Henriette, he'd made her head of the Casamia board of directors. He also signed a prenuptial agreement making her his sole beneficiary, so when he died, she would inherit everything. He was bound hand and foot. Yet the worse she treated him, the more devoted to her he became. He sometimes told himself he'd gotten slapped around so much as a kid that he had developed a taste for it.

And then Josiane had come along. But Marcel was sixty-four, too old to start over. If he got divorced, Henriette would claim half his fortune.

♦ ♦ ♦

"No way *that's* going to happen!" he said aloud, startling Josiane.

"Okay, so we give Chaval a nice contract without any profit sharing. Or maybe just a little slice, so he feels invested in the business."

"A tiny one."

"Got it."

"Christ, it's hot in here. Honeybunch, get me an orangeade, okay?"

Josiane rose from the bed in a rustle of lace and jiggling thighs. Marcel, who liked plump women, smiled.

He took a cigar from the ashtray and rubbed his bald head. *I'd better watch this Chaval character*, he thought. *Not give him too much power or status in the business. I also have to make sure the punk doesn't replace me in Josiane's bed. She's thirty-eight; she must think about younger guys.*

"I can't stay over tonight, honeybunch. Big dinner at my stepdaughter's."

"The prima donna or the wallflower?"

"The prima donna. But the wallflower will be there with her daughters. Hortense, the older girl, is hot stuff, I'm telling you. She's got me pegged, that kid, she really does. I like her. She's got class, too."

"Those females wouldn't have class without your money, Marcel. They'd be like the rest of us, giving blow jobs or cleaning houses."

Marcel didn't want to get into an argument, so he just patted Josiane on the rump.

She handed him the ice-cold orangeade. He gulped it down, rubbed his stomach, and belched loudly. Then he burst out laughing.

"If Henriette heard me do that, she'd have a fit."

"Don't mention that woman if you want me to be your little snuggle bunny."

"All right, already! You know I haven't touched her since forever."

"I should hope not! And I mean it: don't ever let me catch you in bed with that old bat. That stuck-up, self-important bitch!"

Josiane knew that Marcel loved it when she tore into Henriette. It excited him to hear the insults in her deep, husky voice.

"That freeze-dried, wrinkled-assed toothpick! She probably holds her nose when she takes a shit. Maybe Her Holiness doesn't have a hole between her legs like the rest of us? Because she's never been fucked by a nice big prick, never had her plumbing reamed by the giant snake."

That was a new one, and it went straight to Marcel's crotch. He impatiently grabbed Josiane and pulled her close, swearing he was going to eat her up, and then eat her some more.

Josiane stopped ranting and eased herself down on the bed with a sigh of pleasure. She loved this big, fat man. She'd never met anyone so giving or so full of energy. And at his age! He'd chase her around the desk several times a day, and sometimes she had to slow him down, afraid he'd have a heart attack.

"What would I do without you, Marcel?"

"Oh, you'd probably find someone else just as fat, ugly, and stupid to spoil you. You're a love magnet, sweetie-pie. They'd be lining up get a taste of your cute ass."

"Don't say things like that. It makes me feel weird, just thinking about it."

"Oh, stop. Come pay Mister Johnson here some attention. He's feeling lonely."

"Marcel, if anything should ever happen to you, what would become of me? Are you sure you're leaving me something in case you—"

"If I suddenly croaked? Is that what you mean? Don't worry, honeybunch, you'll be taken care of. In fact, you'll be at the head of the line. Make sure you look beautiful that day. Get out all your pearls and diamonds. I want you to do me proud at the lawyer's. God, how I'd love to be there to see Henriette's face! But right now Johnny really needs you."

Josiane hummed as she hungrily took her lover's cock in her mouth. No special talent required: she'd learned very early how to make men happy.

Chapter 3

♦ ♦ ♦

*I*ris dropped her keys in the tray on the hall table. Then she took off her coat, kicked off her shoes, and dropped her purse and gloves onto the large kilim she had bought with Bérengère one bleak winter afternoon. She asked Carmen to bring her a good strong whiskey. She planned to hole up in her study, where no one was allowed, except her ever-faithful housekeeper—once a week—to clean.

"Whiskey?" Carmen asked in disbelief. "In the middle of the afternoon? Are you all right?"

"Not really. And no questions. I need to be alone, to think."

Carmen shrugged and went to get the whiskey. "So now she's taken to drinking alone," she muttered.

Iris curled up on the sofa and looked around her den. *Either I confront Philippe,* she thought, *tell him I can't stand the situation and that I'm leaving and taking my son with me. Or I can wait and pray that this lousy business doesn't go any further. If I leave, I prove the gossips right, expose Alexandre to scandal, hurt Philippe's practice, and therefore myself. If I stay, I'll be denying the fact that we've been living a lie all these years. But at least I don't lose the comfort I've enjoyed for so long.*

Her gaze came to rest on a photo of her and Philippe on their wedding day. They're smiling at the camera. He has his arm on her shoulder, in a loving, protective manner. It looks as though nothing bad could ever happen to her again.

Iris and Philippe were always going to art auctions. They shared a passion for finding undiscovered treasures and bidding on them. They had bought *Still Life with Flowers* by Bram van Velde ten years earlier. They bought the Barceló just after the exhibit at the Fondation Maeght. And the long handwritten letter by Jean Cocteau in which he talks about his love for Natalie Paley.

If I left Philippe, I would lose all this beauty. I would have to start all over again. Alone.

Iris shuddered at the word *alone.* Single women made her skin crawl, and there were so many of them! *Stressed out and pale, always rushing around, forever on the prowl. Terrifying, the way people live these days, burning themselves out.* She sipped the whiskey. Thanks to Philippe—thanks to Philippe's money, that is—Iris wasn't burning out. In fact, she was trying to blossom. For a while now, she'd been writing. One page a day. No one knew. She locked herself in her office and scribbled words onto sheets of paper. When she wasn't inspired, she doodled. It was slow going. She copied out La Fontaine's *Fables* and reread *Madame Bovary* and La Bruyère's *Les Caractères*, trying to figure how they chose just the right word. She tore up almost everything she wrote, but she felt that the work brought some intensity to her life.

She had once written screenplays she wanted to shoot, but she'd dropped everything when she left Gabor Minar behind and married Philippe.

Gabor . . . Gabor . . . He was so tall . . . Long legs, rough language.

"Iris, please, listen to me. Iris, I love you, and it's not for fun, it's for real. For real, Iris." When he said her name, it sounded like "Irish" because of the way he rolled his r's.

Joséphine told her that the twelfth-century marriage motto was "With and under him." Iris wanted to roll right under Gabor. *What's become of him?* she wondered.

Sometimes she fell asleep picturing Gabor ringing her doorbell and sweeping her up in his arms. She would give it all up for him: the cashmere shawls, the prints, the drawings, the paintings. She would run away with him.

But then two little numbers would puncture her fantasy: 44. She was forty-four years old. Her dream was shot. *It's too late now*, she told herself. *I'm married and I'll stay married. But I need a backup plan in case Philippe goes completely nuts and runs off with his young man.*

Iris sighed. She would have to practice pretending—starting now.

Joséphine was relieved that she wouldn't need to take the bus and make the two transfers to get to her sister's. Antoine had left the car for her. She hardly ever drove, and it felt strange to get behind the wheel. She'd forgotten the code for the garage exit gate, and was rummaging in her purse for the notebook where she had jotted it down.

"It's two-three-one-five, Mom."

"Thanks, Hortense honey."

Antoine had called the night before and spoken to the girls. Zoé first, then Hortense. After passing the phone to her sister, Zoé came into her mother's room, where Joséphine was reading. The girl lay down beside her on the bed, sucking her thumb and hugging her teddy bear. After a long silence, Zoé sighed and said, "There are things I don't understand about life, Mommy. It's even harder than school."

Joséphine felt like telling her that she didn't understand much about life, either. But she held her tongue.

"Mommy, tell me Queen Eleanor's story," she said, snuggling even closer. "How she married two kings and ruled over two countries at the same time."

"Should I start at the beginning?"

"Tell me about her first wedding."

"That day, all of Bordeaux rejoiced," Joséphine began, her words filling the room like a Christmas story. "On the embankment, Louis VII waited with his noblemen while Eleanor of Aquitaine finished getting ready in the Chateau de l'Ombrière. . . ." Soothed by Joséphine's voice, Zoé soon fell asleep.

Hortense had remained on the phone with her father for a long time, then gone straight to bed without coming in to kiss her mother good night.

"I suggest we not talk about Daddy's leaving during dinner," Jo told the girls in the car.

"Too late," replied Hortense. "I already told Henriette."

The girls called their grandmother by her first name because Henriette Grobz refused to be called "Grandma" or "Grandmother," which she thought vulgar.

"Oh, God! Why did you do that?"

"Let's get real, Mom. If anyone can help us, she can."

She has Marcel's money on her mind, Jo thought. Two years after the death of Joséphine and Iris's father, Henriette had married Marcel, a very rich, very kind man. He had helped Henriette raise her daughters. He paid for their private schooling, the rent on the Paris apartment, and the chalet in Megève.

"And what did she say?" Jo asked.

"That it didn't surprise her. That it was a miracle that you'd found yourself a husband, but that for you to keep him would have been beyond belief."

"Hortense! That's enough! You didn't give her any details, I hope?"

The moment Joséphine asked the question, she wondered why she had bothered. Of course Hortense had gone into the details, all of them: Mylène's age, height, hair color, what she did for a living. Hortense had probably laid it on thick, to gain sympathy as the poor abandoned little girl.

"Word would have gotten around sooner or later, so why not let it all out? It makes us look less dumb."

"You really think Dad's gone for good?" Zoé asked.

"He's definitely moved on," Hortense said. "He told me he was looking to start a 'project' that 'she' was going to finance. She's crazy about him, apparently. He's looking for work outside France, says there's no future for him here."

Joséphine was stunned: Antoine confided in their daughter more easily than in her. Did he now think of her as an enemy?

"Still, you could have asked me before you spoke about it, Hortense."

"Don't get too worked up about it, Mom. We're going to need Henriette's money, and she loves it when we come to her like lost little ducklings."

"No, Hortense. We're not going to play that game. We're going to make do on our own."

"Oh, really? How do you plan to do that with what you earn?"

Joséphine slammed on the brakes, pulled into a side road, and switched off the ignition.

"Hortense, I forbid you to speak to me that way! If you keep on like this, I'm going to ground you."

"Oh, please, not that!" she sneered. "I'm *so* scared!"

"Now you listen to me, young lady. You may not think so, but I can put my foot down. I've always gone easy on you, but you're crossing the line."

Hortense sat back in her seat and assumed an offended look.

"Go ahead. I dare you. You talk big, but dealing with real life? That's another story."

That was the last straw: Joséphine pounded the wheel and shouted so loudly that little Zoé began to cry. "I want to go home!"

"What's come over you since yesterday, Hortense? You're being awful. I feel like you hate me. What did I ever do to you?"

"You made my father leave because you're ugly and boring and there's no *way* I'm going to be like you. I'll do anything to make sure I won't, even if I have to kiss Henriette's ass so she'll give us money. I don't want to be poor! I hate poor people! Poverty sucks!"

Joséphine was hardly able to breathe.

Hortense turned to Zoé, who was crying quietly in the backseat, her fist in her mouth. "And stop bawling! You're getting on my nerves. Damn! How the hell did I wind up with you two? Now I understand why Dad left."

Joséphine stared at her eldest daughter as if she were an escaped killer who had somehow found her. She forced herself to focus on the Bois road, which was lined with trees in bloom. The gentle swaying of the branches comforted her. Joséphine prayed that she hadn't gone the wrong way and that they would come out at the Porte de la Muette. *Then all I'll have to do is find a place to park—one more problem*, she thought with a sigh.

Mercifully, the family dinner went off without a hitch. Carmen ran everything smoothly, and the serving girl she'd hired was energetic and helpful. Wearing a long white blouse and lavender linen pants, Iris joined the conversation when it faltered. That happened often, since no one was particularly talkative. She seemed a bit withdrawn.

In the old days, when Iris came home, her arms full of shopping bags, she would shout, "Carmen! A hot bath, right away. Hurry, Carmencita! We're going out tonight!" She would drop her parcels and run to find Alexandre in his room. "Did you have a good day? Tell me all about it, my love! How was school? Did you get good grades?"

In the bathroom Carmen would run the water in the enormous blue-green mosaic bathtub, mixing thyme, sage, and rosemary oils with some Guerlain bath salts. When everything was just right, she'd light the little candles and call for Iris to slip into the scented water. Iris would sometimes have Carmen keep her company and pumice the soles of her feet or massage her toes with rose oil. She would talk about her day, like the time she bumped into a homeless woman with her hand outstretched. Iris was so rattled, she dumped all her change into the woman's leathery palm. "Oh, Carmen, I'm so afraid I'll end up like her one day. I don't have anything. It all belongs to Philippe."

"You'll never, ever end up like that, darling," said the maid soothingly, as she spread her mistress's toes and rubbed the soles of her delicately arched feet. "Not as long as I live."

Tonight there had been no bath ceremony. Iris had just taken a quick shower.

Now only Hortense was chattering away, making her aunt and grandmother smile. And she had Marcel practically purring with pleasure every time she complimented him.

"I'm sure you've lost weight, Chief. When you came into the room, I thought, Wow, he looks good! How much younger he looks! So 'fess up. Did you get a facelift?"

Marcel burst out laughing.

"And who would I do that for, you little vixen?"

"I don't know. Me, maybe? I'd be sad if you got all old and wrinkled. I want you strong and tan, like Tarzan."

After being flattered by Hortense, Marcel turned to Philippe to talk about the stock market. Would it go up or down in the coming months? Pull out or invest? Philippe only half listened to his ebullient father-in-law.

The moment dessert was over, Alexandre led his cousin Zoé to his room to play computer games, leaving Hortense on her own. She always hung out with the grown-ups. She knew how to make herself invisible when she needed to.

In the living room, Joséphine sipped her coffee, praying that she wouldn't face a barrage of questions. Marcel read a financial newspaper. Henriette and Iris were talking about changing the curtains in one of the bedrooms. They waved Joséphine over to sit next to them, but she chose to join Marcel instead.

"How's it going, Jo? Life still a bowl of cherries?"

The things Marcel says! she thought. *He must be the only person on earth who still says things like "That's swell!" or "How 'bout them apples?"*

"That would be one way of putting it, Chief."

He winked at her, went back to his newspaper for a moment, and then, noticing that she was still there, realized he had to make conversation.

"What about your husband? Still up a creek jobwise?"

Joséphine nodded.

"If he can't find anything, he can always come see me. I'll find somewhere to put him."

"That's sweet of you, Chief, but—"

"He'll have to tone it down a bit, though. Pretty full of

himself, that husband of yours, isn't he? You can't afford to be proud these days. Me, I fought my way out of the gutter, so . . ."

Joséphine had to make an effort not to confess to Marcel that she wasn't far from the gutter herself.

"But you know what, Jo? If I had to hire a member of the family, I'd hire you. You're a hard worker. I think your husband is afraid to get his hands dirty. At least that's how I see it."

He chuckled.

"It's not like I'm asking him to be a grease monkey."

"I know, Chief. I know."

She patted Marcel's fleshy forearm and looked at him tenderly, which made him uncomfortable. He nodded, cleared his throat, and dove back into his newspaper.

That's the way it always is with Marcel, Joséphine thought. *He'll talk to me for five minutes, and when he feels he's done his duty, he moves on. These family gatherings must be a real drag for him. Just like they were for Antoine.*

She glanced over at Iris, who was talking to their mother while fiddling with the long earrings she had taken off. Jo noticed that Iris's toenails and fingernails matched perfectly. As usual, she felt alien to her sister's relaxed femininity. Iris exuded the ease that comes from having money. Henriette, try as she might to rise to her eldest daughter's station, would always seem to be striving. *Her hairdo is too tight,* thought Jo, *her lipstick too heavy, her handbag too obvious—and why doesn't she ever put it down, anyway?*

The silence was broken only by Marcel turning the pages of

his paper. He wondered what Josiane was doing. Sprawled on her living room couch, watching one of her beloved sitcoms? Or flat on her back, like an enormous blond crêpe, in the same bed they had been rolling around on this very afternoon? The thought gave Marcel a hard-on, and he had to discreetly cross his legs. At Henriette's insistence, he was wearing a pair of tight gray pants that wouldn't hide Mister Johnson's inopportune resurrection.

"A macaroon to go with your coffee, monsieur?"

Carmen was holding out a plate of chocolate, caramel, and marzipan candies.

"No thanks, Carmen. I'm stuffed to the gills."

Henriette overheard and stiffened. Why did he have to talk like that? The vulgarity of the man was the cross she had to bear. She let out a deep sigh, rose, and in silent protest walked over to the window where Joséphine was standing.

"Let's have a little chat," she said, leading her daughter to a couch at the other end of the living room. Iris was next to them in a flash.

"So, my dear, what are you going to do now?"

"Keep going," Joséphine said.

"Keep going?" asked Henriette with surprise. "Keep going with what?"

"Well, um, with my life."

"Really, darling . . ."

When her mother called her "darling," it meant things were really bad.

"Actually, Mom, it's none of your business," Joséphine blurted. "It's my problem."

She sounded more aggressive than she intended—or than Henriette was accustomed to.

"That's no way to speak to your mother!"

"What did you decide to do?" Iris asked in her most soothing voice.

"I'll manage on my own. And I don't want to talk about it anymore. Is that all right with everyone?"

Joséphine's voice was louder, and by the end of her sentence it had risen to a shout, ripping the stuffy atmosphere.

Hm, what's all the ruckus about? wondered Marcel, looking up from his paper. *No one ever tells me anything in this family.*

"When I was left to raise you alone," said Henriette, "I rolled up my sleeves, and I worked."

"But I *am* working, Mom! You always seem to forget that."

"I don't call what you do working, dear girl."

"Just because I do research, and don't work in an office? Because it doesn't fit the way you see things? Well, I'm earning a living, whether you like it or not."

"It's a pittance!"

"I'd like to know how much you earned when you started out with Chief. I bet it wasn't much more."

"Don't you take that tone with me, Joséphine!"

Marcel sat up, suddenly alert. *Hey, the evening's finally getting interesting. And with Her Royal Highness, it'll be balls to the wall. Any second now, she'll play the poor widow who sacrificed everything for her children.*

"It was very hard, that's true," said Henriette. "We really had to tighten our belts. But Chief soon saw how talented I was, and we managed to pull through." Henriette glowed with her astonishing triumph. Bringing up her two girls alone was her Bronze Star, her Legion of Honor. She was Mother Courage.

Marcel went back to his newspaper. *You pulled through because I kept slipping you envelopes stuffed with cash*, he thought, licking his finger to turn the page. *You were as hard-nosed and grasping as any hooker!* But Marcel had already fallen for her, and would have done anything to please her.

Henriette had warmed to her favorite topic.

"My work earned me recognition from one and all, even from Marcel's competitors. But he wanted to keep me at all costs."

That's not the half of it, thought Marcel. *I wanted to sleep with you so badly I would have paid you a CEO's salary without your even having to ask for it. What a fool I was! I ate so much shit, chasing you. And now you're giving sermons! Why don't you tell your daughter how you led me around by the nose? Speaking of which, I better watch my step with Josiane. I don't much like this thing with Chaval.*

"I'll do just what you did, Mom. I'll work. And I'll manage on my own."

"You're not on your own, Joséphine! You have two daughters, in case you've forgotten."

"You don't have to remind me."

"Well, you don't seem very concerned about them, Joséphine. I've always thought that you were too naive for today's world. You're a poor, defenseless child!"

At that, Joséphine exploded.

"You know what, Mom? You can take those inspiring stories of yours and shove them! Do you really think I believe those tales of the noble widow? Don't you realize I see through your pathetic maneuvers? You married Chief for his money. If he'd been poor, you wouldn't have given him the time of day, and we both know it. You always talk to me in that condescending way, as if I were a total failure. I can't stand your hypocrisy! You were just plying the world's oldest profession."

Joséphine turned to Marcel, who was no longer pretending to read. "I'm sorry, Chief. I didn't mean to hurt your feelings." Looking at Marcel's kind, jowly face, she felt ashamed.

"Not to worry, little Jo. I wasn't born yesterday."

Joséphine blushed. "I couldn't help myself. It just all came out."

As she said this, her mother collapsed on the sofa, pale with fury and fanning herself dramatically. She was prepared to faint if it would bring the room's attention back to her.

Joséphine looked at her mother in exasperation. In a moment she would ask for a glass of water, sit up, request a pillow for her back. She was an expert in sowing guilt, waiting until the other person cowered at her feet and begged forgiveness. Joséphine had seen her do it, first with her father and now with her stepfather.

"One more thing, Mom," she added in a firm voice. "I won't ask you for anything, not a penny, not a hint of advice. I'm going to make it on my own—just me and the girls."

Henriette turned her head away, as if the sight of her daughter was too much to bear. Joséphine shrugged and walked out of the room. Pushing open the door to the living room, she nearly knocked Hortense over. Her daughter had been listening at the keyhole.

"Hortense! What are you doing?"

"That was real smart! I hope you feel better now."

Joséphine strode past her into a nearby room, hoping to be alone for a few moments to compose herself. It was Philippe's study. She didn't see him at first, but she heard his voice. He was standing, partly hidden in the shadows of the heavy, gold-rimmed red curtains, and speaking in a hushed voice into his phone.

"Oh, Philippe, I'm sorry!"

He immediately ended the call, saying, "I'll call you back."

"I . . . I didn't mean to disturb you."

She felt her forehead getting sweaty, and waited awkwardly for him to invite her to sit down. He observed her for a moment, apparently unsure of what to say. At the slightest intrusion into his private life, Philippe became cold and prickly. And he hated getting involved in Iris's family matters. He pitied Joséphine, but her almost pathological shyness always made him uncomfortable, and he wanted to get rid of her quickly.

"Tell me, Joséphine, do you speak English?"

"English? Of course! English, Russian, and Spanish." She coughed, embarrassed to seem boastful.

"I might have a job for you translating business contracts. It's pretty boring work, but the pay is good. We used to have a person at the firm doing it, but she just left. Russian, you said? Do you speak it well enough to understand the subtleties when it comes to business?"

"Sure. I speak it quite well."

Philippe remained quiet for a while. Joséphine didn't dare interrupt his thoughts. He had always intimidated her, and yet, strangely, he'd never seemed as human to her as he did at this moment. His cell phone rang, but he didn't answer. Joséphine was grateful for that.

"The only thing I'd ask is that you not to mention this to anyone. Absolutely no one. Not your mother, not your sister, not your husband. I want this to stay strictly between us."

"That's fine with me. You have no idea how sick and tired I am of justifying myself to people who think I'm just a pushover and a ninny."

The words *pushover* and *ninny* made her smile, and all the tension fell away. Philippe smiled as well. Those were exactly the words he would have used to describe her, too. He suddenly felt a wave of affection for his awkward sister-in-law.

"I really like you, Jo, and I respect you. Don't be embarrassed. I think you're very brave, and you're a good person."

"Philippe, stop! I'm going to start crying. I'm kind of fragile right now. If you only knew what I just did . . ."

"I heard Antoine left. Is that true?"

"Yes."

"These things happen."

"Yes, they do," Joséphine said with an ironic grimace. "See? Even in misfortune, I can't manage to be original."

They stood there for a moment, quietly smiling at each other. Then Philippe got up and looked at his calendar.

"How about three tomorrow afternoon at my office? Does that work for you?"

"Sure. Thanks, Philippe. Thanks so much."

He put a finger to his lips to remind her about the secret. She nodded.

In the living room Hortense was perched on Marcel's lap. She was rubbing his bald scalp and wondering how she could somehow undo her mother's incredible screwup.

PART II

♦ ♦ ♦

Chapter 4

♦ ♦ ♦

$\mathcal{I}$t was October, and Joséphine was at the kitchen table, paying bills. School was in session, and she had paid for everything: school supplies, backpacks, gym outfits. She had even paid the insurance, taxes, and maintenance on the apartment.

And I did it all by myself! She sighed, letting her pencil drop.

The translation work she got from Philippe's law firm helped, of course. She'd worked hard right through July and August, skipping her vacation and staying in Courbevoie. Her only distraction was watering the plants on the balcony. The white camellia gave her a lot of trouble. As agreed, Antoine took the girls for the month of July, and Iris invited them to her beach house in Deauville for August. Jo took a week off that month and joined them. The girls seemed in great shape: tan, rested, taller. Zoé had won the sand castle contest and was busy taking pictures with her prize, a digital camera.

Set between the sea and the dunes, the Dupin house was gorgeous. There was fishing every day and a party every night, when they grilled the catch on a barbecue while inventing new cocktails. The girls would flop onto the sand, pretending to be drunk.

Joséphine returned to Paris reluctantly. But when she saw the size of the check that Philippe's secretary handed her, she didn't regret having worked so hard. *There must be some mistake!* she thought. She suspected Philippe of overpaying her. She saw him rarely, but from time to time he would send her a note saying how pleased he was with her work. Once he added a P.S.: "Coming from you, I'm not surprised."

One day the associate she submitted her work to—her name was Caroline Vibert—asked if she felt up to translating full-length books from English for her husband, a publisher.

"Books?" Jo asked, opening her eyes wide. "Real books? Of course!"

Caroline gave her a number to call, and everything was arranged very quickly. Joséphine was given two months to translate a British biography of Audrey Hepburn—352 dense pages. Two months, Jo realized, meant that she had to be done by the end of November!

She wiped her brow. It wasn't like she didn't have other things on her plate besides the translation. She'd signed up for a conference at the University of Lyon, and had to write a fifty-page paper on female weavers in twelfth-century workshops.

Joséphine paused, her pencil in midair. Suddenly a terrifying thought came to her: *I forgot to ask how much I'll be paid for the Audrey Hepburn job! I should have written down my questions before going to a meeting like that. I have to learn to be quicker, to work smarter. I've been living like a studious little snail up to now.*

Shirley turned out to be a great help with the Hepburn translation. Joséphine would jot down the English words and idioms she didn't know, and run next door. Their landing saw a lot of back-and-forth traffic.

Jo would have loved to buy herself a computer, but she knew she couldn't afford it.

In one column in her ledger, Joséphine listed her earnings, in the other, her expenses. She wrote down possible debits and credits in pencil, definite ones in red ballpoint. She tried to build in a small cushion, but in fact, she had no cushion at all. *One unexpected snag, and I'm sunk.*

And she'd have no one to turn to. Before, she had been part of a team. Antoine had taken care of everything. When it involved paperwork, he would point, and she would sign. He'd laugh and say, "I could get you to sign anything."

They still hadn't discussed divorce, and Jo went on obediently signing the various papers he handed her—no questions asked, eyes closed—to keep the bond between them alive. Husband and wife. For better or for worse, for richer or poorer.

When Antoine came to pick the girls up at the beginning of July, it had been very painful for her.

The elevator door slammed shut. " 'Bye, Mom, work hard!"

"Have fun, girls! Enjoy!"

Joséphine ran to the balcony and watched as Antoine loaded the girls' suitcases in the trunk. Then she suddenly noticed something in the front, sticking out on *her* side of the car: an elbow in a red blouse. Mylène!

For a second, Joséphine had an impulse to run downstairs and grab the girls. But she realized that Antoine had a perfect right to do what he was doing. She slid slowly down onto the concrete floor of the balcony. Palms pressed against her eyes, she wept and wept. The same images kept running through her mind, like an endlessly looped film. Antoine introducing the girls to Mylène, Mylène smiling at them. Antoine had rented an apartment. The words "The girls and Mylène . . . Antoine and Mylène" kept coming back, like a refrain.

Joséphine took a deep breath and yelled, "Fuck this blended family shit!" Hearing herself swear startled her. She stopped crying.

That was the moment Joséphine understood that her marriage was really over. *That glimpse of red blouse means it's over,* she told herself. *O-ver. Over and out.* She drew a red triangle on a piece of paper and hung it up over the toaster, where she would see it every morning.

The next day, she went back to her translation work.

It wasn't until later in the summer when she went to Iris's place in Deauville that she learned that Zoé had cried a lot that July.

"Antoine told the girls they'd better get used to Mylène because he was planning to move in with her," Iris said one day in August. "That they had a joint project they would be starting in the fall. What kind of project? No one knows."

"Those poor darlings are getting off to a bad start in life!" declared Henriette magisterially. "Lord, what we put children through these days!"

Joséphine hadn't seen her mother since the scene in Iris's living room in May, or spoken a single word to her. She wondered if their confrontation had given her the energy to work so hard.

"You get positive energy when you're straight with people." That was Shirley's theory. "You were honest that night, and look how much you've accomplished on your own!"

The other day, in the narrow library stacks, Joséphine had bumped into a man she hadn't seen coming. Her armload of books crashed to the floor, and the stranger stooped to help pick them up. He made a funny face at her, and she burst out laughing. She'd had to go outside to pull herself together.

She saw the man in the library another time, and he gave her a wave and a sweet smile. He was tall and skinny, with chestnut hair that fell over his eyes, and hollow cheeks. He carefully hung his navy blue duffel coat on the back of his chair before sitting down. Joséphine thought him handsome and romantic.

She didn't dare tell Shirley about the man, because she knew what she would say: "You should have asked him out for coffee, found out his schedule. You're so pathetic!"

Well, nothing new there, Joséphine thought with a sigh, doodling on her accounts book. *I see all, I feel all, I am the depository of thousands of details that stab me like shards of glass, and that other people don't even notice.* The hardest thing was resisting panic. It always struck at night. Curled up under the covers, she would go over all her expenses in her head until her eyes were wide with terror.

Today, though, to her relief, the numbers written in pencil

and red ink looked okay. *If the money doesn't disappear too fast, I might be able to rent a house at the beach for the girls next summer, buy them nice clothes, take them to plays and concerts. They could eat out once a week. I'll go to the hairdresser, buy myself a pretty dress. Maybe Hortense won't be so ashamed of me.*

Joséphine suddenly remembered that she'd promised to help Shirley deliver an order of cakes for a big wedding.

Shirley was waiting on the landing, tapping her foot. Standing in the doorway, Gary waved good-bye to them.

"I think I just got a glimpse of the man your son will be in a few years," said Jo. "He's so handsome!"

"Don't I know it! Women are already starting to check him out."

"Is he aware of it?"

"No, and I'm not going to be the one to tell him. I don't want him to get too full of himself."

"Tell me, was his father good-looking?"

"Yes, he was. The handsomest man on earth. That was his only real quality, for that matter." She scowled and waved her hand as if to chase a bad memory away. "Okay, let's get moving. You watch the cakes while I get the car. Ring the elevator and hold the door."

Joséphine did as she was told. They stacked the cake boxes in the back of the car, Jo keeping a hand on them so they wouldn't fall.

"I was scheduled to deliver these at five, but they called and said to come at four or to forget the whole thing. He's an important customer, so he knows I'll do whatever he says."

A moped cut in front of her, and Shirley unleashed a volley of choice Anglo-Saxon curses.

"Good thing Audrey Hepburn didn't swear the way you do. I'd have trouble translating that."

"How do you know she didn't curse like a sailor from time to time? It's just not in her biography, that's all."

"But she seemed so perfect. Did you know that she never had a love affair that didn't end in marriage?"

"After what she went through as a teenager, she must have wanted a real home life."

Joséphine had learned that at fifteen, Hepburn had worked for the Resistance in Holland during World War II, carrying notes hidden in the soles of her shoes. One day, on her way back from a mission, she was arrested by the Nazis and taken to the Kommandatur with a dozen other women. She managed to escape, and hid in the cellar of a house. After a month, she finally came out of hiding in the middle of the night and found her way home.

After hesitating for a moment, Joséphine decided to take the plunge.

"There's this guy I met at the library . . ."

Joséphine told Shirley about the collision in the stacks, the books dropping, the laughing fit, and the immediate attraction she'd felt to the stranger.

"So what does he look like?"

"Like a perennial student. He wears a dark blue duffel coat. It's the first time I've looked at a man since, well . . ." Jo stopped herself. She still had trouble talking about Antoine's departure.

"Have you seen him again?"

"Once or twice. He smiled at me. We can't really talk at the library, so we speak with our eyes." Joséphine blushed. "He's so handsome!"

"Look at the map and see if I can turn right somewhere. We're not going to be able to get through this way."

"You can turn. But then you'll have to take a left again."

"I'll take another left. The left side is where the heart is; it's my kind of place."

Joséphine smiled. Life with Shirley was never dull. She knew exactly what she wanted and went straight for it. Joséphine was sometimes shocked by the way she was raising Gary. Shirley talked to her son as if he were an adult, never hiding anything from him. She had even told Gary that his dad ran off the day he was born, but she also told him that she would reveal his father's name if he ever wanted to look him up. She said she'd been madly in love with the man, and that he, Gary, had been wanted and loved.

Shirley usually took Gary to Scotland for school vacations. She wanted her son to know where his ancestors were from, to speak English, to learn about another culture. But this year Shirley had come back in a sad, gloomy mood. She announced that they wouldn't be going back, and never mentioned it again.

"What are you thinking about?" Shirley asked.

"I was thinking about how mysterious you are, about all the things I don't know about you."

"I wonder the same thing, as it happens."

They pulled up at the gate to Parnell Traiteurs at four o'clock sharp.

"You stay in the car and move it if you have to. I'll go deliver these babies."

Joséphine nodded. She slipped into the driver's seat and watched Shirley maneuvering the cake boxes.

Shirley soon came bounding back out and kissed Jo on both cheeks.

"Hooray! I'm loaded! The guy gets on my nerves but he pays well. Want to go to a pub and treat ourselves to a cold one?"

On the drive home, Joséphine was thinking about how to organize her paper for the conference when she suddenly noticed a man crossing the street right in front of them.

"Look!" she shouted, yanking on Shirley's sleeve. "There! Right in front of us!"

A young man with longish chestnut hair was sauntering across the street, hands in his duffel coat pockets.

"It's him! The library guy! You know . . . See how handsome and laid-back he is?"

"Yeah, pretty laid-back, I'd say."

Then the man turned around and waved to someone. The light was about to turn green.

"Uh-oh," Shirley said.

A slim, beautiful blonde ran to catch up with him. She stuck one hand in his coat pocket and stroked his cheek with the other. The man pulled her close and kissed her.

"Oh, well." Joséphine sighed.

"Oh, well, what?" Shirley snapped. "He can change his mind. You're going to be Audrey Hepburn and seduce him. Just stop eating so much chocolate while you're working. You'll lose weight. All he'll see are your big eyes and your tiny waist, and he'll be on his knees in no time. Then you'll be the one slipping a hand into his duffel coat pocket. And you guys will fuck each other's brains out. That's how you must think, Jo. It's the only way."

The minute she got to the office Josiane got a phone call from her brother, saying their mother had died. Josiane cried, even though the woman had never done anything but abuse her. She felt as if she'd been orphaned. Then she realized that she really *was* an orphan, and cried even harder. It was as if she were making up for lost time, crying the way she had never been allowed to cry as a child, when she'd been a slovenly little girl whose stomach ached from fear, hunger, and cold.

"What is going on here, may I ask? Goodness gracious, it feels like a funeral home with all this weeping. And why aren't you picking up your phone?"

Wearing a hat that looked like a big pancake, Henriette Grobz was staring at Josiane, who noticed that her telephone was indeed ringing. She waited a second, and it stopped. She pulled an old Kleenex out of her pocket and blew her nose.

"It's my mother. I just found out that she died."

"That's sad, of course, but we all lose our parents sooner or later. You have to be prepared for it."

Henriette had never liked Josiane. Didn't like her insolence, her catlike walk, her blond hair, and especially not her eyes. Those eyes! Bright, lively, and challenging one minute, deep and seductive the next. She had more than once asked Marcel to fire her, but he always refused.

"Is my husband here?"

"He's upstairs, but he'll be back. You can wait in his office."

"I would watch my manners, girl," said Henriette with vicious condescension. "Don't you use that tone with me."

"And don't you call me 'girl.' I'm Josiane Lambert, not your girl."

Henriette marched into Marcel's office and slammed the door. Josiane allowed herself a smile of satisfaction.

She phoned her brother to find out when the funeral would be. *Could old lady Grobz really get me fired?* Josiane wondered while the phone was ringing. Maybe she could.

Overcome by a sudden wave of sentimentality, she told her brother she would come home for the funeral.

"Mom asked to be cremated," her brother said.

"Really? Why?"

"She was afraid of waking up in the dark."

"I can understand that."

My little mother, she thought, *afraid of waking up in the dark!* She suddenly felt a twinge of love for her mother, and started to cry again. She hung up, blew her nose . . . and felt a hand on her shoulder.

"Something wrong, sweetie-pie?"

"It's my mom, Marcel. She died."

"Come here."

Marcel took her by the waist and pulled her onto his lap.

"Put your arms around my neck and let yourself go, like you're my baby. I've always wanted a baby, you know. But Henriette always said no."

"Well, she's in your office, waiting for you."

Marcel leaped up as if someone had jabbed him in the behind with a rusty nail.

"*What?* Are you sure?"

"Of course I'm sure. We got into an argument."

He rubbed his head, looking chagrined.

"Oh boy! And I need her signature on some papers! You know that crappy Murepain subsidiary? Well, I managed to palm it off on the Brits. Sweetie-pie, couldn't you have chosen another day to pick a fight with her? What am I gonna do now?"

"She's going to ask for my scalp."

"Was it that bad?"

"Christ, Marcel! Does she really scare you that much?"

He smiled sadly.

"I'd better go see what she wants."

"Yeah, go see what she's doing all alone in your office."

"Don't be mad at me, honeybunch."

"Just go."

Josiane knew all about men and their courage. She didn't expect Marcel to go to war with the Toothpick for her. She didn't expect anything from him. Maybe some sweetness, some tenderness when they were in bed. He was a nice guy, and she enjoyed giving him the pleasure he'd been denied, because when you're in love, giving is as good as getting. She loved climbing on top to take him between her thighs, make him practically faint with pleasure.

Josiane stood up, and decided to get some coffee and collect her thoughts. She gave a last worried glance at Marcel's office. What was going on in there? Was he going to knuckle under and sacrifice her on the altar of King Cash? That's what her mother used to call money.

Here I am pretending to be a liberated woman, when I've actually spent my whole life enslaved to King Cash! It paid for my cherry, and it bought and sold me. Yet the moment I see a rich man, I look up to him like he's a superior being, like he's God's gift to mankind.

Still angry at herself, Josiane smoothed her dress and went to the break room to buy a coffee from the vending machine. The plastic cup dropped, and she waited as it filled with hot, black liquid. She squeezed the cup in both hands, savoring its warmth.

"What are you doing tonight? Hanging out with the old man?" asked Bruno Chaval, tapping a cigarette on his pack. Yellow Gitanes, she noticed; he must have seen them in some old movie.

"Hey! Don't call him that!"

"Okay, I got it. You're in a bad mood. I'll shut up."

She shrugged and put the coffee against her cheek. They stood silently for a minute, not looking at each other, sipping their coffee. Then Chaval moved closer, lightly bumping Josiane's hip. She didn't resist, so he leaned close to her neck.

"Mmmmm. You smell good, like fancy soap. I'd like to lay you down and slowly breathe you in."

She moved away, sighing.

Ever since he'd gotten into her pants, Chaval had been acting like he owned her. Josiane had promised to talk to Marcel about a promotion, and he was writhing with impatience. He'd taken to pestering her about it everywhere—in the hallways, the warehouse, the elevators.

He wanted to ask her again about it, but could tell that this was a bad time. "Come on, babe. Truce?"

He put his hand on her hip and pulled her toward him.

"Stop it! Someone'll see us."

"Oh, come on. They'll just say we're good friends having some fun."

"No, I'm telling you. He's in the office with the Toothpick. If he comes out and sees us, I'm history."

For all I know, I'm already history, Josiane thought.

"You do love me a little, don't you?" she asked in a pleading voice.

"You know I do, babe. How can you doubt it? Wait and see and I'll prove it to you."

He slipped his hand under her ass and squeezed.

"But what if the promotion doesn't come through, for some reason? What if you don't get it? Will you stay with me?"

"What are you talking about? Did he say something? Tell me."

"No, it's just that I feel scared all of a sudden."

Chaval stroked her hair absentmindedly. In his arms, Josiane felt like an awkward package he couldn't easily put down.

"C'mon, Josiane, pull yourself together! Now they really *are* going to notice us. You're going to screw this whole thing up."

Josiane stumbled away from him, her eyes red from crying. She wiped her nose and apologized, but it was too late.

Henriette and Marcel Grobz were by the elevator, silently staring at them. Henriette with her pinched lips and face all scrunched up under her big hat. Marcel soft and slumped, his cheeks trembling with sadness.

Henriette was the first to look away. Then she grabbed her husband by the sleeve and pulled him into the elevator. Once the doors were closed, she joyously crowed, "See, what did I tell you? That girl is a slut! When I think of the way she spoke to me! And you're always taking her side. Poor Marcel, you can be so blind sometimes."

Eyes downcast, Marcel was counting the cigarette burns in the elevator floor carpet and struggling to hold back his tears.

The envelope bore a brightly colored stamp and was addressed to "Hortense and Zoé Cortès." Jo recognized Antoine's handwriting. She set it unopened on the kitchen table amid her papers and books. Then she raised it to eye level, trying to see if it had photos in it, or perhaps a check. But she couldn't tell. She'd have to wait for the girls to get back from school.

Hortense spotted it first and grabbed it, but Zoé screamed, "Me too! Me too! I want the letter too!" Joséphine made them sit down and asked Hortense to read it out loud. Jo took Zoé in her lap, hugging her tightly. Hortense slit open the envelope with a knife. She pulled out six thin sheets of paper, opened them, and laid them on the kitchen table, smoothing them with the back of her hand. Then she began to read:

My beautiful darlings,

As you probably guessed from the stamp on the envelope, I'm in Kenya. Have been here for a month. I wanted to surprise you, which is why I only said I was going abroad. But I'm planning to have you visit me as soon as I'm completely settled. Maybe during your school break. I'll talk to Mom about it.

Kenya . . . Does that word mean anything to you? I live between Malindi and Mombasa, the best-known part of Kenya. It was ruled by the sultan of Zanzibar until 1890. The Arabs, the Portuguese, and then the British all fought over Kenya, which became independent only in 1963. But enough history for today! I'm sure you're asking yourselves what Daddy is doing in Kenya? Before answering, I have a question: Are you sitting down, darlings?

Hortense smiled indulgently and sighed. "That's Dad for you!" Joséphine couldn't believe it. *Kenya! Alone or with Mylène?* The red triangle hanging above the toaster seemed to taunt her. She had the impression it was blinking.

I'm raising crocodiles . . .

The girls' jaws dropped in astonishment. Crocodiles! Even Hortense was startled, but she went back to reading the letter, taking a deep breath between each word.

. . . for a Chinese guy! I'm sure you know that China is fast becoming a major industrial power, making everything

from computers to cars. Well, now the Chinese are getting into crocodile farming! Mr. Wei, my boss, established a prototype in Kilifi and hopes that soon this farm will produce lots of crocodile meat, crocodile eggs, and crocodile bags, shoes, and wallets. Mr. Lee, my associate, told me they filled several Boeing 747s with tens of thousands of crocodiles from Thailand. The Thai farmers were struggling because of the Asian crisis, and were forced to sell them: the price of crocodiles had plummeted 75 percent! They got them for a song. They were reduced for quick sale!

"Daddy's funny," said Zoé, sucking her thumb. "But I don't like that he's working with crocodiles. Crocodiles are dumb."

They have them living in the river estuaries, separated by steel netting.

They were looking for a deputy general manager. Well, that's me, my loves! I'm the deputy general manager of Croco Park!

"That's like being a big executive," declared Hortense, after some thought. "That's what I put down on the student-information forms we had to fill out at the beginning of the year when it asks for your father's occupation."

And I rule over 70,000 crocodiles! Imagine that!

"Wow!" Zoé exclaimed. "Seventy thousand crocodiles! He'd better not fall in the water."

The Chinese workers they sent here work long hours and sleep together in cramped bungalows. They laugh all the time. I sometimes wonder if they even laugh in their sleep. They are very funny looking, with skinny little legs sticking out of shorts several sizes too big. The only problem is that they get attacked so often by the crocodiles they have lots of scars on their arms, legs, even their faces. And do you know what? They stitch themselves back up! With a needle and thread! There is a nurse on location whose job it is to sew them back up, but she mostly takes care of visitors.

Because I forgot to tell you that Croco Park is open to tourists: Europeans, Americans, and Australians who are in Kenya for safaris. They pay a small admission fee and are given a bamboo fishing pole and two chicken carcasses to tie to the end of the line. They can have fun dragging the pieces of chicken in the swamp waters and feeding the crocodiles. We keep reminding visitors to be careful, but sometimes they get too close and get bitten. Crocodiles can move very fast and they have very sharp teeth.

"I guess that's bound to happen," said Hortense. "When I go there, I'm only going to look at them through binoculars!"

Joséphine listened to all this, dumbfounded. A crocodile farm?

But don't worry! I don't take any chances, and I keep the crocodiles at a safe distance! I don't get close. I leave that to the workers. The business looks like it's going to do really well. I live in what they call the Master's House. It's a big wooden two-story structure in the middle of the farm, with several bedrooms and a beautifully maintained swimming pool. The pool is surrounded by barbed wire in case a crocodile ever thinks of taking a dip. It happened once! The director of the camp before me found himself nose to nose with a crocodile one day in his pool, and ever since they've beefed up the security.

There you are, darlings. Now you know everything—or almost everything—about my new life. I will write to you very soon and very often because I miss you and think about you a lot. Write to me. Tell Mom to buy you a computer, that way I can e-mail you pictures of the house, the crocodiles, and the little Chinese workers in their shorts.

Hugs and kisses,
Daddy

P.S. Enclosed is a letter for your mother.

Hortense handed the last sheet to Joséphine, who folded it and slipped it into her apron pocket.

"Aren't you going to read it right away?" Hortense asked in surprise.

"No. Do you want to talk about Daddy's letter?"

The girls studied her.

"Why didn't he stay in France?" Zoé asked.

"Because there aren't any crocodile farms here," replied

Hortense. "He was always saying he wanted to go abroad. That's all he ever talked about. I wonder whether she went, too."

Joséphine spoke up quickly, to keep the girls from talking about Mylène. "I hope he's being paid really well and that he's going to enjoy his job."

Jo thought the whole project was crazy, and hoped against hope that Antoine hadn't invested any money in it. *Whose money could he invest, anyway? Mylène's?* Joséphine suddenly remembered that she and Antoine had a joint savings account. She resolved to speak with Monsieur Faugeron, the banker, right away.

"I'm going to go read about crocodiles in my book about reptiles," Zoé declared, jumping down from her mother's lap.

"If we had Internet access you wouldn't have to," said Hortense.

"But we don't," Zoé said. "So I just look things up in books."

"Mom, we need a computer," said Hortense. "All my friends have one. Mom, you're not listening!"

"Of course I am!"

"What did I just say?"

"That you need a computer."

"And what are you going to do about it?"

"I don't know, honey. I need to think about it."

"Thinking about it doesn't mean buying it."

Antoine must feel like he's starting his life over, thought Joséphine. *A new girlfriend, a new house, a new job. We must seem pretty dull to him, the three of us in our little apartment in Courbevoie.*

Just that morning Max Barthillet's mother had come downstairs and asked whether she'd had any news from Antoine. Joséphine said something or other, while noticing that Christine Barthillet had lost a lot of weight. Jo asked if she was on a diet. "You're going to laugh, Madame Cortès, but I'm on the potato diet!" Joséphine indeed burst out laughing, and Christine went on: "I'm serious! You eat a potato every night, three hours after dinner! Apparently this releases hormones that neutralize your brain's craving for sugar and glucose. You don't feel the need to eat between meals. So you lose weight."

"Mom, a computer isn't some luxury, it's a tool," Hortense was saying. "You could use it for research and us for our homework."

"I know, honey. I know."

"You say that, but you're not interested. This is my future!"

"Hortense, listen to me. I'd do anything for you, okay? Anything. When I say I'll think about it, it's because I don't want to make promises I can't keep. I think I may just be able to manage. Can you wait till Christmas?"

"Yes! Thanks, Mom! I knew I could count on you."

Hortense hugged her mother and insisted on sitting on her lap, the way Zoé did.

"Can I still do this, Mom? I'm not too big, am I?"

Joséphine melted.

"I love you so much, honey. Let's try not to fight."

"We don't fight, Mom. We argue. We just don't see things the same way, that's all. And you know, if I get angry sometimes, it's because ever since Daddy left it's been really hard and I take it out on you because you're the one who's here."

Joséphine fought back tears.

"You're the only person I can count on, Mom."

Hortense's trust came as such an unexpected pleasure, it chased away some of Jo's worries, but not all of them.

Since she had started doing translations, Joséphine had put Hortense and Zoé on the school lunch plan, and dinner was almost always the same thing: ham and mashed potatoes. Zoé ate with a frown. Hortense picked at her food, and talked about her latest plans for making her dream of becoming a fashion designer—with her own label—come true. Joséphine finished their plates so as not to waste anything. *That's why I'm gaining weight*, she thought. *I'm eating for three.*

"Mom, Max Barthillet never invites me over anymore. Why?" Zoé asked.

I don't know, sweetie," Joséphine answered, absentmindedly. "Everyone has problems . . ."

"Can you give me some money to buy a Diesel T-shirt, Mommy?"

Joséphine sighed.

After the girls went to bed that night, Joséphine got back to the translation. *What would Audrey Hepburn do in my place?* she wondered. *She would work, keep her dignity, and focus on her children's happiness.* That was how she'd lived her life, with dignity and love—and stayed thin as a rail.

Joséphine decided she would start the potato diet.

Chapter 5

♦ ♦ ♦

*I*t was a cold, rainy November evening, and Philippe and Iris were driving home from a dinner at of one of his partners' houses. The setting had been luxurious, the food excellent, and the evening boring, Iris recalled, leaning back in her seat as they made their way across Paris. Philippe was driving in silence. She hadn't managed to catch his eye all evening.

Iris admired the city—the limestone buildings, the bridges over the Seine, the layout of the grand avenues. When she was living in New York, she missed Paris, missed sitting at cafés and watching the Seine flow by. She used to close her eyes and summon up images of home.

Early in her marriage, Iris had made an effort to keep up with Philippe's friends' conversations, to take an interest in business, in the stock market, profits, dividends, and corporate mergers. At Columbia, she'd reveled in freewheeling conversations about a film, a screenplay, or a book. But around businesspeople she felt awkward and ignorant. Gradually she understood that she was there just for decoration, because she was attractive and charming, because she was Philippe's wife. At first this had offended and hurt her, then she'd gotten used to it.

But this evening had been different.

Gaston Serrurier—a publisher with a reputation for publishing good books and sleeping with beautiful women—had sat across from her at dinner. "So, Iris, are you still tending the home fires?" he asked ironically. "You'll be wearing a chador soon."

Iris was miffed. "Actually, you might be surprised to learn that I've started to write." The words were barely out when she saw Serrurier's eyes light up.

"Is it a novel? What's it about?"

"It's a historical novel set in the Middle Ages," she said, an image of Joséphine and her work on the twelfth century suddenly springing to mind.

"Well, well, that's very interesting! Our readers love history and historical fiction. How far along are you?"

"Oh, I'm making headway," she said, desperately conjuring up what her sister had said about that time. "It's set in the twelfth century, Eleanor of Aquitaine's time. We have so many misconceptions about that period. It's a pivotal era in French history, and a lot like the one we're living through now. Money has replaced barter and has come to dominate people's lives. There is an exodus from small towns, and the cities are growing. France is opening up to the outside world. Trade is flourishing across Europe. Young people are struggling to find their place in society, and are rebelling. The clergy is fanatical and repressive, and they stick their noses in everything. But it's also a time of great public works. Magnificent cathedrals, universities, and hospitals are being built. It's also when the first romance novels appear."

Serrurier watched Iris raptly, his eyes never leaving her face.

"That's fascinating! So when can we have lunch?"

"I'll call you when I have something I'm ready to show."

"You have to promise not to show it to anyone else first, okay?"

He gave Iris his direct number, and, before leaving, reminded her of her promise.

Philippe dropped her in front of their building and went to park the car. Iris hurried to the safety of her bedroom and got undressed, thinking back on the fantastic story she'd just made up. *God, that was brazen of me! Now what do I do? He'll forget all about it,* she reassured herself. *And if he doesn't, I can say I'm just starting out and need more time.*

The brass clock on the bedroom mantelpiece chimed midnight. Putting on an act had felt so delicious. It took her back to her time at Columbia when a group of them had been studying mise-en-scène. Gabor had been very supportive. *Gabor . . .* She kept coming back to him.

Iris shook her head at the memory. For the first time in ages she felt alive. She had told a lie, of course, but it wasn't a very big one. *How wonderful life is when you can be something other than someone's wife or someone's mother.*

She sat at the foot of the bed in a cream-colored negligee, brushing her long black hair. It was a ritual she never missed. In the novels she'd read as a child, the heroines always brushed their hair, morning and night.

She sighed. Another day, and she hadn't gotten anything done; hadn't written, hadn't seen anyone. She'd eaten lunch in the kitchen, feeling very alone. She felt she was spinning her wheels.

If only I could call Bérengère. Iris never saw her anymore, and she felt as if part of herself had been cut off. Maybe not the best part, but she had to admit that she missed the woman and her gossip, with its whiff of the sewer.

I used to look down on Bérengère, Iris thought. *I told myself I had nothing in common with her. But the fact is, I was all a-twitter when we were chattering.* They hadn't seen each other in six months, and Iris no longer knew what was happening in Paris, who was sleeping with whom, who was in and who was out.

Iris had spent most of the afternoon locked in her study. She reread a Henry James short story and was so struck by a passage that she copied it in her notebook:

> What's the most inveterate mark of men in general? Why, the capacity to spend endless time with dull women—to spend it I won't say without being bored, but without minding that they are, without being driven off at a tangent by it.

"Am I a dull woman?" she murmured to the big mirror on her closet door. Before the mirror could answer, the telephone rang. It was Joséphine, and she sounded excited.

"Iris, are you alone? I know it's very late, but I really have to speak with you. Antoine wrote a letter to the girls. He's in Kenya, raising crocodiles."

"Crocodiles? He's nuts!"

"That's what I think, too."

Joséphine read Antoine's letter to Iris, who listened without interrupting.

"So, what do you think?"

"I think he's lost his mind."

"And that's not all. He wrote a little note at the end just for me. You'll never guess . . . Wait, I'll read it to you."

She read aloud:

Joséphine, I know it was cowardly to run away without telling you, but I didn't have the courage to face you. I felt too bad. Here, I can start my life over. I hope it works out that I make some money, and can pay you back a hundred times over for everything you're doing for the children. I have a chance of succeeding, of making a ton of money. I don't know why, but in France I just felt defeated.

You're a good woman, Joséphine. You're intelligent, sweet, and generous. You were a wonderful wife. I'll never forget that. I didn't treat you well, and I want to make it up to you. Make your life easier. I'll send you regular updates. Below you'll find my phone number, where you can always reach me if something comes up.

With much love and all the good memories of our life together, Antoine.

Jo went on: "And there are a couple of PS's. The first one says: 'They call me Tonio here, in case you call and get one of the staff.' The second one says, 'It's weird, but I don't ever sweat anymore, even though it's hot.' That's it. What do you think?"

Iris's thought was, *Poor Antoine, he's just so pathetic!* But she didn't know how much emotional distance her sister had, so she took a more diplomatic approach.

"The important thing is what you think, Jo."

"You used to be much harder on him."

"Before, he was a part of the family. It was okay to abuse him."

"So that's what you think a family is for?"

"You didn't exactly hold back six months ago when you lit into Mother. You were so rough on her, she doesn't want to hear your name mentioned."

"I can't tell you how much better I've felt since then." Joséphine paused, then added, "It's true that with all the work I have, I haven't had much time to think about anything. All I knew is that Antoine had gone abroad somewhere."

"I'm going to have to hang up, Jo. I hear Philippe coming. Big kiss and don't forget: Cric and Croc clobbered the big Cruc as it crept up to crunch them."

Iris looked up to find her husband looking at her from the doorway. *I don't understand Philippe either*, she thought. She sighed and began to brush her hair again. *I feel as though he's spying on me, walking in my footsteps, his eyes boring straight through me. Could he be having me followed? Is he trying to catch me with someone as grounds for divorce?* Silence had settled between them like a fact of life, a wall of Jericho that no trumpet would ever tear down because they never yelled, never slammed doors, never even raised their voices. *Couples that fight are lucky,*

Iris thought to herself. *Everything is clearer after a good argument.*

Philippe sat down on the bed and took off his shoes. First the right one, then the left. The right sock, then the left.

"Do you have a big day tomorrow?" she asked.

"A couple of meetings, a lunch—the usual."

"You shouldn't work so hard. The cemeteries are full of indispensable people."

"Maybe. But I don't see how I could change my life."

They'd had this discussion often.

And now he'll go into the bathroom, brush his teeth, put on his long T-shirt, and come to bed. He'll say, "I think I'm going to fall asleep right away." I'll say . . . I won't say anything. He'll kiss me on the shoulder and say, "Good night, darling." He'll put on his sleep mask and turn toward his side of the bed. I'll put away my brush, switch on my bedside light, and read a book till my eyes close. Then I'll make up a story.

On some nights Iris curled up in the sheets, hugged her pillow, making a little dent in the feathers, and thought of Gabor. They're at the Cannes film festival. They're walking on the beach. He's alone. She's alone, soaking up the sun. They cross paths. She drops her sunglasses. He bends down to get them, stands up, and they recognize one another. "Iris!" "Gabor!" They hug and kiss. He says, "I can't tell you how much I've missed you." She murmurs, "Me too!" He's there for the premiere of his film. She accompanies him everywhere; they walk up the steps together, hand in hand; she asks for a divorce . . .

On other nights, Iris chose a different fantasy. She's just

written a book, and it's a huge success. Translated into twenty-seven languages, rights sold to MGM. Tom Cruise and Sean Penn are fighting to play the lead. Little green stacks of dollar bills stretch out as far as the eye can see. The reviews are ecstatic. Iris is photographed in her study, in her kitchen. She's quoted about everything.

Suddenly Alexandre was standing at the bedroom door.

"Mom, can I sleep with you guys?"

Philippe turned over and snapped, "No, Alexandre! We've discussed this a thousand times. By the time a boy is ten, he doesn't sleep with his parents anymore."

"Mom, say yes—please!"

Iris could see the panic in her son's eyes. She got up, took him by the hand, and said, "I'll put him to bed."

"That's no way to raise the child. You'll just turn him into a sissy who's afraid of his shadow."

"Oh, come on, Philippe, I'm just taking him back to bed. Don't make such a big deal out of it." To Alexandre she said, "Let's go, honey."

"It's very unhealthy," said Philippe. "The boy will never grow up."

Iris led Alex to his room. She switched on the nightlight and pulled back the covers. Alexandre slipped under the sheets.

She put her hand on his forehead. "What are you afraid of, honey?"

"I'm just afraid."

"You're still a little boy, but you'll be a man soon, Alexandre.

You'll be living in a world of bullies. You have to be tough. You won't be able to come crying to your parents' bedroom."

"I wasn't crying!"

"No, but you let yourself be afraid. You let your fear overcome you, and that's not good. You have to conquer it, honey, or you'll always be a baby."

"I'm not a baby."

Alex looked sad. He was frustrated with his mother for not understanding him. "You're being mean!"

Iris didn't know how to respond. She didn't know how to speak to her son.

She kissed Alex on the forehead and stood up.

"Mom, will you stay till I fall asleep?"

"I'll stay, but next time, promise me that you'll be strong and that you'll stay in your own bed."

Alexandre sighed and closed his eyes. Iris softly stroked his shoulder. Slender body, long eyelashes, curly black hair—Alex had the fragile grace of a fretful child. He frowned even in sleep, and his chest rose and fell as if under some great weight.

Alexandre came into our bedroom because he knew I needed him, thought Iris. *Children know. I'm a wreck. The relaxed, easy veneer I've maintained for so long is cracking, and the jumble of contradictions is showing through. Life doesn't make sense anymore, and it's slipping through my fingers. Once you start to live according to other people's rules, going along with what other people think, your soul shrivels and dies. Is it too late? Have I become the woman I see reflected in Bérengère's eyes?*

Iris shuddered. She took Alexandre's hand and squeezed it tightly. In his sleep he returned the squeeze, mumbling, "Mommy . . ." Iris's eyes filled with tears. She lay down next to her son, put her head on the pillow, and closed her eyes.

"Josiane, did you book my tickets for China?"

Marcel was standing directly in front of Josiane, but staring over her head, as if he were looking at a road sign. Josiane felt her chest tighten, and she sat up stiffly in her chair.

"Yes. It's all . . . Everything's on your desk."

She didn't know how to talk to Marcel anymore. He was painfully formal with her, and she stuttered and groped for words in response. He had been avoiding her ever since catching her with Chaval at the coffee machine three weeks ago. He walked by her blindly, locked himself in his office from morning till night, and then called, "See you tomorrow," while looking the other way.

I'm gonna be left high and dry, thought Josiane. *Marcel will fire me any day now. He'll pay my unused vacation time, give me a severance package, and wish me all the very best with my "future endeavors." Then it's bye-bye, don't let the door hit you on the ass on your way out!*

She sniffled and choked back tears. *What an asshole that Chaval is! Why did he have to go waving his dick right under Marcel's nose? Couldn't help it, I guess. Probably high on testosterone. And then he had to go and dump me!*

I had it all: my big old snuggly bear, my hot young lover, and money about to start pouring in. All I had to do was pull the strings and the knot was tied. Now I can't even think straight. I wore sunglasses at Mom's funeral last night, and everyone thought I'd been bawling my eyes out.

Her mother's funeral . . . Josiane had taken the train down to Culmont-Chalindrey, then splurged on a cab to the cemetery—35 euros, plus a tip. It was pouring rain, and when she arrived, there they were, clustered under their umbrellas: all the people she'd left behind twenty years earlier. It probably hadn't been such a good idea to show up without putting on more of a show—a few trumpets or a little fanfare to shut them up.

"What, you came by train?" a cousin asked. "Don't you own a car?" In her family, owning a car meant you had it made.

"No, I don't have a car. In Paris it's considered cool to walk."

She broke away from the others and went over to the hole where they'd put the little urn of ashes. That's when the dam burst.

Marcel, Mom, Chaval! she silently wailed. *I'm alone, I'm broke, and I don't have a future. I am so screwed! I feel like I'm eight years old and I'm going to get slapped. I'm eight years old and I'm so scared, I'm about to shit my pants. I'm eight years old, and Grandpa is quietly sneaking into my room while everyone is asleep. Or pretending to be asleep.*

Josiane was crying, but she wasn't crying for her mother. She was crying for herself.

After the service they partied. The wine flowed like water; there were sausages and rillettes, pizzas and pâtés, Caprice des Dieux cheese and heaps of potato chips. Her relatives came over to Josiane in waves, checking her out.

"How's life in Paris?" they asked. "You making out okay?"

"Like a bandit," she'd replied, showing off the diamond and ruby bracelet Marcel had given her, and stretching her neck so they could admire the South Sea pearl necklace.

"What kind of work do you do? Is the pay good? Does your boss treat you all right?"

"He's the best," she answered, her teeth clenched. "He treats me just fine."

The questions kept coming, and she gave the same answers over and over. Each time her relations saw how well she was doing, they looked surprised and went off to get another drink.

After a while Josiane began to feel light-headed and asked if someone could open a window.

"Having dizzy spells? You knocked up? Who's the dad?" A chorus of raucous laughter followed that seemed to fill the room, with people nudging each other as if they were about to break into a funky line dance.

A baby! A baby with Marcel! Why didn't I think of that before? Josiane's mind was suddenly racing. He'd always dreamed of having a kid, anyway. He never stopped talking about how the Toothpick had denied him that rightful pleasure. He would get teary-eyed at ads showing little buggers stumbling around in spilled baby food or smelly Pampers.

Josiane's revelation was so powerful that time seemed to stop. The words became flesh. *A ba-by. A little ba-by. A baby Jesus. A plump little Grobz, born with a silver spoon in its mouth. A spoon? What am I saying? A whole place setting!*

Josiane looked tenderly at her brothers and her aunts and

uncles and their snotty children. How she loved them for giving her this brilliant idea. How she loved their mediocrity, their dreary lives, their ruined faces. She had been living in Paris for too long. It was back to basics now. How do you keep a man? Simple: with a bun in the oven. How could she ever have forgotten the age-old wisdom that had created dynasties and filled treasure chests?

The hardest part would be convincing Marcel that her fling with Chaval hadn't meant anything. Just a moment of weakness, a screwup, a bit of female fickleness. It was so momentary she'd already forgotten about it. That wouldn't be easy, but Josiane wasn't afraid of a challenge. She'd been through worse and come out on the other side.

"We're meeting them inside, you're sure?" asked Hortense in the car. "This is so cool! I wouldn't miss it for the world! An afternoon at the Ritz swimming pool, the height of luxury!" She sighed, stretching. "I don't know why, but the moment we leave Courbevoie and cross the bridge into Paris, I feel I'm coming back to life. I hate the suburbs. Why did we go live there anyway, Mom?"

Joséphine ignored the question. She was looking for a parking spot. It was Saturday, and Iris had invited them to meet at her health club. "It'll do you good, Jo. You seem so stressed out." But finding a place to park near the Ritz was no easy task—and not exactly the most relaxing way to spend the afternoon. Everyone was out Christmas shopping. Joséphine kept driving around, craning her neck, as the girls grew more and more impatient.

"There, Mom! Right there!"

"No! That's a no-parking zone, and I don't want to get a ticket!"

"Oh, Mom, you're such a buzzkill."

That was their latest word for her, buzzkill. And the two of them used it constantly.

Just then, a car pulled out of a space right in front of them. Joséphine braked and put on her turn signal. The girls bounced up and down.

"Go for it, Mom! You can do it!"

Parallel parking wasn't one of Joséphine's strengths, but she managed to squeeze into the space. The girls clapped as she mopped her brow.

She sweated even more at the thought of walking into the hotel and dealing with the hotel staff. She was sure they would look down their noses at her, wondering what she was doing there. She found herself following Hortense, who seemed perfectly at ease, nodding distantly at the doormen in their livery.

"Have you been here before?" Joséphine whispered.

"No," Hortense whispered back, "but I imagine the pool must be downstairs. And if we're wrong, we'll just turn around. These people work here. They're paid to give us directions."

Joséphine stuck close to her daughter, feeling as much out of her element as Hortense clearly felt in it. Zoé, meanwhile, was gazing in wonder at the glass cases filled with jewels, watches, and handbags.

"Wow, look at that one! I'll bet it's really, really expensive! Max Barthillet says that you can steal from the rich if you're poor, because they don't notice it, and it's only fair."

Joséphine was starting to think that maybe Hortense was right about this Max kid.

"Mom, look! A diamond egg!" exclaimed Zoé. "Do you think a diamond chicken laid it?"

At the club's front desk, a beautiful young woman asked them their names, checked a big ledger, and confirmed that they were expected by Madame Dupin poolside. A scented candle flickered on the desk, and classical music wafted in from hidden speakers. Glancing at her feet, Joséphine felt ashamed of her cheap shoes. The young woman showed them to the dressing room and wished them a good afternoon. The three of them disappeared into their changing stalls.

Joséphine got undressed. She folded her bra carefully and rubbed at the marks it had left on her skin. She took off her tights and rolled them up, folded her T-shirt, sweater, and pants, and put everything into the locker reserved for her. Taking her bathing suit out of the plastic pouch where she'd stored it in August, she felt a stab of anxiety. She'd gained weight since last summer; would the bathing suit still fit her? She looked around and noticed a white bathrobe on a hanger. Saved!

She put on the robe and went looking for her daughters, who had gone ahead to find Iris and Alexandre.

Iris was lying on a wooden deck chair, looking sumptuous in her white bathrobe. A book was open on her knees. She was deep in conversation with someone Joséphine could see only from behind—a slim girl in a sparkling, skimpy bikini. Her suit bottom was so tiny that Joséphine thought it was almost superfluous. Everything about the girl exuded grace and beauty, a perfect match for the refined decor of the pool, its blue water reflected in undulations along the walls. All of Jo's self-consciousness returned, and she drew the bathrobe tighter around herself. *This time, I swear I'm going to stop eating, effective immediately, and I'll do sit-ups every morning. I was a slender young girl once, too.*

She saw Alexandre and Zoé in the water and waved at them. Alex started to get out to say hello, but Joséphine waved him off. He dove back underwater, grabbing Zoé's legs and making her shriek.

The girl in the red bikini turned around. It was Hortense.

"Hortense! What in the world are you wearing?"

In her astonishment, Joséphine said this louder than she'd intended.

"Come on, Mom, it's a bathing suit. And don't shout like that. This isn't the public pool in Courbevoie."

"Hello, Jo," Iris said, sitting up to put herself between mother and daughter.

"Hello," said Joséphine, immediately turning back to her daughter. "Hortense, will you tell me where that bathing suit came from?"

"I bought it for her last summer, Jo. There's no reason for you to get all worked up about it. Hortense looks amazing."

"Hortense, go change. Immediately."

"No way! Just because you wear a burlap bag doesn't mean I have to."

Hortense met her mother's furious glare without blinking. Strands of hair had escaped from her barrette and her face was flushed, partly spoiling her femme fatale look. Joséphine spluttered with rage at her daughter's insult.

"Okay, girls, let's calm down," Iris said, smiling to ease the tension. "Your daughter's growing up, Jo. She's not a baby anymore. I know it's a shock to you, but there's nothing you can do about it. Unless you plan to stick her on a shelf between two dictionaries."

Feeling faint, Joséphine sat down on the deck chair nearest Iris. Confronting her sister and her daughter at the same time was more than she could handle. She slumped there for a moment, feeling shaky and defeated. She stared at the watery reflections, the plants, the white marble columns, and the blue mosaics without really seeing them. Then she got up and took a deep breath to hold back her tears. *The last thing I need is to make a fool of myself.* She turned around, ready to confront her daughter. But Hortense was over on the pool steps, testing the water with her toe.

"You shouldn't get so worked up in front of her, you know," muttered Iris, rolling over onto her stomach. "You lose all your credibility."

"Easy for you to say. She's awful to me."

"It's called adolescence, and she's in the thick of it."

"It's still awful. She treats me like dirt."

"Maybe that's because you let people walk all over you."

"What do you mean?"

"You let people treat you any way they please. You have no self-respect, so how do you expect others to respect you?"

Joséphine gaped at her sister.

"I mean it," Iris continued. "Remember when we were little, and I used to make you kneel in front of me and balance your most prized possession on top of your head. You had to bow and offer it to me without letting it fall. Otherwise, you'd be punished! Remember?"

"That was just a game!"

"Oh, it was more than a game. I was testing you. I wanted to see how far I could go, what I could get you to do. You should have put up a fight, but you never did. So don't be surprised your daughter treats you that way."

"Stop it! Next you're going to tell me it's my fault."

"Of course it's your fault!"

That was too much for Jo. Big tears rolled down her cheeks. She wept in silence as Iris regaled her with stories of their childhood, of the humiliating games she had invented to keep her sister enslaved.

Here I am back in my beloved Middle Ages, thought Joséphine. *I have and always will be a humble serf to my sister and to other people. Today, it's Hortense; tomorrow it'll be someone else.*

Having made her point, Iris rolled onto her back again, and their conversation continued as if nothing had happened.

"What are you doing for Christmas?"

Joséphine gulped, swallowing her tears. "I don't know. I haven't had time to think about it. Shirley asked if I wanted to go to Scotland with her."

"To stay with her parents?"

"No. She doesn't want to go back there, for some reason. We

would stay with friends of hers. But Hortense thinks Scotland is a total drag."

"We could spend Christmas together at the chalet."

"I'll have to think about it. It'll be the first Christmas without their father." Joséphine sighed. Then she had a terrible thought. "What about Mother Courage? Will she be there?"

"No, or I wouldn't have suggested it. I figure we'd better not let you two near one another without calling the bomb squad."

"Very funny. Did you mention it to Hortense?"

"Not yet. I only asked her what she wanted for Christmas. Same for Zoé."

"And she told you what she wanted?"

"A computer. But she said that you'd already offered to buy her one, and didn't want to hurt your feelings. See how thoughtful she can be?"

"That's one way of putting it. She practically bullied me into promising. And if I give her such an expensive gift, what can I give Zoé? I hate being unfair."

"That's where I can help, Jo. You know it's not that big a deal for me. If you like, I won't even tell the girls. I'll just give them a little present on the side and let you have all the glory."

"That's generous of you, but it wouldn't feel right."

"Come on, Jo. Lighten up."

"No, I mean it."

"Fine, I won't insist," Iris said with a smile. "But remember, Christmas is in three weeks and you don't have much time left to earn your millions. Unless you win the lottery."

Don't I know it! thought Joséphine to herself. *Don't I damned well know it! I was supposed to hand in the translation a week ago. I don't have time to do the research for my postdoc scholarship, and I'm lying to my sister about working for her husband. My life was once as neat as a musical score, and now it's just a big, noisy mess.*

While Joséphine continued her inner monologue, Alexandre was waiting patiently for Zoé to quit splashing about so he could ask her the questions buzzing in his head. Zoé was the only one who would know the answers. He couldn't confide in Carmen, or in his mother, or in Hortense, who always treated him like a baby. So when Zoé finally came to rest her elbows on the edge of the pool, Alex swam over and said:

"Zoé, listen to me. This is important."

"What's up?"

"Do you think that when grown-ups stop making love, it means they don't love each other anymore?"

"I don't know. Why?"

"Because Mom and Dad don't sleep together anymore. It's been two weeks. Dad sleeps in his study. In a little cot."

"Oh boy! Your parents are getting a divorce, for sure! And just wait, they'll start sending you to a shrinker. A kid in my school says that's a person who opens up your head to see what's going on inside."

"I already know what's going on in my head. I'm scared all the time. Before Dad started sleeping in his study I used to get up at night and listen at their bedroom door. And it was so quiet in there, it scared me! Before, they used to make love sometimes. It was noisy, but it made me feel better."

"So they don't make love at all anymore?"

Alexandre shook his head.

"And they aren't sleeping together?"

"Nope. Not for the last two weeks."

"Then you're going to end up just like me: divorced!"

Hortense, who had been practicing swimming underwater the length of the pool, popped up next to them just as Alexandre said, "Mom and Dad, divorced!" She floated on her back and pretended not to be listening, but Alexandre and Zoé stopped talking right away.

If they stop talking, it has to be something big, Hortense thought. *Aunt Iris and Uncle Philippe, divorced? If he left her, she'll have a lot less money, and she won't be able to spoil me the way she does.* Hortense thought about the computer. She'd been a fool to turn down Iris's offer. It would probably have been ten times better than the one her mother would choose. *Mom always talks about saving money. She's such a buzzkill with all her talk about saving. Life sucks big-time.*

Hortense observed the people around her. The women were elegant, and their husbands were . . . somewhere else. Too busy working, earning money so their gorgeous wives could lounge around the pool in the latest Eres bathing suits and Hermès pareo wraps. Earlier, Hortense had dashed out of the changing room to go hang out with her aunt, so those beautiful women would think Iris was her mother. She was ashamed of her own mom. At least her father was elegant and chic, and hung out with important people. He knew all the brands of Scotch, spoke English, played tennis and bridge, knew how to dress. Hortense's eyes came back to rest on Iris. *She doesn't look all that sad. Maybe Alexandre's wrong; he's such a dummy. Just like Mom, sitting there, wrapped in her bathrobe. I bet she never gets in the water now. I've made her ashamed.*

"Aren't you going in?" Iris asked Joséphine.

"No, when I was in the changing room I noticed that I had . . . that it's not a good time of the month for me."

"You're such a prude! You mean you have your period?"

Joséphine nodded.

"Well, let's go have some tea, then."

Iris pulled her bathrobe closed, grabbed her bag, and headed toward the tearoom, which was behind a hedge. Joséphine followed.

"Do you want a piece of cake or pie to go with your tea?" Iris asked as she sat down. "The apple tart's delicious."

"Just tea. I started a diet when I walked in the door of this place, and I feel thinner already."

Iris ordered tea and a slice of tart. As the waitress left, two smiling women approached the table. Iris stiffened, and Joséphine was surprised at her sister's obvious discomfiture.

"Hello!" the women exclaimed in unison. "What a surprise!"

"Hello," Iris replied. "My sister Joséphine . . . These are friends, Bérengère Clavert and Nadia Serrurier."

The women flashed a brief smile at Joséphine and promptly ignored her, turning back to Iris.

"So what's this Nadia tells me? That you've taken up writing?" Bérengère's face was taut with envy.

"My husband told me about it after that dinner the other

night," Nadia explained. "I couldn't go because my daughter had a fever. He was all excited." To Joséphine she said, "My husband's a publisher."

"Bravo, darling!" said Bérengère. "I think it's fantastic! You've been talking about it forever and now it's really happening. So when will we get to read it?"

"I'm just toying with the idea right now," said Iris fiddling with the belt of her bathrobe. "I'm not actually doing any writing."

"Don't say that!" exclaimed Nadia. "Gaston expects a manuscript soon. You really hooked him with your stories about the Middle Ages! That's all he talks about these days."

Joséphine stifled a cry of surprise when her sister kicked her under the table.

"And you're so photogenic, Iris," said Bérengère. "All they have to do is put those big blue eyes on the cover and it'll be a best seller! Don't you think so, Nadia?"

"Last I heard, eyes don't write books," Iris snapped.

"No, but Bérengère is right. Gaston always says that it's not enough to *write* a book, you have to *sell* it. And that's where your eyes will make a big impression. With your eyes and your connections, you're bound to have a hit."

"All you have to do is write it, darling!" Bérengère clapped her hands to show how exciting she thought it all was. "Whoops! I have to hurry. I'm late! Bye, darling. We'll talk."

The women left in a little flurry of friendly waves.

"Great!" Iris said with annoyance. "Now all Paris will know I'm writing a book."

"A book about the Middle Ages? Was that some kind of joke?"

"Take it easy, Jo. It's not a big deal. I was at a dinner party the other night, and I was so bored that I made up this story about writing a book. When they asked what it was about, I started blathering about life in the twelfth century. Don't ask me why. It just came out."

"But you always said that stuff was so hokey."

"Yeah, I know. I was caught off guard. But it really hit home. You should have seen Serrurier's face. He got all worked up about it. So I kept on talking, and I got excited too, the way you do when you talk about it. Funny, isn't it? I must have repeated some of the things you've spouted over the years, word for word. I don't know what I'm going to do now. I'll just have to keep them in suspense."

"You can read some of my work. I can give you my notes, if you want. The twelfth century is full of stories that would make wonderful novels."

"Jo, get serious! I can't write a novel. I'd love to, but I can't even string five sentences in a row."

"Have you actually tried?"

"Yes, I have. I've been trying for the last four months, and all I have is a couple of lines to show for it. I'm not even close!" Iris laughed sarcastically. "I just need to keep up the pretense long enough for everyone to forget about the whole thing."

Baffled, Joséphine stared at her sister.

"You think I'm ridiculous, don't you?" Iris asked. "Go ahead, say it. You'd be right."

"No . . . I'm just sort of surprised, really. Telling people something like this isn't like you, that's all."

"Well, yeah. But let's not make too much of it. I'll find a way. I'll make something up. It wouldn't be the first time."

Joséphine was taken aback. "What do you mean, it wouldn't be the first time? That you told a lie?"

"Not the first time I've been in deep shit, you twit!"

There was an edge to Iris's voice, a combination of spite and irritation. Joséphine had never heard her sister sound that nasty. But what really surprised her was the hint of jealousy she sensed. She felt guilty for even noticing it.

"I'll help you! I'll find a story for you to tell. Next time you see your publisher, you'll dazzle him with medieval culture."

"Is that so? Dazzle a highly educated man with my ignorance? I don't think so."

"Listen to me! You know the story of Rollo, the leader of the Normans, don't you? They said he was so tall that when he rode horseback, his feet dragged on the ground."

"Never heard of him."

"He was a tireless explorer and a great sailor. From Norway. Terrorized people wherever he went. Claimed the only way a warrior could get to heaven was to die in battle. Doesn't that ring a bell? You could create a character based on him. He's the founder of Normandy, for goodness sake!"

"I couldn't pull it off, Jo. I don't know a thing about that period."

"Wait, I have an idea! Tell the publisher that *Gone with the*

Wind—you know, the Margaret Mitchell novel—got its title from a poem by François Villon."

"Is that really true?"

"Sure is! 'Autant en emporte le vent' is a line from a Villon sonnet."

Eager to get her irritated sister to smile, Jo stood up and began reciting, like a Roman tribune haranguing the masses:

> *Princes à mort sont destinés*
> *Et tous autres qui sont vivants*
> *S'ils en sont chagrins ou courroucés*
> *Autant en emporte le vent.*

"There you have it: Gone with the wind."

Smiling weakly, Iris gazed at Joséphine. She'd gotten completely into the recitation. She seemed to glow with a soft light of indefinable charm. She'd become knowledgeable and confident, totally unlike the Joséphine Iris knew! Iris looked at her with a touch of envy. It appeared and vanished in a flash, but it lasted just long enough for Joséphine to notice.

"Come back to earth, Jo. They don't give a good goddamn about François Villon!"

Joséphine sighed.

"I was only trying to help."

"I know, and it's very sweet of you. You're a nice person, Jo. Completely out of it, but very nice."

There was resentment in Iris's voice, and a hint of that jealousy Joséphine was sure she'd glimpsed. *I can't be all that hopeless if Iris is jealous of me*, Jo thought, sitting up taller. *And I didn't order that apple tart. I've probably lost a few ounces already.*

Joséphine looked triumphantly around her. *I have something my sister doesn't have, and she covets it! And if a publisher ever asked me, what stories I could tell! Thousands of them! I'd bring them to life, too. The gleaming brass trumpets, the galloping horses, the sweat of battle . . .*

Joséphine shivered with pleasure. She suddenly felt a powerful urge to rummage around in her notebooks, to immerse herself in the centuries that so enchanted her.

She glanced at her watch. "I'm afraid I have to go home. I have work to do." Iris looked up and nodded glumly. "I'll get the girls on the way. Thanks for everything!"

Jo was eager to leave, to get out of a place where everything suddenly seemed fake and pretentious.

"Let's go, girls," she called. "We're going home. And no whining."

Hortense and Zoé climbed out of the pool and followed their mother. Joséphine felt a foot taller. She was dancing on air, moving like a queen across the spotless white carpet, catching her reflection in the mirrors. On her way to the changing room, she gave the woman at the front desk a triumphant smile. Just as she did, her bathrobe fell open.

"Oh, congratulations, madame!" said the young woman warmly.

"Congratulations? What for?"

"I hadn't noticed that you were pregnant. I so envy you! My husband and I have been trying for three years."

Joséphine gaped at her in disbelief, then looked down at her belly and reddened. Now her feet felt leaden as she stumbled into the changing room.

In the stall next to her mother's, Zoé was mulling over what Alexandre had said. *Iris and Philippe simply mustn't break up!* Her aunt and her uncle were the only family she had left. She'd never known her father's family. "I don't have any relatives," her dad used to whisper, kissing her on the neck. "You're all I've got!" Zoé had to come up with a bright idea, some way to keep Iris and Philippe together. She would tell Max Barthillet about it! A big smile lit up her face. She and Max made a great team. He had taught her so many things. Thanks to him, she wasn't such a scaredy cat. Zoé could hear her mother's voice, calling impatiently.

"Coming, Mommy!" she cried.

Chapter 6

♦　♦　♦

The screams woke Antoine up. Mylène was clinging to him, shaking and pointing at something.

"Antoine! Look there! There!"

Her lips were white and her eyes bulging with fear.

"Antoine, do something!"

Antoine had trouble getting his bearings. Even after more than three months at Croco Park, he still woke up half dazed every morning, searching for the curtains of his room in Courbevoie. He looked at Mylène, surprised that she wasn't Joséphine in her nightie with the blue forget-me-nots, surprised that the girls weren't bouncing on their bed, yelling, "Get up, Dad! Get up!"

Each morning, he had to go through the same process of remembering. *I'm in Croco Park, on the east coast of Kenya between Malindi and Mombasa, and I'm raising crocodiles for a big Chinese company. I've left my wife and my two daughters. And I'm not going back. I'm raising crocodiles and I'm going to be rich as Croesus. I'll double my money, and people will flock to me with other investment projects, and I'll smoke a big cigar and choose the one that will make me even richer! And then I'll return to France. I'll pay Joséphine back a hundred times over, I'll dress the girls like Russian princesses, and I'll buy them each a beautiful apartment. We'll be a happy, prosperous family. When I'm rich.*

Every morning, he got up, took a shower, shaved, dressed, and went down to breakfast, prepared by Pong, his manservant. To please him, Pong had learned a few words of French. "Dejeuner est prêt, patron," he would say. "Mangez! Bon appétit!"

Mylène would fall back asleep under the mosquito netting.

At seven o'clock, Antoine met the workers with Mr. Lee, who gave them their orders for the day. Forever smiling, they stood ramrod-straight, their skinny legs in baggy shorts, like soldiers at attention.

"Yes, sir!" they would chorus, their chins up.

But that morning, Antoine knew things weren't going to go as usual. "What is it, darling? Did you have a nightmare?"

"Antoine. Look over there! I'm not dreaming! It . . . it licked my hand!"

There weren't any cats or dogs on the plantation. The Chinese fed them to the crocodiles.

"Mylène, darling, go back to sleep. It's still early."

But she dug her nails into Antoine's neck. He rubbed his eyes. Then, leaning over her shoulder, he saw a fat, shiny crocodile, its yellow eyes fixed on him in the half-light.

"Right," he said, gulping. "We have a problem here. Don't move, Mylène. Whatever you do, don't move! Crocodiles attack if you move. If you stay still, they won't bother you."

"But look at it! It's staring at us!"

"If we don't move, it'll be friendly."

Antoine stared at the animal. The crocodile stared back. Yawning, it revealed a row of sharp, powerful teeth. Then it waddled closer to the bed.

"Pong!" Antoine yelled. "Pong, where are you?"

Now the crocodile was looking at Mylène and making a strange whining sound deep in its throat. Antoine burst out laughing.

"I think it's courting you, Mylène."

He heard hurrying footsteps on the stairs, then a knock at the door. It was Pong. Antoine told him to deal with the animal. He pulled the sheet up over Mylène's breasts, which Pong pretended not to see.

"Bambi! Bambi!" he squealed affectionately. "Come here, my beautiful Bambi! Those people are friends!"

The crocodile slowly swung its yellow eyes around, paused for a moment, and sighed. Then it ambled toward Pong, who stroked it tenderly between the eyes.

"Good boy, Bambi. Good boy."

He pulled a chicken thigh out of the pocket of his shorts and held it out for the animal, who snapped it out of the air. That was too much for Mylène.

"Pong," she said hoarsely, "take . . . that thing . . . Bambi out! *Now!*"

"Yes, ma'am. Come on, Bambi."

The crocodile swaggered off after him. Shaking with fury, Mylène gave Antoine a long look that meant, *I never want to see that animal in the house again, get it?* Antoine nodded, threw on shorts and a T-shirt, and took off after Pong and Bambi.

He found them in the kitchen with Ming, Pong's wife. Antoine had learned to be careful never to confront the Chinese directly. They were hypersensitive, and even a slight reprimand could cause a feeling of humiliation that lasted a long time. So he calmly asked Pong where the animal had come from. Charming though the crocodile was, he said, it was threatening and had no place in the house.

Pong explained that Bambi's mother had died on the flight from Thailand. At the time, Bambi was no bigger than a tadpole and so cute that he and Ming became attached to the little creature and adopted him. Growing up, Bambi had never once attacked them. Usually he lived in a fenced pond, but this morning he had managed to escape.

Antoine sighed as he wiped the sweat from his forehead. *As if I didn't have enough problems already.* He made Pong promise to lock Bambi up securely and to keep an eye on him. He didn't want him in the house again. Pong smiled and bowed, thanking Antoine for being so understanding.

"Nevermore, Mr. Tonio, nevermore!" he rasped, bowing deeper and faster.

The Croco Park plantation consisted of the coop where they raised chickens to feed the crocodiles and staff; the crocodile farm proper, whose pens extended from the coral reefs across several hundreds of acres and included a number of man-made canals; the canning factory, where the crocodile meat was canned; and the factory where the crocodile hides were removed, treated, and prepared to be shipped to China. There they were turned into suitcases, bags, card holders, wallets, and purses—and stamped with the logos of famous designers. That was the part of the business that most concerned Antoine, who worried there would be an international backlash if it were discovered that the trafficking started on his plantation. When owner Yang Wei had come from Beijing to Paris to meet and hire him, he hadn't told Antoine about that part of his job. Wei had mostly emphasized the crocodile breeding and the meat and egg production business, both of which needed to be state-of-the-art and on a solid financial footing.

Wei had mentioned "ancillary" activities, but without going into detail. Grinning broadly, he promised Antoine a percentage on everything that left the plantation, "dead or alive."

It was too late to make a stink now, and Antoine knew it. Morally and financially, he was in up to his neck.

Antoine had big dreams. Burned by what happened at Gunman & Co., he had promised himself he would become someone to be reckoned with. He had taken out a loan and bought 10 percent of the Croco Park business. To do that, Antoine had gone to see their banker Faugeron at Crédit Commercial and shown him the plans for Croco Park and its anticipated profits over one, two, and five years. Faugeron was skeptical at first, but he knew Antoine and Joséphine, and figured that Marcel Grobz's fortune and Philippe Dupin's reputation would serve as security. In the end, Faugeron loaned Antoine 200,000 euros. The first monthly loan payment had been due October 15, but Antoine hadn't been able to make it; he hadn't been paid himself yet. Administrative issues, Yang Wei explained once Antoine finally reached him on the phone after several attempts.

"I'll pay you three months all at once next time," Antoine promised Faugeron. "By December fifteenth at the latest." He could tell from the banker's voice that he was concerned, and used his most upbeat tone to reassure him. "Don't worry, Monsieur Faugeron, we're talking big business here! China is on the move. It's the place to be. I make deals that would make your employees green with envy. Millions of dollars pass through my hands each day!"

"I trust that the money is clean, Mr. Cortès," the banker responded coldly.

Antoine awoke every morning with the same anxiety, haunted by Faugeron's comment. And every morning he checked the mail to see if his paycheck had arrived.

He hadn't lied to Hortense and Zoé. He really was in charge of seventy thousand crocodiles. He read everything he could about crocodile behavior, hoping it would help him boost their output and breeding.

"They're not aggressive just for the fun of it," he explained to Mylène, who was frightened of them. "It's instinct. They eliminate the weakest and clean up the environment around them as they go. They literally vacuum junk from rivers."

"Sure, and if they catch you, they gobble you down in the blink of an eye. They're the most dangerous animal in the world, Antoine!"

"And completely predictable. We know how and why they

attack. If you splash about in the water, crocodiles think you're an injured animal and it's all over. But if you just slip slowly in, they won't stir. Want to try?"

Mylène shuddered visibly at the idea, and Antoine burst out laughing.

"No, really, Pong showed me. The other day he got right next to one and stayed very still, and the crocodile didn't do a thing."

"I don't believe you."

"It's true, I swear! I saw it with my own eyes."

"You know, Antoine, at night sometimes I get up to watch them and I see their eyes in the dark. They look like flashlights or little yellow lanterns floating on the water. Don't they ever sleep?"

Antoine laughed, and hugged her tight. Mylène was good company. She wasn't used to their new life yet, but was eager to make the best of it. "I wish I could be doing something useful," she said, "like Meryl Streep in *Out of Africa*. Remember that movie? She was so beautiful! I could do what she did and open an infirmary. I got my first aid certificate when I was in school. I could learn to disinfect wounds, to sew them up. At least I'd keep myself busy. Or—I know!—I could be a tour guide for the tourists that come through."

"Except that they aren't coming anymore. Too many accidents."

"That's too bad. I could have opened a souvenir shop. It would have brought in some cash."

The biggest problem Antoine faced was feeding the crocodiles. The canals dug for them extended into rich hunting territory, but the antelopes and other prey animals had grown wary and went farther upriver to drink. So the crocs depended more and more on the food provided by the plantation workers. Mr. Lee had been forced to initiate "feeding rounds," where the staff would walk along the canals, dragging strings of chicken carcasses in the water. When they thought no one was looking, the workers would quickly unhook a chicken and eat it. They tossed the bones away and continued walking.

The plantation soon had to start raising more chickens.

The crocodile parks farther inland didn't have that problem. The land they were on had been left wild, and the crocodiles caught their own prey at the water holes.

The local breeders would get together in Mombasa, the closest city to Croco Park, in a place called, appropriately enough, the Crocodile Café. Antoine listened to the conversations between these old breeders, toughened by Africa, experience, and the sun. They swapped the latest news, talked about the price of meat, the latest market for hides. They also shared their views about the crocodiles themselves. "They'll outlive us, that's for sure," one breeder said. "They communicate among themselves, see. They're always showing who the new leader is. It's very important to them to know who the strongest one is. Just like men, right?"

"So, how are you getting along with your boss?" asked another, turning to Antoine. "Does he pay you on time, or does he bullshit you and string you along? They're always trying to screw us. Raise a ruckus, Tonio! Don't let yourself be cowed. Make them respect you!"

The others laughed. Antoine watched as their jaws worked. A trickle of sweat ran down his back.

He ordered a round of drinks, and lifted a cold beer to his sunburned lips. "Here's to us, guys!" he said loudly. "And to the crocs!" They raised their glasses, drank deeply, and rolled themselves cigarettes. "There's good shit here, Tonio. You should try it. Helps to soften the blow on a bad night when you haven't made your quotas and you're freaking out." Antoine turned down the offer. He was dying to ask them what they knew about Mr. Wei, or why the previous plantation director had left, but he didn't dare.

They gazed at him out of the slits of their yellow crocodile eyes.

The hardest part was hiding his anxiety from Mylène when he came back from his trips to Mombasa. She would question him about what he had seen, what he had learned. He knew she was seeking reassurance. She had used up all her savings to pay for the trip and what she called "the basics" they needed for their new house—the previous owner had stripped the place when he left. "I'm so happy to be part of this adventure," she'd sighed, handing him her credit card. Nothing was too good for their "little love nest," she said. And thanks to her, the house had become a home. She bought a sewing machine—an old Singer she found at the market—and made curtains, bedspreads, table-cloths, and napkins. Some of the Chinese workers started bringing her things for mending, which she did cheerfully. At times, when Antoine came home unexpectedly and wanted to kiss her, she would have a mouth full of pins. On the weekends they went to the white beaches of Malindi and went scuba diving.

But three months had gone by, and Mylène was no longer sighing with happiness. Every day she waited anxiously for the mail to arrive. Antoine could see his own anxiety reflected in her eyes. On December 15 there was nothing in the mail. The day passed in gloomy silence. Pong went about his duties without a word. Antoine didn't touch his breakfast; he was sick of eggs. *In ten days it'll be Christmas, and I haven't been able to send anything to Joséphine or the girls. In ten days it'll be Christmas, and I'll be sitting here with Mylène, mournfully sipping cold champagne, all our hopes ground to dust.*

Tonight I'm calling Wei, and this time I'm going to do some yelling! Given the time difference, Antoine was sure to catch Wei at home. But in the evening, reality didn't have such a jagged edge, and the yellow eyes of the crocodiles were a thousand points of light. The wind picked up, and the stifling heat of the day over the grasslands and the swamp eased. A light mist was rising. You could breathe again. Contours softened, and hope rose anew. Antoine smiled at Mylène. Relieved to see him relaxed, she smiled back.

The publisher was delighted. He'd opened the folder, rubbed his hands, and said, "Let's just take a quick look." Wetting his index finger, he leafed through a dozen pages, nodding with satisfaction. "You write very well, Madame Cortès. The prose flows, it's elegant and simple. Like an Yves Saint Laurent dress!"

Joséphine blushed, unaccustomed to such praise. "Audrey inspired me," she stammered.

"Don't be so modest. You have real talent. Would you consider taking on other projects like this one?"

"Yes, of course."

"In that case, I'll be in touch soon. You can stop by the accounting department, one floor down, and they'll give you your check."

He stuck out his hand, and Joséphine gripped it like someone clinging to a lifeboat in a storm.

"Good-bye, Madame Cortès."

"Good-bye, monsieur."

Joséphine was too shy to say anything or look at the check when the bookkeeper handed her the envelope. She just tucked it away. She'd been in a cold sweat. Only when she was in the elevator did she gently peel open the envelope, unsticking one corner, making the opening bigger. She had plenty of time coming down from the fourteenth floor, detaching the check from the letter it was stapled to. When she saw the amount, her head began to swim and she had to lean against the side of the elevator cage.

The check was for 8,012 euros—four times her monthly salary at the CNRS! Eight thousand and twelve euros for translating the life of the adorable Audrey Hepburn.

Joséphine held her purse tightly under her arm and decided to deposit the check at the bank right away. "Hello, Monsieur Faugeron!" she would say. "Guess what I have in my purse? Eight thousand euros!"

She decided to splurge and take a taxi.

At the bank she filled out the deposit slip, beaming with pride as she wrote the numbers. When she got to the teller's window, she asked if Faugeron was there. She was told that he was with a client, but that he'd be there around five thirty. "Tell him to call me," Joséphine replied, closing her bag. "I'm Madame Cortès."

Leaving the bank, Joséphine decided to head straight for the mall at La Défense. She would shower the girls with Christmas presents. *My little darlings will get everything their hearts desire. Better yet, they'll get as many gifts as their cousin Alexandre!*

She peered into the expensive boutique windows. Zoé and Hortense wouldn't have a father at Christmas, but she would dazzle them with presents. With the swipe of her credit card, she, Joséphine, would be Daddy, Mommy, and Santa Claus all in one. *I want them to fall asleep at night thinking, Mom is here, Mom is watching over us, nothing bad will happen to us.*

As she wound her way through the rows of shops decked out in tinsel, Christmas trees, and Santa Clauses with billowy white beards, she thanked God, the stars, and the heavens for her good fortune. Then she remembered that she had to put some of the money aside to pay her taxes. Joséphine wasn't the kind of woman to lose her head.

Yet within an hour at the computer store, she'd spent a third of her check. Her head was spinning. Salespeople buzzed around her, offering soothing advice, like the sirens that enchanted Ulysses. She wasn't used to it, and didn't dare say no. Any question she asked was quickly and smoothly deflected.

For a few more euros, they would install the necessary software on the computer. For a few more euros, they could deliver it all to her home. For a few more euros . . .

Feeling half drunk, Joséphine agreed to everything. "You can deliver everything today because I work at home. And could you do it during the day, during school hours, to keep it a secret from my girls?"

"No problem, madame."

Jo walked home in the wind that howled along the wide avenues of La Défense, her collar turned up and her head down. She could have bought herself something warmer, she thought. *Maybe I'll splurge and buy myself a new coat after the next translation. Antoine gave me this one ten years ago.*

Antoine wouldn't be home for Christmas. Their first Christmas without him.

The other day, at the library, Joséphine had looked at a book on Kenya and found Mombasa, the white beaches, the old neighborhood of Malindi, the small craft shops. Everyone looked friendly and welcoming. What about Mylène? Was she warm and welcoming, too? Joséphine snapped the book shut.

She never saw Duffel Coat Man at the library anymore. He had probably finished his project and was strolling the streets of Paris with a pretty blonde's hand slipped into his pocket.

In front of her apartment building, Joséphine ran into Christine Barthillet, and instinctively pulled back. The woman had the look of a trapped animal. She stared at her shoes when she saw Joséphine, and they passed each other in tense silence. Joséphine couldn't bring herself to ask how things were. She had heard that Monsieur Barthillet had left.

Her happy mood from earlier in the afternoon had vanished. The phone was ringing when she opened the door to her apartment; she answered it wearily. It was Faugeron, calling to congratulate her for the check she had deposited at the bank. Then he said something she didn't immediately grasp.

"This deposit is very timely, Madame Cortès. As you know, you've been overdrawn for the past three months."

Joséphine's mouth went dry, her hands suddenly gripping the telephone. Overdrawn? For three months? But she'd been balancing her checkbook every day. She couldn't possibly be overdrawn.

"As you know, your husband opened an account before leaving for Kenya. He took out a big loan and hasn't made any payments since October fifteenth."

"A loan? Antoine?"

"The account is in his name, Madame Cortès, but you're a cosigner of the loan and responsible as the loan's guarantor."

Jo's silence told Faugeron a great deal.

"You must have signed some papers, Madame Cortès. Try to remember."

Concentrating with great effort, Joséphine recalled that, indeed, Antoine had had her sign some bank papers before he left. He had talked about some sort of plan, an investment in the future. That was at the beginning of September. She had trusted him. She always signed with her eyes closed.

"I'm sorry to say this, but you are responsible for his debts. Now, if you could stop by the bank, we can find a way to restructure the loan. Perhaps you could ask your father-in-law for help."

"Never, Monsieur Faugeron! I'll never do that."

"I'm afraid you may have to, madame."

"I'll find a way. I'll manage."

"That's fine. In the meantime, we'll apply the eight thousand and twelve euros to the shortfall your husband left."

"It's just that I bought some things this afternoon. For the girls. For Christmas," she finally managed to say. "I bought a computer and . . . Wait, I have the credit card receipts."

She dug around in her bag, found her wallet, and took out the receipts. She slowly added the amounts and gave Faugeron the total figure.

"Well, it'll be awfully tight, Madame Cortès. Especially if your husband doesn't make the January fifteenth installment on time."

Joséphine didn't know what more to say. Her gaze lit on the kitchen table and the old IBM Selectric typewriter that Marcel had given her.

"I'll deal with this, Monsieur Faugeron. Just give me some time to get on my feet. I was offered another well-paid job this morning. It'll only be a matter of days."

Joséphine was babbling. She felt she was drowning.

"Of course, Madame Cortès. I'm sure you'll manage. In the meantime, do you and your family have any Christmas plans?"

"I'm going to my sister's place in Megève," she said, sounding like a groggy boxer being given the referee's ten count.

"That's nice. It's good to have family. People shouldn't be alone during the holidays. Merry Christmas, Madame Cortès."

Joséphine hung up and stumbled out onto the balcony, where she'd taken to hiding of late. She liked looking at the stars, and whenever she saw a twinkle or a shooting star, she took it as a sign that someone or something was watching over her. That night, she kneeled on the concrete pad, put her hands together, and prayed aloud:

"Stars, please, please make it so that I'm not alone anymore, or poor, or tired. Give me strength. Send me someone to love, who will love me. I don't care if he's tall or short, rich or poor, young or old. But I can't live without love." Joséphine bowed her head to the cement floor and gave herself up to an endless prayer.

Chapter 7

♦ ♦ ♦

$\mathcal{M}$any years before, Marcel Grobz had fallen in love with a two-story building with a private courtyard that was festooned with wisteria vines, and bought it. He'd been looking for a classy place to start his company, and was amazed that they sold it to him for so little. It felt monastic, yet the kind of place that would bolster his authority. He was happy as a flea in a doghouse.

Marcel bought it all: the main building, the workshop, the courtyard, and the wisteria vines, as well as an old stable with broken windows that he fixed up.

It was there, at 75, avenue Niel, that Casamia took off.

It was also there that, one October day in 1970, René Lemarié showed up. René was ten years younger than Marcel, and had a narrow waist and broad shoulders. He had a shaved head, a deep tan, and a broken nose.

What a guy! thought Marcel as the younger man made his pitch.

"I can do anything under the sun, no bullshit," said René. "And I don't screw around. I may not have a big name or a fancy diploma, but I know how to make myself useful. Take me on probation, and you'll be begging me to stay."

René had recently married a tiny, cheerful blonde named Ginette. Marcel hired them both, giving Ginette a job in the warehouse. She had wanted to be a singer, but it was either René or the stage, and she chose René. Every so often the mood would hit her and she'd go stand under the big shop windows and belt out a song while imagining a horde of screaming fans at her feet. She'd sung backup for Rocky Volcano, Dick Rivers, and Sylvie Vartan, and every Saturday was karaoke night at René and Ginette's place.

Ginette had never outgrown the sixties; she wore flats and checkered capris and big hair, like Sylvie Vartan in the old days. She owned every back issue of *Salut les copains* and *Mademoiselle age tendre* and would flip through them when she was feeling nostalgic.

Marcel let René and Ginette have the space above the stables. They turned it into a real home, and raised their three children there: Eddy, Johnny, and Sylvie.

When Marcel first hired René, he put off defining his job too exactly. "I'm starting out," he said. "You can start out with me." Since then, the two men had grown as close as the wisteria vines twining up the building facade.

Every night before leaving work, Marcel would head down to the warehouse to have a glass of red wine with René. René would bring out some sausage, a Camembert, a baguette, and some salted butter. They would shoot the breeze while looking at the wisteria vines through the windows. In thirty years, the wisteria had grown from young tendrils into thick, knotty vines, covering everything.

But Marcel hadn't come down to hang out with René for a month now.

And when he did come, it was because of some problem or other. He would storm in, grumpily ask a question or bark an order, then leave, avoiding René's eye.

At first René had been offended. So when Marcel showed up in one of his black moods, René would jump on a forklift and go off to inventory crates in the back of the warehouse. This little game lasted three weeks. Three weeks without a hunk of sausage or a shot of red wine, without any gossip under the wisteria. Eventually René realized that he was playing Marcel's game, and that Marcel wasn't going to make the first move.

So he swallowed his pride and went upstairs to talk to Josiane.

"What's going on with the old man?"

To his surprise, she just shrugged.

"Ask him yourself. He's been giving me the cold shoulder."

Josiane looks like hell, René thought. *She's thinner, pale, and that dab of color on her cheeks looks like cheap blush.*

"Is he in his office?"

Josiane nodded.

René pushed open the office door to find Marcel slumped in his armchair, head down, sniffing a piece of fabric.

"You testing a new product?" René walked over and grabbed it out of his friend's hands. "What the heck is this?"

"Josiane's pantyhose."

"Why the hell are you sniffing that?"

Marcel looked both miserable and angry. René sat down on the desk, looked him in the eye, and waited.

Away from his office and his financial success, Marcel reverted to the unhappy boy he'd once been, wandering the streets of Paris alone. He'd become rich and powerful, but once he'd achieved that, he lost his purpose in life. The richer Marcel got, the more he lost his common sense. And he'd been taken for a ride by Henriette Grobz.

René had thought that marrying Henriette was a bad idea, that signing the prenuptial agreement was stupid, and that making her head of his board of directors was insane. Marcel couldn't make a single major business decision without her consent.

"You're nuts!" René yelled when he learned the terms of the contract. "It's highway robbery. The woman's a crook. And you think she loves you, you poor idiot?" Marcel stormed out of the warehouse, slamming the door behind him.

They went a whole month without speaking that time. And when they patched things up, they tacitly agreed not to raise the topic again.

And now Marcel was slumped on his desk, sniffing an old stocking.

"You just gonna sit there forever? You look like a toad on a matchbox."

Marcel didn't answer. He had lost a lot of weight, and his cheeks sagged like empty bags. He had become a dazed, pale old man on the verge of tears. His eyes glistened, their lids red.

"Pull yourself together, Marcel. You look pathetic. Show some self-respect."

Marcel shrugged helplessly at "self-respect." He gave René a rheumy look and lifted a hand, as if to ask, *What's the point?*

René stared at him in disbelief. This couldn't be the man who had once taught him business as war, who could stare down the toughest union boss in Poland. In those days, Marcel had it all: success, money, and the girl.

"I've got it made!" he'd say, slapping René on the back. "And soon I'll be bouncing little Marcel Junior on my knee."

But Junior never showed up, and René would sometimes catch Marcel looking sadly at his kids, especially Eddy and Johnny. He would lift a heavy hand to wave, as if he were saying farewell to a dream.

René brushed cigarette ash off his overalls.

"All right, out with it. What the hell's going on? The way you've been looking for the last month, it better be good!"

Marcel hesitated, then slowly looked up at his friend and told him everything: Chaval and Josiane together at the coffee machine, Henriette's efforts to get Josiane fired, and his loss of interest in the business.

"René, I barely manage to get dressed in the morning. I've lost it. Seeing the two of them all over each other reminded me how old I am. It was like having my birth certificate shoved down my throat. It killed me to see my sweetie-pie in the arms of a guy who's younger and sexier. And especially Chaval, who would steal a gold tooth out of his mother's mouth!"

Marcel stood up and swept everything off the desk. Files, telephone, lamp, went crashing to the floor.

René was silent for a moment. Then gently but firmly, the

way you would speak to a child having a tantrum, he said to his friend:

"Well, I think your sweetie-pie isn't doing much better than you are. Her thing with Chaval didn't mean a damn thing. A little taste on the side, a quick fuck behind the counter. Don't tell me you've never done that."

"That's different!" Marcel sat up straight.

"Why? Because you're a man? That's old hat, Marcel. Women have changed, you know. Josiane's in love with you! Do you ever even look at her, moping behind her desk? No, you march right by, proud as a peacock. Haven't you noticed that she's lost weight, she's swimming in her clothes, and the rouge she's slapping on her face is all fake?"

Marcel shook his head.

Suddenly René had an idea. He crossed his arms and told Marcel that his greatest fear had become a reality: their Chinese manufacturer had made a mistake with his orders. They'd confused inches and centimeters!

"I noticed it when I was going over the order slips for the Beijing factory. You better come see right now!"

"What? Goddamn it!" Marcel roared. "That could cost us a bundle! Why didn't you tell me right away?"

He jumped up, grabbed his jacket and glasses, and clattered down the stairs to René's office.

René followed, and as they passed Josiane's desk, he shouted, "Grab your steno pad, Josiane. We've got yellow fever in Beijing!"

In his office, René opened the ledger on his desk, then slapped his forehead. "Damn, wrong ledger! I left the big one at the loading dock desk. You stay put. I'll go get it."

He left, pulled the door closed behind him, and—click!—locked the two of them in. He walked off, rubbing his hands.

In the office, Josiane and Marcel waited. It was the first time they had been face-to-face and alone since the coffee machine incident. They could hear vans pulling up to the loading docks and workers yelling at the drivers.

"What's René doing?" Marcel grumbled, looking out the window.

"Not a damned thing. He's already done what he wanted—getting us together. That story about the messed-up Chinese order was bullshit."

"You think so?"

"Just try the door. I bet it's locked. We're caught like rats in a trap."

Marcel turned the handle, then jiggled it. The door wouldn't open. He kicked it hard.

"As if I have nothing better to do!" Marcel yelled.

"How about me? I'm busy too."

The air in the office smelled of old cigarettes, the electric heater, which was going full blast, and a sweater drying on a chair. Josiane wrinkled her nose and sniffled. She turned to look at the wisteria vine outside the window and saw Henriette striding in their direction.

"Shit!" she hissed. "It's the Toothpick!"

"Hide, in case she decides to come this way."

He pulled her close, and they crouched down against the wall below the window.

"Why are you so scared of her?"

Marcel put his hand on her mouth and squeezed her tightly against him.

"You keep forgetting that she signs off on everything."

"Because you were dumb enough to give her the power."

"Give me a break! You weren't looking so cool yourself the other day, draped all over that stud muffin at the coffee machine."

"I was just getting some coffee, that's all."

Marcel almost choked.

"Oh, for Christ's sake! Are you saying you weren't in Chaval's arms?"

"Well, yeah, we did fool around a little. But it was just to get a rise out of you."

Marcel shrugged and started polishing the tips of his shoes with his jacket cuff.

"I'd had it with you, Marcel."

"Oh, really?" he said, pretending to be preoccupied with his shoes.

"I'd had it up to here with seeing you every night with the Toothpick! It drives me crazy. My life is zooming by, and I don't have a grip on it. You and I have been together for years, and we're still sneaking around. You never ever take me out in public, or anywhere nice. I'm what you do in the dark, a nice warm place to park your johnson.

"I make little Johnny happy, but before I know it, you're

packing your bags and heading home. You slip me some jewelry when I threaten to freeze you out, but otherwise, it's nothing but promises. So I cracked, that day. And on top of it all, she was really mean to me. I'd just learned my mom had died, and she told me I shouldn't be crying on company time. I could have strangled her!"

Leaning against the wall, Marcel listened. He could feel himself melting. Josiane felt Marcel's body relax, and she continued in a whisper. "It was really hard to lose my mother, you know. I thought I'd be okay about it, but it really knocked the stuffing out of me."

She took Marcel's hand and laid it between her breasts.

"It was like I was two years old again," she said. "When you look up trustingly at the one person who should protect you, and all you get is a slap. You never really recover from those kinds of hurt, ever. You pretend you're fine, you hold your chin up, but . . ."

"Oh, sweetie-pie, it's so good to hear your voice again. Go on, tell me more. I love hearing you talk."

Henriette had gone up to her husband's office and, finding neither Josiane nor Marcel, went in search of René. She found him in the warehouse. René turned when he saw her, but a glance at his office window reassured him that the bickering lovers had hidden. He asked Henriette what he could do for her.

"I'm looking for Marcel," she said curtly.

"Must be in his office."

"He isn't there."

René assumed a surprised air and pretended to think.

Henriette's pink face powder raised dry patches on her skin and emphasized the fine lines around her mouth and the sag of her jowls. She had an old lady's face with a beak of a nose framing lips so thin and pursed that her lipstick looked smeared. *God, what a woman!* René thought. *Stiff as a fucking poker. Needs to have a stick of dynamite shoved up her ass.*

"I'll be waiting for him in his office," Henriette hissed as she walked away.

"Right. If I see him, I'll tell him you're there."

Meanwhile, kneeling in René's darkened office, Marcel and Josiane continued their whispered reunion.

"Did you cheat on me with Chaval?"

"I let myself go one night when I was feeling blue. It only happened because he was there."

"You do love me a little, don't you?"

He'd moved closer, and his thigh now touched Josiane's.

"Of course I love you, you big teddy bear."

Josiane sighed and let her head rest against Marcel's shoulder.

"I've missed you so much, you know."

"Me, too. You have no idea."

The two of them were whispering like a pair of schoolkids who'd cut class to go sneak a cigarette.

Suddenly, Marcel sat up.

"Watch out!" hissed Josiane. "She might be behind the door!"

"I don't give a damn! Sweetie-pie, get up. It's stupid to be hiding like this. I have something I want to ask you. Something too serious to ask when you're sitting down."

Josiane stood and brushed off her skirt.

"What is it?" she asked with a laugh. "Are you going to ask me to marry you?"

"Better than that, sweetie-pie! Better!"

"What then? I'm thirty-eight, and the only thing I haven't done yet is get married. And it's not as if I haven't dreamed of it."

"Do you love me, sweetie-pie?"

"You know I love you, Marcel."

"If you love me, if you *really* love me, then prove it: give me a child, a child to carry on my name. A little Grobz."

"Say that again, Marcel," Josiane murmured. "Say that again."

Marcel said it again, and again, and again. He was telling her that he had wanted this child for ages, and that he already knew what it would look like—the shape of his ears, the color of his hair, his tiny hands, the wrinkles on his feet, the dimples on his butt, the itty-bitty nails, and the little nose that wrinkles when he's nursing.

"Mind if I sit on the floor, Marcel? My knees are dancing the Charleston."

She slid down the wall onto her behind, and he crouched down beside her, grimacing when his knees hurt.

"This child . . . would you recognize him? Make him legit? He wouldn't be some shameful little bastard?"

"He'll sit at the family table, carry my name: Marcel Grobz Junior."

"You swear to God?"

"I swear on my balls," said Marcel, putting his hand on his crotch.

"See, you're making fun of me!"

"No, no! It's just the opposite. In the old days, you swore on your balls. Testicular, testament. Joséphine taught me that when you swear on your balls, it's dead serious. Because if it isn't true, your nuts shrivel and fall off. And honeybunch, that's something I don't want."

Josiane started to laugh, then burst into tears.

A hand with sharp red nails dug into Iris's. She cried out and, without turning around, jabbed an elbow at the hand's owner, who squealed in pain. *How dare you!* Iris fumed, clenching her teeth. *The nerve! I was here first.* The stranger seemed to covet a cream-colored silk outfit with brown trim. *Well, I saw it first, so it's mine,* thought Iris. *Not that I need it, but since you're so determined to have it, I'm taking it.*

She grabbed the precious items, and struggled to free herself from the crowd. The sale was taking place on the first floor of the Givenchy store, and it was a mob scene. The hand with red nails appeared again, trying to grab anything within reach. Iris saw it coming her way, like a stubborn crab, and decided this was her moment. Taking careful aim, she stabbed the hand with the clasp of her bracelet.

"What the— Are you out of your mind?" screamed the owner of the hand as she tried to identify her attacker.

Iris smiled without turning around. *Serves you right! You'll be scarred for months, and you'll have to wear gloves to hide the damage.*

She straightened up and broke free of the pack of anonymous

rumps. Brandishing her booty, Iris escaped to the shoe department, where she snapped up three pairs of evening pumps, a pair of flats, and some crocodile-skin boots. The boots were a bit punk, but the leather was very good quality, she noticed, running her hand inside. *Should I find a tuxedo to wear with these little boots?* Glancing at the furious mob, she decided against the idea. After all, she already had a whole closetful of them—and Saint Laurents, besides. Hardly worth getting ripped to shreds over one more.

Her phone rang, but she ignored it. Shopping required total concentration. Her laserlike gaze scanned the shelves, the racks, and the floor bins. She scooped up some earrings, bracelets, sunglasses, scarves, a tortoiseshell comb, a black velvet handbag, a few belts, some gloves—Carmen loves gloves!—and reached the checkout counter disheveled and out of breath.

"You need a lion tamer in here," she said to the clerk, laughing. "With a big whip!"

The saleswoman smiled politely. Iris threw her bounty on the counter and fanned herself with her credit card while tucking a few strands of hair in place.

"That will be eight thousand four hundred and forty euros, madame," said the clerk, as she folded the items in tissue paper and placed them in big white paper bags with the Givenchy logo.

Iris handed over her card. Her telephone rang again; Iris hesitated, but let it ring.

She counted the number of bags she would have to carry and felt exhausted. Luckily she had booked a car for the day. It was double-parked outside.

Turning her head, she noticed Caroline Vibert paying at another counter. Vibert was a member of Philippe's firm. *How did that woman manage to get a sales pass?* wondered Iris, as she flashed her warmest smile. They traded sighs of mutual sympathy and held up their bulging bags. Iris made a coffee-drinking gesture with a quizzical look, and soon the two women were at Chez Francis.

"This kind of thing is getting dangerous," said Iris. "Next time I'm bringing a bodyguard with a Kalashnikov!"

"Well, I got slashed by some psycho bitch! She jabbed me with her bracelet. Here, look!"

Caroline removed her glove, displaying a deep red furrow on the back of her hand.

Iris was startled to realize who her victim had been. "God, those women are crazy, aren't they?" She sighed. "They'd kill for a scrap of fabric."

"Did I tell you I met Joséphine this summer? I would never have guessed that you were sisters! It sure isn't obvious."

"Where'd you meet, at the Courbevoie municipal pool?" asked Iris jokingly as she signaled to the waiter. "What would you like, Caroline?"

"Fresh orange juice."

"Ah, good idea. Two orange juices, please . . . I need some vitamins after an expedition like this one. By the way, what were you doing at the Courbevoie pool?"

"Nothing. I've never been there."

"Didn't you tell me you'd met Joséphine this summer?"

"Sure, at the office. She's been working for us. Didn't you know?"

Iris slapped her forehead, pretending suddenly to remember.

"Oh, yes, of course. I'm such an idiot."

"Philippe hired her do some translation work. And in the fall I put her in touch with a publisher who gave her a biography of Audrey Hepburn to translate. He praises her to the skies. Says her writing is elegant, and the work she hands in is clean. She doesn't charge much, either. Just takes her check and practically kisses your feet on the way out the door. A little worker ant, quiet as a mouse. Did you two grow up together, or was she raised in a convent?"

Caroline burst out laughing, and Iris wished she could shut her up.

"You talk about her as if she were some kind of half-wit," she snapped.

"I didn't mean to make you angry. I thought it was funny, that's all."

Iris bit her tongue. She didn't want to make an enemy of Caroline Vibert, who had just been made a partner in the firm. Besides, she might know some things about Philippe. Iris decided to move her pawns carefully.

"Don't worry about it. I love my sister, but at times she seems like she's from another planet. She does research at the CNRS, you know. Another world altogether."

"Do you see each other often?"

"Mostly at family get-togethers. This year we're spending Christmas together at the chalet."

"That'll do your husband good. He seems tense, these days. A nice week in Megève, and he'll be in great shape. But don't let him work. Take away his laptop and cell phone."

"That's impossible." Iris sighed. "He sleeps with them—on them, even!"

"Then he should be well rested, because he's totally on top of his cases, as sharp as ever. A real shark. Though he seems softer lately, not so hard-nosed. The other evening I caught him daydreaming in the middle of a meeting. There were about ten of us in his office, all talking at once, waiting for him to cut to the chase. Philippe had a big file open in front of him and everyone hanging on his every word, and suddenly he was somewhere else entirely. He looked serious, hurt. There was something vulnerable in his eyes. In twenty years of working together it's the first time that I've seen him like that. I'm so used to the ruthless warrior, it felt weird."

"I've never found him ruthless."

"Well, of course not! He's your husband and he adores you! When he talks about you his eyes light up like the Eiffel Tower. You dazzle him."

"Oh, I wouldn't go that far!"

Was Caroline being sincere? Iris studied her face as she sipped her orange juice, but didn't detect any duplicity in the woman.

"Philippe says you're writing a book."

"He told you that?"

"Yeah, is it true?"

"Not really. I have an idea I'm toying with."

"Philippe must be very proud. He's not the kind of husband to be jealous of his wife's success."

Iris didn't respond. Her worst nightmare was becoming a reality: everyone was starting to talk about her book, everyone was thinking about it—except her. She not only had no idea how to begin, but she felt incapable of writing it in the first place. She'd made up a little story at a dinner party, and now it was taking over her life.

"I need to find a husband like yours," Caroline sighed, not realizing that Iris was feeling unnerved. "I should have nabbed Philippe before you married him."

"Are you still single?" Iris asked, trying to sound interested.

"Afraid so. My life is just a big nonstop party. I leave my house at eight in the morning, get home at ten at night, heat some instant soup, and go off to bed to watch TV or read a trashy novel. I avoid reading mysteries so I don't have to stay up till two in the morning to find out who did it. Talk about a fascinating life! No husband, no children, no lover, no pet. Just an elderly mother who doesn't recognize my voice when I call her. Last time she hung up on me, saying she'd never had any children." She laughed mirthlessly.

Caroline suddenly struck Iris as pitiful, exhausted and used up, whereas half an hour earlier she was a harpy ready to kill to get her hands on a silk Givenchy top.

We're the same age, Iris thought, *and I have a husband and a child drifting away from me. Why didn't Jo mention the translations? Why didn't Philippe tell me about it?*

My life is falling apart, and I'm watching it dissolve. I put all the energy I have left into seasonal sales on the first floor of Givenchy. I'm just another rich chick with a pea-size brain. And in my circles, that makes me one in a long line of them.

"Iris, I'm sorry. All this talk has made me feel bad. I don't usually go on like that. Maybe I'll go back and risk my life at Givenchy again. Provided that crazy woman with the box cutter is gone."

The two kissed each other good-bye.

Iris had to jump over puddles to reach the cab. She thought of the crocodile boots, congratulating herself on buying them.

Settling into the backseat of the car, she watched Caroline join the queue for a taxi on place de l'Alma. The line was long, and it was raining; Caroline had stuffed her purchases under her coat to keep them dry. Iris thought of offering her a ride, and was leaning out the window to call her over when her phone rang again.

"Alexandre, darling, what is it? Why are you crying, love? Tell me."

He was cold and wet and had been waiting in the rain in front of the school. Iris was supposed to have picked him up for a dentist appointment an hour ago.

Chapter 8

✦ ✦ ✦

"Zoé, what's wrong? Tell Mommy. You know that mommies understand everything, forgive everything, and they love their children even if they're cold-blooded murderers. You do know that, don't you?"

Zoé was standing straight and had a finger up her nose.

"Don't pick your nose, love. Even when you're feeling very sad."

Zoé pulled the finger out regretfully, inspected it, and wiped it on her plaid pants.

Joséphine glanced at the kitchen clock. It was four thirty. She had a date with Shirley at five to get her hair done. She had only a half hour to get Zoé to talk. Hortense wasn't around, so she had to strike while the iron was hot.

"Can I sit on your lap?"

In Zoé, Jo could see herself as a child in family photos. A pudgy little girl bundled in a cardigan sticking her stomach out and looking suspiciously at the camera.

"There you are, my love, my little girl, whom I love truly

madly deeply," she murmured, holding Zoé tight. "You know that Mommy is always here, don't you? Always, always?"

Zoé nodded and snuggled against her mother. *She must be feeling sad with Christmas approaching, and Antoine being so far away.* The girls never talked about him, and they didn't show her the letters they received. They drew a clear line between their mother and their father.

She started gently rocking Zoé, whispering to her.

"My, how my baby has grown! She's no longer a baby at all, is she? She's a beautiful young girl with beautiful hair, and a beautiful nose, and a beautiful mouth."

She stroked Zoé's hair, continuing in the same singsong voice:

"A beautiful young girl, and all the boys will fall in love with her. All the boys in the world will come lean their ladders against the wall of the castle where Zoé Cortès lives, to climb up to get a kiss."

At those words, Zoé burst into tears.

"Mommy, that's not true! You're lying! I'm not a beautiful young girl, and no boy wants to lean his ladder against me!"

Uh-oh, thought Joséphine, *here we go: the first heartbreak. I was ten when it happened to me. I used to cake my eyelashes with gooseberry jam to make them grow longer. And the boy ended up kissing Iris anyway.*

"First of all, sweetie, you don't say, 'You're lying!' to your mommy."

Zoé nodded.

"And second, I'm not lying. You're a very pretty girl."

"No, I'm not! Max Barthillet and Rémy Potiron made a list, and I'm not on it! He put Hortense on it, but not me."

"What was the list, sweetie love?"

"A list of girls who are vaginally exploitable, and I'm not on it."

Joséphine almost dropped Zoé on the floor. She took a deep breath.

"Do you even know what that means?"

"It means girls who can be fucked. He told me so."

"He explained that to you, did he?"

"Yes, but he said not to make a big deal out of it because I'd eventually have an exploitable vagina too, just not right away."

Zoé began chewing on the sleeve of her sweatshirt.

"First of all, lovey, a sensitive boy doesn't use a girl like a piece of merchandise. You should tell him you're proud not to be on his list."

"Even if that's a lie?"

"What do you mean, a lie?"

"Well, yeah. Because I'd like to be on his list."

"Really? Well, tell him it isn't nice to classify girls that way, that men and women don't talk about vaginas, they talk about desire."

"What's desire, Mommy?"

"It's when you love someone, when you really want to kiss them, but you wait and wait . . . All that waiting, that's desire. It's when you haven't kissed them yet, but you dream about them when you fall asleep, tremble when you think of them, and it's so wonderful. Zoé, you tell yourself maybe someday maybe—maybe—you'll kiss them."

"So you must be sad."

"No! You wait, and the day he kisses you fireworks go off in your heart, and fill your head, and you feel like singing and dancing, and you fall in love."

"So I'm already in love?"

"You're still very young, Zoé. You have to wait."

Joséphine tried to think of a way to convince Zoé that Max wasn't the right boy for her.

"It's as if you talked to Max about his wee-wee," she said. "As if you said to him, I'll kiss you but I want to see your wee-wee first."

"He already offered to show it to me. Does that mean he's in love too?"

Joséphine felt her heart racing. *Stay calm, don't show you're upset, don't start yelling about Max.*

"And did he show it to you?"

"No. I didn't want him to."

"Zoé, there's something you have to understand. Max is fourteen, almost fifteen. He's Hortense's age. He should be her friend, not yours. Maybe you need to find yourself a new friend, sweetie."

Zoé thought this over for a moment, and released her sleeve.

"That means I'll be all alone," she said matter-of-factly.

"Or you'll find other friends."

Zoé sighed, got off her mother's lap, and pulled up her slacks.

"Do you want to come to the hairdresser with Shirley and me? He'll give you those beautiful curls you love."

"No, I don't like the hairdresser. He pulls your hair."

Zoé had resumed sucking on her sweatshirt sleeve.

"You know, Mommy, life hasn't been easy since Daddy left."

"I know, sweetie."

"You think he'll ever come back?"

"I don't know, Zoé. I really don't know. In the meantime you're going to make tons of friends now that you aren't always stuck with Max. I'm sure there are many boys and girls who'd like to be your friend but who thought Max took up all the space."

"That's not the only way life is hard." Zoé sighed. "It's hard every way."

"Come on!" Joséphine shook her and laughed. "Think of Christmas, think of the presents you're going to get, think of the snow, of skiing. Won't that be fun?"

"Can't we take Max with us? He'd like to go skiing too, and his mother, she hasn't got the money for—"

"No, Zoé!" Joséphine struggled not to lose her temper. She calmed herself and began again. "We're not bringing Max to Megève. We're Iris's guests, and we can't just show up with extra people in our suitcases."

"But it's Max Barthillet!"

Two quick rings of the doorbell saved Joséphine from losing it completely. Bending down to kiss Zoé, she sent her to review the reading for her history test.

Joséphine watched her daughter go to her room. Soon she wouldn't be able to handle the girls anymore. Wouldn't be able to handle life in general.

If only she could go back to the days of courtly love and its mysteries, forbidden caresses, enchanted sufferings, stolen kisses, and knights who rode into battle with their lovers' favors on their lances. *I was made to live in that world*, Jo thought, *not this one.*

She sighed, grabbed her bag and keys, and went out.

At the salon, Joséphine and Shirley were having their hair highlighted.

"I look pretty funny, don't I?" asked Jo, catching a glance of herself in the mirror, her head covered in little twists of aluminum foil.

"You've never had highlights done?"

"Never."

"If it's your first time, you get to make a wish."

Joséphine looked in the mirror and said, "I wish that my girls not suffer too much in life."

"Was Hortense being mean again?"

"No, it's Zoé. She's lovesick for Max Barthillet."

Joséphine told her the "list of exploitable vaginas" story, and Shirley burst out laughing.

"I don't find that funny at all!" snapped Jo. "It worries me!"

"It shouldn't, since she told you about it. Zoé got it off her chest, and she trusts you."

"You're not shocked?"

"So many things shock me, I can hardly breathe. So I've decided not to be shocked. Otherwise I'd go mad."

"This is a world where fifteen-year-olds classify girls by access to their vaginas! I mean, my God!"

"Calm down, Jo."

"I don't want that little pervert abusing her!"

"He won't do a thing to her. If he does anything, it'll be with another girl. I'll bet you anything he did it to impress Hortense! They're all fantasizing about that little minx. And my son more than any of them. Gary can't take his eyes off her, and he thinks I don't notice."

"When I was young, it was the same thing with Iris. All the boys were crazy about her."

"Yeah, and look what it got her."

"I don't know. She's got it made, wouldn't you say?"

"She married well, if you call that making it. But without her husband's lolly, she's nobody."

Joséphine recalled Iris's aggressive tone at the swimming pool. And the other night, on the phone, when Jo had tried to give Iris ideas for her book. "I'll help you," she'd said. "I'll find you stories and documents. All you'll have to do is write! Hey, did you know what the word for taxes was in those days? 'Banalities'! Isn't that funny?"

But Iris had snapped, "You're such a drag, Jo! You're just too—" and hung up.

Too what? Jo wondered, puzzled at the nastiness behind Iris's remark. She wouldn't mention it to Shirley; it would just prove her right.

"She's nice to the girls."

"Because it doesn't cost her anything."

"You've never liked her, and I don't know why."

"And that Hortense of yours: if you don't rein her in, she'll end up just like her aunt. Being so-and-so's wife isn't a career, Jo. The day Philippe dumps her, Iris won't have a pot to piss in."

"He'll never dump her. He's madly in love with her."

"What makes you so sure?"

Jo didn't answer. Since starting working for Philippe, she'd gotten to know him better. When she went to the law firm on avenue Victor-Hugo, she would peek into his office if the door was open. She'd made him laugh, the last time. Standing in the doorway, she asked, "Do I have to press a remote to get you to look up from your files?" He waved her in.

"Another fifteen minutes, and I'll rinse you," said Denise the hairdresser, as she parted the foil strips with the tip of her comb. "Hey, the color is taking really nicely. It's going to look great!"

She walked off, hips swaying under her pink smock.

"Mylène used to work here, didn't she?"

"Yes. She did my nails once. Get any news from Antoine?"

"No, but the girls have."

At the sound of Antoine's name, Joséphine felt her stomach tense. The loan! Fifteen hundred euros every month to Monsieur Faugeron! Once she paid the January installment, there would be nothing left of her 8,012 euros. Jo had spent her last penny on gifts for Gary and Shirley. She figured that at this point a few euros more or less wouldn't make much difference.

She slumped in the salon chair, messing up her rows of silver twists.

"Are you okay?" Shirley looked worried.

"Yeah."

"No, you're not. You're as white as a sheet. Do you want a magazine?"

"Sure, thanks."

Shirley handed her a copy of *Elle*. Joséphine opened it but couldn't read. All she could think about was the loan repayment. *Fifteen hundred euros!*

Denise came to get Shirley to rinse her out.

"It will be your turn in five minutes, madame," she said.

Joséphine nodded vaguely and flipped through the magazine. Suddenly she shrieked: "Shirley, Shirley! Look!"

She ran over to the sink, waving the magazine in the air.

Her head back, eyes closed, Shirley said, "I can't exactly read at the moment, Jo."

Joséphine was waving the magazine around, and Shirley had to crane her neck around to see it.

"Look at the man in the photograph!"

Shirley squinted.

"Not bad. Not bad at all."

"Is that all you have to say?"

"I said he wasn't bad. You want me to fall on my knees?"

"Shirley, it's the man from the library! The guy in the duffel coat! He's a model. And the blond woman in the photo is the one from the crosswalk. They were shooting that photo when we saw them. God, he's so handsome!"

"It's weird, but on the crosswalk he didn't make much of an impression on me."

"You're just not that into men."

"Correction: I used to love them too much. That's why I keep them at a distance."

"I'm going to cut out the photo and put it in my wallet. Oh, Shirley, it's a sign!"

"A sign of what?"

"A sign that he's going to come back into my life."

"You actually believe that kind of crap?"

Joséphine nodded. *Yes, and I talk to the stars.*

"It's your turn, madame," said Denise. "Follow me, and we'll rinse you out. You're going to be a new woman."

Joséphine leaned her head back against the basin. *Maybe I'll turn out like Iseult la Blonde, with her gleaming golden locks.*

The big hand of the clock came to rest at half past five. Iris found herself watching the door anxiously. What if he didn't come?

On the phone, the head of the detective agency had been courteous and precise. Iris explained what she needed. He asked a few questions, then said, "Do you know our rates? We charge two hundred and forty euros a day during the week, double on weekends."

"That's fine."

"Very well, madame. In that case, let's make a first appointment, say a week from now. It should be in a neighborhood you don't usually visit, where you're not likely to run into anyone you know."

She suggested the thirteenth arrondissement, and they decided on the café on avenue des Gobelins near rue Pirandello. To Iris it sounded mysterious and clandestine, even slightly louche.

"Our man will be easy to recognize. He'll be wearing a Burberry rain hat. He'll say, 'It's freezing out there,' and you'll answer, 'You can say that again.' "

"I'll be there. Good-bye, monsieur."

It had been so easy! She had hesitated for so long before making the call, and then suddenly it was all arranged.

She looked at the people seated around her. Students reading; a couple of women, waiting; a few men drinking at the bar and staring into space. She heard a coffee percolator, orders being shouted.

At five thirty on the dot, a man wearing a plaid Burberry hat entered the café. He was young and good-looking, with an easy smile.

The private detective glanced once around the café, and his eyes quickly found Iris's. She nodded in acknowledgment. He pretended to look surprised as he approached.

"It's freezing out there," he said quietly.

"You can say that again."

He shook her hand and gestured that he'd like to sit down on the chair next to her, if she would move her purse and coat.

"It's probably not a good idea to leave your purse on a chair for all the world to see," he said, noting the Vuitton logo.

Iris waved away his concern and looked meaningfully at her watch.

"I can tell you're eager to get started, madame, so I'll begin. As you requested, we followed your husband, Philippe Dupin, continuously from Thursday, December 11, at 8:10 a.m. from in front of your residence, until last night, December 20, at

10:30 p.m., when he went back into your residence. I was assisted by two colleagues."

"So I gather," said Iris in a dull voice.

"Your husband keeps to a very regular routine, so following him was quite easy. I was able to identify most of the people he met except for one man, who is giving us some trouble."

"Ah," said Iris, feeling her heart speed up.

"A man he saw on two occasions, three days apart, in a café at Roissy–Charles de Gaulle. The first was at eleven thirty a.m., the other at three p.m. Each meeting lasted an hour, at most. The man showed Monsieur Dupin various things—photographs, documents, newspaper clippings. At these meetings your husband nodded, let the other man do most of the talking, then asked many questions. The man listened and took notes."

"Took notes?"

"Yes. So I figured it must be a business meeting. I managed to obtain a Xerox of his datebook—don't ask how, we have our ways—but there is no record of those meetings anywhere in it. And he didn't mention them to his secretary or to his closest colleague, Caroline Vibert."

"How can you know all this?" asked Iris, shocked by such an invasion into her husband's private life.

"As I said, madame, we have our ways. But in short, I know these are not business meetings."

"Do you have pictures of the man in question?"

"Yes." The detective pulled a sheaf of photos from a folder, and spread them out for her. Iris leaned over them, her heart pounding. The man looked to be in his thirties, had short brown hair, thin lips, and wore tortoiseshell glasses. He was neither handsome nor ugly. The kind of man who could fit in anywhere. Iris racked her brain trying to remember him, but couldn't recall ever seeing him before.

"I followed the man after both meetings. The first time, he flew off to Basel; the second, to London. That's all I could find out. I could learn more, but we would have to follow him."

"So he came to Paris especially to see my husband."

"We don't know why he is making the trips. We could find out, but following someone that way is a major undertaking. You should think about it and call if you want us to go ahead."

"Yes," replied Iris distractedly. "That's probably best."

There was still one question she was dying to ask, and she didn't dare. She needed to summon her courage. She hesitated, sipped some water.

"I need to ask you . . . ," she stammered. "I'd like to know if there were any gestures . . ."

"Physical contact that might suggest intimacy between them? No, none. But there was definitely a shared understanding. The men spoke to each other very directly. Each seemed to know exactly what he expected of the other."

Iris glanced at the clock on the café wall. It was 6:15. She'd found out all she was going to, she realized, and felt suddenly let down. She was both disappointed and relieved not to have learned more. So Bérengère's gossip had been wrong, thank God. But for some reason, Iris now felt vaguely threatened.

"I need to think about all this," she murmured.

"Of course, madame. I'm at your disposal if—"

"Thank you," Iris interrupted, without looking at him.

She extended a hand absentmindedly, and he shook it. She watched the detective walk away.

The night before, Philippe had come back to sleep in their bedroom again. He merely said, "I think Alexandre is worried. It's not good for him to see us sleeping apart." He spoke in a perfectly matter-of-fact way, but for the first time, Iris thought she detected a note of indifference, almost of contempt.

Iris watched the man in the plaid hat turn the corner. Somehow, and by any means within her power, she had to regain her husband's esteem.

Chapter 9

♦ ♦ ♦

It was 6:30 when the two women left the hairdresser's. Shirley grabbed Jo's arm and forced her to look at her reflection in a furniture store window. "I want you to see how smashing you are. Look!"

Joséphine looked at her reflection and had to admit she didn't look bad. The hairdresser had layered her hair in a way that caught the light, making her look younger.

"It's true. That was a good idea, Shirley. I never go to the hairdresser. I always thought it was a waste of money."

"What about me? How do I look?" Shirley said, spinning around and patting her short platinum curls. She lifted the collar of her long coat, titled her head back, and launched into an old Queen tune.

> *We are the champions, my friend . . .*
> *We are the champions . . .*
> *We are the champions of the world!*

Shirley skipped down the empty streets with their cold, gray buildings, her long legs leaping, singing for the pleasure of having made Joséphine beautiful.

"From now on, I'm treating you to the hairdresser every month!"

A sharp gust of wind interrupted her song-and-dance performance. She took Jo's arm for warmth, and they walked along for a moment without speaking. Night had fallen, and the few pedestrians they met hurried blindly past, heads down, eager to get home.

"Tonight's no night to catch anyone's eye," said Shirley. "They're all staring at their feet."

"You think he'll look at me, the man in the duffel coat?"

"If he doesn't, then he's got shit for brains."

"Can I ask you a question, Shirley? It's kind of personal. You don't have to answer if you don't want to."

"Oh, come on, Jo. Just ask."

"All right, here goes. Why don't you have a man in your life?"

Joséphine regretted the question the second she asked it. Shirley jerked her arm free and strode quickly ahead.

Joséphine ran to catch up to her.

"I'm sorry, Shirley, really. I shouldn't have asked, but you're so beautiful, and seeing you by yourself, I—"

"You're not going to get an answer on that one. Okay?"

"Okay."

Another blast of wind hit them, and they hunched over, clinging to each other.

"This is scary weather," Shirley muttered. "You'd think it was Judgment Day!"

"You're right. They could put in a few more streetlights, too, don't you think? We should write city hall."

Joséphine was saying whatever came to mind to change her friend's mood.

"Okay, I have another question, a more ordinary one. Why do you wear your hair so short?"

"I'm not answering that one, either."

"But that isn't a nosy question!"

"No, but it relates directly to your first question."

"Oh. I'm so sorry! I'll stop talking."

They walked on in silence, Joséphine wishing she had kept quiet.

Lost in thought, Jo didn't notice that Shirley had stopped, and she bumped into her.

"Want me to tell you something, Jo? Just one thing?"

Joséphine nodded.

"Long hair can get in your way. You can think about that—"

Out of nowhere, three young men rushed up and grabbed their purses. Joséphine took a hard punch in the face and yelped. When she touched her nose, she felt blood.

Shirley erupted in a volley of English curses and raced after the three punks. Joséphine watched dumbstruck as Shirley unleashed her fury on them. In a blinding flurry of elbows, kicks, and punches, she knocked the three sprawling to the ground. One pulled a knife, but she sent it flying with a roundhouse kick.

"Had enough, or you want some more?"

The three boys were rolling on the ground, clutching their chests, as Shirley picked up the purses.

"You broke my tooth, you bitch!" muttered the biggest.

"Just one of them?" She kicked him in the mouth again.

He screamed and curled up in a ball to protect himself. The other two got up and took off as fast as their legs could carry them. Moaning, the one still on the ground started crawling away on his elbows.

"You fucking whore!" he muttered, spitting blood. Shirley bent over and grabbed him by his jacket collar. Forcing him up onto all fours, she methodically began to strip him. Piece by piece, she ripped off his clothes until he was down to his underpants and socks, and lay huddled on the sidewalk.

"Why'd you attack us, you scummy piece of shit? Because we're two women on our own, is that it?"

"It wasn't my idea, m'dame. It was my friend who—"

Shirley slammed his head against the ground. He started yelling, swore he'd never do it again, would never again attack a woman alone. Holding an arm up to shield himself, he staggered to his feet and went to pick up his clothes.

Shirley shook her head. "You're going home just the way you are. In your socks and shorts. Now beat it, you little arsehole."

He took off without another word. Shirley waited till he was gone, then bundled up his clothes and tossed them into a Dumpster. She straightened her blouse and pants and brushed off her coat.

"Fucking toe rags!"

Joséphine gaped at Shirley, stunned by the violence she had seen her unleash.

Shirley shrugged. "That's also part of why I don't have a boyfriend. Clue number two."

She leaned close and inspected Joséphine's bloody nose, then pulled a Kleenex from her pocket and dabbed at it. Jo winced.

"It's okay. It's not broken, just battered. It'll be black and blue tomorrow, though. You can tell people you ran into the door on your way out. But not a word to the kids, okay?"

Joséphine nodded numbly. She wanted to ask Shirley where she learned to fight like that, but didn't dare. Her knees were wobbly, and she suggested they stop for a minute so she could collect herself.

"Sure. Don't worry about it. That was your first fight. You get used to it after a while."

"I need a drink. My head's spinning."

In the lobby of their building they found Max Barthillet sitting on the stairs by the elevator.

"Um, I don't have my key, and my mom's not home yet."

"You can wait in my flat. Go leave your mum a note."

Jo and Shirley got into the elevator.

"It's Christmas Eve, and I don't have a gift for Max!" said Jo. She looked at her nose in the elevator mirror. "Goodness gracious! My face is a mess."

"Jo, when are you going to start saying 'shit,' like the rest of the world? I'll slip him some money in an envelope. It's what the Barthillets need most right now."

Joséphine took the presents down from where she'd hidden them on the top shelf of her closet and went to get the girls, who hooted with laughter at their mother's clumsiness and swollen nose. Ringing the bell to Shirley's apartment, they could hear Christmas carols. Shirley opened the door with a big smile, and Jo had trouble recognizing the avenging angel from earlier in the evening.

Hortense and Zoé squealed when they opened their gifts. Gary jumped for joy when he unwrapped the iPod Joséphine had bought him. "This is so cool!" he exclaimed. "Mum didn't want me to have one. You're the best, Joséphine." He leaped up and hugged her, mashing her nose.

Zoé was gazing at the Disney movies and the DVD player. Hortense was in shock. Her mother hadn't bought some discounted, crappy computer; this was the latest Mac. And Max Barthillet was staring at the hundred-euro bill Shirley had slipped into an envelope with a little card.

"Wow! Thanks for thinking of me, Shirley. That's why Mom's not around. She knew you were having a party and didn't say anything, so it would be a surprise."

Joséphine held out her gift to Shirley: an early edition of *Alice's Adventures in Wonderland* with the John Tenniel illustrations. She'd found it at a flea market. Shirley gave her a black cashmere turtleneck.

"To strut your stuff in Megève."

Joséphine hugged her, and for a moment Shirley relaxed in her arms. "We two make quite a team, don't we?" she murmured. Jo hugged her tighter.

Gary had taken over Hortense's computer and was showing her how it worked. Max and Zoé were absorbed in the Disney movies.

Joséphine had been dreading this party because of Antoine's absence, but it was going better than she could have hoped. Shirley had trimmed a Christmas tree and decorated the table with holly, cut-out snowflakes, and gold paper stars. Tall red candles flickered in wooden candlesticks. It looked like a dream.

They uncorked the champagne and devoured the turkey with chestnut stuffing and the chocolate-and-coffee *bûche de Noël* (a secret Shirley recipe). When dinner was over, they pushed the table aside and danced.

Gary did a slow dance with Hortense as the two mothers watched, sipping their champagne.

"They look cute," said Joséphine, who was a little tipsy. "See that? Hortense didn't need much convincing. I even think she's dancing a bit too close to him."

"Because she knows he's going to help her with her computer."

Jo playfully poked Shirley in the ribs, and Shirley yelped in surprise.

Jo wished she could stop time, just take this moment of happiness and preserve it in a bottle. Glancing out the window, she saw stars in the sky and raised her glass to them.

They were leaving Shirley's when Christine Barthillet came to fetch Max. Her eyes were red, and she claimed she'd gotten dust in them as she was stepping off the Metro. Max showed her his hundred-euro bill, and she thanked Shirley and Jo for taking care of her son.

Jo had trouble getting the girls to settle down. They were bouncing on their beds and squealing with excitement about leaving for Megève in the morning. Zoé wanted to check her suitcase for the tenth time to make sure she had everything she needed. Joséphine finally managed to cram her into her pajamas and stuff her into bed.

In the bathroom, Hortense was washing her face with the expensive cleansing lotion Iris had bought her. She turned around to Jo. "Mom . . . all those presents. Did you pay for them?"

Joséphine nodded.

"Does that mean we're rich now?"

Joséphine burst out laughing and sat on the edge of the bathtub.

"I'm doing some extra work, translations. I got eight thousand euros for that biography of Audrey Hepburn. With any luck, I'll do many more of them."

"So we'll have plenty of money?"

"We'll have plenty of money."

"And I'll be able to get a cell phone?"

"Maybe."

"And we'll move?"

"Do you really not like living here?"

Hortense frowned.

"I'd like to live in a nice neighborhood in Paris," she said. "Meeting the right people is just as important as getting an education, you know."

Hortense looked beautiful in her camisole and pink pajama bottoms.

"Honey, once I've earned enough money, we'll go live in Paris. I promise."

Hortense dropped the cotton makeup ball and threw her arms around her mother's neck.

"Oh, Mom, I love it when you're like this, all strong and decisive . . . By the way, I like your new cut and highlights. You look really pretty!"

"So you do love me after all?" Joséphine made an effort to sound light, not needy.

"I love you so much when you're sure of yourself. When you act all pitiful and sad, it bums me out. Worse, it scares me. I feel like we're not gonna make it."

"Hortense, honey, I promise we're going to make it. I'm going to work like crazy and earn lots of money, and you'll never be scared again."

Joséphine wrapped her arms around her daughter's soft, warm body. This moment—this very moment—was the best Christmas gift ever.

The next day, Jo, Zoé, and Hortense were gathered on Platform F at the Gare de Lyon, waiting to board the Lyon–Annecy–Sallanches train, which was due to leave in ten minutes. Joséphine was looking every which way, hoping to see her sister and little Alexandre. Instead she glimpsed a couple down the platform. *Oh, no*, she thought. It was Marcel kissing his secretary Josiane, then fussily helping her aboard the train. *He looks ridiculous! You'd think he was transporting the crown jewels.*

To distract Zoé and Hortense, she sent them ahead to look for car 33, which fortunately was at the front of the train.

Dragging their suitcases and checking the car numbers they passed, the girls moved away from Marcel and Josiane.

Jo turned around and spotted Iris and Alexandre in the distance, racing toward them.

They all plopped down in their seats as the train started to move. Hortense carefully folded her down jacket and put it on the coat rack. Zoé and Alexandre started vividly describing their respective Christmas eves. This annoyed Iris, who snapped at them.

"They're going to grow up to be morons, I swear . . . God, Joséphine, what happened to you? Your face is a mess! Have you been taking judo? You're too old for that, you know."

As the train started, she pulled Jo aside.

"Come on, let's go grab a coffee."

"Now, right away?" asked Jo, worried that they would run into Josiane and Marcel in the dining car. Then she remembered that Marcel was spending Christmas with his mother in Paris, and wouldn't be on the train. Reluctantly, she got up and followed Iris. She was missing her favorite part of a train ride: the moment when the train passed through the outskirts of Paris, picking up speed as it flashed through a landscape of row houses and little suburban stations.

At the dining-car bar, Iris kept stirring her little plastic spoon around in her coffee. She looked gloomy and tense.

"Are you okay?"

"I'm in deep shit, Jo. Really deep shit."

Joséphine said nothing, but thought that Iris wasn't alone.

I'll be in deep trouble too, in about two weeks. On January 15, to be exact.

"And you're the only person who can help me."

"Me?" Joséphine was astonished.

"Yes, you. So listen to me and don't interrupt. This is hard enough to explain."

Jo nodded.

Iris sipped her coffee and turned her violet-blue eyes on her sister.

"You remember the story I made up that night, about pretending I was writing a book?"

Joséphine nodded again. Iris's eyes always had the same hypnotic effect on her. She would have liked to ask Iris to turn her head away, but Iris kept staring into her sister's eyes.

"So guess what? I *am* going to write a book."

"Hey, that's great news! I'm surprised that—"

"Don't interrupt. Believe me, I need all my strength to tell you what I'm going to say next."

She took a deep breath, then exhaled sharply.

"I'm going to write a historical novel set in the twelfth century, just as I boasted I would, that night. I phoned Serrurier yesterday. He's thrilled. To whet his appetite, I fed him a few of those anecdotes you kindly gave me the other day—you know, about Rollo, William the Conqueror, taxes being 'banalities,' and all that. He sounded delighted. 'How soon can you have it for me?' he asked. I said I had no idea. So he promised me a big advance if I gave him fifty pages to read as soon as possible. Just to see how I write and if I can pull it off. Because to write a book like that, he said, you need both knowledge and staying power."

Jo nodded.

"The only problem is that I don't have the knowledge or the endurance. And that's where you come in."

"Me? No offense, but I don't see how—"

"You come in because you and I are going to make a secret deal. Remember when we were kids, and we used to do that blood oath thing?"

"Yeah, and after that I did anything you wanted. I was always terrified I might break the vow and die on the spot."

"It's simple. You write the book, and you get the money. I put my name on it and talk it up on TV, the radio, the newspapers. You produce the raw material, and I pitch the product. I'll handle public relations, getting people talking, photo shoots, and author appearances. That's all about how your hair and your makeup look, and what you're wearing. Having your picture taken when you're shopping, in your bathroom, under the Eiffel Tower, whatever. All the things that have nothing to do with the book but make it sell. I'm great at that stuff, and it terrifies you. If we work together, the book will be a hit. For me, it's not about the money; you'll get all that. For me, it's about waking up, feeling alive again."

"But Iris, that's fraud!"

Iris let out an exasperated sigh. Her eyes swept over Jo and came to focus on her face like a bird of prey's.

"I knew you'd say that. But tell me, where's the fraud if I give you what you most need at the moment—money—and all I'm asking in a return is a tiny lie? Not even a lie, a secret."

Joséphine looked doubtful.

"You just have to trust me."

"Like when we were little."

"Exactly."

Joséphine watched the countryside racing by.

"Jo, I'm begging you. Do this for me. What do you have to lose?"

"I don't think in those terms."

"Oh, stop it! Don't tell me you never hide anything from me! I heard you were working for Philippe's office, and you didn't tell me. You think that's a good thing, sharing secrets with my husband?"

Joséphine blushed.

"I'm not proud that I hid that from you," she stammered.

"Yeah, but you did! You did it, Jo. Are you saying you'll do it for Philippe but not for me, your own sister?"

Iris could sense Jo weakening, and assumed a softer, almost pleading tone.

"Listen, Jo, you'd be doing me a huge favor—me, your sister. I've always been there for you. Cric and Croc, you remember? Ever since we were little . . . I'm all the family you've got. You don't have anyone else! No mother, since you've stopped seeing her and she's seriously pissed off at you, no more father, no more husband."

Joséphine shuddered and wrapped her arms around herself. She felt alone and abandoned. In her elation over her first check, she'd assumed that the translation jobs would keep coming, but they hadn't. The editor who'd congratulated her on her work hadn't called. On January 15, she'd have to make a loan payment—unless Antoine miraculously turned up, checkbook in hand. Then again on February 15, March 15, April 15, May 15, June 15, July 15 . . . An ominous cloud of misfortune suddenly descended on her. The feeling of dread gripped her, and she could hardly breathe.

Noticing that Joséphine now looked worried, Iris bore on.

"And I'm not talking chump change, either! I'm talking fifty thousand euros, minimum."

"Fifty thousand euros!"

"Twenty-five thousand as soon as I hand in the first fifty pages and an outline. Another twenty-five when the book's done."

"Fifty thousand euros!" repeated Jo, who could hardly believe her ears. "Serrurier must be out of his mind!"

"No, he's not out of his mind. He's thinking, he's calculating. He's a publisher; he's running the numbers."

"Yes, but . . . ," protested Jo, more weakly now.

"You write it. You know that period by heart. For you, it'll be a breeze. And in six months—listen carefully—in six months you'll have fifty thousand euros! You won't have any more worries. You can go back to your old parchments and your François Villon poems, your *langue d'oïl* and *langue d'oc*."

"You're mixing it all up!"

"Who cares? I'll only have to talk about what you write!"

Joséphine felt a tingle of pleasure deep in her chest. Fifty thousand euros! Enough to pay—she quickly calculated—at least thirty loan installments. Thirty months of relief! Thirty months of being able to sleep at night and tell stories by day. She would bring them all to life: Rollo and Arthur, and Henry and Eleanor and Enide! She would set them off on a mad whirl of balls, tournaments, battles, castles . . . and conspiracies.

As the train pulled into the Lyon-Perrache station for the three-minute stop, Joséphine agreed.

"Okay," she said with a sigh. "But just this once, okay, Iris? You promise?"

"I promise: just this once. Or the big Cruc will crunch me."

PART III

♦ ♦ ♦

Chapter 10

♦　♦　♦

The train hadn't even come to a complete stop at the Lyon station, and Iris was already kissing Jo.

"You have no idea what a jam you're getting me out of! I know I've wasted my life, but it's too late, I can't go back now. I have to make do with what's left. It's not very glorious, I'll admit, but that's the way it is."

Iris kissed her again, then withdrew into her composed, older-sister self. She gave Joséphine a searching glance.

"You're looking pretty, Jo. Those little blond streaks . . . very nice. Are you in love? You will be soon. I see so much good in your future: beauty, talent, wealth." Iris snapped her fingers, as if conjuring fate. "Your time has come, Jo. I was born with more than you, but I've squeezed every drop out of life, and all I've got left is the dried-out rind. Remember when people used to say that I had talent, that I was a true artist, that I would be somebody? Take Hollywood by storm?" Iris laughed bitterly. "Hollywood, hah! Turns out you're the real writer in the family.

I remember those letters you sent when you were away at camp. My friends all said you were a great writer, like Mme de Sevigné!"

Jo was moved by Iris's unusual candor, but still felt intimidated. Could she really pull this off?

Iris snapped her out of her reverie. "First thing I'm going to do is buy you a new laptop computer and get you hooked up to the Internet."

Joséphine protested, but Iris insisted. As usual, Jo gave in.

So now Jo was staring at that computer, its screen staring blankly back at her. The kitchen table was littered with a week's worth of books, bills, markers, pens, sheets of paper, plus the remains of breakfast. *I simply have to make room to write*, she told herself. *Put everything else out of my mind*. She sighed deeply, and when she did, all her resolve vanished at the thought of the effort she'd have to make.

How do you come up with a plot for a book? How do you create characters? Who should she bring to life? William the Conqueror, Richard the Lionheart, or Henry II? Should she try to channel the early writers of romances, like Chrétien de Troyes? Maybe she should use the people in her daily life: Shirley, Hortense, Iris, Philippe, Antoine, even Mylène. *Can I put hennins and clogs on the women, and helmets and pointy shoes on the men? Just dress them up in twelfth-century attire and drop them into a farm or a castle?*

Is there a recipe book for writers? Joséphine wondered. *Mix one cup of love with a dash of adventure, a few ounces of historical references, and two pounds of sweat. Let simmer on low heat, stir, sauté so it doesn't stick, let sit for three months, six months, a year.*

Stendhal supposedly wrote *The Charterhouse of Parma* in three weeks. Georges Simenon could bang out a book in ten days. But how long had they carried those books around inside as they got up in the morning, sipped their coffee, read the mail, watched the morning light on the breakfast table?

Every writer had a trick. Drink coffee, the way Balzac did. Write standing up, like Hemingway. Lock yourself away, like Colette. Prowl the mean streets, like Zola. Take opium, like Coleridge. Yell, like Flaubert. Run, go nuts, sleep . . . or maybe not sleep, like Proust.

And what about me? Joséphine stared at the sink, the clock, the remains of breakfast, and the bills. The writer Paul Léautaud used to say, "Write as if you're writing a letter, and don't reread what you've written."

Who should she write her letter to? Maybe write to some man she would invent . . . A man who would listen to her.

The computer was sitting before her, its screen still blank. Iris had bought it for her in Megève, the day after Joséphine got there. At the chalet, Philippe bent down and asked in a whisper if she had bought it with the money from the translations. Joséphine turned beet red. Iris was busy lighting a fire in the fireplace.

"The whole firm's delighted with your work," he said. "You saved us from a real blunder on the Massipov contract."

I'm becoming the queen of secrets and lies, Joséphine thought to herself. *I can manage translating contracts for Philippe, but what if the Audrey Hepburn publisher asks me to do another book? I'll have to hire a ghost translator!* She laughed aloud at the thought, and Iris turned around.

"Is what Philippe's saying that funny?" asked Iris, turning around. "You should let us in on the story."

Joséphine mumbled an explanation.

She was feeling more and more at ease with Philippe. They weren't exactly close and probably never would be, but she was beginning to notice a strange kindness in Philippe that she found comforting. He seemed to be coming out of his shell, much as she had herself had started to.

The sun went behind a cloud just then, and the cold light of January dimmed. Joséphine sighed. She really needed to clean up the place if she wanted to make a work space for herself. She pushed the kitchen table aside and spotted the red paper triangle she'd made when she saw Antoine and Mylène together for the first time; it had fallen behind the toaster. Jo picked it up. She closed her eyes and went back in time to that July day when Antoine had picked up the girls, and she'd felt like jumping off the balcony.

Joséphine tore up the red triangle and threw it in the trash. *It's my fault,* she thought. *I bored him with my love.* She looked up at the clock and gasped. It was seven o'clock already! She'd sat down to work at three. The four hours had flown by. The girls would be home from school at any moment, and she hadn't even started dinner.

Jo filled a pot with water, dropped in some potatoes, put in lettuce from the fridge to soak, and set the table. *No point in panicking,* she told herself. *You'll manage. A writer doesn't need to be a genius, just has to have a way to translate what she feels. I have to find the words that will express those feelings. Who do I feel like writing to?*

Jo started on the salad dressing. *Sunflower or olive oil? Once I get the money from the book, I'll use only top-quality olive oil. Cold-pressed, extra virgin, the most expensive stuff, the kind that wins competitions. I won't be short on money now. Jesus, fifty thousand euros! Those publishers are crazy. Did I really lose weight, or did I misread the scale? I'll weigh myself again tomorrow.*

Anyway, why do you have to be thin to please men? In the twelfth century, women were built like tanks. What shall I call my heroine? Careful not to put too much mustard in the dressing, Hortense doesn't like it. Will there be children in my book? When Antoine and I got married, we wanted four kids, but we stopped at two and I regret it now.

What the hell was he thinking, taking out that loan without telling me? And here I am, stuck with it!

So how do you come up with a name for a character? Eleanor? Too predictable. Gertrude, Mary, Cécile, Sibylle, Florence? What about the man? Eustache, Baudouin, Arnoud, Thierry, Guibert? And why should my heroine only have one lover, anyway? She's not the fool I am. Or maybe she's a fool who ends up wildly successful anyway. That would be funny: a girl who only hopes for a little happiness and winds up rich because everything she touches turns to gold.

A drop of boiling water from the pot splashed Joséphine's hand, and she jumped back with a yelp. She poked the potatoes with the tip of a knife to see if they were done.

"Hi, Mommy!" Zoé bounded into the kitchen. "We walked home with Mme Barthillet. She's so skinny! Mom, if I ever get fat, will you put me on that diet of hers?"

"Hello, Mom," said Hortense. "Guess what? They told us there won't be any hot lunch tomorrow. Can I have five euros to buy a sandwich?"

"Yes, honey. Give me my wallet. It's in my purse," she said, pointing to the bag on the radiator. "Zoé, don't you want a sandwich too, for tomorrow's lunch?"

"I'm eating at Max's. He invited me over. I got an 81 on my history quiz."

Joséphine observed her younger daughter. She would definitely put a little Zoé in her story. She could picture her as a village child with ruddy cheeks, bringing in the hay or stirring the soup as it bubbled in a big cauldron hanging over the fire. Joséphine would change Zoé's name, but keep her humor and her love of life. And her way of saying things. And what about Hortense? She would make her a princess—very beautiful and haughty . . . She'd live in a castle while her father was off on a crusade and—

"Hey, Earth to Mom!"

Hortense was holding Joséphine's purse out to her. "My five euros, remember?"

Jo took her wallet, and handed a five-euro bill to Hortense. As she did, a clipping fell to the floor, and Joséphine bent to pick it up. It was the photo of the man in the duffel coat. She suddenly knew who she would write her letter to.

That night, when the girls were in bed, Joséphine wrapped her quilt around her shoulders and went out onto the balcony. She looked up at the stars and asked them for strength and for ideas. She wanted them to forgive her for agreeing to Iris's scheme. *I don't have any choice. What was I supposed to do?*

She studied the night sky carefully, looking for the last star on the handle of the Big Dipper. That had been her star when she was little. Her father had given it to her one night when she was feeling sad. "You see that little star at the very tip of the dipper, Jo?" he'd said. "If it went away, the whole dipper would lose its balance and fall. If we lose you, our family will fall apart. Because you bring it joy, good humor, and a big heart. In each family, there are some people who don't seem important, but without them, there would be no life, no love. You and I, we're that type."

The little star at the end of the dipper never sparkles, Jo thought, *but I bet it made the photograph of the man in the duffel coat fall out of my wallet. Thank you. I'll write my story for him.*

"Hey, Jo! You're hiding something from me, aren't you?"

Shirley was standing in the doorway, hands on her hips. Joséphine had spent the past hour and a half in front of her computer, vainly waiting for inspiration. Taped next to the keyboard, the photo of the man in the duffel coat wasn't any help. As a muse, he'd been a complete failure. Jo thought of Iris's failed attempts to write. *Will I experience the same blank hopelessness? Better not start counting those euros before they hatch.*

"You've been avoiding me, Jo."

"This isn't a good time, Shirley. I'm in the middle of something."

Just when I was ready to dive in! she fumed. *Just when I was going to overcome my writer's block!* She looked up, and decided that Shirley's nose was much too small. To her dismay, Jo suddenly wanted to punch it.

"You're avoiding me, aren't you? Ever since you got back from the mountains three weeks ago, I've hardly seen you." She pointed at the laptop. "Is that Hortense's?"

"No, it's mine," Joséphine said through clenched teeth.

"Since when do you have two computers? Did Steve Jobs leave them to you in his will?"

Joséphine smiled despite herself. She was beginning to accept that she wasn't going to get any work done.

"Iris gave it to me for Christmas, actually." She immediately regretted saying so.

"What's the catch?"

"What do you mean?"

"Come on, Jo. Your sister never gives something for nothing, not even the time of day. So go on, tell me."

"Shirley, I can't. It's a secret."

"And you don't think I can keep a secret?"

"A secret is meant to stay secret, right?"

Shirley smiled.

"Okay. You scored a point. Are you going to offer me some coffee? Black with two lumps of brown sugar, please."

"I only have white. I haven't had time to go shopping."

"Too busy working?"

Joséphine bit her lip.

"You didn't ask how my holiday went. Remember? In Scotland?"

Joséphine knew that keeping her secret would be tough. Shirley didn't give up just like that. At Christmas it had been easy not to tell her about Antoine and the loan; Shirley's thoughts were all about decorations, the stuffed turkey, and the *bûche de Noël*. But the holidays were over now, and Shirley's radar was fully operational again.

"All right, I'll ask. How was your vacation?"

"Awful. Gary was in the doldrums the whole time. Ever since dancing with your daughter, he's been off his rocker. He wandered around my friend Mary's house spouting gloomy poetry and threatening to hang himself with his turtleneck. In his room I found twenty-four drafts of love letters to her that were as torrid as they were desperate! Some were even written in iambic pentameter. He didn't send any of them."

"And a good thing, too. Hortense doesn't have much patience with whiners. If he wants to attract her, he better become a big shot. Hortense is a material girl. She wants it all and she doesn't like waiting."

"Thanks for the warning."

"She loves beautiful dresses, fine jewelry, fancy cars. Her ideal man is Marlon Brando in *A Streetcar Named Desire*. Gary might try working out and wearing a ripped T-shirt. That doesn't cost much, and it might catch her eye."

"Brando! When I was her age, it was Robert Mitchum. I was mad for him! Speaking of which, *What a Way to Go* was on the telly last night. It stars Mitchum and Shirley MacLaine. When they were shooting it, the two were having a hot love affair."

"Oh, really?" said Joséphine absentmindedly, looking for an excuse to get Shirley out of her kitchen.

Unbelievable! she thought to herself. *This is my best friend, and I love her dearly, but at this very moment I'd chop her up and put her in a stew just to get rid of her.*

Shirley had finished listing the movie's cast and was describing the plot when something she'd just said caught Joséphine's attention.

"She doesn't want to be rich, so she tries to marry the most modest, unassuming bloke she can find, one who will guarantee her a nice quiet life. She thinks that money can't buy happiness, see? It just makes you unhappy. Anyway, it's so funny, Jo! Because she keeps marrying these poor blokes, and thanks to her, each one hits it big, makes loads of money, and kills himself working. She ends up a widow every time. Proving her theory that money doesn't bring happiness!"

"Wait a minute!" said Jo. "Tell me the story again, from the beginning. I wasn't listening." Shirley recapped the plot again.

Excited, Jo clutched her arm.

"But that's my idea exactly! I thought of it yesterday!"

"I've never seen you so excited over a movie," said Shirley teasingly.

"That's not just a movie, it's the story I want to tell in my stupid novel! . . . Oops!"

Jo turned pale.

"It's a secret, Shirley. I mean it."

"I won't say a word, Jo. I swear," said Shirley, crossing her fingers behind her back. She planned to tell Gary, of course. Shirley told her son everything he needed to understand life, so he could beware and protect himself. She claimed that children know everything before the adults do. They know their parents are going to split up before the parents do, that Mommy drinks in secret and that Daddy is screwing the supermarket checkout girl. Also, that Grandpa didn't die in bed of a heart attack, but atop a stripper in Pigalle.

"I knew something was up the minute I walked in."

"You really can't tell a soul. Iris would be furious if she knew you knew. When she suggested I write it for her, at first I said no. . . ."

"This novel you want a plot for . . ."

"Yeah. Iris suggested I trade my so-called talent for cash. For fifty thousand euros! That's an awful lot."

"You need that much money?" Shirley asked, now genuinely surprised.

"There's something else I didn't tell you."

Afterward, Shirley folded her arms across her chest and looked at Joséphine.

"You'll never change," she said with a sigh. "You let yourself get taken in by the first con artist to come down the pike! But what I don't get is why Iris needs you to write a novel."

"She wouldn't tell me."

"For God's sake, Jo, you're an accomplice to a swindle and you don't want to know why? I'll never understand you!"

Joséphine looked like a deer in the headlights.

"Next time you see her, at least ask. It's important, Jo. She's going to put her name on a book you wrote, and what does it get her? Fame? Your book's going to have to make a big splash for that to happen. Fortune? She's giving you all the money—unless she's planning to cheat you, which I wouldn't put past her. She promises you the money, then gives you only a small part of it and flies off to her lover in Venezuela."

"Shirley, stop it! Now you're the one writing a novel! Don't put thoughts like that in my head. I'm stressed enough as it is."

Joséphine looked anguished, and Shirley regretted upsetting her.

"I recorded that film last night," she said. "Want to watch it?"

"What, right now?"

"Sure. My class at the conservatory isn't for an hour and a half, and if the movie isn't over, you can finish watching it alone."

They went to Shirley's apartment and played the tape. Onscreen, Shirley MacLaine appeared, dressed all in black and looking lovely. She slowly walked down the staircase of a pink mansion, followed by eight men in black carrying a coffin.

"Did you see the photo of the man in the duffel coat on my keyboard?" Joséphine asked as the credits rolled.

"Yeah, I did. I figured you must be up to something big to have stuck it in front of your face. Probably for inspiration."

"It didn't work. He hasn't inspired me at all!"

"Make him into one of the five husbands and it'll work."

"Thanks a lot! You told me that they all die."

"Not the last one."

"Oh . . . But I don't want him to die," Jo said very quietly, her eyes glued to the screen. Shirley MacLaine had calmly walked offscreen. The funeral parlor attendants lost their grip on the coffin, which went tumbling down the stairs behind her.

♦ ♦ ♦

Antoine couldn't sleep anymore. He awoke with his pillow and sheets soaked, imagining he saw Faugeron wagging his finger at him. He tossed and turned some more. Finally, he relaxed and breathed in the cool night air. Then he took a shower and went downstairs. He grabbed a bottle of whiskey and went out onto the porch.

Sitting on the steps, he took a sip of whiskey, and another, and then another, while his eyes adjusted to the darkness. Gradually, shimmering yellow spots emerged, lighting up one after the other, until they seemed to be converging on him: the yellow eyes of crocodiles. Like lanterns bobbing on the swamp's dark, gleaming surface, the eyes watched him.

These creatures have been on earth for fifty million years, he thought. They had survived every natural disaster as the planet split, folded, shattered, burned, and congealed. The crocs had seen dinosaurs, primates, and humans arise and be struck down, and they were still here, watching.

Antoine felt incredibly alone. Besides Mylène, he had no one to talk to. And still nothing from Mr. Wei. No news, no check, no explanation.

He was living off Mylène's savings now. When he called his daughters in France, he made up stories about how things were going, spoke of fabulous profits, promised to send for them soon. *And what about Jo?* he wondered, as another crocodile joined the row of yellow footlights shining up at him. *Faugeron must have told her.* Looking back out at the yellow dots in the night, he felt his eyes watering. He was such a coward. Where was the fine self-confidence he used to feel after a safari, when he'd sit with the other men under a canvas tent drinking whiskey like one of the guys?

Joséphine . . . Mylène . . . Somehow those two have gotten tougher just as I'm going soft. Mylène exuded calm and serenity. She'd figured out how to cook buffalo meat, marinating it in a delicious mint and wild verbena sauce. It made a nice change from chicken. She wanted to keep busy, and was always making plans: to learn Chinese, make bracelets and necklaces like those worn by the women in the market, use grains and dyes from native plants to create beauty products. Mylène had a new idea every day.

And Joséphine hadn't even bothered picking up the phone to call him a coward and a thief.

Those two are alike, he thought, with hides as thick as a crocodile's. Antoine refilled his glass, smiling at the connection he'd dared make between them.

He felt a little breeze rising, and he patted his hair down. A crocodile had come out of the water and was lumbering closer on its short legs. It rested its snout on the sturdy wire fence and tried to bend it, emitting a hoarse cry. It snapped at the fence a few times. Then it lay down and slowly closed its yellow eyes, like someone reluctantly lowering window blinds.

Last night, Mylène had told him that she'd like to go to Paris, maybe for a week. "You could see your daughters," she said. That's when the fear started to gnaw at Antoine's stomach, and he began to sweat. He would have to face Joséphine and the girls and admit that he had made a mistake, that raising crocodiles wasn't such a good idea after all. That he'd messed up once again.

Now the crocodile was banging against the fence. Its yellow

eyes seemed narrowed in anger and its claws plowed the dirt, as if it were trying to dig its way out. *That's got to be a male*, thought Antoine. *I have to get that one to breed. This breeding thing has to work, goddamn it! I'm forty fucking years old, and if I don't make it this time, I am really and truly screwed!*

He started to swear, feeding the anger rising inside him. He hated Mr. Wei, he hated the crocodiles, he hated having to live in a world where if you hadn't made it by his age, it was all over.

Antoine expected that the thought of Wei would bring the knot back into his stomach, but something very different happened. Not only didn't he feel fear, he was overcome by joy, the joy of a man who suddenly knows exactly how he's going to get back at the guy who has been trying to pull the wool over his eyes.

I'll go to Paris, work out a repayment plan with Faugeron, and get my money from Wei. There has to be a way to wring some cash out of this flea-bitten crocodile park. Who do they think is running this crummy plantation, anyway? Me, Tonio Cortès, not some punk in cargo shorts. A real man, with a real pair of balls. A guy tough enough to go kiss that snarling croc over there, if I felt like it.

Antoine laughed out loud and raised his glass to the crocodile's health.

The light of dawn had extinguished the yellow eyes. Feeling emboldened, Antonio opened his fly and sent a hot, golden stream of urine at the crocodiles. He would show them. Not only was he not ashamed any more, he wasn't scared, and they'd better behave.

"You really think that'll impress them?" asked a sleepy voice behind him. He turned to see Mylène coming down the steps, a sheet around her hips. He stared at her, bewildered.

"You look just great," she said with a laugh.

He laughed a little too heartily. Did he imagine it, or did he detect a note of disdain in her voice?

"Meet the new Tonio!"

"The old one was fine."

"Yeah, right. But I know what I know, and I know we can't go on like this much longer."

"Okay, just as I suspected," Mylène said with a sigh. "Come on. Let's go have breakfast. Pong's already in the kitchen."

As Antoine staggered toward the house, Mylène snapped, "I wish you would act this brave with that thieving Wei character. When I think of how fast we're going through my life's savings, I'm scared shitless."

But Antoine couldn't hear her. He'd missed the first step and lay sprawled facedown on the porch. The whiskey bottle rolled down the steps and came to rest on the lowest one, spilling its contents in an amber puddle that caught the first rays of the morning sun.

"So I told Mother what a shame it was that the two of you aren't speaking, and she said, 'No, not till she says she's sorry, and means it—says it from the heart, not just rattles it off. Joséphine is the one who insulted me, she's my daughter, she owes me respect!' I told her I would pass the message along."

"I've had it with her, Iris. I'm not about to apologize."

"Then you won't be seeing each other anytime soon."

"I'm doing just fine without her."

"Jo, you haven't seen her in eight months. What if something happens to her? She is your mother, after all."

"Nothing's going to happen to her. She's too mean to die. Dad died of a heart attack at forty. She'll live to a hundred. And you know what? Ever since I stopped seeing her, I've been doing just great."

Iris didn't answer.

"Okay, Iris, you didn't really make me come all the way out to Porte d'Asnières just to lecture me about our mother, did you?"

"No. I stopped in to see Marcel before coming here. Hortense was in his office. She's looking for an internship for June, for school. From the minute she walked in the door, the warehouse guys couldn't stop drooling."

"I know. She has that effect on everyone."

Joséphine and Iris were having lunch in the working-class Café des Carrefours. Trucks rumbled by, and when they braked before taking the on-ramp to the Périphérique, the restaurant's windows rattled. Iris ordered fried eggs with ham, Joséphine a green salad and a yogurt.

"I saw Serrurier. You know, the publisher."

"And?" whispered Joséphine, suddenly anxious.

"He's delighted with your plot idea and the fifty-page writing sample. He went on and on. You should have heard him!"

Iris opened her purse, pulled out an envelope, and held it up.

"He gave me the advance. The rest will follow when I hand in the finished manuscript. I deposited it and wrote you a check for twenty-five thousand euros. Here you go. But keep it under your hat!"

Joséphine accepted the envelope reverently. But as she put it in her purse, a thought suddenly struck her.

"What will you do about taxes?"

"You've got a bit of lettuce stuck right there," Iris said, gesturing at her own teeth.

Joséphine picked it off and repeated her question.

"Don't worry about it," said Iris. "Philippe won't ever notice. He doesn't prepare his own return; an accountant does it. Anyway, he pays so much in taxes that a little more won't make much difference!"

"Are you sure? What if they ask me where all that money came from?"

"You'll say it's a gift from your rich sister."

Joséphine looked skeptical.

"Oh, stop being such a worrywart, Jo. Our project passed with flying colors!"

For a moment, Joséphine was tempted to order something rich, like a choucroute with sausages.

"Isn't it terrific, sis?" Iris asked, a yellow gleam in her eyes. "We're going to be rich and famous!"

"Rich for me. Famous for you."

"Does that bother you?"

"No, just the opposite, actually. When I see what people have to do and say to get on television, I want to crawl under my bed."

"See, to me that's the best part. I can't stand my image as the good little wifey-poo anymore! I'm going to put on a show that'll knock their socks off. I intend to milk this thing. Serrurier keeps saying to me, 'With your eyes, your connections, your beauty, blah, blah, blah.' Well, let's put it to the test!"

Iris tossed her black hair and stretched her arms in the air as if she were opening a path to the heavens.

"God, I've been so bored, Jo." She sighed. "So totally bored."

"Is that why you're doing this?" Joséphine asked timidly.

"Well, sure. Why else?"

"The other day on the train you said that I'd be getting you out of a sticky situation. I have the right to know about it."

Iris considered her sister carefully. Jo was changing, she thought. She was becoming more forceful and persistent. Iris let out a long sigh and looked away.

"It's Philippe," she said. "I feel he's avoiding me, that I'm not the eighth wonder of the world anymore. I'm afraid he's thinking of leaving me. I figured that by writing this book, I might seduce him all over again."

Iris pushed her plate aside and lit a cigarette.

"When did you start smoking?"

"It's part of my new image! I'm practicing. Chief's secretary Josiane said she was quitting, and she gave me her pack."

Joséphine remembered the scene on the station platform: Marcel kissing his secretary and helping her onto the train as though she were the crown jewels. Jo hadn't mentioned it to anyone. She thought of Henriette and shuddered. What would become of her mother if Marcel started a new life with someone else?

"Are you really afraid Philippe's going to leave you?" she asked gently.

"Until recently, it had never crossed my mind. But lately, yes. I feel like he's drifting away. I was even jealous of the way you two were talking at the chalet. He talks to you with more feeling than he does to me."

"That's nonsense!"

"No, sadly, it's not. I have plenty of faults, but blindness isn't one of them. I can tell when people are interested in me or not. And I can't stand being ignored."

Gazing at the smoke from her cigarette curling upward, Iris thought back to her meeting with Serrurier in his office. The outpouring of praise, the eyes bright with excitement . . . The man was so attentive and respectful, she'd felt alive again. The smoke from his cigar filled the room as he followed the ins and outs of the plot Joséphine had concocted.

"The idea of the girl who wants to join a convent but is forced to marry—that's terrific!" Serrurier had said. "And I love that she outlives all her husbands, and winds up a rich widow every time. I really like what I've read so far. To be honest, I wouldn't have thought such a pretty head would hold so much skill and talent. And where did you unearth that material about the degrees of humility? It's wonderful! A woman who does everything she can to be humble, but becomes a heroine despite herself. Very ingenious."

Iris had come out of Serrurier's office feeling weak in the knees, her heart pounding wildly.

"By the way, where did you get that stuff about the degrees of humility?" she now asked, trying not to sound too admiring.

"That's from the Rule of Saint Benedict. I thought it would

fit the character of a girl who dreams only of devoting her life to God."

"And what is this rule, exactly?"

"Well, according to Saint Benedict, you have to go through various degrees of self-denial to reach perfection and God. It's what he called the Ladder of Humility. On the lowest rungs, you're asked to put your desires and your selfishness aside, and to obey God in all things. Then you learn to give, to love those who criticize or slander you, to be patient and good. The sixth rung is to be content with the most humble of circumstances. And so on until the twelfth rung, where you're nothing but a miserable insect willing to put yourself entirely at the service of God and mankind, and you achieve greatness through abnegation."

"I see," said Iris dubiously. "Tell me, Jo, you aren't turning into some sort of mystic, are you? You'll end up in a convent if you're not careful!"

After a moment, Iris continued. "In case you've decided to climb the ladder of saintly redemption, why don't you make your peace with Mother?"

"Because I'm only on the first rung; I'm just a humble novice! And remember, we're talking about my book's character, not about me. Don't confuse the two."

Iris shook her head, laughing.

"Serrurier loved your character's name, by the way: Florine. Very pretty! Want to drink a glass of champagne to Florine's health?"

"No, thanks. I have to work this afternoon. When does he want to publish my book?"

"*Our* book! Jo, don't forget! And when it comes out, it'll be *my* book. We can't afford a mistake."

Joséphine felt a pang. She was already so attached to her story—to Florine, and to her parents and her husbands. In bed, she would go over their names, the color of their hair and eyes, their personality traits. At times she felt as if she was living their lives, and it kept her awake at night. She would have liked to tell Iris that it was *her* story.

"Let's see," said Iris, "it's February now. . . . If you can deliver the manuscript in July, he'll publish it sometime next winter. That gives you six, seven months to write it. That's enough time, isn't it?"

"I don't know, maybe," said Joséphine, feeling stung. Her sister was talking to her like a secretary.

"You'll manage fine. Stop worrying! And above all, not a word to a soul! If we want our plan to work, we can't tell anybody, Jo. No one, absolutely no one. You understand, right?"

"Yes," said Joséphine weakly.

She sighed. She felt like telling Iris that this wasn't some plan they were talking about, but her book, her baby . . .

Chapter 11

♦ ♦ ♦

"So, still nothing?"

"Not a thing. I'm starting to give up hope, Ginette."

"Relax, it's normal. You've been on the pill for years, and now you think you can just snap your fingers and bingo, you're pregnant? Be patient! The baby will come in its own time."

"Maybe I'm too old, Ginette . . . Thirty-nine, soon. And the wait's driving Marcel crazy! He makes me take all these tests to make sure the plumbing's in order. Before now, you just looked at me, and I got pregnant."

"You mean you've been knocked up before?"

Josiane nodded gravely.

"Yeah, and I've had three abortions, so—"

"You ditched a kid of Marcel's?" Ginette was shocked.

"Well, did you think I was going to be the Virgin Mary without a Joseph to stand by me? You know Marcel's scared shitless of the Toothpick. Who's to say that he'll even give my baby his name?"

"He said he would. He promised."

"Sure, promises: easy to make, hard to keep."

"Come off it, Josie. It's not true in this case, and you know it. This baby is all Marcel talks about these days. He's gone on a diet, rides a bicycle, eats organic food. He stopped smoking and takes his blood pressure morning and night. He's even starting to pick onesies out of catalogs."

Josiane looked unconvinced.

"Well, we'll see what happens once I'm pregnant. If he caves in to her again, I'm blowing everything away, him and the kid!"

"Quiet! Here he comes!"

Marcel was coming upstairs, followed by a heavyset man who panted at every step. They came into Josiane's office, and Marcel introduced the women to Monsieur Bugalkhoviev, a Ukrainian businessman. Josiane and Ginette nodded and smiled. Marcel quickly kissed Josiane on top of her head once the man had gone ahead into his office.

"Everything okay, sweetie-pie?"

He put his hand on her stomach, but she brushed it away.

"Stop treating me like a mother hen. I'll end up laying an egg."

"Still nothing?"

"You mean since this morning?" she asked sarcastically. "Nope. There's nobody in sight."

"Don't tease me, honeybunch."

"I'm not teasing, I'm fed up. There's a difference!"

Marcel straightened and walked into his office. Before closing the door, he turned around and whispered: "I love you! I'm the happiest man in the world."

The door closed, and Josiane gave Ginette a helpless look. Since Marcel had suggested she have his baby, everything had changed. At Christmas, he sent her to the mountains to get some fresh air. He phoned every day to see if she was breathing properly, worried when she coughed, and told her to go see a doctor right away, to take vitamins, to sleep ten hours a night.

She spent hours walking in the snow. *Will I be a good mother?* she wondered. *Who knows, considering the mother I had . . . Is a person born a mother, or do you become one? What if I start acting just like my mom, without intending to?* Josiane shivered at the thought, pulled her collar tight, and set off walking again.

She thought of Chaval at times, of his lean, taut body, of his hands on her breasts, of the way he would bite her until she begged him to stop. She shook her head to drive him from her thoughts.

"I'm going nuts!" she said aloud, and sighed.

"Is it my imagination, or has Marcel gotten hair implants?" Ginette asked.

"You're not imagining it. And once a week he gets a facial at a beauty parlor. Wants to be the handsomest daddy in the world, he says."

"That's so cute!"

"No, it's scary."

As Ginette was leaving Josiane's office, she ran into Chaval coming in.

"Is she there?" he asked abruptly.

" 'She' has a name, may I remind you."

"Oh, give me a break. I'm not going to eat your pal alive or anything."

He shouldered his way past her and went into Josiane's office.

"Hi, beautiful! Still playing the senior circuit?"

"Where I park my fanny is none of your business."

"Okay, take it easy. Is he around? Can I see him?"

"He doesn't want to be disturbed under any circumstances. You'll have to come back when he's free."

"That'll be too late."

Chaval smiled cockily, his grin accented by the pencil mustache over his upper lip.

"I might as well say it, since he tells you everything," he said, sounding casual. "I'm outta here. I've been asked to run IKEA France, and I said yes."

"They want *you*? Are they trying to sink the company?"

"Go ahead and laugh. You were the one who wanted to push me to the top, so I can't be all bad. I was headhunted, babe! Didn't have to lift a finger. They came to me. Twice the salary and lots of perks, so I said yes. Since I'm a decent guy, I came to tell the old man in person. But you can tell him, and we'll have a meeting later to sort everything out. I plan to blow Casamia out of the water."

"Ooooh! You really scare me! I'm getting goose bumps, Chaval."

"Speaking of bumps, I met Mademoiselle Hortense this morning. Pretty hot stuff."

"She's fifteen, Chaval."

"She is? Well, she could pass for twenty. That must get you down, seeing's you're getting close to menopause."

He gave a nasty laugh and left.

Josiane shrugged and wrote Marcel a memo: "Chaval wants to meet with you. IKEA made him offer. He accepted."

Barely a year earlier, she'd been sleeping with Chaval. *There's something rotten about that guy*, she thought. *But he drives me wild. I must be rotten, too.*

The trouble with outsourcing is that you have to keep on doing it, thought Marcel, as he studied the Ukrainian's heavy eyelids and houndstooth overcoat. *No sooner do you find a nice little country where wages are low, benefits nonexistent, and workers begging for jobs than the place joins the EU or some damned thing, and there goes your profit margin.*

Marcel had been forced to keep moving east, toward the sunrise. First Poland, then Hungary, now it was Ukraine's turn. *What the heck*, he thought, *may as well go straight to China!* But China was far away, and a tough place to do business. He'd already set up a couple of factories there. He needed a right-hand man, but Marcel Junior was taking his sweet time about showing up. *I won't live to see him get old enough to vote*, Marcel thought gloomily.

He sighed and brought his attention back to the points the Ukrainian was making. Marcel poured him another shot of whiskey, and added ice. Smiling, he handed it to him and pushed the contract across the desk. The man shifted in his seat to take the proffered glass, pulled out a fountain pen, and unscrewed the cap. *This is it!* thought Marcel. *He's going to sign!* But the Ukrainian instead drew a thick envelope from his breast pocket and handed it to him.

"These are my travel expenses," he said in a thick accent. "Please you will take care of them?"

Marcel opened the envelope and glanced quickly through the crumpled wads of paper. Receipts for a restaurant, a hotel, a case of champagne, Yves Saint Laurent perfume, and a ring and a bracelet from Mauboussin. All the bills were made out to Marcel Grobz. He could cover this fat pig's crazy expenses with one stroke of his pen.

"No problem," he said. He winked at the Ukrainian, who was still holding his fountain pen in the air. Marcel smiled even more broadly, to signal that everything would be settled. The man was waiting, his hooded eyes shining with impatience.

"No problem," Marcel repeated. "You're my friend, and whenever you come to Paris, you'll be my guest." The Ukrainian smiled and relaxed, his eyes now shrunk to lifeless slits. He put his pen to the contract and signed it.

Philippe put his feet up on his desk and skimmed the file Caroline had sent him. The cover memo read: "We're in a jam, and only a merger will save the situation." He sighed and started reading from the beginning. Textile manufacturing in France was finished, that was certain, but a company like Labonal had survived by specializing in luxury hosiery. To make it in the age of globalization, each European country had to focus on its own special abilities. The question was, how do you make clients understand that? They counted on Philippe to come up with the arguments.

He took off his shoes and wiggled his toes in his socks—

Labonals, as it happened. *The British figured this out this years ago*, he thought. *They gave up their heavy industries and turned into a service economy, and now their country's going great guns.* Philippe sighed. France was a beautiful country and he loved her, but he hated to see her greatest industries go under for lack of flexibility, imagination, and guts.

His secretary rang.

"It's a Mr. Goodfellow," she said. "He insists on speaking to you."

"Put him through."

He heard a click, and John Goodfellow came on, speaking a rapid mix of English and French.

"We've been spotted, Philippe."

"What do you mean, spotted?"

"Someone put a private detective on my tail. So I turned around and followed him. He wasn't very good—an amateur. I have his name and the address of his agency in Paris. We just need to figure out who he's working for. What shall we do?"

"Wait and see. Give me his name and number, and I'll take care of it."

"Do we keep going or do we stop?"

"We keep going, Johnny. I'll take care of the rest. See you next Monday at Roissy, as agreed."

"Okay."

Philippe hung up. So he was being followed; who would want to do that? He and Goodfellow weren't doing anyone any harm. It was a strictly private matter. Was it a client poking into his private life so as to blackmail him? Anything was possible. The firm's clients were often involved in major deals where hundreds of jobs might depend on his recommendation. He looked at the detective's name and his agency's phone number, and decided to make the call later. He wasn't worried.

Philippe picked up the file again but had trouble concentrating. He was tempted to just quit the law sometimes. He was forty-eight years old and had made his mark. He wanted to spend more time with his son. Alexandre was growing up and becoming a stranger to him. He was a gangly kid with headphones on his ears who would say, "Hey, Dad, what's up?" and disappear into his room.

Anyway, who could blame him? thought Philippe. *Most evenings I come home with a stack of files and lock myself in my study. And that isn't counting the nights when Iris and I go out.*

"I don't want to lose touch with my son," he said out loud.

The other day, he'd had an idea. He would write a long letter to Alexandre. Everything he couldn't say to him in person, he'd put in writing. It wasn't good for a boy to be around women all the time—his mother, Carmen, his cousins Hortense and Zoé. Alexandre was surrounded by females! *He's about to turn eleven; it's high time I sprung him from that harem. We should be going to soccer games and rugby matches, to museums. I've never even taken him to the Louvre, for God's sake! And that's not something that would ever occur to his mother.*

How do you begin a letter to your son? Dear Alex? Dear Alexandre? Dear son? Maybe he would ask Joséphine; she'd know. Philippe found himself turning to her more and more. He would say things to Jo that he wouldn't to anyone else. "I think

I'm going to close the firm and retire," he'd told her the other day. "Lawyering bores me, the work's getting harder, and I'm tired of my colleagues."

"But Philippe," she protested, "your people are the best in Paris!"

"Yes, they're a good team, but they're losing their edge, and as people, they're not that interesting any more. You know what I'd love to do?"

Joséphine shook her head.

"I'd like to be a consultant. Give advice occasionally and have some real time for myself."

"What would you do with it?" she asked.

That's when he told her about Alexandre.

"Alex is worried," Joséphine said. "He needs you to spend time with him. People think that what matters is spending quality time with your kid, but quantity counts, too. Kids don't just open up when you press a button. Sometimes you can spend a whole day with them, and it's only that evening on the way home that they suddenly open up and share a secret or a fear, or they confess something. Here you'd thought you'd wasted all this time, but it wasn't wasted, because it was worth it for that."

Joséphine blushed. "I don't know if I'm making much sense."

She's looking tired, Philippe thought.

"Is there anything you need, Jo?" he asked. "You sure you're managing okay?"

She assured him she was doing just fine. Then she said, "Iris knows that I'm working for you."

"How did she find out?"

"From Caroline Vibert. They had tea together. Iris was kind of annoyed that you hadn't told her, so maybe you should."

"I will, I promise. It's stupid, but I don't like mixing work and family. Especially since as conspirators, we're not very good at lying."

He'd burst out laughing. Joséphine looked at him, feeling awkward, and backed out of his office.

Philippe was jolted out of his reverie by Caroline Vibert.

"Did you come up with a strategy for that file I sent?"

"No, I've been daydreaming. I don't feel like working today. It's Wednesday; I think I'm going to take my son out to lunch."

Caroline stared at him in disbelief as he dialed Alexandre's cell. The boy was thrilled at the prospect of going to his favorite restaurant with his dad.

"Then I'm taking you to the movies and you get to choose what we see."

"No, let's go to the Bois and practice penalty kicks!" Alexandre shouted.

"All right. It's your call."

Caroline twirled her finger at her temple in a you're-crazy gesture.

"The French hosiery industry can wait," Philippe said. "If you'll excuse me, I have an appointment with my son."

First, the sound of his footsteps in the hallway. The pale yellow tile walls with the blue trim, the big full-length mirror. The mailbox, with the card that Joséphine hadn't changed: "M. et Mme Antoine Cortès." The smell of the elevator. Finally, his footsteps on their landing. He didn't have the key, and raised his hand to knock, but Joséphine had already opened the door.

There they were, face-to-face.

Nearly a year had passed, and they studied each other with cautious curiosity and surprise.

How much has changed in a year, thought Joséphine, observing the bags under Antoine's eyes, the burst capillaries on his cheeks, the furrows in his forehead. *He's taken to drinking . . .*

Nothing has changed, thought Antoine, who wished he could stroke the blond hair framing Joséphine's face, which looked thinner and firmer.

You look beautiful, darling, he wanted to whisper.

You look tired, dear, she almost said.

A smell of sautéing onions wafted in from the kitchen.

"I'm making chicken with onions for dinner. The girls love it."

"Actually, I was thinking of taking them out to eat. It's been such a long time."

"They'll like that. I didn't say anything to them, I wasn't sure if . . ." What Joséphine didn't say: *I wasn't sure if you would be alone, if you were free for dinner, if she was going to be with you.*

"They must have changed a lot," said Antoine. "Are they doing okay?"

"It was a little hard at first."

He felt like sitting down and watching her make dinner. Joséphine so often had that effect on him; she soothed him. He needed a break from the misery of the last months. Antoine had gone to see Faugeron, but the banker took three phone calls during the scant ten minutes he'd granted him. "Please excuse me, Monsieur Cortès, this is important." Antoine felt like yelling, "So you're saying I'm not important?" But he held his tongue and waited for Faugeron to hang up and continue their talk.

"Your wife is handling everything just fine. There are no problems with your account, Monsieur Cortès. I think you should discuss all this with her." Then he stood up and shook Antoine's hand, again saying, "No problems at all, as long as your wife is around." Antoine never got a chance to tell Faugeron about his problem with Mr. Wei.

Night was falling. Streetlights were winking on, and a soft white glow lit the dark sky. Through the kitchen window, you could see the lights of Paris. When Jo and Antoine first moved to Courbevoie, they used to look at the city and make plans. "When we live in Paris, we'll go to the movies and out to restaurants," they'd say. "We'll take the Metro and drink coffee in smoky cafés." Paris had become the repository of all their dreams.

"We never did wind up living in Paris," Antoine said, so sadly that Joséphine felt a stab of pity for him.

"I'm perfectly happy here," she said. "I've always been happy here."

"Did you do something to the kitchen? It looks different."

"Just more books, that's all. Oh, and the computer. I made myself a work space."

"That must be it."

He remained silent, slumped in his chair. Jo noticed some gray hairs on the nape of his neck, and found herself thinking that people usually started going gray at the temples.

"Antoine, why did you take out that loan without telling me? That wasn't right."

"I know. Nothing I've been doing lately seems right. I have no excuse. When I left for Africa, I thought I'd be successful, make a lot of money, pay you back double or even triple. I figured everything was going to work out perfectly, but then . . ."

"It's not over. Things might still work out."

"It's Africa, Jo! It eats people alive. It rots you from the inside. Only the big cats survive in Africa. And the crocodiles."

I can't let the girls see Antoine in this melancholy state, thought Jo. Then she had a terrible suspicion. She leaned over and smelled his breath.

"Antoine, you've been drinking! Listen, you're going to go take a shower and change your clothes. I still have some shirts and a jacket of yours in the closet. I want you to stand tall and be cheerful if you're going to take the girls to a restaurant."

"You kept my shirts?"

"They're beautiful shirts. I certainly wasn't about to throw them out."

Suddenly he felt better. The old familiar ease was returning. He would shower and change, the girls would come home from study hall, and he could act as if he'd never left. The four of them would go out to dinner, the way they used to. He stood under the shower, feeling the water run down the back of his neck.

Joséphine was surprised at how painless seeing Antoine had been. The moment she opened the door, she knew: Antoine would never be a stranger; he would always be the girls' father. The worst part of the separation had been how quietly it had happened, without any yelling or screaming. During the time she was struggling all alone, he had simply tiptoed out of her heart.

"I've always thought some people are completely happy, and I've always wanted to be one of them," Antoine admitted, once he was showered, shaved, and dressed. "You, for example. You seem to be one of those happy people now. Nothing scares you. Faugeron told me that you've been paying back the loan on your own."

"I have a second job. I'm doing translation work for Philippe's firm, and he pays me very well. Too well, in fact."

"You mean Philippe Dupin, Iris's husband?"

"Yeah. He's changed, become more human. Something must have happened in his life. He pays attention to people now."

I have to hold on to this moment, Joséphine thought. *I need it to last a little longer so that it stays imprinted in my memory. The moment when Antoine stopped being the man I loved and became just a companion, not quite yet a friend. I've changed too. I've grown. I've suffered, but it hasn't been in vain.*

"How do they do it?" Antoine asked. "I mean, people who are successful. Are they just lucky, or do they have a secret formula?"

"I don't think there's any formula. Nobody succeeds all at once. You set one stone on top of another and you keep on going. When you go back to your crocodiles, try to take things as they come, one at a time."

He was listening to her as if her words could save his life.

"It's the same with drinking," she went on. "Every morning

when you wake up, tell yourself, 'I'm not having a drink until this evening.' Take a small step every day, and you'll get there."

"The Chinese guy I work for isn't paying me."

"So what are you living on?"

"Mylène's money. That's why I wasn't able to pay the loan back."

"Oh, Antoine!"

"I wanted to discuss it with Faugeron. I hoped he'd help me find a way, but he barely listened."

"What about the Chinese workers? Are they being paid?"

"Wei pays them peanuts, but yeah, they're paid. From a separate budget. I'm not going to steal their pennies from them."

Joséphine thought for a moment, tapping her teaspoon against the cup.

"Listen to me, Antoine. People like this Mr. Wei only do things if they're forced to. If you go on working without being paid, how do you expect him to respect you? Whereas if you leave, he'll send you a check posthaste. Think about it. He won't risk letting thousands of crocodiles die. He'd be in a real bind."

"Maybe you're right." Antoine took Joséphine's hand and squeezed. "Thank you."

The doorbell rang.

"Now pull yourself together. Smile and be cheerful tonight. They mustn't know. It's not their problem. Understood? And don't let Hortense dominate the conversation. Get Zoé to talk. She always lets her sister overshadow her."

He gave her a weak smile and nodded.

The reunion was joyous. The girls took turns jumping on

their father. They were about to head out the door when Antoine asked, "Aren't you coming to dinner with us?"

Jo shook her head. "No, I've got work to do. Have fun and don't get back too late. It's a school night!"

Joséphine closed the front door and smiled. *I have to start writing right away*, she told herself. *I have to get this scene down and put it in the book. I'm not sure where it'll fit, but it's one of those moments where a character's feelings drive the whole story forward.*

In the meantime, Mylène had gone back to the room at the Ibis Courbevoie Hotel that Antoine had reserved in the name of M. and Mme Cortès. What would have thrilled Mylène a year earlier now left her cold. She was carrying so many packages she had trouble getting her room key into the lock. She had made the rounds—Monoprix, Sephora, Marionnaud, Carrefour, and Leclerc—hunting for cheap beauty products. In Kenya, she noticed that whenever she made herself up, the Chinese women would follow her, whispering among themselves. In broken English, they asked how to get those reds, greens, pinks, ochers, and "cocoa for the eyelashes." She also noticed that they loved products labeled "Paris" or "Made in France." This gave Mylène the idea of opening a beauty parlor in Croco Park. She could give facials and beauty treatments, and sell cosmetics from Paris. She'd just have to set her prices high enough to cover shipping and travel, and also make a profit.

She knew that she couldn't count on Antoine anymore. He was gradually falling apart, had become a gentle, resigned alcoholic. If she didn't take things in hand, they'd soon be flat broke. Maybe seeing his wife and daughters would bring him to his senses.

Mylène undressed and went to bed. She was eager to go back to Kenya and open her beauty salon. She drifted off to sleep thinking up a name for her salon: Paris Beauty? Paris Chic? Vive Paris? Suddenly, she jerked awake. *My God, what if it doesn't work, and I wind up stuck with all these cosmetics? I've spent everything in my savings account, and I don't have anything left!* She groped around in the dark for some wood to knock on, then fell back asleep.

A black marker in hand, Joséphine studied her kitchen calendar and crossed out the next two weeks. *Today is April 15,* she thought; *the girls will be back on the thirtieth. That means I have two weeks to devote to my book. Two weeks, meaning fourteen days of ten hours of writing a day. Twelve, maybe, if I drink a lot of coffee.*

When Antoine had suggested taking the girls for Easter vacation, she had hesitated. The idea of their going off with him to Kenya with only Mylène to keep an eye on them made her very nervous. What if the girls got too close to the crocodiles? But Shirley'd said she and Gary could go along. "I love traveling and adventures, and I can take off for two weeks," she said. "I don't have any classes at the conservatory, and I don't have any big orders to fill."

Jo had dropped everyone off at Roissy–Charles de Gaulle the night before.

Now I need to set myself a schedule, she thought, *and stick to it. Eat meals between chapters. Spread out my books and my notes, and write and write . . .*

Joséphine decided to start by concentrating on her novel's setting, a village in the south of France, near Montpellier.

In the twelfth century, there are 12 million people living in France, and only 1.8 million in England. France is split between the Plantagenet kingdom, headed by Henry II and Eleanor of Aquitaine, and that of Louis VII. Trade is expanding through markets and fairs. Money has replaced barter as the preferred medium of exchange. In the towns, Jews are tolerated but shunned. Because Christians are forbidden from lending money at interest, the Jews are bankers, and often usurers. They are seen as profiting from others' hardship, and despised. They are forced to wear the yellow star.

In high society, a woman is valued only for the virginity she offers up on her wedding day. Her future husband thinks of her as a womb to impregnate—with boys. He is not supposed to show love for her. Under church law a man who loves his wife too passionately is guilty of adultery. For this reason, many women dream of retiring to a convent. In the eleventh and twelfth centuries, convents proliferate.

Florine understands all this. She doesn't want to be one of those women who are led to marriage like a lamb to the slaughter. She would rather give herself up to God.

For Jo, Florine was beginning to come to life. She is tall, blond, and shapely. She has a slender neck and almond-shaped green eyes with long lashes. Her skin is clear, her lips full, and her cheeks red. She wears an embroidered headband above a high, rounded forehead, and blond tresses cascade down around her face. She has long, soft hands the color of ivory; the hands of an aristocrat.

Not like mine, thought Joséphine, glancing with dismay at her scabby fingers and nails.

Florine's parents are bankrupt nobles who live in a drafty house with a leaking roof. They dream of regaining their past glory by marrying off their only daughter.

The story begins one evening . . .

The whole family—grandparents, children, grandchildren, and cousins—is gathered around the fire when word reaches them that Guillaume, the rich and handsome count of Castelnau, has just returned from the Crusades. He has decided to marry, and everyone wonders who the future countess will be. This is the evening Florine plans to tell her parents that she wants to observe the Rule of Saint Benedict and enter a convent.

Florine's mother is an ambitious, hard-hearted woman who dominates Florine's kindly father.

Florine tries to get her father's attention and join the conversation, but in vain. Children are allowed to speak only when spoken to, so she waits for the moment when she can speak up. At long last the master of the house asks his daughter to bring him his pipe.

Florine fills the clay pipe with his favorite hemp blend, and announces her plan. Her mother cries out that a convent is out of the question. Florine is to marry the count of Castelnau!

Florine stands up to them, declaring that God is her intended.

Her father orders her to her room, to meditate on God's commandment to honor thy father and thy mother.

Now I describe Florine's room, thought Jo, *with its chests, tapestries, icons, benches and footstools, and of course, her bed.* Florine's chests and sideboards all have locks, and having the keys to so many locks is a sign of status in the household. After everyone has gone, Florine can overhear her parents in the next room. They're talking about her, and her duties as a daughter. A daughter from a good family bakes bread, makes the beds, washes, cooks, takes care of all the linens and sewing, and embroiders purses.

"She'll marry Guillaume," insists her mother, "and that's all there is to it!"

Her father remains silent.

When Florine walks into the kitchen the next morning, her wet nurse sees her and faints. Hearing the commotion, her mother runs in—and promptly faints as well!

Florine has completely shaved her head.

"I won't marry Guillaume," she says. "I want to enter a convent."

Her mother comes to and locks Florine in her room. General hysteria. Threats and accusations rain down. She loses her keys and her freedom, and is put to work as a scullion in the kitchen.

Word of Florine's reputation reaches Guillaume, and he demands to see her. Her mother covers her shaved head with an embroidered wimple hung with jewels.

The presentation takes place. Guillaume is captivated by Florine's silent beauty and by her slender white hands. He asks her to marry him. Florine must obey. She decides that this will be her first degree of humility.

Guillaume wants a big wedding. He builds a stage big enough for five hundred people to spend a week in feasting. It is adorned with tapestries, expensive furniture, armor, and fabrics brought back from the Orient. Florine keeps her eyes downcast on the wedding day. She has obeyed. She has promised God to be a good wife. She will keep her word.

Now I get to describe Florine's first night with Guillaume, thought Joséphine. *Those medieval wedding nights must have been horrible, with child brides handed over to drunken brutes.*

During his marriage to Florine, Guillaume becomes very wealthy. *How does he do that?* Jo wondered. *I'll have to think about it. And later, her second husband—*

Just then, the doorbell rang. She tiptoed over and looked out the peephole. It was Iris. Reluctantly, she opened the door.

"Hi, Jo! I thought I'd drop by to see how things were coming with my book. How's our Florine doing?"

"Well, she shaved her head," Joséphine retorted, wishing she could do the same to her sister.

"I want to read all about it!"

"I don't know, Iris. I'm right in the middle of—"

"I won't stay long, I promise. Just a quick peek."

They went into the kitchen and began to read on the computer screen.

Iris's cell phone rang, and she answered it.

"No, no, you're not interrupting anything. I'm at my sister's. Yes, in Courbevoie! Can you believe it? I had to take a compass and bring my passport! Ha, ha! . . . Really? Are you serious? Go on, tell me about it!"

Joséphine could feel her blood boiling. She snatched the laptop from Iris and glared at her.

"Uh-oh, I'm going to have to call you back. Joséphine is giving me the hairy eyeball."

Iris shut her phone.

"Are you mad at me?"

"Yes, I am! First you show up without warning, you interrupt me when I'm working, and then you spend the time making fun of me to some stupid society bitch! If you're not interested in what I'm writing, don't come bothering me, okay?"

"All right, all right! Calm down! Can I at least read a little bit of it?"

"Only if you turn off your phone."

Iris agreed, and Jo handed her the computer back.

Iris read for a moment in silence. When she looked up, she looked hard at her sister and said, "This is good. It's really good."

Jo didn't answer.

"Do you want me to leave now?"

"If you don't mind."

"I'm happy to go. I'm delighted you're taking this so seriously." Iris grabbed her purse and phone and left, trailing a cloud of perfume.

Joséphine slumped against the front door for a moment, then took a deep breath and returned to the kitchen. She'd completely lost her train of thought!

Raging, she screamed and yanked open the refrigerator door.

Chapter 12

♦ ♦ ♦

"*D*addy, will the crocodiles eat me up?"

Antoine squeezed Zoé's little hand and assured her that they wouldn't.

He remembered Joséphine's advice. "Be sure to spend some time alone with Zoé, one on one. Don't let Hortense monopolize you."

Shirley, Gary, and the girls had arrived the night before, exhausted from the trip and the heat, but excited at the thought of being in Kenya and seeing Croco Park, the lagoons, and the coral reefs.

Mylène was delighted to have company, and Antoine felt happy for the first time since moving to Kenya. He was happy to have his daughters with him, happy to have a family. Mylène and Hortense seemed to get along really well. Hortense promised to help sell her beauty products.

"I'll do your makeup," said Mylène, "and you can be a walking advertisement for the salon. But don't get the Chinese men too turned on!"

Hortense curled her lip in disdain. "They're too small," she said. "I want a real man, with big muscles."

Gary discreetly felt his biceps. He was doing fifty push-ups twice a day, morning and night, and Hortense noticed.

"Keep at it, beanpole," she scoffed. "Maybe you'll get lucky."

Shirley scowled.

Zoé and Antoine walked along in silence. Antoine was showing her the park's features, teaching her the names of trees and birds. He had been careful to slather her with sunscreen and give her a big hat to wear. She brushed away a fly and sighed.

"Are you going to stay here a long time, Daddy?"

"I don't know yet, Zozo."

"Once you've killed all the crocodiles and put them in cans and made bags out of them, then you can leave, right?"

"They'll be more of them. They're going to have babies."

"When is a crocodile all grown up?"

"When it's twelve years old it stakes out its territory and finds a mate."

"So it's kind of like us."

"Sort of, yeah. The mommy crocodile lays about fifty eggs in a nest and she spends three months sitting on them. The warmer the nest, the more male crocodiles she'll have. That's not like us."

"So she'll have fifty babies? That's a lot of children to look after!"

"Well, ninety percent of baby crocodiles die when they're little. It's a law of nature."

"Does that make the mommy sad?"

"She knows that's the way it is. But she fights to protect the ones who survive."

"She must be a little sad, though. She sounds like a good mommy. She goes to a lot of trouble. Just like Mommy. She works really hard."

"You're right, Zoé. Your mom's wonderful."

"So why did you go away?"

She had stopped and was looking at him gravely from under the brim of her hat.

"That's a grown-up problem, Zoé. When we're little, we think life is simple, but when we grow up, we find out it's more complicated."

Antoine didn't know what else to say. He'd been asking himself the same question: Why had he left? After bringing the girls home from dinner the other night, he would have been happy to stay there with Joséphine. They would have slipped into bed together, gone to sleep, and life would have picked up again, comfortable and sweet.

"When you sleep with Mylène, do you wear all your clothes?"

Antoine was startled; there was a question he didn't expect! He took his daughter's hand, but she pulled free and repeated her question.

"Why are you asking? Does it matter?"

"Do you make love with Mylène?"

"Zoé!" he stammered. "That's none of your business!"

"Yes, it is! Because if you make love with her, you're going to have lots of little babies and I don't want that."

He knelt down and took her in his arms. "I don't want any children besides you and Hortense, Zozo."

"Promise?"

"I promise. You're my two wonderful daughters, and you fill my heart with love."

Zoé looked concerned, and seemed to be thinking. Antoine was afraid that she'd ask more awkward questions, and was eager to change the subject.

"Do you like your room here?"

"Yeah, it's okay."

They walked back to the house in silence. Zoé was pouting, but she let Antoine take her hand again.

They spent the afternoon at the beach, but without Mylène, who opened her salon at four o'clock. When Hortense took off her T-shirt and pareo, Antoine got a shock. She had the body of a woman: long legs, a slim waist, nice round buttocks, a taut stomach, and breasts that her bathing suit barely contained. The way she lifted her long hair and pulled it back, the way she rubbed sunscreen on her thighs, shoulders, and neck, unnerved him. Antoine looked away, scanning the beach to see if any men were checking her out. He was relieved to see that they were alone, apart from a few children playing in the waves.

Shirley noticed his discomfort. "She's something else, isn't she? She's going to drive men mad! The minute he sees her, Gary starts tripping over his own feet."

"When I left Courbevoie, she was still a little girl."

"Better get used to it. This is just the beginning."

The kids rushed into the water, screaming with delight.

"Want to join them?" he asked. "You'll see, the water's great."

As he dove in, Antoine realized he hadn't had a single drink since his daughters arrived.

Henriette was on the warpath.

In front of her mirror, she made the final adjustments to her hat, jabbing it with a long pin so it would stay straight on her head and not blow off at the first gust. She smeared bright red lipstick across her mouth, patted her cheeks with dark blush, clipped a pair of earrings on her wrinkled earlobes, and stood up. She was ready to begin her inquiry.

It was the first of May, a holiday, a day when no one goes to work.

No one except Marcel Grobz.

At breakfast he had announced that he was going to the office, wouldn't be back until late in the evening, and not to wait for him for dinner. He told Henriette this very casually, while slicing off the top of his soft-boiled egg.

Her suspicions had first been aroused at dinner the night before. She and Marcel were seated at opposite ends of the long dining room table. As he did every night when they ate together, Marcel asked if she'd had a good day. But then he added a word that rang out like a pistol shot: *darling*.

"Did you have a good day, darling?"

And then he went on eating his beef carrot daube, blissfully unaware of the storm he'd just triggered.

It had been at least twenty years since Marcel last called Henriette "darling." In the past, he'd been so put down every time he did that he eventually started using more neutral terms, like "dear," or simply "Henriette."

But last night he had called her "darling."

And it hit Henriette like a slap in the face.

Because that "darling" hadn't been meant for her.

Later, she spent hours tossing and turning, alone in her big bed. (Marcel, claiming that his snoring would keep her awake, slept in the guest bedroom.) She got up at 3:00 a.m. for a glass of red wine to help her sleep, and quietly opened his bedroom door. The room was empty. She switched on the light. No doubt about it, the bird had flown the coop: the bed hadn't even been slept in! She inspected the bathroom. Along with a razor, aftershave, comb, brush, shampoo, and toothpaste was a complete line of men's beauty products: day cream, exfoliant, smoothing cream, moisturizer, eye cream, firming lotion, even a cream designed to shrink love handles. To Henriette, the array of beauty products felt like a taunt.

She shrieked. *Marcel has a mistress! He's diddling someone, supporting a hussy, sneaking around!*

She ran to the kitchen and finished the bottle of vintage Bordeaux she had opened at dinner.

So when Marcel claimed at breakfast that he was going to work on May Day, Henriette decided to investigate. First she would go to his office to see if he was really there—he wouldn't be, of course. Then she would go through his mail, look at his appointment calendar, and examine his check stubs and credit card statements.

She tugged at the skin at her throat to minimize the wattles, and left the apartment, lips pursed.

Downstairs, she nodded and gave the concierge a big smile as she passed. Henriette was vicious with those close to her, but courteous to strangers. She suspected that her family—and Joséphine in particular—had probed her heart and found it empty. She figured that she had nothing left to gain from the people in her family circle, so she exercised a ruthless tyranny to keep them under her yoke. But Henriette was also very proud, and she needed strokes and flattery. So she made a laudable effort to win strangers over. What she got from them renewed her sense of worth and reinforced the high opinion she already had of herself.

Henriette was surprised not to find the chauffeur waiting downstairs with the car as usual, and then remembered that Gilles didn't work on May Day. "All these days off and holidays just encourage laziness and hurt the country's progress," she muttered, deigning to hail a taxi.

A gray Opel pulled over.

"Avenue Niel!" she barked.

Seated comfortably at her husband's desk, Henriette looked through the papers in Marcel's in-box, opened one binder after another, checked every meeting on his calendar. No woman's name, no suspicious initials. Undeterred, she rummaged through the drawers in search of a checkbook or credit card receipts.

She was beginning to lose hope when her hand happened on a fat envelope marked "Miscellaneous Expenses" at the back of one of the drawers. When she opened it, she could feel a wave of warmth; she'd hit the jackpot! Among other things, it contained a hotel bill for four nights at the Plaza for two, with caviar and champagne for breakfast. *Well, well, what do you know? Marcel certainly enjoys himself when he's with his floozy.* There was also a stiff bill from a jewelry store on place Vendôme, and others for designer perfumes and clothes. *My heavens! The old goat is paying through the nose to get his jollies. That's what you have to do when you're old: you pay and pay!*

Suddenly a photograph fell out of the sheaf of bills, and Henriette's flinty heart skipped a beat. Apparently taken in front of the Lido, it showed a beaming Marcel hugging a gorgeous brunette. The word "Natasha" was scrawled on the back, in the traitor's own handwriting. Henriette was first shocked, then jubilant: "I've got you this time!" she exulted.

She went into Josiane's office to Xerox her finds. As she was copying them, she suddenly wondered why Marcel had bothered to keep all those bills. *Did he pay them from the business checking account? If so, he's embezzling from the company, and I can nail him on two fronts!*

Back in Marcel's office, she was continuing her search when her foot struck a cardboard box under his desk. She opened it, staring in disbelief at its contents: dozens of velour, silk, and terrycloth onesies in pink, blue, and white; burping cloths; baby mittens to keep newborns from scratching themselves; wool socks in every possible shade; and Swiss, English, and French catalogs for cribs, baby carriages, and toy mobiles. She studied the box and its contents. *So Chief is planning to start a line of baby products! Maybe his consolation for not having a child of his own.* She kicked the box back under the desk.

Henriette hurried away, clutching the incriminating envelope under her arm. *Go ahead, have your fun*, she raged. *I've got you right where I want you.*

"So *that's* why we don't see you anymore? You've shut yourself away to write?"

Iris assumed a mysterious look and nodded. Remembering the scene in Joséphine's kitchen, she was describing the agony of the creative life to Bérengère, who couldn't believe how much her friend had changed.

"It's exhausting, you know," said Iris. "I hardly leave my study. Carmen brings me meals on a tray. She makes me eat, because I completely forget."

"It's true, you've lost weight."

"All those characters living in my head! They inhabit me. They're more real to me than you are, or even Alexandre or Philippe. You think you see me, but I'm not really here at all, I'm with Florine, my heroine."

Bérengère listened, mouth agape. "How do you come up with the Middle Ages stuff?"

"The twelfth century, darling; a turning point in the history of France. I bought tons of books and I just read and read: Georges Duby, Georges Dumézil, Philippe Ariès, Dominique Barthélemy, Jacques Le Goff . . . I'm also reading Chrétien de Troyes, Jean Renart's novels, and that fabulous twelfth-century poet Bernard de Ventadour!"

Iris sat slumped in her chair, as if weighed down by all that learning.

"Do you know what they called lust back then?" she asked.

"No idea."

"Lechery. And do you know how they aborted? With ergot."

Bérengère was amazed by her friend's knowledge.

It's working! Iris silently congratulated herself. *If all my readers are as easy to fool as Bérengère, this'll be a breeze.* Iris had reconciled with Bérengère for the sole purpose of testing her mastery of facts. She scheduled regular lunches to practice answering questions the way she would later when dealing with reporters.

"What about the Decretum? Do you know about the Decretum?"

"You know I never went to college, Iris. I barely graduated from high school!"

"It was a very crude questionnaire drawn up by the church to regulate women's sexual behavior. Some of the questions are pretty scary: 'Did you make an instrument of suitable shape, strap it over your private parts or that of another woman, and fornicate with other sinful women using that instrument or any other?'"

"They had dildos back then?" asked Bérengère in disbelief.

"'Have you fornicated with your little boy? Have you placed him on your private parts and simulated fornication?'"

"Oh, gross!"

"'Have you given yourself to an animal? Have you provoked it into copulation by any means? Have you tasted your husband's semen so that he would burn with greater love for you? Have you made him drink your menstrual blood or eat bread kneaded with your buttocks?'"

"That's a new one."

"'Have you sold your body to lovers for their enjoyment, or sold those of your daughter or granddaughter?'"

"It all sounds so modern!"

"That makes it easier, in a way. The clothes, the food, and the pace of life have changed, but feelings and personal behavior are still the same, unfortunately." That was another point she'd heard Joséphine make.

Iris knew that Bérengère had had several abortions. For her coup de grace, she leaned close.

"'Have you killed your unborn child? Expelled the fetus from the womb by the use of spells or herbs?'"

Horrified, Bérengère begged her to stop, but Iris went on. "Aha, damned soul! Repeat after me: 'I renounce sex and the vanities of this world and I offer my body as a living sacrifice to God!'"

"Amen," said Bérengère, eager for all this to end. "What does Philippe think of your writing?"

"He was pretty surprised, I must say. But he respects my need to be left alone to work. And he's been a love, takes care of Alexandre all the time."

That part was true. Philippe seemed perplexed by his wife's new project, and never discussed it with her. On the other hand, he had started to spend much more time with Alexandre. He came home every night at seven and hung out in the boy's room, going over schoolwork, helping with math problems, taking him to soccer and rugby matches. Alex never looked happier.

Iris phoned the detective agency to tell them to stop their

investigation. "I got all worked up over nothing," she said, hoping to keep the conversation short. "It was just a business matter of my husband's."

As it happened, the head of the agency had decided to close the case even before the lovely Madame Dupin called. Philippe Dupin had dropped by and warned him that if they didn't stop following him, he would get their license revoked. He could do that, he said, and he meant it.

Her lunch over, Iris drove home to work on polishing her image as a best-selling novelist. Not a single detail could be left to chance. She had to be ready to answer any and all questions with crisp, penetrating answers. And she had to read as much as she could. Iris asked Jo to list a few essential works on the period, and she studied them, taking notes. Carmen was allowed to bring her tea—in silence—while she read.

At times, she thought of Gabor. *I wonder if he'll read the book. Maybe it will occur to him to pitch it as a film. We could work on the screenplay together, like in the old days.* Iris sighed.

Joséphine had sought refuge in the library. Its windows, open to a classic French garden, let in soft light along with birdsong and the regular pulse of a water sprinkler.

She spread her notes around her on the table and worked on her outline. Florine was about to be widowed for the first time.

After six months of married bliss, Guillaume once again rides off to war in the Orient. He finds a treasure, and quickly arranges to have it sent back to Florine. Then he dies, his throat slit by a jealous Moor. Florine weeps over her pile of gold ecus, and veils herself in mourning and devotion. But her status as a grieving young widow unleashes her neighbors' covetousness.

They want to force her to remarry. She is besieged by suitors and threatened with the loss of everything she owns. She had no time to produce an heir who could protect her and demand that his father's name be respected.

What's more, her trusty servant Isabeau informs her of a plot brewing against her. Her neighbor Etienne le Noir has hired a band of mercenaries to kidnap and rape her, so he can seize her lands.

Florine resolves to marry, and chooses the suitor she thinks will least impede her devotion to God: Thibaut de Boutavant, known as the Troubadour. He is from a good family, honest and upright. The real challenge will be getting the other feudal lords to recognize the marriage!

Florine decides to present them with a fait accompli. She secretly marries Thibaut in the castle's chapel one night. Next day, she throws a banquet at which she presents her new husband to the flummoxed suitors. Thibaut raises his banner on the ramparts to show that he is master of the house.

As she wrote, Joséphine endowed her characters with the traits of people she knew—a few details, sometimes just a brief impression. In this way she had modeled Florine's father after her own father. At times memories came to her that she didn't understand, like pieces of driftwood in a pattern she couldn't discern. And her father's frightening, silent rage that stormy summer day in the Landes. She clearly remembered being carried off in her father's arms. He smelled of salt: was it the sea or his tears? *Someday I'll figure out the secret of the floating driftwood*, Joséphine thought to herself. But Thibaut was a puzzle. Who could she use as a model for the gentle poet? She was chewing on her pen when she looked up and realized that the man in the duffel coat was sitting at the other end of the long table. *He'll be my Troubadour!*

Moved by her new husband's gentleness, Florine discovers love and neglects God, then prays long and hard for forgiveness. She also discovers the pleasures of the marriage bed. Joséphine found herself blushing as she started to describe the wedding night, and decided to put off writing the scene until later, when she wouldn't be sitting right across from Duffel Coat Man!

Though he is a lord, Thibaut pens pamphlets protesting the king's power. A born troublemaker, he gives voice to the serfs' and vassals' discontent. Weary of Thibaut's tirades against injustice, Henry II has him poisoned.

Joséphine sighed. She would just have to accept the Troubadour's death. Time flew by, and she worked the whole afternoon, inspired by the man in the duffel coat.

Joséphine barely noticed that he was putting away his things and getting ready to leave. She hesitated for a moment, torn between Thibaut and Duffel Coat Man, then followed him out through the big double doors.

When she caught up to him at the bus stop, he seemed lost in thought.

Standing next to him, she dropped one of her books. When he picked it up, he recognized her and smiled.

"Are you always dropping things?"

"I'm sorry. I'm very absentminded."

He laughed softly. "But I won't always be around."

He said that without any flirtatiousness, and Jo was immediately ashamed of her ploy. He let her board the bus first, assuming they were both going in the same direction. *Oh, God!* she thought. *This isn't at all where I want to go.* The bus was heading away from Courbevoie, not toward it. But she sat down anyway, and he joined her.

"Are you a teacher?" he asked politely.

"I work at the CNRS," she said. "My field's the twelfth century. What about you?"

"I'm working on a book about the history of tears. It's for a foreign publisher, a university press. Not very cheerful, as you can imagine."

"Oh, but it must be fascinating!"

She felt like kicking herself. *What an idiotic thing to say!*

"In those days, men and women used to cry a lot. It was a way of expressing yourself, in public or private."

He sank back into his duffel coat. *This guy doesn't like cold weather*, thought Joséphine, who decided to use that detail in describing Thibaut. He would have weak lungs.

Glancing out the window, she saw that she was traveling farther and farther out of her way. She really had to think about getting home.

"Do you come to the library often?" she asked, gathering her courage.

"Whenever I need peace and quiet. When I'm working, I can't stand the slightest noise."

He's married with children, thought Joséphine. She needed to find out more, and was wondering how to question him without seeming too nosy when he stood up.

"This is my stop. I'm sure we'll see each other again," he said awkwardly.

She nodded and watched him get off.

Now she had to take the same bus going back the other way. *I even forgot to ask him his name! He's hard to talk to. For someone who poses for photographs, he sure isn't very outgoing.*

When Joséphine got to her own street, she saw a crowd in front of her building, and her heart started to pound. Something had happened to the girls! She pushed through, to find Christine and Max Barthillet sitting on the front steps.

"What's going on?" Joséphine asked her third-floor neighbor.

"They're being evicted. Too many months of unpaid rent."

"Where are they going to go?"

The woman shrugged. Christine was weeping quietly, her head down. Max looked grim. Joséphine caught his eye.

"Do you have someplace to go tonight?"

Christine shook her head.

"They can't just throw you out on the street! Not with a child!"

"You think they give a damn?"

"Come stay with us. At least for tonight."

Christine looked up. "You sure?"

Joséphine took the boy by the arm.

"Come on, Max. Get your things and follow me."

The third-floor neighbor shook her head in dismay.

"That poor woman has no idea what she's getting into! She's opening a can of worms."

"Mum, when will I get to have sex?"

On the phone, Shirley said a few words in rapid English, then hung up. She was going to have to go out of town, and her son's question caught her off guard.

"You're only sixteen, Gary! There's no rush."

"There is for me."

She looked at him. *He's a man now*, she thought, almost with surprise. He stood over six feet tall, had slender arms and legs, a deep voice, and a shock of black hair. Gary had started to shave, took hours in the bathroom, refused to go out if he had a pimple, and spent all his money on gels and lotions.

It must be confusing to feel a man's body growing inside that of a child, Shirley thought. *I remember when my breasts started growing, I used to bind them. And when I got my first period, I thought that maybe if I just squeezed my legs tight enough . . .*

"Listen, Gary, we'll talk about this again when you're in love."

"Do you really have to be in love?"

"It's better that way. Sex isn't something casual, and your first time is a big deal. You don't want do it with just anyone. You always remember your first time."

"There's Hortense, but she never even looks at me."

During their spring break in Kenya, he had followed Hortense around like a puppy. She'd pushed him away. "Gary! Do you have to always be in my face all the time? Back off! Give me some space!"

One evening, Shirley explained to Gary that he was going about it all wrong. "A woman needs mystery and distance. She needs to desire the person she's attracted to. Hortense will never desire you if you trail behind her like that."

"Mum, I can't help it. She drives me bonkers!"

But Shirley couldn't revisit the topic today.

"Listen, Gary, this just isn't a good time to talk. I have to go to London, it's an emergency. I'll be gone for a week. You'll have to get by on your own."

"It's never the right time to talk to you!"

"That's not true, love. I'm always there for you. But I can't right now."

Gary huffed loudly and went to his room. Shirley felt torn. Sex was a subject that needed time, which was exactly what she didn't have. She had to pack a bag, book a flight, and warn Jo that she was leaving.

When she rang at Joséphine's, Christine opened the door.

"Is Joséphine there?"

"Yes, she's in her room."

As she went in, Shirley noticed two big suitcases in the entry.

"What's Christine Barthillet doing here?" she asked quietly.

"She was just kicked out of her apartment. I told her to come stay with me until she gets back on her feet."

"Hm, bad timing. I was going to ask you a favor."

"Try me."

"I have to go to London right away . . . for a job. I wondered if you could watch Gary while I'm away."

"Of course I will. At this point I might as well put on a little Red Cross cap!"

"I'm really sorry, but I can't turn this job down. I'll help you with Christine when I get back."

"I hope she'll be gone by then. I have two more months before my manuscript is due, and I'm only on husband number two. There are still three more to go!"

"Thanks, Jo. I won't forget this!"

When the girls got back from school, Zoé clapped her hands on hearing that Max was going to be living with them. But Hortense angrily dragged Joséphine into the bathroom to talk.

"Is this some sort of joke?"

"No, it isn't. We're can't let them sleep under a bridge!"

"Omigod! You mean we have to make room for those retards? You know Madame Barthillet is a nut case, right? You'll be sorry, just you wait. In any case, there's no way they're taking over my room! Or touching my computer!"

"Please don't be selfish, honey," said Joséphine gently, trying to take Hortense into her arms. "Anyway, it's Zoé's room too."

Hortense roughly shoved her away.

"I wish you'd stop acting like Mother Teresa," she snarled. "It makes me want to puke!"

Joséphine slapped her before realizing what she was doing.

Hortense put a hand to her cheek and glared. "I can't stand

living here anymore! I can't stand living with *you*! All I want to do is get out of here, and I'm warning you—"

Joséphine slapped her again, this time putting her rage into it.

"You're going to start behaving," she muttered through clenched teeth, "or you're going to be very sorry."

Hortense stared at her, swayed for a moment, then plopped down on the edge of the tub and smirked. "You're such a fucking loser!"

Joséphine felt like throwing up. She felt like crying. She hated herself for letting her anger run away with her.

"You despise me, don't you?"

"Oh, Mom, give it a break! You and I have nothing to say to each other. I would have done better to stay in Kenya with Dad. I even get along better with Mylène than I do with you. Just imagine!"

"What did I ever do to you, Hortense?"

"I hate everything you stand for. Your hangdog look, all that bullshit you come up with!"

Looking balefully at her mother, Hortense rubbed her cheek.

"I'm sorry. I shouldn't have slapped you, honey, but you pushed me over the edge."

Hortense shrugged. "It's okay. I'll try to forget about it."

Someone knocked on the door. It was Zoé, announcing that dinner was ready, and that everyone was waiting for them.

Joséphine pulled herself together and wiped her eyes. She headed for the kitchen, but stopped in the hall. With the Barthillets there, she realized, she wouldn't be able to use the kitchen to work—or the living room, for that matter. Where will I put my

THE YELLOW EYES OF CROCODILES

books? My papers? The computer? *When we move, I'm going to get an apartment with my own study.*

"Don't you have a TV?" asked Max when she came into the kitchen.

"That's another of Mom's ideas," Hortense said with a sigh. "She put it down in the basement. At night, she wants us to go to bed and read. A real blast!"

"We're missing Charles and Camilla's big ball at Windsor Castle," said Christine. "The queen will be there, Prince Philip, William, Harry, all the crowned heads of Europe!"

"I know, we'll go over to Gary's!" exclaimed Zoé. "They have a TV. But we have the Internet here. Aunt Iris had it put in so Mom could work."

"If anyone touches my computer, I'll bite their head off," said Hortense. "I'm warning you."

"Don't worry. I managed to keep mine," said Christine. "I bought it at the Colombes thieves' market."

This was the bargain basement of an electronics store where you could buy stolen goods for a third of their retail price. Joséphine felt a shiver go down her spine. *That's all I need*, she thought, *having the police knocking at the door!*

"They took all your things?" Zoé asked, a pitying expression on her face.

"Everything," Christine said with a sigh. "We don't have anything left."

"Okay, enough with the self-pity," snapped Hortense. "You're going to look for a job, and work. For those who really want to, there's always work. You just have to get up early! I heard about my internship, by the way. Chief's taking me on for ten days in June."

"That's great, honey!" said Joséphine.

"Is the pasta ready? I have tons of homework to do."

Jo drained the noodles and served them, careful to give everyone an equal portion. As she did, she wondered if taking in the Barthillets hadn't been a huge mistake.

Chapter 13

♦ ♦ ♦

$\mathcal{T}$heir appointment with the fertility specialist was for 3:00 p.m., but Marcel and Josiane arrived at the elegant avenue Kléber office at 2:30, dressed to the nines and as nervous as newlyweds.

Dr. Troussard had asked them to have some tests done beforehand and said he would go over the results—a whole page of tiny printing—with them. The two were now perched nervously in the waiting room, intimidated by its ornate furniture and heavy drapes.

"I'm scared, Marcel! Feel my hands. They're like ice!"

"Read a magazine. It'll distract you."

Marcel handed one to Josiane, but she waved it away.

"I'm not in the mood to read stuff."

"Come on, sweetie-pie, read something."

Marcel flipped his magazine open at random and read: "At forty, women are three times as likely to have a miscarriage than at twenty-five. The risk of a miscarriage goes up thirty-five percent when the father is over thirty-five, and that risk increases steadily with age."

He closed the magazine in a panic. Josiane watched as he turned pale, and started licking his lips.

"You feeling okay, Marcel?"

Crushed, he handed her magazine.

She read the article, then put the magazine down. "No point in getting all worked up about it, honey. The doc's got our tests, and he'll tell us what's what."

Troussard reassured Marcel and Josiane right away. Everything was in working order with both of them, he said. The test results looked like those of parents half their age. All they had to do was roll up their sleeves and get to work.

"But that's all we ever do!" Marcel exclaimed.

"And it's not working," moaned Josiane. "Why not?"

The doctor raised his hands, as if to say that there was nothing he could do about it. He stood up, handed them their file, and ushered them out.

"But—," Josiane began.

Troussard cut her off. "Just stop thinking about it so much. Otherwise we'll have to examine your head, and believe me, that's far more complicated and expensive."

Out on the street, Marcel took Josiane by the arm, and they walked in silence. "Here's what we do: We don't talk about it anymore. We live it up, we fuck like bunnies, and if you're still flat as a flounder in six months I'll have you put in a test tube!"

They strolled back to the office arm in arm. The weather was beautiful. The Arc de Triomphe stood out sharply against the sky, and little tricolor flags fluttered from rearview mirrors. The women's arms were bare, and the men's arms were around the women's waists.

"We almost never walk this way," Josiane remarked. "You know, like lovers. We're usually too afraid we'll run into someone."

"That kid Hortense is doing an internship with us in June."

"Yeah, I know; Chaval told me. When's he leaving, anyway?"

"End of June. I'd love to cut him loose sooner, but I need him. Gotta find his replacement."

"Good riddance! I can't stand the guy anymore."

Marcel shot her a worried glance. Was that the truth, or was there a hint of disappointment in her voice? He would have preferred to hang on to Chaval, to keep an eye on his appointment and travel schedule.

"You never think about him anymore?"

Josiane shook her head and kicked a beer can into the gutter.

They were gathered around Shirley's television, all except Hortense, who said she didn't care to watch a bunch of crowned heads parading around. When they'd rung, Gary opened the door, grumbling.

"You're going to watch that crap? Be my guest. I'll be in my room."

Joséphine, Zoé, Max, and Christine sprawled in front of the TV amid bags of chips, Cokes, and strawberry gumdrops. Using their fingers, they spread pâté on slices of baguette.

I should be home working, thought Joséphine. *Florine's second husband is still alive!* Jo had grown fond of him, and was having trouble killing him off. She dutifully went to the library every day, but hadn't made much headway. She had too many things on her mind. Zoé had cut classes twice in a week to follow Max on his dubious adventures. Her adorable little Zoé was out of control, a wild nymphet in the making. She once locked herself in the bathroom and emerged wearing a miniskirt and sporting coal-black eyeliner and vampire-red lipstick. Joséphine scrubbed it off with a washcloth and soap while Zoé struggled and screamed about child abuse.

Meanwhile, Christine spent her days sprawled on the living room sofa, surfing the Internet. She had found a dating Web site and was trading e-mails with panting admirers. When Joséphine came home from the library, she described her online hookups.

"Don't worry, Madame Joséphine, I expect I'll be finding a new place real soon."

Jo listened to her stories in dismay. "But you don't know a thing about these guys, Christine. You're not going to jump right back into the same mess you were in before, are you?"

"Why not? For years I walked the straight and narrow, and look where it landed me. I got nothing left—no home, no money, no husband, and no job! This time, I'm gonna work the system. Sign up for welfare and unemployment, and then find some rich old fart to support me!"

"But you're a responsible adult!" Jo stammered. "You have to set an example for Max!"

Christine just laughed. "Those days are over. Being honest doesn't get you squat. For me, it's party time!"

"But not in my house."

♦ ♦ ♦

Jo would head off to the library with a knot in her stomach. Each evening when she returned home, she felt a moment of panic when she put her key in the lock. Even Duffel Coat Man couldn't cheer her up.

"Is something wrong?" he'd asked over coffee the previous afternoon. "You aren't dropping things anymore."

He'd told her that he was passionate about religious history, and spoke at length about tears—holy tears, profane tears, tears of ecstasy, tears of joy, tears of sacrifice. The talk made Joséphine herself start crying.

"See, something is wrong," he said, observing her keenly.

"What you're telling me about isn't very cheerful," she said, smiling through her tears.

"But you must know all about this stuff, given how pious the twelfth century was. Convents spreading like wildfire, preachers roaming the country warning about eternal damnation if people didn't repent of their sins."

"That's true," she said, swallowing her tears for want of a tissue.

At times, Joséphine told herself that the most oppressive part of her arrangement with Iris was its secrecy. She worried about that at night, unable to sleep. *I bet it blows up in our faces*, she thought. *The whole scheme will be uncovered, and I'll end up homeless and broke, like Christine Barthillet.*

"You shouldn't take what I tell you so much to heart," he was saying. "You're too sensitive."

"I don't even know your name!" she blurted.

He smiled. "Luca, Italian origin, age thirty-six. I have all my teeth, and I'm a hopeless bookworm."

"Is your family in France or in Italy?" Jo ventured. She had to know if he was married.

"I don't have any family," he answered seriously.

She left it at that.

The broadcast had begun, and Christine licked her fingers and popped another gumdrop into her mouth. Windsor Castle appeared onscreen, all lit up, with Charles and Camilla at the top of the stairs, greeting friends and family.

"Gosh, it's beautiful!" said Christine. "And they're so cute! Look at how everything is sparkling. Isn't that something, Madame Joséphine, waiting thirty-five years for your true love? Not everyone can say that about themselves."

Certainly not you, thought Jo. *You're ready to shack up with someone you meet on the Net after thirty-five seconds.*

"What's your latest prince charming called?" she whispered.

"Alberto. He's Portuguese. Oh, look! It's the queen and Prince Philip! I've always thought he was dreamy. Look at that big strong chest! A real fairy-tale prince!"

Now Queen Elizabeth was coming forward. She was wearing a turquoise evening gown and carrying a black purse. Philip followed close behind her, in tails.

Suddenly Joséphine gasped. "Look! Just behind the queen! Right there, there!"

She jumped to her feet and pointed at the TV screen, repeating, "Right there!" But no one reacted, so she went over and tapped the screen, on a young woman in a pink gown who was walking near the queen.

"Did you see?"

"No," they all answered.

"There, I'm telling you. Right there!"

Now Joséphine was jabbing her finger on the screen. "Look at the woman with the short hair!"

The woman seemed to be trying to remain in the queen's shadow while staying close to her.

"Well, yeah . . . That black bag doesn't go with the turquoise dress."

"Not the queen! The person next to her!"

Joséphine shouted toward the back bedroom: "Gary! Gary! Come out here!"

He shambled into the living room. "What's wrong? Why are you yelling like that?"

"It's your mother!" Jo cried. "She's at Windsor Castle! Right next to Queen Elizabeth!"

Gary ran a hand through his hair, went to stand in front of the television, and mumbled, "Oh, yeah . . . Mom."

"What is she doing there?" Jo yelled at him.

"It *is* Shirley!" roared Christine, a gumdrop suspended in front of her mouth. "What the hell is she up to?"

"That's what I'd like to know," said Jo, watching as the figure in pink mingled with the crowd of guests.

"I'll be damned!" mumbled Christine. "I smell a rat."

"And I smell the blood of an Englishman," joked Zoé.

Shirley's going to have some explaining to do, thought Joséphine.

Could she really be connected to the English royal family? If she is, what in heaven's name is she doing baking cakes in a Paris suburb?

Shirley didn't return on Monday—or Tuesday, Wednesday, or Thursday. Gary ate his meals at Joséphine's, where the girls peppered him with questions.

"I don't know what you think you saw," he told them, "but you're wrong."

"Oh, come on, Gary. You saw her, too!"

"No, I saw someone who looked like her, that's all. The world's full of women with short blond hair. Besides, what the heck would she be doing there?"

"That's true," Christine agreed. "You've been working too hard, Madame Joséphine. Maybe you're getting confused."

"But you all saw her! It wasn't my imagination!"

"I think Gary's right. We just saw someone who looked like her."

Jo stuck to her guns. It *was* Shirley, and Jo was furious with her. *Here I tell her everything, and she doesn't tell me a damned thing. I can't even ask her questions.* She felt like a fool. Everyone was playing her for a fool—Iris, Antoine, Christine and her legion of virtual lovers, Shirley at Windsor Castle, Hortense hating her, and Zoé running wild. *They all treat me like a well-meaning dolt, which is exactly what I am.*

Anger inspired her. She coldly dispatched Thibaut the gentle Troubadour, poisoned soon after joyously witnessing the birth of his son. Florine no longer had to fight to survive anymore. She now had a legitimate son and heir, Thibaut the Younger.

Joséphine then introduced the third husband, Baudouin, a knight who was kind, strong, and pious. *How am I going to do away with this one? He's young and healthy, doesn't drink or overindulge, is moderate in his lovemaking.* Then she thought back to the Windsor Castle ball, and how Shirley had lied to her, and turned her anger on poor Baudouin.

He and Florine are invited to a great feast by the king of France, who is hunting on land near Castelnau. The king notices Baudouin in the midst of the glittering assembly, and turns pale. At the end of the evening, the young couple is walking down a hall toward their rooms. Suddenly a group of armed men attack Baudouin and cut his throat in front of his horrified wife. There is blood everywhere. Florine faints, collapsing across her husband's lifeless body. We learn later that Baudouin was one of the king's bastard sons, and would have been in line for the throne. Fearing he might claim to be his heir, the king decided to have him killed.

Widowed once again, Florine implores heaven to avert its wrath and let her peacefully climb the last rungs of the ladder.

Joséphine was now in a bloodthirsty mood. *That takes care of number three!* she thought grimly, encouraged by all the pages she had written.

"You seem to be doing better these days," Luca said as they sat in the library cafeteria together. "You have a mischievous look on your face."

"I'm giving up on being so conventional. You know, good friend, good sister, good mother."

"You have children?"

"Two daughters, but no husband. He left me for another woman. I must not have been a good wife."

She laughed awkwardly and blushed. She hadn't meant to say that.

"Would you like to go see a movie on Saturday? A theater on rue des Écoles is showing *Wild River*. It's an Elia Kazan film that never runs in France. I thought maybe—"

"Sure, I'd love to!"

Saturday night, Joséphine got to the theater early. She wanted time to compose herself before Luca showed up. She found him very attractive physically, and that troubled her. Until now her experience of sex had been pretty bland. Antoine had been gentle and considerate, but he didn't send the wave of heat shooting through her that a single glance from Luca could spark. *I have to keep cool and not lose my head*, she thought. *I still have a solid month of hard work ahead, and I can't afford to lose my way in a fling. Florine needs me.*

She was amazed by how easily the writing was going, by the pleasure she took in making up stories, and by the importance the book was taking on in her life. Florine was a strong woman, devout, courageous, and beautiful, but a woman nonetheless. Being a bride of Christ wouldn't have been enough for her; Florine would have felt the prickly temptations of the flesh. *How do we act when we're head over heels in love?* Jo wondered.

She took out her pen and notebook—she never went anywhere without them anymore—to jot down her thoughts.

She had just closed the notebook when she glanced up and found Luca leaning over her. He was looking at her with his usual affectionate detachment. Startled, she dropped her purse, spilling its contents. They knelt down together to pick everything up.

"Aha! Now I recognize the woman I met that first day," he said with a mischievous glint.

"I was thinking about my book."

"You're writing a book? You never told me!"

"Well, no . . . I mean my postdoc research . . ."

When they got to the counter, Joséphine opened her purse, but Luca gently waved it away. Joséphine blushed.

The lights in the theater went down and the movie began. Right away, there were shots of water, powerful muddy water that made Jo think of the crocodile swamps in Kenya. Hanging vines, sun-scorched bushes. Suddenly Antoine seemed to appear before her. She could almost hear his voice, picture him hunched over her kitchen table, his hand reaching for hers, inviting her to join him for dinner with the girls. She blinked to make the image go away.

The movie was so beautiful that Joséphine quickly found herself carried away to the island with the farmers. She marveled at Montgomery Clift's wounded beauty, and the gentle, wild determination in his eyes. When the farmers beat him up, she squeezed Luca's arm. He patted her on the head and whispered reassuringly in the darkness: "He'll be fine, don't worry." She forgot everything except that moment, Luca's hand on her head and his comforting tone. She waited, suspended in the darkness, for him to pull her closer, to put his arm around her shoulder, to bring their faces together. She waited and waited . . .

Joséphine wept. She wept from the sadness of not being the kind of woman a man pulls close. She wept from disappointment. She wept from exhaustion. She wept in silence, sitting up straight, not trembling. She was surprised to be weeping with such dignity, her tongue catching the tears streaming down her cheeks, savoring them like some salty vintage. On the screen, a flood was washing away the farmers' homes—and washing away the old Joséphine, the one who never dreamed she would ever find herself weeping in a darkened movie theater, sitting next to a man other than Antoine.

After the movie, they walked the city streets. She looked at the lights of the cafés, felt the energy of people hurrying, yelling, laughing—the nervous pulses of Paris nightlife. The image of Antoine came back to her. They had dreamed of coming to live in Paris for so long.

How many lives are we allowed during our time on earth? she wondered. *They say cats have nine lives. Florine has five husbands. Why shouldn't I have the right to a second love?*

Luca grabbed her by the arm, startling her out of her reverie.

"That car almost ran you over! You really are very absent-minded. I feel like I'm walking with a ghost!"

"I'm so sorry. I was thinking about the movie."

"Will you let me read your book when you finish it?"

"But I'm not—"

Luca smiled. "Writing a book is always a mysterious process. You're right not to talk about it."

He walked her to her front door, glanced up at her apartment building, and said, "Let's do this again sometime, all right?"

He shook her hand gently, holding it for a long time, as if he thought it would be rude to let it go too quickly.

"Well, good night then."

"Good night, and thanks so much. The movie was really beautiful."

Luca strode briskly away, a man escaping the dreaded front-door good-bye ritual.

Jo watched him go. A terrible feeling of emptiness came over her. Now she understood what "being on your own" meant. Not being on your own as in paying bills or raising children by yourself, but being on your own because the man you hoped would take you in his arms is walking away. I'd rather be alone with the bills, she thought as she pushed the elevator button. At least you know where you stand.

The lights in the living room were still on. The girls were crowded around the computer with Max and Christine, giggling and shouting, "Look at this one! Look at that one!" while pointing at the screen.

"Why aren't you all in bed?" demanded Joséphine. "It's one o'clock in the morning!"

Absorbed by whatever it was they were looking at, they barely glanced up.

"Mommy, come see!" yelled Zoé.

"What's going on? You look like you're about to burst!"

"We can't tell you, Mommy," said Zoé seriously. "You have to see with your own eyes."

Jo went over to the table with the computer.

"Are you ready, Mommy?"

"You better sit down, Madame Joséphine. This might come as a shock."

"It's not porn, I hope." Jo didn't exactly trust Christine's judgment.

"Of course not, Mom!" said Hortense. "It's much better than that."

Christine clicked on an icon, and some photographs of little boys appeared on the screen.

"Okay, so what?"

"Don't you recognize them?" Zoé giggled.

She looked more closely. "It's William and Harry, the princes."

"Yeah, but what about the third one?"

Concentrating, Joséphine now recognized the third boy. *It was Gary!* Gary on vacation with the two little princes, Gary holding Princess Diana's hand, Gary on a pony being led around by Prince Charles, Gary playing soccer in a big park.

"Gary . . . ?" she murmured.

"It's him!" exclaimed Zoé. "Can you believe it? Gary's a prince."

"You're sure those pictures haven't been Photoshopped?"

"We found them online. They're in a bunch of family pictures posted by a careless valet."

"Careless is certainly the word!"

"Doesn't that blow a hole right through your ass?" asked Christine.

Joséphine stared at the screen, clicking on one photo after another.

"What about Shirley? Aren't there any pictures of her?"

"No," said Hortense. "But she's finally back home. She got in while you were at the movies. Speaking of which, how was the movie?"

Joséphine didn't answer.

"How was the movie you saw with Luca, Mom?"

"Hortense, stop it."

"He called right after you went out, to say he'd be a little late. Mom, you were early! You should *never* be early! I'll bet he didn't even kiss you. Nobody kisses women who are on time."

Hortense ostentatiously stifled a yawn to show how bored she was with her mother's lack of basic smarts. She knew perfectly well that Joséphine wouldn't do anything to her in front of Christine Barthillet. She would have to endure her daughter's humiliating remark—which she did, gritting her teeth and struggling to retain her composure.

"He's got a nice name, Luca Giambelli," said Hortense. "Is he as handsome as his name?" She yawned again, tossing her hair. "Actually, I don't know why I even bother asking. I bet he's one of those library geeks you like so much. Does he have dandruff and yellow teeth?"

Hortense laughed and looked over to Christine for support, but Christine felt embarrassed for Jo, and stayed out of it.

"Hortense, I want you to go straight to bed!" Jo shouted. "The rest of you, too. It's late, and I'm tired."

As the others filed out of the living room, Jo yanked the sofa bed open so hard, she broke a nail. She flopped on the mattress, thinking, *Boy, was that date ever a bust! I'm so insecure, I make no impression on people. And Hortense could tell right away. That girl can smell a loser a mile away.*

The next morning, Max and the girls went off to a neighborhood flea market while Joséphine cleaned the kitchen. It was market day in Courbevoie, and she made a shopping list: butter, jam, bread, eggs, ham, cheese, lettuce, apples, strawberries, a chicken, tomatoes, string beans, potatoes, cauliflower, artichokes. . . . She was still writing when Christine dragged herself in.

"Man, I am so hung over," she mumbled, rubbing her head. "We had too much to drink last night." She was holding a radio to her ear, searching for her favorite station. She can't be that deaf, Joséphine thought to herself.

"When you say 'we,' I hope that doesn't include my daughters."

"You're very funny, Madame Joséphine, you know that?"

"Can't you just call me Joséphine?"

"No, you intimidate me too much. We're too different."

"Please, just try."

"I'm sorry, I already thought about it and I just can't."

Jo sighed." "'Madame Joséphine' sounds like someone who runs a whorehouse."

"What do you know about whorehouses?"

Something in her tone caught Joséphine's attention. She stared at Christine, who had set her radio down and was swaying to a South American tune. "The question is, what do you?"

Christine solemnly drew her robe across her chest.

"From time to time, to make ends meet."

Joséphine gulped. "Well, I—"

She was desperately trying to think of something to say when the phone rang, rescuing her. It was Shirley, who wanted her to come over.

Joséphine handed Christine the grocery list and some money, and told her to get dressed and do the shopping.

"And don't buy candy instead of fruits and vegetables!" she called as she went out. "It's bad for your teeth, bad for your skin, and bad for your butt."

"I don't care," said Christine with a shrug. "I eat my potato every night." She was peering at the list as if trying to decipher a user's manual.

Joséphine almost said something, but stopped herself.

Shirley was disheveled and had bags under her eyes. She looked so exhausted that the resentment Joséphine had been nursing all week melted away.

"It's nice to see you. Did everything go okay with Gary?"

"Are you kidding? Your son's smart, kind, and handsome. What's not to like?"

"Thanks for saying that. Cuppa tea?"

Joséphine nodded, while staring at Shirley as if she'd never seen her before in her life.

"Jo, why are you looking at me like that?"

"I saw you on television the other night. . . . At Windsor Castle, next to the queen of England, with Charles and Camilla. And don't tell me it wasn't you, because I swear I'll—" Joséphine struggled for words. "Shirley, you're my only friend, the only person I confide in, and I don't want that trust and friendship jeopardized. So please, don't lie to me."

"Yes, that was me. That's why I had to leave at the last minute. I didn't want to go, but—"

"You were forced to go to a ball with Queen Elizabeth?" Jo asked, incredulous. "So you know Charles and Camilla? William and Harry, the whole royal family?"

Shirley nodded.

"Princess Diana too?"

"I knew her very well. Gary grew up with her kids, and—"

"Shirley, you owe me an explanation!"

"I can't, Jo."

Shirley was looking at her with a mix of tenderness and great sadness.

Joséphine, on the other hand, was practically choking with rage.

"I hated you all week, Shirley! I spent all week feeling you'd stolen something from me, that you'd betrayed me. And now you won't even explain?"

"It's for your protection," Shirley said levelly. "What you don't know, you can't talk about. Knowing too much can be dangerous; it sure is for me! But I have to live with it. You don't."

"Is it that bad?"

Shirley came over to sit next to Joséphine and put her arm around her.

"Haven't you ever wondered why I decided to live here—in this suburb, in this building? Why I was all alone in France, with no husband, no friends, no real job? I came here to hide. Someplace where I was sure not to be recognized or tracked down while I waited for things to settle down back home.

"I put all that behind me when I moved here. I changed my personality, I changed my name, I changed my life. Here I can bring Gary up without panicking when he's late coming home from school. I can go out without checking to see if I'm being followed. I can sleep at night without being afraid that someone's going to break down my door."

"Does Gary know?"

"Yes. I told him. I had to. He'd already figured out a lot of things, and I wanted to tell him that he was right. He handled it pretty well. It's made him a lot more mature. Sometimes I feel he's the one protecting me!"

She hugged Joséphine tighter, and went on.

"And in the middle of all that misfortune, I found happiness here. A quiet happiness, without any fuss or drama. And without a man."

Shirley shivered. She would have liked to say "without *that* man." She had been with him again, which is why she'd extended her stay in London. He'd phoned and given her his room number at the Park Lane Hotel. He just said, "Room six-sixteen. I'll be waiting," and immediately hung up. She stared at the phone, silently repeating to herself, *I'm not going there.*

Then she ran to the hotel, near Piccadilly and Green Park, behind Buckingham Palace. Inside, the decor scrolled by her as if in a movie. The big beige-and-pink hall with Venetian chandeliers shaped like bunches of grapes. The enormous bouquets of flowers. The bar. The elevator. The long hallway with beige walls, thick carpet, the sconces with their little skirted lampshades. Then room 616.

This was how they always met, in hotels next to parks. "Leave Gary in the park and come join me," he would say. "He can watch the squirrels and the lovers and learn about life."

Gary got to know every park in London.

Once, when he was eleven, he went over to Speakers' Corner at Hyde Park and discussed the existence of God with a grumpy man on a soapbox. "If God exists," the man asked him, "why does he make mankind suffer?"

Shirley asked her son what he'd answered.

"I told him about that movie, *Night of the Hunter*, and good and evil, and how you have to choose, and how can you choose if you haven't experienced suffering and evil?"

Gary hadn't been waiting in some park this time, and Shirley was free to stay locked away with her lover. She didn't notice the hours passing, or the days. Food trays piled up at the end of the bed. The chambermaids who rapped at the door were told to go away.

Never again! Shirley told herself. *This has to stop!*

She had to stay away from him. He always found her. But he never came to France. They were after him. In France, she was safe. In England, she was at his mercy. And it was entirely her own doing; she was unable to resist him. She always felt ashamed when she came back downstairs, to find Gary trustingly waiting in front of the hotel, or sitting in the lobby when it rained. They would walk home through the park together.

"So how's it going with Christine?" asked Shirley.

"Does that mean you don't want to tell me more?"

"I'm tired, Jo. I need a break. I'm happy to be home, believe me."

"That doesn't change the fact that we all saw you on television. What will you say if the girls or Max ask about it?"

"That I have a look-alike in the court."

"They won't believe you. They found photos of Gary with William and Harry on the Internet. Some servant posted them."

"I'll just say it isn't Gary. I'll say that all little boys look alike. I can handle it, trust me. I've dealt with much worse."

"You must find my little life awfully boring."

"Your little life is going to get complicated, with this whole book thing. Once you start lying and cheating, you go off on all kinds of strange adventures."

The kettle began to whistle, and Shirley got up to make the tea.

"I brought some Lapsang souchong back from Fortnum and Mason. I'd like to know what you think of it."

Joséphine watched Shirley warm the pot, measure out the tea, pour the boiling water, and let it steep, all with the seriousness of a true Brit.

"Do they make tea the same way in Scotland?"

"I'm not Scottish, Jo. I'm pure English."

"But you told me—"

"I thought it was more romantic."

Joséphine almost asked Shirley what other lies she had told, but decided not to. They sipped their tea and talked about the kids, and about Christine's Internet dating.

"Is she helping you financially?"

"She's flat broke."

"You're such a pushover," Shirley said, giving Joséphine a little tap on the nose.

Jo shrugged.

"I spend all my time at the library. I went to a movie with Duffel Coat Man. Turns out he's Italian; his name's Luca. Still doesn't talk much, which actually suits me just fine. I have to get the book done first . . ."

"How far along are you?"

"On the fourth husband."

"Who is?"

"I don't know yet. I'd like Florine to have a hot love affair, a real physical passion."

"Like Shelley Winters and Robert Mitchum in *The Night of the Hunter*. Remember? He's a fake preacher who quotes scripture and robs and kills women. Evil incarnate. He marries Shelley Winters, but on their wedding night, he gives her a sermon about the sins of the flesh and turns his back on her. Finally he kills her."

"Yeah, that would work," said Joséphine, holding her teacup. "The fourth husband could be a preacher. Just the other day, Luca was talking about what preachers in that period were like."

"Did you tell him you were writing a book?" Shirley sounded concerned.

"Not exactly, but I really goofed." Joséphine looked down, flustered. "I'll have to be really careful when the book comes out."

"Don't worry, Iris will make sure she gets all the attention. How is she, by the way?"

"Busy rehearsing for the big day. She comes over from time to time to look at what I've written, and reads the books I recommend. Sometimes she gives me ideas. She wanted me to write about the Paris student riots. In those days the students were clerics, and being in the clergy protected them from civil justice. Even the king couldn't lift a finger against them."

Joséphine paused for a moment to reflect.

"Sometimes I feel like I'm just a big funnel. I listen to everything, collect anecdotes and little snippets from everyday life, and pour them into the book. I won't be the same after this book is finished, Shirley. I'm changing a lot, even if it isn't apparent."

"Sounds like writing's taking you places you'd never go otherwise."

"The biggest thing is, I'm not afraid anymore."

Jo giggled, hiding her face in her hands.

"I just have to be patient and let the new Joséphine grow up a little. One of these days she'll take over, and she'll give me her strength. For now, I'm learning. . . . I've learned that happiness doesn't mean living a safe life without screwups or mistakes, without taking risks. Happiness means accepting effort and doubt, and keeping on moving forward, overcoming obstacles.

I've accepted that life has a dark side. It doesn't get to me or scare me anymore."

Joséphine smiled shyly, as if surprised to have made such grand pronouncements about herself.

Then she held out her cup for a refill and asked, chuckling, "So, what's Queen Elizabeth really like?"

Shirley poured the tea. "No comment."

Christine was back from the market, her arms aching and her palms sore from carrying plastic grocery bags. *I gotta get out of here!* she thought. *Start a new, cushy life. Take it easy, find some nice guy who'll pay the rent and let me watch TV all day. Max can manage on his own. It's every man for himself!*

At five, she was going to meet Alberto at La Défense, and she needed to shower and get ready. *I wanna look pretty*, she thought. *That picture he sent of himself was so blurry, you can't see shit. I bet he's no beauty.*

When Hortense came in, Christine was waiting for her. She was in her bathrobe on the living room couch, watching a talk show.

"You guys find any cool stuff?" she asked, sitting up.

"Oh, just some junk, but it was fun," said Max. "We went and played pinball and drank Cokes."

Christine turned to Hortense.

"Hey, Hortense, you promised to help me choose an outfit for my date, remember?"

Hortense looked her over.

"What do you have to work with?"

"Not much," she said with a sigh. "I'm not big on designer labels, you know. I buy my clothes from catalogs."

"Okay, go get them."

She came back with a couple of bundles. Hortense picked up the clothes one by one, spread them out on the sofa, and studied them.

"Just wait and see," Zoé whispered to Max. "She's going to turn your mom into a bombshell."

Standing in front of Max and the girls in her panties and bra, Christine covered her breasts in embarrassment. Max and Zoé shrieked with laughter. Then Hortense went into action.

"The safari jacket is a must. Rule number one: you wear it on top of Adidas tracksuit pants with the white stripes, which you happen to have. In fact, that's the only way to look good in a tracksuit."

"A safari jacket?"

"Absolutely."

Hortense held out the clothes and had Christine put them on, then looked her over.

"Okay, not bad . . . Not bad at all." She worked on Christine as if she were a dress-shop dummy. She stepped back to examine her, rolled up a sleeve, adjusted the collar, added a necklace, and perched a pair of aviator sunglasses on Christine's head.

"Put on running shoes, and you've got it," she declared, satisfied.

"Running shoes!" protested Christine. "That's not very feminine!"

"Do you want to look like a mess or a mannequin? You asked

me to help you. If you don't like it, you can wear your stilettos and look like a hooker."

Christine put on the running shoes.

"You're all set!" said Hortense.

"Wow, I love it!" Christine cried. "I look like a whole other person! Thanks, Hortense!"

She whirled around the living room, then plopped down on the couch, slapping her thighs with glee. "Amazing, what you can do with a couple of old rags!"

"It takes skill," Hortense replied. "Do you know what this Alberto guy looks like?"

"No idea. He said he'll be carrying a copy of the *Journal du Dimanche*. I'll tell you all about it later. All right, I'm off. Ciao, everyone!"

As Christine was heading downstairs, Max and Zoé yelled after her to take a picture of Alberto so they could see what he looked like.

"He might be your stepfather someday, see," Zoé whispered.

Chapter 14

♦ ♦ ♦

Joséphine was writing in the kitchen with the shutters closed against the heat. Her July deadline was approaching fast. Iris came every day to take Max and Zoé to the movies, for walks around Paris, or to the Jardin d'Acclimatation amusement park. The children's school was being used for *baccalauréat* prep classes, leaving Max and Zoé at loose ends. Joséphine had made it clear to Iris that if she were ever to finish the novel, she had to have the apartment completely to herself, without worrying about what the kids were doing. Hortense was working at Casamia, but Zoé and Max needed to be kept busy.

"And I can't let Zoé just hang out with him," she said. "She'll end up stealing cell phones or selling marijuana!"

Iris had been none too happy. "What am I supposed to do with them?"

"You figure it out. Either that, or I don't write!"

Meanwhile, Christine Barthillet was pursuing her romance with Alberto. They would meet at sidewalk cafés but hadn't slept together.

"Something's going on, and I don't know what it is," she said. "Something weird. Maybe he's impotent. Or maybe he's mental. He can't bring himself to make his move. And you know what? I've never seen him standing up! I feel like I'm dating a midget."

"It's romantic!" said Zoé. "He's taking it slow."

"Yeah, but I don't have any time to waste. I don't even know his last name! I'm telling you, I smell a rat."

Joséphine had no time to waste either. She was dealing with scary Guibert the Pious, Florine's fourth husband.

Guibert rides up to Florine's castle on a big black charger. He is incredibly handsome, with long brown hair, a broad chest, powerful arms, and piercing blue eyes. When he preaches the Gospels in his deep, resonant voice, Florine feels a fire in her belly.

Guibert can recite the Decretum by heart and rails against sin in all its forms. He moves into the castle and imposes his rules on its occupants. He makes Florine wear sackcloth. "You claim to want to follow the Rule of Saint Benedict, yet you hesitate when I order you to sleep on the ground in a shift," he thunders.

Florine eagerly drinks in his words. *This man has been sent to put me back on the path of righteousness*, she thinks. She obeys him in everything. Her faithful servant Isabeau becomes so fearful of Guibert's fanaticism that she flees one night, taking the young count with her. Florine is left alone, with only a few terrified servants. But one evening, Guibert puts his arm around her shoulder and asks her to marry him. Thanking the Lord, Florine agrees. The wedding is sad and austere. On their wedding night, Florine slips into the conjugal bed trembling with anticipation.

But Guibert lies down next to her wrapped in his cloak. He has no intention of consummating their marriage. That would be to commit the sin of lust.

Guibert chops off Florine's long golden hair and marks her forehead with two streaks of ash. He works her to exhaustion and makes her fast continuously. He demands that Florine tell him where she hid the gold that the king of France gave her. "That money is cursed," he says. "Give it to me, that I may throw it in the river." Florine resists. She doesn't want to disinherit Thibaut the Younger. Guibert tortures her.

Florine has nearly given up all hope when Isabeau returns with a troop of knights and rescues her. Searching the castle, they discover a real treasure: the money Guibert stole from the widows he duped before meeting Florine.

Guibert is burned at the stake as a heretic, and Florine weeps to see the man she loved so much die in the flames. "He will go straight to hell," says Thibaut the Younger, "as he so richly deserves."

Whew! Joséphine thought, mopping her brow. *It was high time he died. What a self-righteous creep!*

So Florine is a widow again, and wealthier than ever.

She's a bit like me, thought Joséphine. *I'll soon be richer, but I'm still lonely.* She hadn't heard from Luca in ten days. She rubbed her back and sat down at the computer again. Florine had only one more husband to go—the last one, Tancrède de Hauteville. *This one will be Mr. Right*, she decided. *I want the book to have a happy ending, and I think I know how to make that work out.*

Tancrède is a neighbor of Florine's. He returns from a crusade and asks her to marry him. She agrees, leaves the castle to her grown-up son, and goes to live with Tancrède in a cottage in the Poitou region. Their life is very simple: they pray, grow their own vegetables, and wear furs. They are happy, and love one another dearly. But one day when Tancrède is fetching water, he discovers a tremendous vein of silver ore. They will be rich! Florine is initially devastated, but comes to see her fateful, recurring wealth as a sign from God. She and Tancrède found a hospice for the poor, they have many children, and live happily ever after—The End.

At last! Jo exulted. *All I have to do is write it. One last effort and I'll be done, and then . . .*

Then she would have to turn the manuscript over to Iris. She was dreading this. The book had become her friend. The characters spoke to her, and she listened, traveling with them along their path. How could she let them go?

So as not to think about that, she checked her e-mails. There was a long one from Antoine.

> Dear Jo,
>
> Just a quick note to give you the latest news. I took your advice and went on strike. The hungry crocodiles knocked down fences and killed two of the workers. The crocs that escaped had to be shot. It made the front page of the local news. Wei sent me a big check for all the money he owed me!
>
> In the process, I realized that Lee was on Wei's side. I caught him whispering on the phone a few

times. Ever since then I've been wary of him. I got myself a dog, and I let him taste all of my food before I eat it.

While I was on strike, I gave Mylène a hand in her boutique. The grand opening was a huge success and the place has been going strong ever since. She's had to fly back to France twice to restock. I ran the store while she was away, and it gave me some great ideas. I'm determined to get rich, even if I have to go live in China!

Joséphine was dismayed. *Oh my, Antoine is getting grandiose ideas again! He hasn't learned a thing.*

I hardly drink anymore, just a shot of whiskey in the evening when the sun goes down, but that's it, I promise. In short, I'm a happy man and things are finally paying off.

We should talk about the upcoming summer vacation. Tell me what you have planned and I'll work around it.

Kisses,

Antoine

The e-mail filled Jo with such conflicting emotions, she just stared blankly at the screen.

Then she checked the time. Soon Iris would be back with the

kids, Christine from her date with Alberto, and Hortense from her job at Casamia. Good-bye, peace and quiet!

She closed the computer and got up to start dinner. The phone rang. It was Hortense.

"I'm going to be a little late, Mom. There's a party at the shop after work. Don't hold dinner for me."

"How will you get home?"

"Someone'll give me a ride."

"Someone who?"

"I don't know. I'm sure to find someone. Mom, sweetie, please don't spoil my fun. I'm so happy to be working, and everyone seems pleased with me. I get tons of compliments."

Joséphine looked at her watch. It was seven o'clock.

"Okay, but don't be home later than . . ."

She hesitated. This was the first time Hortense had asked her for permission to stay out, and Jo didn't know what was appropriate.

". . . ten o'clock, okay?"

"Okay, Mom, don't worry. See, if I had a cell phone it would be much easier. You'd be able to reach me any time, and you wouldn't worry."

Joséphine could picture the pout on Hortense's face as she hung up.

Jo now sensed a new challenge looming: how to manage Hortense's freedom. She smiled grimly. *Manage* and *Hortense* were two words that really didn't go together. She'd never been able to manage Hortense. In fact, she was always amazed when her daughter did what she asked her to.

She heard a key in the lock. Christine came into the kitchen and plopped down on a chair.

"I finally got it."

"What did you finally get?"

"His name's Alberto Modesto, and he has a clubfoot."

"Nice name, Alberto Modesto."

"Sure, but a clubfoot isn't nice at all. And I only noticed it 'cause I was clever; otherwise he would've gone on fooling me. So I get to the café, and there he is, all dressed up, turned out real nice. We kiss hello, and he says nice stuff about my getup. He orders a mint soda, gets me a cup of coffee, and we talk and talk. It's nice, okay? After a while I tell him I have an appointment and gotta go. So Alberto kisses my hand! I get up and leave, but I go hang out at the corner and watch for him, and I see him go limping by. With his clubfoot. It's like he's got his foot caught in a toolbox. He limps, Madame Joséphine! He's all lopsided!"

"So what? He has the right to live, doesn't he?" Joséphine was shouting. "You know what? You make me sick! If it weren't for Max, I'd kick you out! You live in my house, you don't lift a finger to help. You don't do a damned thing except troll for guys on the Internet, chew gum, and watch TV. And now you're bitching because your boyfriend isn't perfect? You're pathetic, you know that?"

"Jeez! A person can't even say what's on their mind around here!"

"Listen, I'm swamped with work, and I don't need this nonsense. Today's June tenth. I want you out of here by the end of the month. Max can stay until you get settled, but I'm never taking care of you again. You hear me? Never!"

"Yeah, yeah, I get the picture," mumbled Christine, sounding aggrieved.

Josiane watched as the Cortès girl entered the courtyard, and noted that she was right on time, as she was every morning. Hortense walked as elegantly as a fashion model. When she was on the job, she pulled her long auburn hair back into a ponytail. At the end of the day, she released it with a theatrical gesture, tucking the strands behind her ears, the better to show off the neat oval shape of her face, the glow of her skin, and the delicacy of her features.

Still, I have admit she's a hard worker, thought Josiane. Ginette had taken Hortense under her wing and shown her how they tracked inventory. She knew how to use a computer, so she caught on fast. Now she wanted to move on to something else, and was buzzing around Josiane.

"Who handles the purchasing?" Hortense asked, with a bright smile that didn't quite reach her eyes.

"Bruno Chaval," Josiane said, fanning herself.

"I'd like to work for him. Stock management I get, but it's not all that fascinating. I want to learn something new."

That damned fake smile, said Josiane to herself. *She must think I don't see though her. She's got Ginette and René fooled, and the guys in the warehouse can't even stand up straight when she's around.*

"Just ask him," she said. "I'm sure he'll take you on, but you better hurry. He's leaving for a new job at the end of the month."

Hortense thanked her, flashing another smile that left Josiane cold. *Bruno and Hortense—that's gonna be interesting*, she thought. *Wonder who's gonna swallow who?*

She looked out the window to see if Chaval's red sports car was there. It was, parked right in the middle of the courtyard, as usual. The rest of them could just find parking spaces as best they could.

While Hortense was learning the ropes at Casamia, Zoé, Alexandre, and Max were prowling the Musée d'Orsay. Iris had taken them early that morning, hoping the Impressionist masterpieces would help burn off some of their energy. She was sick of the hot, dusty Jardin d'Acclimatation with its screaming kids, long lines, and cheesy rides. Plus she had to lug around the tacky stuffed animals that the children won at the shooting gallery.

It's high time Jo finished so I can get my life back, Iris thought. *I'm tired of being around teenagers in heat. Alexandre is all right, but sweet little Zoé acts out all the time now. Max's influence, I guess.*

Iris told the children she planned to quiz them later. They each had to pick three paintings and talk about them. She would buy a present for the one who discussed them the best. *That way I can do a little shopping, too*, she thought. *It'll relax me.*

So the three were wandering the halls of the museum. Alexandre looked at the paintings, came close, stepped back, tried to make up his mind. Max dragged his feet on the parquet floor, making his sneakers squeak. Zoé couldn't decide whether to act like her friend or her cousin.

She went to stand next to Alexandre, who was examining a Manet.

"Ever since Max moved into your place, you don't talk to me anymore," he said.

"That's not true. I still like you the same."

"No. You've changed. I don't like that green stuff you put on your eyes. It's vulgar. Makes you look older and sort of weird."

"Which paintings did you choose?"

"I don't know yet."

"I'd really like to win," said Zoé. "I'd ask your mom to buy me an outfit so I can dress up and be pretty, like Hortense."

"You're already pretty!"

"Not like Hortense."

"Don't you have a personality of your own? You just want to do everything like Hortense."

"Yeah, well, you don't have any personality either. You want to do everything like your father. You think I haven't noticed?"

They separated, annoyed with each other. Zoé went off to find Max, who'd stopped dead in front of a Renoir nude.

"Me, I like the women this guy paints," said Max. "They're relaxed. They look friendly and happy."

In the museum cafeteria, Iris had a hard time getting Max to talk.

"You don't have a very big vocabulary, do you, sweetheart? Not that it's your fault. It's a question of education."

"Yeah, well, so what? I know things you don't. Things you don't need words for."

Iris dropped the subject. There was a gulf between her and this boy, and she wasn't sure she wanted to bridge it. So that nobody would feel left out, she decided to let all three children choose presents, and they set out for the Marais to look in the stores. *I can't wait for this thing to be over!* she thought. *For Jo to finish the book so I can take it to Serrurier and we can all leave for Deauville. Carmen will be there, and I won't have to deal with moody brats every day.*

Iris had managed to convince Joséphine to spend the month of July with them. "That way, if Serrurier wants any changes, you'll be right there. It'll be very convenient."

Joséphine had agreed reluctantly.

"Don't you like our Deauville house?" asked Iris.

"Sure I do. It's just that I don't want to spend all my vacations with you guys. I feel like a third wheel."

As they walked through the Marais, Zoé began to feel guilty. She caught up with Alexandre and slipped her hand into his.

"What do you want?" he grumbled.

"I'm going to tell you a secret."

Alexandre weakened. Having to share his cousin with the Barthillet kid who came along everywhere they went pained him.

"What's your secret?"

"Ah, so now you're interested! But first, promise you won't tell anyone. Cross your heart and hope to die?"

"All right."

"Shirley's son Gary is a prince!"

Zoé told Alexandre the whole story: the evening watching TV, and then the Internet pictures of William and Harry and Charles and Diana. Alexandre shrugged and said it was bullshit.

"It is not bullshit! Honest, Alex. I swear! Anyway, this'll prove it: Hortense believes it too. Suddenly she's being all nice to Gary."

"You shouldn't tell lies, Zoé."

"They aren't lies!" she yelled. "It's true!"

She ran to get Max and asked him to back her up.

"Sure, I saw them," he said. "On TV and the Internet. I may not have a big vocabulary, but I've got eyes."

Alexandre grinned at him. "Did my mom hurt your feelings?"

"Yeah, she did. Just 'cause she's farting through silk doesn't mean she can shit on people who don't have any money."

Joséphine was the first one up, and she went downstairs to make herself breakfast. She loved those summer mornings in Deauville when she got to be alone in the big kitchen with the bay window looking out onto the beach. She put some bread in the toaster, heated water for tea, and set out the butter and jam.

She missed her characters: Florine, Guillaume, Thibaut, Baudouin, Guibert, Tancrède, Isabeau, and the others. *I really wasn't very fair to poor Baudouin,* she reflected. *He'd barely made his appearance when I bumped him off just because I was angry at Shirley. Guibert still gives me the shivers. Men were so violent in those days!*

Joséphine had given the manuscript to Iris, who in turn delivered it to Serrurier. Now every time the phone rang, the two sisters jumped.

That morning, Philippe joined Joséphine in the kitchen. He was an early riser, too. He usually went into the village to buy the newspaper and some croissants, had a cup of coffee, then returned to finish breakfast at home. His vacation wasn't until August, so he only drove out to Deauville on weekends, arriving Friday evening and leaving on Sunday. He took all the kids fishing except Hortense, who preferred to hang out on the beach. Joséphine felt she ought to meet Hortense's friends, but she didn't dare ask to be introduced.

Hortense was going out in the evenings, too. "Come on, Mom, I deserve to go out!" she'd say. "I'm on vacation, I worked hard all year, and I'm not a baby anymore."

"All right, but I want you to make like Cinderella and be back by midnight." Jo knew her teasing tone didn't hide her nervousness, and she was afraid Hortense would rebel. But to her relief, she agreed. Joséphine didn't bring it up again, and Hortense always came home on time, right at midnight.

In August the girls would go to Kenya to be with their father. *It'll be Antoine's turn to be the bad cop*, she thought. *Right now, all I want is not to exhaust myself in endless arguments with Hortense.*

"Want a warm croissant?" Philippe asked, putting the newspaper and the bag of pastries down on the table.

"I'd love one."

"What were you thinking about just now, when I came in?"

"About Hortense and her nightly outings."

"She's a tough cookie, that daughter of yours. She would have needed a father with an iron fist."

"Probably," she said, and sighed. "But you know what? I'm not too worried about her. Hortense knows exactly what she wants."

"Were you like that at her age?"

Joséphine almost choked on her tea.

"You're kidding, right? I was the same as I am now, but even more clueless." She stopped, sorry she'd said that. It felt like she was asking for pity.

"What didn't you get when you were little, Jo?"

She thought for a moment. She'd never really asked herself that before, but ever since she'd started writing, childhood memories had begun to come up, bringing tears to her eyes. Like the day she was in her father's arms and he yelled, "You're a criminal!" at her mother. It was late on an oppressive afternoon, with pounding waves and dark clouds in the sky. *I'm starting to sound like a bad romance novel*, she thought. *I have to get a grip on myself.*

"I didn't lack for anything," she said. "I got a good education, had a roof over my head, and two parents. But no one paid me much attention. Nobody told me that I was pretty, or smart, or funny. People didn't do that in those days."

"But they said those things to Iris."

"Iris was so much more beautiful than me, I got used to being in her shadow. Mom always used to hold her up to me. I knew she was proud of her, and not of me." Reddening, Joséphine took a bite of croissant.

"What about now, Jo? Today?"

"I guess my writing gives my life meaning these days. When

I'm actually writing, that is, not when I'm reading what I've written. Ugh! That's when I want to throw it all out!"

"You mean your postdoc scholarship?"

"Uh, yes, that's right," Jo stammered, then quickly went on. "You know, I sometimes wonder if I'm missing my chance to break free, but at the same time I'm not even sure what that chance would be. You don't know what that's like, Philippe. You've never let anyone push you around."

"Nobody's ever really free, Joséphine. Not me, not anybody. And I see you changing. Someday you'll be living exactly the life you want, and you'll have done it all by yourself."

She gave him a fleeting smile. "Do you really think so?"

"You're your own worst enemy, Jo." Philippe picked up the newspaper and his coffee mug. "Mind if go out on the deck and read?"

"Not at all."

How easy it is to talk to Joséphine, Philippe thought as he opened the *International Herald Tribune*. With Iris these days, he just clammed up. The night before, she'd suggested they go for a drink at the Royal Hotel bar, and he let her have her way. In fact, what he really wanted to do was hang out with Alexandre. A month before, he'd finally written the letter to his son, and it changed their whole relationship.

Carmen told Philippe about it.

"You should have seen him," she said. "He ran into the kitchen shouting, 'I got a letter that Dad wrote me! He says he loves me, and is going to spend all his free time with me! Isn't that great, Carmen?' He practically made me dizzy, racing around the kitchen waving the letter in the air!"

Philippe kept his word. He'd promised Alexandre to teach him to drive, and every Saturday and Sunday morning he took him out, sat him on his lap, and showed him how to handle the steering wheel.

Iris ordered two glasses of champagne. A young woman in a long gown was playing the harp.

"What did you do in Paris this week, darling?"

"Just work. The usual."

"Tell me about it."

"Iris, it's really not that interesting. Anyway, you know I don't like talking about my cases when I'm out here."

Their table was at the edge of the terrace. Philippe was watching a bird trying to fly off with a piece of bread.

"Would you mind if I took off my jacket?"

Iris smiled at him and gave his cheek a pat. The gesture was affectionate, but it was also a way of treating him like an impatient child. Philippe was thinking: *I know you're beautiful, and you rule over me and my love. But that beauty leaves me cold, because it's built on lies. I first met you because of a lie, and you haven't stopped lying since.*

"You never tell me anything," she said petulantly.

"What do you want me to tell you?" asked Philippe, watching the bird struggle with the bread.

She threw an olive pit at the bird, which was flopping around, unable to take off with its prize.

"That was mean!" he exclaimed. "That might be dinner for its whole family."

"You're the one who's mean! You never talk to me anymore."

He looked at Iris. She was sulking. He knew that attitude, the one that said: *Look at me, pay attention to me! I'm the center of the universe.* But Iris wasn't the center of his universe anymore. Had she changed, or had he? *Either way, it's all over,* he thought. *Some marriages exude a boredom so sweet and gentle, it puts you to sleep. But I woke up a few months ago. Was it my meeting with John Goodfellow that did it? Or did I meet with him because I'd already woken up?*

Having managed to break the bread in half, the bird flew away so quickly, it seemed to melt into the blue sky. Philippe looked at the part left on the ground. *He'll come back for it,* he thought. *You always come back for what is yours.*

"Hey, Dad! Will you take me driving today?" Alexandre had spotted his father sitting on the deck.

"Sure. Whenever you like."

"Can we bring Zoé? She doesn't believe I know how to drive."

"If her mother says it's okay."

Alex went into the kitchen and asked Joséphine, who was happy to say yes. Ever since Zoé quit hanging around Max, she'd gone back to being a little girl. She was acting her age, and had stopped talking about makeup and boys. She and Alexandre were thick as thieves. They'd invented a secret pseudo-English language that was no secret at all. "The dog is barking" meant *Watch out!* "The dog is sleeping": *Everything is fine.* "The dog is running away": *Let's get out of here.* They snuck around looking mysterious, and the adults pretended not to understand.

Joséphine received a postcard from Christine. Her clubfooted boyfriend Alberto had rented her a furnished room on rue des Martyrs, not far from his company. The card read: "All's well. The weather is nice. Max is spending the summer in the Massif Central with his dad, who makes goat cheese with his girlfriend. He loves working with animals, and his dad may keep him. That suits me fine. Best regards, Christine Barthillet."

"What day is it today?" asked Joséphine, as Carmen walked into the kitchen.

"July the eleventh. Not quite time for the fireworks."

That's just what Daddy said, Jo thought, *a little before he died.* In two days, it would be the anniversary of his death. She never forgot the date.

Carmen laid a cell phone on the table. "This is Hortense's."

"You must be mistaken. The girls don't have cell phones."

"Well, it was in her jeans. I checked the pockets before I did the laundry."

Joséphine looked at the phone. "Do me a favor and don't say anything. We'll see how she reacts."

The housekeeper gave her a conspiratorial look. "You don't know where it's from, do you?"

"No. And I don't want to fire the first shot, so I'll wait for her to show her hand."

♦ ♦ ♦

Two days later, Joséphine came in from a run in the woods just before noon. A sea breeze ruffled her hair, and her orange T-shirt was dark with sweat.

She looked at her watch: forty-five minutes! Running helped Jo think. As she ran she heard a bird chirping, *Quick-er! Quick-er! Quick-er!*, and picked up her pace. She talked aloud to her father. "Send me a sign, Daddy. . . . Any sign at all . . . When's the publisher going to get back to us? . . . What's he doing, anyway? . . . We gave him the manuscript two weeks ago . . ." Somewhere off to her left, a heron called.

Henriette had phoned the day before and spoken at length with Iris, who promptly reported to Joséphine.

"Mom thinks Chief has a mistress!" Iris said gleefully. "She says he's completely changed! He seems younger, livelier. Apparently he's using beauty creams and dyeing his hair. He's lost weight, and he isn't sleeping at home. Mom's sure there's another woman. She found a photo of him hugging some voluptuous babe at a dinner at the Lido. Can you believe it, at his age? Mom claims he's spending money on this chick like there's no tomorrow and writing it off as business entertainment."

Remembering the scene on the platform at the train station, Jo was puzzled. Josiane Lambert was blond and plump, and well past the age of being called a chick. *Could Marcel have more than one mistress? What a man!*

"So what does she plan to do?" Jo asked.

"She says she has a secret weapon against him. She couldn't

care less about his cheating, but says if Chief tries to divorce her, she'll blow him out of the water."

"What kind of secret weapon?"

"Something about embezzling company funds. Mom apparently found a very incriminating file. Says he better do right by her if he doesn't want to end up bankrupt and splashed all over the newspapers."

Poor Marcel, thought Joséphine. *He has every right to fall in love. Being with our mother couldn't have been a million laughs.*

Iris was waiting for Joséphine on the front steps of the house. She was wearing white capri pants and the latest Lacoste blouse, and was beaming triumphantly.

With a pitying glance at Joséphine's sweaty outfit, she proudly announced: "Cric and Croc clobbered the big Cruc creeping up to crunch them."

Joséphine collapsed onto the steps and mopped her forehead with her T-shirt.

"Let me guess: You finally managed to bake a soufflé?"

"Cold."

"Alex drove around the house by himself for the first time?"

"Colder."

"You're pregnant?"

"At my age? You're out of your mind!"

Joséphine looked up at her sister. "Serrurier called?"

"Bingo! *And he loves it!*"

Joséphine rolled onto the ground and lay there, arms outflung, staring up at clouds that formed the phrase AND HE LOVES IT. She had done it!

Iris came and stood over her, her long brown legs forming an upside down V—a V for Victory.

"You did it, Jo! You did it! He was dazzled, blown away! You're amazing, and wonderful, and unbelievable! Thank you!"

"We should thank Daddy," she said. "He died thirty years ago today. The day before Bastille Day."

"Has it really been thirty years?"

"To the day. I was thinking of him as I was out running. I asked him to help the book, and—"

"Joséphine, stop it!" Iris snapped. "You wrote the book, not him!"

Poor old Jo, she thought. *Such a sucker for cheap sentiment. Jo and her insatiable need for love, her tendency to trust everyone except herself. Never able to give herself credit for anything.* Iris gave a mental shrug, and her thoughts returned to the book. It was her move now.

"From now on, I'm a writer!" she declared. "I have to think like a writer, eat like a writer, sleep like a writer, wear my hair like a writer, dress like a writer. How am I going to manage all that?"

"No idea. We said we'd divide the roles, and you're on now." Joséphine said this as casually as she could, but her heart wasn't in it.

That night, Philippe, Iris, and Joséphine went to dinner at Cirro's, on the Deauville boardwalk. Iris ordered champagne and made a toast to the book.

"Tonight I feel like I'm christening a ship about to be

launched into the world," she said pompously. "I wish it a long and prosperous life."

They all clinked glasses and sipped their pink champagne in silence. Philippe's cell phone rang, and he looked down to see who was calling.

"I'm sorry, I have to take this," he said, getting up from the table.

When Philippe went out to the boardwalk, Iris drew a heavy white envelope from her handbag.

"This is for you, Jo. So that tonight will be a celebration for you, too!"

Joséphine took the envelope, opened it, and pulled out a pink-trimmed card. In Iris's loopy handwriting it said, "Happy You! Happy Book! Happy Life!" in gold ink. A check was folded inside the card, for 25,000 euros. *The price of my silence*, thought Jo, mortified. She turned beet red and stuffed everything back into the envelope. As she bit her lip to keep from crying, she caught Philippe watching her from afar.

Suddenly Iris stood up and waved at a girl heading for a table near the beach.

"I think that's Hortense over there!"

"Hortense?" asked Joséphine, peering in that direction.

Iris called out, and Hortense turned and came over to them.

"What are you doing here, darling?"

"I wanted to come say hello. Carmen told me you were having dinner here, and I didn't feel like staying home alone with the two brats. I'm going to meet some friends at the bar next door."

She looked at Joséphine.

"Can I please, Mom, sweetheart? You're looking all radiant tonight!"

"You think so? I didn't do anything special. Well, yes, I did; I went for a run this morning."

"That must be it. Okay, see you later. Have fun!"

Joséphine watched her daughter gracefully walk off. *She's hiding something from me*, she thought. *It isn't like Hortense to pay me compliments for no reason.*

"All right, here's to the book's health!" said Philippe. "Oh, by the way, what's the title?"

Taken aback, the sisters looked at each another.

"Rats!" said Jo. "You know, I never thought of a title!"

Iris jumped in to cover Joséphine's gaffe. "But we've talked about it often enough! Ever since I gave you the manuscript, I've been begging you for suggestions, and nada! You promised me, Jo. I can't believe you forgot!"

Philippe was glaring at Iris in silent fury, remembering a similar situation from fifteen years earlier. *What Iris isn't able to do herself, she gets others to do for her, then swoops in and steals the glory*, he thought. *She tried it once. Now she's doing it again, only this time the victim is willing.*

He glanced over at Joséphine, who was hiding behind her menu.

"You're looking at the wrong menu, Jo. That's the wine list."

"Sorry," she muttered. "My mistake."

"No problem," said Philippe, turning back to Iris. "We won't let it spoil your party, will we, darling?" His voice rose with mordant sarcasm on the word *darling*.

"Come on, Jo, smile!" he continued. "We'll come up with a title, don't you worry."

They clinked glasses again as the waiter came to take their order. A light wind had picked up, blowing the sand and shaking the fringes of the umbrellas. You could smell the sea, invisible beyond the big white wooden planters surrounding the terrace. A sudden chill descended on the diners.

Iris shivered.

PART IV

◆   ◆   ◆

Chapter 15

♦ ♦ ♦

"What's the secret of your success?"

"I'm still being breast-fed."

"What would satisfy you?"

"A nun's habit."

"Are you happy?"

"As happy as anyone can be, considering I think about committing suicide every day."

"What have you given up on?"

"Ever being blond."

"What do you do with your money?"

"I give it away. Money brings bad luck."

"What would you like for your birthday?"

"An atomic bomb."

"Name three contemporaries you hate the most."

"Me, myself, and I."

"What are you capable of doing for love?"

"Anything."

"What is art to you?"

"It gets me through the day."

"What do you like the most about yourself?"

"My long black hair."

"Would you sacrifice your hair for a cause?"

"Yes."

"If I asked you to sacrifice your hair now, would you do it?"

"Yes."

"Bring me some scissors!"

Iris didn't flinch. Looking into the TV camera with her big blue eyes, she showed no sign of apprehension. It was 9:30 p.m., and half of France was watching the variety show *On ne peut pas plaire à tout le monde*. Iris had answered the rapid-fire questions, and made the most of the interview. The host's assistant now brought out a pair of scissors on a silver tray. He picked them up and came over to Iris.

"Do you know what I'm about to do?"

"Your hands are shaking."

"You're going to let me do this, and you agree not to sue us, right? Say, 'Yes, I swear.' "

Iris held up her hand. "Yes, I swear," she said, very calmly.

The host showed the scissors to the TV camera. The audience held its breath. Then he took Iris's glossy black hair, spread it over her shoulders, and made the first cut. There was a dull creak, then a sound like ripping silk. The host took a hank of hair, turned, and held it up like a trophy. The audience gasped. Iris didn't stir. She sat up straight, eyes open, a faint smile on her lips. The host lifted more hair and cut it. The other guests on the show instinctively pulled back, as if they wanted no part of this ritual execution.

Now the silence was total. Between each snip, the director showed reaction shots of stunned members of the studio audience.

The show host was now hacking at Iris's hair like a gardener trimming a hedge. The ratings were going to go through the roof.

At last, he put the heavy scissors down triumphantly.

"Ladies and gentlemen, Iris Dupin has just proven that fiction and reality are one and the same, because—"

He paused for a roar of applause, as the audience released its pent-up nervous tension.

"Because in Iris Dupin's debut novel, she introduces us to Florine, a twelfth-century woman who shaves her head rather than submit to a forced marriage. It's called *A Most Humble Queen*, and it's published by Éditions Serrurier."

Looking radiant and serene, Iris ran her fingers through her ruined hair. What did a few inches of hair matter? Tomorrow *A Most Humble Queen* would be flying off the shelves. Every bookseller in France would be begging Serrurier to rush-deliver thousands of copies. Eyes downcast, she savored her triumph. Then she gravely bowed her thanks, gracefully slid down from her stool, and went offstage into the wings.

Talking on her cell phone, the book's publicist smiled broadly and gave her a thumbs-up: You did it!

"That was a knockout, darling!" she cried, muffling the phone with her hand. "You were fantastic! Absolutely fabulous! Everyone's calling—the newspapers, radio, the other stations. They all want you, darling!"

♦ ♦ ♦

Joséphine, Hortense, Zoé, and Gary were in Shirley's living room, gathered around the television.

"Are you sure that was Aunt Iris?" Zoé asked worriedly.

"Of course it was."

"Why did she let him do that to her?"

"To sell books, silly," said Hortense. "And they will! Everybody's going to be talking about this! What a great idea! Think they planned it ahead of time, Shirley?"

"Nothing your aunt does surprises me. But I have to admit, that was pretty amazing!"

"It sure was!" Gary said. "I've never seen anything like it on television. Except in a movie, that is. I saw the Joan of Arc thing, but that was just an actress, and she was wearing a wig."

Zoé looked at her mother, who'd remained silent. "That's awful, Mommy! I'm never gonna write a book, ever! And I never want to be on TV!"

"You're right, it's awful," Joséphine managed. Then she ran into the bathroom and threw up.

"Show's over for now," said Shirley, switching off the television. "But stay tuned! This is just the beginning, if you ask me."

The toilet flushed, and Joséphine came out, looking pale.

"Why's Mommy sick?" Zoé whispered to Shirley.

"She's upset at seeing your aunt behave the way she did. All right, everyone go set the table and I'll serve the chicken. I almost forgot it was in the oven. Good thing Iris was the first guest on the show. Otherwise we'd be eating free-range charcoal!"

Gary stood up and went into the kitchen. He was almost

seventeen, on the verge of adulthood. Longish black hair framed his face, highlighting his green eyes and even white teeth. He had broad shoulders, and his voice had changed.

Joséphine still wasn't used to how tall Gary had grown. When he came back to Courbevoie in September, she'd hardly recognized him. Now she admired his natural grace. *Maybe he really is some sort of prince*, she thought.

"I don't think I can eat a thing," she mumbled, sitting down at the table.

Shirley leaned close. "Pull yourself together," she whispered. "Or they'll wonder why you're so upset."

During their vacation, Shirley had told Gary that Joséphine had written the book, and made him swear not to tell a soul. She knew he could keep a secret.

The two of them had spent a wonderful summer together: two weeks in London, then a month in Scotland, in a manor house a friend loaned them. They went hunting and fishing, and took long walks in the hills. Gary spent most of his evenings with Emma, a young woman who worked in the village pub. One night he came back wearing a satisfied grin.

"Well, I did the deed!" he announced.

He and Shirley drank a toast to this new stage in his life.

In the evening when Gary was out, Shirley lit a fire in a great hall lined with hunting trophies and Highland antiques, and curled up with a book. She'd spent some nights with her lover, who came to the house a few weekends. They met late at night, in the west wing of the manor house.

Now Shirley caught Hortense looking at Gary appraisingly as he set the table, and felt a surge of pride. He wasn't an eager young puppy anymore.

Hortense has changed too, thought Shirley. *She used to be merely pretty; now she's dangerous—sexy and unsettling. Jo is the only one who hasn't noticed; she still treats her like a little girl.*

Shirley basted the chicken with pan drippings, relieved to see that it was nicely browned and crisp. She set it on the table.

"Didn't the book come out awfully fast?"

"The publisher moved it up to get it into the fall catalog," said Joséphine.

"He must have been pretty sure it would sell."

"And sure of Iris, too. Looks as if he was right."

"Any news from the Barthillets?" Shirley asked, eager to change the subject.

"None, and that's just fine with me."

"Max isn't a bad guy," Gary said. "He's just a little lost. Of course, with parents like his, he didn't get dealt much of a hand. He's herding sheep for his dad now. Probably not a lot of laughs."

"At least he's working," said Hortense. "Hardly anybody's able to get jobs nowadays. I've decided to major in theater. It'll be a help, later on. Speaking of which, Mom, I need to subscribe to some magazines. I have to keep up with the trends. Yesterday a friend and I went to Colette; it was so cool!"

"No problem, honey; we can get the subscriptions. And what's Colette?"

"A super-awesome store. I saw the cutest Prada jacket there.

Kind of expensive, but beautiful. I'd stick out in Courbevoie, but it would be perfect when we're living in Paris."

"What? You're moving?" cried Shirley, dropping the chicken leg she was eating.

"That's not even close to happening," said Joséphine. "I'd have to make a lot of money first."

"That might happen sooner than you think," she said, glancing toward the TV.

"Shirley!"

"I'm sorry, it's just that this is upsetting news. You're my family. You guys are all the family I've got. If you move, I'm coming with you!"

Zoé clapped her hands.

"That would be so great! We could get a big apartment and—"

Joséphine interrupted: "Hey, calm down, everyone! We're not there yet. Eat, girls, or it's going to get cold."

The chicken was delicious, and Shirley was explaining how to buy a good free-range chicken when she was interrupted by a ringing cell phone.

No one moved to answer it.

"Is that your phone, Gary?" Jo asked.

"No, it's in my room."

"Is it yours, Shirley?"

"No, that's not my ringtone."

Joséphine then turned to Hortense, who wiped her mouth with her napkin and said calmly, "It's mine, Mom."

"Since when do you have a cell phone?"

Jo couldn't understand how Hortense had replaced the one Carmen found in her jeans.

"A friend lent me his. He has two of them."

"And who's paying the phone bill?"

"His parents. They're loaded."

"Well, you're going to return it right away! I'm not at all happy about this, but I'd rather buy you a phone myself."

How can Mom afford to be so generous? Hortense wondered. *Maybe she's started a new translation. In that case I'd better ask her to raise my allowance.* There was no hurry, though. For the time being her boyfriend was buying her whatever she wanted, but when the day came and she dumped him, she'd be happy to have a little money saved up.

It was October 1, a day Josiane would remember for the rest of her life. She was the first one in the office, and she ran upstairs to the bathroom to use the pregnancy test kit that she'd bought at the avenue Niel drugstore. Her period was late: she should have had it ten days ago!

Every morning, Josiane had been getting up feeling anxious. She would lift her nightgown, slowly spread her legs, and examine the little white cotton patch on her panties. Nothing! She put her hands together and prayed that this was it: a baby Grobz in blue or pink booties. *Little angel, if this is you, I'm gonna give you a beautiful place to live!*

She waited ten minutes, sitting on the toilet and reciting every prayer she knew, praying to God and all the saints, her eyes raised to the ceiling as if the skies would open up. Finally, she looked at the test strip: Bingo! A bubble of joy burst in her chest.

She let out a triumphant yelp, jumped up, and raised her arms to heaven. Then she sat back down again, overcome with emotion, tears rolling down her cheeks. "I'm going to be a mommy!" she said over and over, rocking and hugging herself. Tiny pink and blue booties danced before her eyes. Then she ran to pound on Ginette's office door.

"It's a go! The baby's here!"

She pointed to her stomach.

"Are you sure?" asked Ginette, wide-eyed.

"I just did a test: *pos-i-tive*!"

At the thought that she would soon be holding her baby, Josiane started bawling again. Ginette took her in her arms.

"Come on, kiddo, relax. This is good news, isn't it?"

"Oh, man, you have no idea how shaken up I am. What can I say? It's taken us so long, I'd given up hope."

She was suddenly seized by a terrifying thought.

"Oh, God, I hope the baby stays in there! They say you can lose it during the first three months. Can you imagine how heartbroken Marcel would be if I screwed this up?"

"Hey, stop talking like that! You're pregnant!"

Ginette poured Josiane a cup of coffee.

"You want a sandwich with that?" she asked. "You have to eat for two now!"

"I'd eat for four if it makes the baby come out all nice and chubby. I'm almost forty, Ginette! Can you believe it? Is this a miracle, or what?"

Ginette smiled and patted her friend's arm. "I know, Josie, I know. The best part of your life is about to begin. Marcel's gonna treat you like royalty."

"He'll be so happy, he'll go bananas. In fact, I gotta be careful how I break the news, 'cause his heart might burst."

"Oh, come on! With all the exercise he's getting, I'm sure his heart can take it."

Josiane returned to her office, powdered her nose, and was just putting her compact away when she heard Henriette Grobz's distinctive footsteps on the stairs. *God, the way that woman walks!* she thought. *The Toothpick clamps her legs together so tight, the insides of her thighs must have calluses.*

"Good morning, Josiane," said Henriette, much more sweetly than usual.

"Good morning, Madame Grobz. How are you?"

What the hell is she doing at the office at the crack of dawn, all gussied up? Josiane wondered. *And what's with the sweet talk? She must want something.*

Henriette began hesitantly.

"Josiane, I want to ask you something, but it must remain strictly between the two of us. I don't want my husband to know. He might be annoyed that I'm going around him on a matter that concerns the business."

Henriette took a snapshot from her purse and held it out to her.

"Do you recognize this woman? Have you ever seen her at the office?"

It was a photo of a gorgeous, busty brunette. Josiane glanced at it and shook her head.

"No, not that I can recall."

"Are you sure?" Henriette asked. "Here, take another look."

Josiane took the photo and studied it—and got a shock. A grinning Marcel was standing next to the brunette, his arm around her waist.

Henriette noticed the change in Josiane's expression.

"So, do you recognize her?"

"No, it's just that . . . Would you mind if I make a copy of this?"

"What for?"

"I want to see if it matches anything in our files."

"All right, but don't leave it lying around. I know Monsieur Grobz is in Shanghai, but I wouldn't want him to come across it when he returns."

Josiane put the snapshot facedown on the Xerox machine and studied the back of the photo. There was a neatly drawn little heart and, in Marcel's handwriting, the words "Natasha, Natasha, Natasha." Josiane gulped. She couldn't let the Toothpick see that she was upset.

"I'll take a look in the files later," she said. "I may have seen that woman once before. It was here in the office, with your husband. I think her name was something like Sasha."

"Natasha, perhaps?"

"That's it, Natasha! Listen, Madame Grobz, I'll check, and if I find anything of interest, I'll let you know."

"Thank you, Josiane. That is very sweet of you."

"It's my pleasure, madame. I'm at your service."

She gave Henriette her most obsequious smile and walked her to the door.

"Can I trust you not to tell Monsieur Grobz anything?"

"Not to worry. I know how to keep secrets."

"You're very kind."

Yeah, well, I'm not going to be so kind with that fat son of a bitch when he gets back from China, thought Josiane as she sat down at her desk. *That's it! No more red carpet for that bastard when he shows up, fresh from a jog and all hot and bothered. I'll show that two-timing prick!*

She took her pen and jabbed it through Natasha's beautiful eyes.

"Pull over right there!" Hortense ordered, pointing at the corner.

"What if I don't feel like it?"

"You want to keep going out with me, or not?"

"Hey, I was just kidding. Of course I do."

"Well, if Mom or Zoé sees me with you, it'll be all over."

"But your mother doesn't know who I am. She's never even seen me."

"Yeah, but she knows me, and she'll make the connection. She may be slow, but she can put two and two together."

Bruno Chaval parked the car and turned off the engine. He put an arm around Hortense's shoulders and pulled her to him.

"Give me a kiss."

She gave him a quick peck and reached for the door.

"You can do better than that!"

"Quit bugging me!"

"You didn't say that earlier when you were waving my credit card around."

"That was earlier."

He buried his face in Hortense's long hair, inhaling the smell of her skin and perfume.

"God, you drive me crazy!" he murmured. "Don't be mean. I can't help myself. I want you so badly. . . . I'll buy you anything you want."

Hortense rolled her eyes. What a drag Chaval was. He even took the fun out of shopping!

"It's seven thirty. I have to get home."

"I have two invites for a Galliano party on Friday night. Want to go?"

Hortense's eyes became as big as saucers. "John Galliano, the designer?"

"Himself. I can take you, if you like."

"Okay. I'll make up some excuse so I can go."

"But you have to be really, really nice to me."

Hortense sighed and stretched, like a bored cat.

"Always conditions! If you think that turns me on, you're—"

"I'm sick and tired of this shy virgin routine, Hortense!"

"Listen, I'll sleep with you if and when I feel like sleeping with you. And right now, there's no way. Get it?"

"Well, at least you're direct. I'll give you that."

Hortense grabbed a big white Colette shopping bag from the

backseat and got out. She strolled down the sidewalk like a fashion model. Chaval watched her go. *What a bitch!* he thought. *She's driving me crazy.* The way Hortense's soft lips parted when they kissed made his blood race, and that darting tongue of hers . . . He closed his eyes and leaned back in his seat. *That little cunt is making me as horny as a three-balled tomcat.*

Our little fling's been going on since June, he thought. *No girl ever treated me this way, ever! Usually they worship the ground I walk on. This one polishes her shoes on my trousers, smears lip gloss on my seat cushions, and sticks old chewing gum in my glove box. And when she gets pissed, she pounds the hood with her Dior handbag! What have I done to deserve this?* Chaval inspected himself in the rearview mirror. *It's not like I'm the son of Frankenstein. I'm a good-looking guy with lead in his pencil, but she doesn't even care enough to take a picture of me!*

He sighed and switched on the ignition.

As if she could read Chaval's mind, Hortense turned around just then, her luxuriant hair swinging just so, and blew him a kiss.

Guys are so easy! she was thinking. *They're such pushovers. When they get the hots, they park their brains at the door. Even the really old ones, like Chaval. He's thirty-five and can't live without sex, goes around begging for it like a dog. Still, he probably has lots of experience. Should I sleep with him? I don't really feel like it, but if I don't, he might lose interest. I want to make it with someone I care about, at least a little. Especially the first time.*

At her building, Hortense ducked into the superintendent's supply closet to change out of her sexy clothes before she went upstairs. She traded her miniskirt for a pair of jeans, pulled on a big sweater over her belly-baring T-shirt, and wiped her makeup off. *Here I am, Mommy's little girl again*, she thought. *She's so clueless!*

Hortense shoved a tub of floor wax aside to hide her clothes and noticed an unfolded newspaper with Aunt Iris's face on the front page. The headline read, "Before and After: A Star Is Shorn." Just below it were pictures of Iris, first with long hair, then with her Joan of Arc crew cut. Hortense gave a low whistle of admiration.

She was about to head upstairs when she realized she was still carrying the big Colette bag with the Prada jacket. After a moment's thought, she carefully cut off the Prada label and saved it. She would tell Joséphine that she'd bought the jacket at the flea market the previous week.

Antoine scowled at the huge crocodile sprawled on the grass in front of them. They had stopped the Jeep in the shade of an acacia tree, and he watched the animal basking in the sunshine, its skin glistening and its eyes half closed. *What do you think you are?* he asked in irritation. *A leftover dinosaur? A walking handbag? Why are you taunting me with those sleepy yellow eyes? Isn't it enough that you're making my life a living hell?*

Antoine's problems at Croco Park were getting worse. He had been forced to host a team of scientists who came to the plantation to study crocodile blood with an eye toward creating new antibiotics. Crocodiles are immune to nearly everything, it turns out. When they get hurt, instead of getting infections, they grow scar tissue and go on their merry way. Some compound in their blood gives them a very robust immune system. Antoine had to feed and house the scientists, and find work space for them. It was another moneymaking scheme for Mr. Wei, and another headache for him.

Also, the crocodiles were proving highly unreliable: obese and picky. They would eat nothing but chicken or human flesh. Anything not to their taste they left to rot in the sun. Worse, Antoine had discovered that the females the Thai suppliers shipped were almost all menopausal. Not exactly a recipe for fruitful multiplication. The output of the leather goods factory had slowed, and the meat canning had dropped by half. *With my luck*, he thought, *the only money to be made from these damned reptiles will be mass-produced antibiotics, and there I'm screwed, because it isn't covered under my contract!*

That evening, as Pong silently served them dinner, Mylène announced that she'd sent a proposal to Mr. Wei and was thinking of going into business with him.

Antoine's shrewd boss was quick to spot an opportunity. The moment he heard about Mylène's boutique, he called and offered to become her partner. Together, they could launch a line of beauty products called Belles de Paris. Wei suggested having the packaging manufactured in France so they could put "Made in France" on the labels. This would guarantee success in the Chinese market, he said.

"Have you signed a contract yet?" Antoine asked.

"No, but we're nearly there."

"You never told me about this!"

"Yes I did, lovey, but you didn't listen. You thought it was some tea party for little girls. Well, there's a lot of money to be made."

"Did you get any legal advice before drafting the contract?"

"During my last trip to Paris, I went to see a business lawyer on the Champs-Élysées who specializes in this kind of thing."

"How did you find him?"

"I called Josiane, your father-in-law's secretary. She's very nice, and we got along really well. I told her I was calling on your behalf."

"And so?"

"She gave me the name of someone they use, and I called him. Since I was referred by Marcel Grobz, he agreed to handle my case. He even took me out to dinner. We went to a Russian cabaret near his office."

"Mylène, I can't believe you did that! You used Chief's professional connections without even knowing him? For all you know, he hates you."

"Why should he? I never did him any harm."

"Have you forgotten that I left my wife and two daughters because of you?"

"I never asked you to leave them, Antoine. You did that on your own. And you're the one who got me involved in this whole Kenya thing!"

"Do you wish I hadn't?"

"No, I have no regrets. I loved you so much, I would have gone anywhere with you. It's just that I need to keep busy. I'm not used to sitting around doing nothing. I've always worked, ever since I was very young." She looked at Antoine with unnerving candor. "Please don't be mad, lovey. The cosmetics thing is just something for me to do. Plus, you never know. If it doesn't pan out, Mr. Wei will be the only one to lose money, because I haven't invested anything. And if it does work, my little business will make lots of money and you can be my manager."

Antoine gaped at her. She was thinking about hiring him! She was probably already figuring his salary and his year-end bonus! Sweat began to trickle down his back. No, not that! He threw his napkin on the table and got up to go change.

"You really shouldn't get angry, lovey," she said. "It's a gamble. If it works, I'll be rich! Wouldn't that be funny?"

Antoine stopped at the door to the house. Mylène hadn't said "we." She'd said "I." He peeled off his sweaty shirt and went inside.

Philippe sat down heavily on the couch in Iris's study and sighed. He couldn't believe he would ever be rifling through his wife's things like some jealous husband. Whenever he saw a man doing that in a movie, he always found it pathetic.

Philippe, Alexandre, and Carmen had watched the hair-shearing broadcast together while eating in front of the TV. When Iris returned from the studio, she planted herself in front of them, looking triumphant. "So what did you think?" she asked. "Was I terrific, or what?" They didn't have the heart to contradict her.

The next day, she ran to her salon and for a cool 165 euros got a proper haircut. The short hair made her blue eyes look even bigger and more soulful. Her long neck, the perfect oval of her face, and her tanned shoulders stood out as vividly as a monogram on a tapestry. She looked like a pageboy.

"Mom, you look like you're fourteen!" Alexandre exclaimed.

Seeing her new look, Philippe felt an almost forgotten sexual stirring. If he hadn't been so disgusted by the rest of her behavior, he might have been turned on.

He found a pink binder on Iris's desk. On it, she had written NOVEL in big letters, and below that, "A Most Humble Queen" in green marker.

Is she planning to write more books? Philippe wondered as he opened the binder. *Or will she have someone else write them?* He couldn't help it, he just had to know. Confronting her would have been nobler, but you couldn't confront Iris. She always found a way to wriggle off the hook.

The pink binder was full of newspaper clippings. The magazines hadn't come out yet, but when they did, the reviews would be full of Iris and her lies. Philippe looked over the first articles, some by journalists he knew. They all spoke of Iris and her boldness. "A Star Is Bared" read one headline; another, "Heading for Glory." One thoughtful critic wondered where spectacle ended and literature began, but he admitted that the book was well written. "Iris Dupin seems to know the twelfth century intimately, and she brings it to life with great skill. Readers will find themselves following the Rule of Saint Benedict as closely as they might the plot of a Hitchcock movie."

After the reviews came articles quoting Iris on writing and writer's block. She was very articulate, talking about her years as a Columbia student and beginning screenwriter, and citing André Gide's advice to young writers: "So as not to be tempted to go out, shave your head!" She said: "What I hadn't dared to do out of vanity was forced on me."

In the photos she wore low-waisted jeans and a T-shirt that ended above her navel. With her new tomboy haircut, she looked like a rebellious teenager. In one picture, she was photographed with her head bent, "Love" and "Money" written in lipstick on her neck. The caption read: "She carries her novel's plot and the future of the world on her shoulders." Philippe groaned.

I've been supporting a monster, he thought. But the realization wasn't painful. That's how you know that love is gone: it doesn't hurt anymore. You take a long, hard look at the person you once loved, and you realize she's simply the way she is, and that you can't change her. You're the one who has changed. And it's over.

All Philippe felt now was disgust and anger. For years he'd been obsessed with Iris, wanting only to please and impress her. He wanted to be the best corporate lawyer in Paris, then the best in France, then a player on the international stage. He began collecting art, buying rare manuscripts, underwriting ballets and operas, starting a foundation—all to make her proud of him.

His gaze moved around the room, lingering on each work of art. *The record of our love*, he thought. *No*, he corrected himself, *of my love. She never really loved me.*

It was all over. He had just one final, dramatic thing to do, and then he'd leave her. It was a bit ridiculous, he knew, but it was big. He would go out in grand style. It would be his own piece of performance art.

A last newspaper clipping caught his eye, an article about the New York Film Festival. Iris had highlighted one name: Gabor Minar, who was to be the festival's guest of honor; they would be screening his latest film, *Gypsies*, a prizewinner at Cannes. "So it's still Gabor Minar," Philippe murmured thoughtfully. "The flashy movie director. It's always Minar."

He snapped the binder shut and checked the time. It was too late to call Johnny Goodfellow. He would phone him tomorrow.

When Iris got home that night, she was holding a copy of *L'Express*.

"Number four on the best-seller list!" she cried. "In only two weeks! I called Serrurier and they're shipping forty-five hundred copies a day. And that's on top of the initial print run. Can you believe it? Every day, forty-five hundred people are buying Iris Dupin's book! I bet I'm at the top of the list next week! And you wondered whether getting myself shorn in public was worth it?"

Her eyes were alight as she devoured the review. Surprised by her husband's silence, she lowered the magazine, gave him a big smile, and took a bow, awaiting his congratulations. Philippe bowed politely back.

I must be dreaming! thought Joséphine. She blinked, but the scene on the 163 bus didn't change. The woman sitting across the aisle really *was* reading her novel. Not just reading it, but devouring it. She sat bent over, turning each page carefully, apparently savoring every line, as if she didn't want to miss a single word. Around her, people were getting off and on, making phone calls, coughing and chatting, but the woman didn't move. *A Most Humble Queen* was riding the 163!

Every time Jo read a good review of the book, she felt like whooping and screaming and leaping about. She would run to Shirley's, the only place she could give free rein to her feelings of joy.

Then, as the days passed, a feeling of emptiness began to overcome her. Iris was everywhere; her smile was all over town, her blue eyes gazed out from every newsstand. One day, Jo even heard an interview in which her sister invoked divine inspiration to explain why her writing was so fluid. "It's not me writing," Iris said. "I'm being told what to write."

Joséphine collapsed onto a stool, shouting, "She has a hell of a nerve!"

That night she rang Shirley's doorbell, but no one was home. Zoé had left a note saying that she was going to stay at Alexandre's and that Carmen was coming to pick her up. Also, that Hortense was going out, would be back late, and not to worry. Joséphine was alone.

She reheated some leftover quiche, ate a little salad, and watched as night fell. She felt sadder and sadder. When it was fully dark, she went onto the balcony and looked at the stars.

"Daddy?" she asked quietly. "Can you hear me?"

She went on, in a little-girl voice: "It's not fair! Why is she always first, huh? Once again, I've been left behind."

Jo could still hear her father yelling, "You're a criminal! A criminal!" She remembered feeling his arms around her, the salty taste of his skin as he ran, carrying Jo as if to save her. They were on the beach; it was summer. *I was coming out of the water—my eyes stung. I was spitting up water, and sobbing. Daddy never again slept in the same room as Mom after that, I remember. He took refuge in the crosswords, in his awful puns, in his favorite pipe. And then he died. He piped down for good.* Joséphine chuckled; the pun was so terrible her father would have liked it.

"Daddy, Daddy," she sang to the stars in the darkness. "Someday I'll find the missing piece of the puzzle. In the meantime, thank you for making the book a success. You must be proud of me, since you know I'm the one who wrote it."

Joséphine looked up again. A peaceful feeling came over her. *I'll get back to doing the research for my postdoc scholarship. I'll go back to the library, back to my illuminated manuscripts and my histories.*

And someday I'll write another book.

A book that will be mine, and mine alone.

Chapter 16

♦ ♦ ♦

At the airport, Marcel threw his bags into the trunk of the car and got in front next to his driver.

"God, I'm exhausted! I'm getting too old for these long trips. What do you think, Gilles? Do I look ready for the scrap heap?"

Gilles Larmoyer glanced over at him.

"You look pretty shipshape to me, boss."

"Nice of you to say. And thanks for not noticing the ship's extra cargo around my waist. Did you buy the newspapers for me? What's happening?"

"They're on the backseat. Your stepdaughter, Madame Dupin, really hit the jackpot with that book of hers."

"*What*? She wrote a book?"

"Yeah. My mother bought it, and she loved it!"

"Oh, great! I'm sure to get an earful about that one. Anything else?"

"Not much. I took the car in for a tune-up, like you asked. Everything's fine. Where are we going, boss?"

"To the office."

I really have to see Josiane, thought Marcel. *Each time I've gotten her on the phone, she's been distant. Maybe she's seeing Bruno Chaval again. That sex-crazed* schnorrer *is as bad as they come.*

"Any news about Chaval?" he asked casually.

Marcel knew that Bruno and Gilles were buddies who went out clubbing together. The chauffeur would regale his boss with tales of swingers' parties and lap dances. They would stumble out at dawn to straighten their ties and tuck in their shirts, and Chaval would head to the office, and Gilles to go drive the car. The chauffeur seemed free of any ambition. Marcel had tried to give him a leg up, but Gilles loved only cars. To keep him happy, Marcel got a new one every couple of years.

"So you haven't heard about Chaval? He's head over heels in love with your niece."

"Little Hortense?"

"That's the one! And I'm telling you, it's killing him. He's been trying to get her into the sack for six months, but no luck! Has to go home and finish the job by hand. She's driving him batshit."

Marcel snorted with laughter, partly from relief. So Chaval wasn't screwing around with Josiane. He took out his cell phone and called the office.

"Sweetie-pie, it's me! I'm in the car, on my way. Are you okay?"

"I'm fine."

"Aren't you glad to be seeing me?"

"I'm jumping for joy." She hung up.

When Marcel walked into the office, Josiane didn't so much

as smile. Didn't even look up from her desk. He spread his arms to give her a hug, but she stayed where she was.

"Your mail's on your desk. Your list of phone messages too. I sorted through everything."

Marcel sat down at his desk to find a pile of letters—and a Xerox of a photograph right on top. It was the brunette from the Lido, and her eyes had been poked out. He snatched it up and ran to the outer office, chuckling.

"Sweetie-pie! Is this why you've been giving me the cold shoulder since forever?"

"I don't see what's so funny. I'm not laughing, anyway!"

"You've got it all wrong! I planted that picture months ago, to fool Henriette! René said she'd come prowling around here on the first of May, when the place was closed! That sounded fishy, so I carefully looked though my files, and I noticed that a big envelope had been opened and probably Xeroxed. It was the one with that fat Ukrainian's expenses in it. Poor old Toothpick! She probably figured she could nail me for cheating on her, and embezzling from the company to boot!

"The snapshot was taken at the Lido when I took a big client out one night you didn't feel like going. I just made up a name for the girl. When Henriette saw it along with the expenses en-velope, I bet she swallowed the story hook, line, and sinker. Have you really been stewing all this time because of that?"

Josiane looked at him suspiciously.

"You think I'm going to buy that crap?"

"Why would I lie to you, sweetie-pie? I don't even know the girl. I posed with her for laughs, that's all. Try to remember. It was about a year and a half ago, and you said you were too tired to come along."

Actually, Josiane did remember: she'd been with Chaval that night. The old guy was right.

Walking over to her desk, he bumped into a suitcase.

"What's this?"

"I was planning to leave, Marcel. I was gonna wait for us to talk things out, then I was splitting."

"You're crazy! Listen, honeybunch, you'd better get used to this, 'cause I'm here. I'm really here for you."

He took her in his arms and rocked her, murmuring, "She's silly, she's so silly."

Josiane leaned against him, waiting for him to stop so she could give him the news about her pregnancy. One emotion at a time, she figured. I'll let him come back to earth, and then announce the arrival of Baby Grobz. That'll send him to seventh heaven.

"With that photo I figured I could kill two birds with one stone," Marcel was saying. "This way, Henriette won't get suspicious in case you get pregnant and start to show. She'll be thinking about Natasha, not about you."

Josiane slowly stepped out of his arms. She didn't like what she'd just heard.

"So you're not planning to tell her when I do get knocked up?"

Marcel turned crimson.

"No, it's not that! I just . . . I just need a little time to get everything straightened out."

"Seeing how long we've been talking about this kid, you've had plenty of time to get things straight!"

"I'll be honest, sweetie-pie. I don't know how to handle it without her turning around and screwing me. But I'll do it when the time comes, I promise!"

At that, Josiane stood up, grabbed her purse, and waved an arm dramatically at her office.

"Take a good look around, Marcel Grobz, 'cause you're never going to see me again. You're such a coward, you make me sick! I'm throwing in the towel. I've had it!"

"Sweetie-pie! I promise—"

"I've been eating promises out of the air for so long, I wanna puke! I don't believe a word you say anymore."

She picked up her suitcase and strode out of the office. Heels clicking as she went downstairs. Josiane Lambert quit Marcel Grobz's company on October 22, at exactly 11:50 a.m.

She didn't stop to say good-bye to René.

She didn't stop to hug Ginette.

She didn't look at the wisteria.

When she went out the front gate, she didn't look back.

She looked straight ahead, thinking, *If I stop now, I'll never leave.*

That night after dinner, Alexandre showed Zoé his secret hiding place: a big armoire his father had bought in Saint-Valéry-en-Caux, a little seaport in Normandy. Alex had gone there with his parents. His dad had to meet an English client, and the man had sailed over on his boat. After their meeting, the family went for a walk around the little seaport and stopped in a secondhand shop. The moment Philippe saw the armoire, he had to have it.

Iris objected that it didn't match the rest of their furniture. It was old-fashioned, she said, tacky. It would look all wrong. But Philippe insisted.

He put it in his study, where it soon became Alexandre's favorite hiding place. It smelled of furniture polish and lavender, and if you listened really, really hard, you could hear the rumble of the ocean and the clicking of mast halyards. Alex would pull the doors closed, put on headphones, and travel to SSIW—his Super Secret Imaginary World. That was a country where everyone lived according to the lyrics in John Lennon's song "Imagine." The other essential piece of SSIW equipment was a pair of round glasses that let you see things that were invisible.

He often invited Zoé in with him. "In the SSIW," he said, "there's no teachers, no money, no school, no grades, no traffic jams, no divorced parents. Everyone loves everyone else, and the only rule is that you can't bother the other SSIW inhabitants."

Also, you had to speak English.

Alexandre insisted on that. He spoke it fluently, because his parents sent him to school in England for a few weeks every summer. At first it was hard for Zoé, but she did her best to keep up with her cousin. When she didn't understand something, he translated.

That night Carmen made them dinner early, Iris went to a book party, and Philippe had a business dinner. Alexandre and Zoé snuck off to the study and slipped into the magic armoire. He had created a regular ritual. First they had to put on the little round yellow glasses and say "Hello, John" three times. Then they sat down, closed their eyes, and sang "Imagine."

After that, they held hands and waited for an emissary of the SSIW to come.

"Concentrate," said Alexandre. "Let's call the White Rabbit."

Zoé closed her eyes, and he said the magic words: "Hello, White Rabbit. Where are you?"

"Here I am, children," Alexandre answered in a deep voice. "Where do you want to go today?"

He glanced at Zoé, and said, "To Central Park in New York. To the Imagine circle in Strawberry Fields."

"Okay, children. Fasten your seat belts!"

They pretended to fasten their seat belts.

"I've never been to New York," Zoé whispered.

"I have. You'll see, it's great. Central Park has horse-drawn carriages, lakes with ducks, and a statue of Alice in Wonderland. There's even a statue of the White Rabbit!"

After playing for a while, the two children were about to leave the armoire when they heard the study door open, then footsteps.

"Is it your dad?"

"Shh! We'll see."

It was indeed Alex's father, and he was on the phone, speaking English.

"Is he pretending to be playing with us?" asked Zoé. "Does he know about the SSIW?"

"Shh!" Alex put his hand over her mouth, and they held their breath and listened.

"She didn't write the book, Johnny. Her sister wrote it for her. I'm sure of it."

"What's he saying?"

"Wait!" Alexandre hissed.

"Yes, she pulled a stunt like this before," said Philippe. "She's such a liar! She made her sister write the book, and now she's pretending she did! It's a huge hit here in France. . . . No, really. I'm not kidding!"

"*What's he saying?*" Zoé asked plaintively

"Shut up! I can't hear with you whispering in my ear!"

"So let's do it in New York, at the film festival. I know for sure that he'll be there. Can you manage everything? Okay, we'll talk soon. Let me know."

He hung up.

In the armoire, the two children were afraid to move, or even whisper. But then Philippe put on some classical music, and they were able to speak

"Alexandre, what did he say?" Zoé demanded, taking off her round glasses.

"He said that my mom didn't write that book. Your mother wrote it. He said my mom's done that before, that she's a big liar."

"Do you believe him?"

"If he says so, yeah. Dad doesn't tell lies."

"Well, the Middle Ages is certainly more my mom's thing. So she wrote it and your mother . . . But why, Alex?"

"No idea."

They could hear Philippe moving about the study. Then he

stopped, and the smell of tobacco began to fill the room. He had lit a cigar.

"Yuck, that stinks!" complained Zoé. "We gotta get out. It makes my nose itch."

"Wait until he leaves first. We can't let him see us. Otherwise, no more SSIW. If a secret place is discovered, it doesn't exist anymore."

They didn't have to wait long. Philippe left the study to go ask Carmen where the children were.

They crept out of the armoire and ran to Alexandre's room. When Philippe found them, they were sitting on the floor, reading comic books.

"You all right, kids?"

They looked at each other nervously.

"Want to watch a movie together? There's no school tomorrow, so you can stay up late."

Relieved, they agreed. Then they got into an argument over what to watch. Alexandre voted for *The Matrix*, and Zoé, for *Sleeping Beauty*. Philippe settled the matter by choosing a comedy, *The Murderer Lives at Number 21*. "You'll like it, Zoé. It's a little scary, but it all turns out okay in the end."

They settled in front of the television. As Philippe was starting the movie, Zoé and Alex exchanged a meaningful look. They were in this together now.

Six months earlier, Luca had told Joséphine about the colloquium that would be held in Provence that fall.

"It's a conference on the sacred in the Middle Ages, in Montpellier in October. I'm presenting a paper. You should too. It's a good idea to build up your list of publications."

October had arrived, and Joséphine was now on the Montpellier train to join him. Luca had given his talk yesterday, Friday. Jo had signed up to speak this afternoon.

When Luca came to the station, he seemed very happy to see her. He was wearing the same old blue duffel coat, and his thin cheeks were dark with a three-day beard. He picked up Joséphine's suitcase and steered her toward the exit, his hand resting lightly on her shoulder.

They passed a bookstore, and Joséphine was startled to see a big window display of *A Most Humble Queen*.

"A real best seller," said Luca. "I bought a copy to see if it lived up to all the hype, and you know what? It wasn't half bad. I couldn't put it down, in fact. Very well written. Have you read it?"

Joséphine mumbled yes, then immediately asked how the conference had been going. The other participants were interesting, Luca said. Yes, his talk had gone well; yes, there would be a publication.

The afternoon went by quickly. Joséphine spoke for twenty minutes in a lecture hall to thirty people. She made her points clearly, surprised by her new self-confidence. A few colleagues stayed afterward to congratulate her. One mentioned the success of *A Most Humble Queen*, and said he was glad the twelfth century was back in the spotlight, and presented free of the usual clichés. "Nice job!" the man said before leaving. Joséphine wondered whether he meant her talk or the novel, then reminded herself that she'd written both.

She met Luca back at the hotel. They took a cab to a restaurant on the beach at Carnon, and chose a table near the water.

Joséphine felt cheerful and relaxed. She glanced at the menu, and decided to just get whatever Luca was having. After careful study, he ordered the wine. *This is the first time I've seen him look so at ease*, she thought. *Maybe he's happy to be with me after all.*

Luca asked about her daughters. Had she always wanted children?

"Actually, I didn't used to think about my life very much. I just lived day to day."

"And you had a rude awakening?"

"Yes, pretty rude."

"Remember that time we went to the movies? You started to say you were writing a book, and then you caught yourself. I always wondered if you misspoke, or what."

"Did I say that? I don't remember."

"Yes, you did. And I think you should be writing. You have a very lively way of talking about history. I remember how much I enjoyed listening to you that afternoon."

"What about you? Why don't you write a book?"

"Because to write, you have to have a point of view. Have an opinion. Know who you are. And that, I don't know yet."

"But you give just the opposite impression."

He raised an eyebrow. "Really? Well, appearances can be deceiving," he said, playing with his wineglass. "You know, you and

I have something in common: we're both loners. I watch you at the library; you never speak to anyone. So I'm very flattered that you've taken an interest in me."

Joséphine blushed. "Now you're making fun of me!"

"No, I'm serious. You settle down to work, never raise your eyes from your materials, and then you leave, as quiet as a mouse. Except when you drop your books all over the place!"

Joséphine laughed.

"Luca, can I ask you a personal question?" Joséphine chalked up her boldness to the wine and the fresh sea air. She felt good. She had the feeling—unusual for her—of being in harmony with her surroundings. Happiness felt within reach, and she didn't want to let it get away.

"Have you ever been married? Ever wanted to have kids?"

"I'd rather not answer that, Joséphine."

Once again, she felt she had blundered. "I'm terribly sorry. I didn't mean to offend you."

"You didn't offend me. I'm the one who started asking personal questions."

But we'll never get to know each other if we only talk about generalities and the Middle Ages, Jo protested silently.

That summer, she'd been flipping through a magazine when she spotted Luca in an advertisement for men's cologne. He had his arms around a tall brunette, her head thrown back in laughter and her slim, muscular midriff bare. In the photograph, his eyes glowed with an intensity Jo had never seen before, a look of grave desire. She wondered if maybe she should let her hair grow long, like the brunette's.

"I saw you in an ad this summer," she ventured, trying to change the subject. "For a cologne, I think."

"Let's not talk about that, if you don't mind."

Luca's gaze had become impenetrable. The friendly, engaging man who had been chatting with her moments before had gone, and left a stranger in his place.

"It's getting chilly," he said. "Do you feel like going back?"

In the taxi to the hotel, Joséphine studied him, then spoke. "I'm very sorry. I shouldn't have asked you those questions. We were having such a good time, and I let my guard down, and—"

Luca gave her a tender look, pulled her close, and slipped his arm around her waist.

"You're wonderful, Joséphine. You have no idea how much you mean to me. Don't change, please, whatever you do."

She put her head on his shoulder and relaxed, breathing in the smell of his cologne. *What was in it?* she wondered. *Verbena, lemon, sandalwood, maybe orange blossom . . . Was it the cologne from the advertisement?* She stopped thinking when he kissed her. A long, tender kiss that ended only because the taxi had stopped in front of the hotel.

In silence, they took their keys and went up to the third floor. When he made a move to enter her room, she let him. She let him put his hands on her shoulders and start kissing her again.

She let him slip his hands under her sweater, and caress her. She let him. . . .

But just as she was about to surrender, the image of the brunette in the ad came to her mind. Jo could see the woman's slender waist, her toned, tanned stomach, her slim arms thrown back. Joséphine tensed, imagining herself standing naked against Luca. A mother of two with thin, flat hair, little pimples on her back, a thick waist, and plain white cotton underpants.

She pushed him away, murmuring, "No, no . . ."

Startled, Luca straightened, then collected himself.

"I'll stop bothering you," he said lightly. "Let's forget all about it. Shall we meet for breakfast tomorrow?"

Jo nodded, her eyes full of tears, and watched as he left the room.

"Pathetic, Shirley! I was pathetic! There he was, holding me and kissing me, and it felt great, and all I could think of was my love handles and my stupid white cotton panties. When he left, I cried my eyes out. This is the man of my dreams, and I pushed him away! I think I'm crazy. That's it. Nothing's ever going to happen to me again. My life is over."

Shirley was rolling pastry dough for an apple tart on the tabletop.

"Your life isn't over," she said firmly. "It's only just beginning. Problem is, you don't realize that yet. You just wrote a best seller—"

"Yes, but—"

"And you didn't know you could write. So cheer up! Your sister did you a favor. Plus, you're going to earn tons of money."

"Seems that way."

"So forget about the bloody book. Let it go. Write for yourself now, not for Iris. You want a man, and you push him away. You want to write, and you hesitate. For God's sake, Jo, you drive me mad with your doubts. And above all, stop thinking that you're ugly and fat. You're not."

"So why do I see myself that way?"

"Audrey Hepburn thought she was ugly. We all think we're ugly."

"You don't."

"I started out with more love in my life than you did. I had a mother who adored me, even though she had to hide it. And so did my father."

"What was your mother like?"

Shirley was poking holes into the rolled dough with a fork. She hesitated for a moment before answering.

"She didn't say much, but all I had to do was walk into the room for her face to light up and her worries to fall away. She didn't hug or kiss me, but she would look at me with so much love, I could feel it with my eyes closed. She raised me without a kiss or a touch, but she gave me a foundation so solid that I don't have any of the doubts you do."

"What about your father?" asked Joséphine. Surprised to have Shirley speaking about her childhood, she was determined to make the most of it.

"Same thing. He was as silent and reserved as my mother. He never kissed or hugged me in public. He couldn't. But he was always there for me. They both were, and it wasn't easy for them,

I can tell you. You didn't have that luck. You grew up on your own, without much support. You're still stumbling around today, but you'll get there in the end!"

"Think so? After what happened last night with Luca, I don't have much hope."

"These things happen. But it's not over. And if it doesn't happen with him, it'll be with someone else."

Shirley put the apple tart in the oven and set the timer.

"Let's open a good bottle of wine to celebrate your new life."

They were toasting Joséphine's newfound boldness when Gary entered the kitchen, followed by Hortense. He had a motorcycle helmet under his arm.

"Have you finished your tarts, Mummy?" he asked, giving his mother a kiss. "I can deliver them for you, if you like. I borrowed a friend's scooter."

"Gary, I don't want you riding scooters. They're too dangerous!" Shirley slapped the tabletop. "I've told you a hundred times!"

"I'll be along, and I'll keep an eye on him," Hortense said.

"Right! With you behind him he'll drive with his head screwed on backward. No thanks! I'll handle the pies on my own, or Joséphine will go with me. Okay, Jo?"

Joséphine nodded. The teenagers looked at one another and rolled their eyes.

"Is there any tart left over?" Gary asked. "I'm starving!"

"Enunciate when you speak, honey, I can't understand a word you're saying. You can have that little piece there; it's overcooked. Do you want some too, Hortense?"

She wet the tip of her finger and picked up some crumbs.

"Pie makes you fat," she said.

"You've got nothing to worry about," Joséphine said, smiling.

"Mom, to stay thin you have to watch what you eat all the time. Come on, Gary, let's go try the scooter. Shirley, I promise we won't do anything stupid."

"Where are you going?"

"Iris suggested that we come see her at Studio Pin-up. She's doing a photo shoot for *Elle* in about half an hour. Gary can take me there, and we'll hang out for a while."

"I don't like this one bit," Shirley grumbled. "You be careful, okay, Gary? Promise? And wear your helmet! And be back for dinner, the two of you!"

Gary kissed his mother on the forehead, Hortense waved at Joséphine, and the two teens bolted for the door.

"I really don't like Gary riding scooters. And also I don't like that Hortense is buzzing around him. This summer in Scotland he forgot all about her. I'd hate to see his obsession for her starting again."

Wearing a heavy tweed coat and a yellow scarf, Marcel was sitting on a bench in the courtyard. He gloomily gazed at the knotty wisteria vines as water droplets beaded on them. Josiane had been gone for two weeks, and it was tearing him to pierces.

Ginette noticed him from the warehouse window. She parked her forklift, wiped her hands on her overalls, and came outside. She gave Marcel a friendly thump on the back and sat down beside him.

"Not doing so great, huh?"

"No. I'm a total wreck."

"You shouldn't have let her go. You pushed her over the edge, Marcel! I understand her. She couldn't stand waiting anymore, poor kid. And you're the only one who can set this right. You've been talking about it since God knows when, but you don't do diddly-squat! Just file for divorce, and everything'll work out."

"I can't ask for a divorce right now, Ginette. I'm onto something really big." He paused. "I'll tell you, but you've got to promise not to say a word about it, okay? Not even to René."

"I promise. You know me, talkative as a tomb."

"I'm just about to buy the biggest home furnishings manufacturer in Asia. It's a huge deal, huge! To pull it off, I've had to mortgage everything I own. I'm so exposed I can't afford a separation from Henriette. She would immediately claim half my assets! You think I just spent a whole month in China for the fun of it?"

"Why didn't you tell Josiane this?"

Marcel frowned and hunkered down in his coat.

"Ever since that thing with Chaval, I don't trust her the way I used to. It's not that I don't love her as much, I'm just more careful. So I'd rather she think I'm being a coward."

"Well, she sees you shitting bricks whenever you're around Henriette. She figures you'd never dare leave her."

"Once everything's signed, sealed, and delivered, I'll be able to do as I please. I made sure to structure the deal so Henriette won't have anything to do with the new organization; no share of the profits, no say in the management. But I'll give her a nice allowance, and I'll let her have the apartment. She'll lack for nothing, believe me. I won't be an asshole about it."

"I know, Marcel. You're a good guy."

"Yeah, but if I don't have Josiane, what's the point?"

He bent down and picked up a dead leaf, twirled it between his fingers, then tossed it to the ground.

Ginette stuffed her hands in the pockets of her coveralls and took a deep breath.

"Okay, Marcel, listen to me. I have good news and bad news. Which do you want first?"

"The bad news. The way things are going . . ."

"The bad news is, I have no idea where Josiane is. Not a clue."

Marcel slumped, his head between his knees. He waited for a moment, then sat up.

"So what's the good news?" he asked numbly.

"The good news is, she's pregnant. Three months. She was about to tell you before you had that fight."

Marcel's jaw dropped. He looked as innocently surprised and delighted as a child. He grabbed her hand so hard she winced.

"Say that again, Ginette! Say it again!"

"She's pregnant, Marcel. And she's over the moon. She found out soon after you left for China. If Henriette hadn't brought in the photo of that Russian babe, she would've shouted it over the phone so loud, it would've blown your eardrums."

"She's pregnant! Oh my God, she's pregnant! I'm going to be a dad, Ginette, do you realize? Oh my God!"

Marcel had his arms around Ginette and was rubbing her head.

"Calm down, Marcel. Calm down! And leave me some of my hair."

"This changes everything! I'd given up. I stopped working out and taking my vitamins. As of today, I'm starting again. If she's pregnant, that means she'll come back. I've got everything we need in my office—crib, stroller, breast pump, baby monitors. I even have an electric train! Josie knows this. She'll come back. She can't keep all that happiness to herself. She knows how much this kid means to me."

Ginette looked at him and grinned. Marcel's joy was so touching. But she wasn't so sure that Josiane would be coming back. The woman didn't scare easily, and raising a child on her own didn't frighten her. She'd probably been saving her salary, and with what Marcel had given her over the years, she would be okay.

Before they went back to work, Ginette made Marcel swear not to say anything to Josiane in case she decided to come out of hiding.

"Cross your heart, Marcel?"

He nodded, and put a finger to his smiling lips.

"But promise you'll let me know the moment she calls you," he said.

"Come on, Marcel! She's my friend. I'm not going to give her away!"

"You don't have to tell me where she is. Just say something like, 'Oh, by the way, Josiane called and she's doing fine. She gained five pounds, her back aches, she's craving candied chestnuts.' Things like that. And don't forget to ask her if her belly is pointed out or spread sideways. The first shows it's a boy, and the second, a girl. Oh, and tell her to eat well—plenty of red meat—and to go to bed early. And to sleep on her back so she doesn't crush the baby. And to take it easy!"

"Listen, Marcel, I had three of 'em, and I survived. Calm down. And now I'm going back to work. Last I heard, you don't pay me to stand around waiting by the phone."

Marcel abruptly stood up, wrapped his arms around a branch of the wisteria vine, and kissed it. Raindrops ran down his cheeks. It looked as if he was crying for joy.

Iris threw the magazine onto the coffee table and frowned. She'd been set up. She had invited the writer to her home for the interview; she had Carmen serve tea on the big wooden tray and treated the woman to lemon meringue pie. She answered her questions calmly and objectively. Everything had gone perfectly, or so she'd thought. But Iris's nonchalance had been seen as arrogance.

She practically calls me a nouveau riche show-off, she fumed, rereading the article. They were always the same old questions: How did relations between men and women in the twelfth century differ from today? What did women suffer from most in those days? Are they really happier in the twenty-first century than in the twelfth? What has really changed? In the end, doesn't modernity and equality between the sexes wind up killing passion?

"Women don't have any more emotional security than they did in the past," Iris said. "They just deal with it better, that's all. The only real security would come from turning our backs on men altogether—not needing them anymore. But that would be a kind of death. At least that's how I see it."

What was so bad about that? she wondered. *And it wasn't the least bit arrogant.*

"There is no ideal man," Iris had continued. "The ideal man is the one you're in love with. He can be eighteen or eighty-eight—there's no rule, as long as you love him. I don't know any ideal men. I know men. Some I love, others I don't."

"Could you fall in love with an eighteen-year-old?"

"Why not? When you're in love, age doesn't count."

"How old are you?"

"I'm as old as the man I love wants to think I am."

Iris had struggled to hide her annoyance.

For the next novel, Joséphine will have to work in a more sophisticated vein, she thought. *This business about dying husbands making Florine rich one after the other is all well and good, but it reads like chick lit. No wonder people think I'm a bimbo.*

She kicked at the pile of magazines on the floor. *Next time, I want them to talk to me like a real writer. Stop asking these idiotic questions. What do I know about relations between men and women? I've been married for fifteen years, and been so faithful it's bored me to tears.*

She had to admit that she didn't even know where the only man she'd ever loved was. The press said Gabor was always off someplace between London, New York, and Budapest; maybe Mali. He wandered wherever he pleased, and probably slept with anyone he liked. Stopped filming when he got death threats, and came skipping back home to actors who adored him and would do whatever he said.

I see he's still wearing the same old jeans and knitted cap, thought Iris. *That's what I should have told that idiot! That the handsome, famous movie director Gabor Minar was my lover, and that I still love him.*

And she was finally going to see him again.

It was Philippe who had suggested they go to New York for the film festival, where Gabor would be the guest of honor. Iris pulled her shawl tightly around her. *Is it Gabor's love I miss, or is it the fame, the celebrities, and the glitter? After all, he was a nobody when we met.*

She drove that thought from her mind. She and Gabor were made for each other. Her marriage to Philippe had been the mistake.

I'm going to see him again, she thought. *I'm going to see him, and my life will change. What's fifteen years of absence when we loved each other the way we did? He won't be afraid. He'll carry me off and smother me with kisses, the way he did when we were students at Columbia.*

She snuggled in her shawl and admired her perfectly manicured nails.

At the Hotel George V, Josiane had developed a routine. She woke up every morning around nine, had room service bring her breakfast, stepped on the bathroom scale and noted her weight, sprayed herself with Chance by Chanel, then went back to bed to listen to her horoscope on the radio. The astrologer was never wrong, and always gave her a feel for what the day would bring. Josiane ate a few croissants. She couldn't bring herself to eat eggs, even though her gynecologist urged her to have protein in the morning.

"Those greasy things may be fine for the English," she said aloud, "but I can't stomach 'em." Having no other company, Josiane had gotten into the habit of talking to herself.

She had the newspapers sent up with breakfast. After leafing through them, she would turn on the TV, stretch her arms a little out on the balcony, and take a shower.

Later, she went down to the Restaurant des Princes, where she ordered the most extravagant dishes on the menu. She wanted to taste things she'd never tried before.

"This is my education," she told herself as she bit into another blini with caviar. "I'm here to forget my troubles, and eating helps."

In the afternoons, Josiane went out for a walk, wearing the mink coat she'd bought one day when she'd been window shopping on avenue George-V. What fun, she remembered, to see the look of surprise on the salesgirl's face when she pulled out her platinum credit card and pointed to the coat, saying, "I want that." She enjoyed revisiting the event, like a scene from a movie.

Josiane strolled down the avenue, holding the soft fur collar to her cheeks, and turned onto avenue Montaigne. She whipped out the platinum card at the slightest temptation. It tickled her no end to see the same pinched expressions on the clerks' faces. Only one gave her a big smile, saying, "You're going to love this sweater, madame!" Josiane asked the saleswoman's name—Rosemary—and bought her a beautiful cashmere scarf on the spot. They became pals, and after work, Rosemary would join her for dinner at the Restaurant des Princes.

Josiane was happy to have the company. She sometimes felt lonely, especially at night. And she wasn't the only one, she noticed. There were lots of lonely hearts living "chez George," as she called the hotel. From time to time Rosemary would stay the night. She would put her head against Josiane's stomach and speculate whether it was a boy or a girl. They would try to think of names. "If it's a boy, he'll be Marcel. If it's a girl, I get to choose."

"Where do you get all the money?" Rosemary asked, disconcerted by her friend's spending.

"From my sweetie. He gave me a platinum card one Christmas Eve when he ditched me to go spend it with the Toothpick, as usual."

"What's he like, this Marcel of yours?"

"He's no spring chicken, but I like him. We both come from the streets."

"You gonna stay here a long time?"

"Until I get the call from the big guy. The day I know he's finally dumped that bitch. Then I'll come back, same way I left, with my little suitcase."

"And your mink coat."

"I want my baby surrounded by comfort. Even squeezed in my belly, I want him to be in the lap of luxury."

"You know what? You're gonna be an amazing mom."

Josiane loved hearing that.

Returning mink-clad from her daily stroll one day, she spotted Bruno Chaval standing at the hotel bar. She came up behind him and put her hands over his eyes.

"Guess who?" she shouted. Josiane was happy to see a familiar face—even Chaval's. "Buy a girl a drink?"

He glanced at the entrance to the bar, then at his watch, and waved her to a stool.

"What brings you here?" Josiane asked.

"I'm waiting for someone."

"Is she late?"

"She's always late. So, what are you up to?"

"I'm living here in the hotel."

"What? Did you win the lottery?"

"Almost. I hit the jackpot, sort of!"

"Oh, yeah? Who's the guy?"

"Santa Claus!"

As Josiane hoisted herself onto the bar stool her coat opened, revealing her round belly.

"Hey, you've got a bun in the oven! Congratulations! So, you left Casamia?"

"Yeah. My boyfriend doesn't want me to work anymore. Wants me to take it easy."

"Did you hear about old man Grobz?"

Josiane's heart missed a beat. Something had happened to Marcel!

"What? Did he . . . die?"

"Of course not, dummy! Don't you know? He just pulled off the deal of the century. He bought the world's largest manufacturer of home goods. It was like a mouse swallowing an elephant, and nobody saw it coming. Old Grobz must've had the deal cooking for months."

Suddenly, Josiane understood everything. Marcel hadn't been afraid of the Toothpick, he'd just been waiting for this deal to go through. Until everything was signed, Henriette had him by the short hairs, she realized. *And now he's beat her. What a guy! And to think I ever doubted him!*

Josiane ordered a whiskey straight up, apologized to Junior for the alcohol, and drank to her man's success.

Chaval, on the other hand, wasn't doing so well. He sat slumped on his stool, and kept glancing anxiously at the front door.

"Come on, Chaval, buck up. You never knuckled under to a woman before!"

"Josiane, if you only knew. I can barely drag myself out of bed in the morning. I didn't realize it could be so bad."

"Breaks my heart, Chaval."

"Yeah, well, shit happens."

"But things work out in the end. I'm drinking to things working out. And to think I used to be crazy about you!"

Josiane asked the front desk to prepare her bill for the next day. Then she went up to her room to take a bath.

She was relaxing in the tub, popping soap bubbles and talking to the mirrors about her future happiness, when she suddenly felt something kick inside her. For a moment, she was so happy she couldn't breathe, then tears started rolling down her cheeks, and she whooped for joy.

Chapter 17

♦　♦　♦

*L*egs were parading past Joséphine's face: black legs, beige legs, white legs, green legs, plaid legs. If she craned her neck, she could see polo shirts, jackets, raincoats, overcoats.

Joséphine and Hortense were sitting in the first row at the fashion show, right below the runway. The models were passing by them close enough to touch.

Before Iris left for New York, she told Jo she had two tickets to the Jean-Paul Gaultier men's fashion show at the Intercontinental Hotel. "Why don't you go, and take Hortense? It would interest her, and maybe it'll give you inspiration for the next novel. We aren't going to stay in the Middle Ages forever, are we, darling? Let's skip ahead a few centuries for the next one."

Jo glanced at her daughter. Hortense had her sketchpad out, and was carefully jotting down details of linings, sleeves, shirt collars, and the occasional necktie. *I didn't know men's fashion interested her so much*, Jo thought. Hortense's solid work ethic always surprised her.

I'm definitely not writing another book for Iris! she thought.

In interviews, Iris had started spouting nonsense. Now she was giving out recipes and beauty tips, and recommending charming hotels in Ireland. Joséphine was mortified. *I just yielded to the temptation of easy money.* She sighed. *On the other hand, life has certainly become pleasant.* At Christmas she would take the girls somewhere sunny, someplace picked out of a glossy travel brochure.

The sound of Hortense turning the pages of her sketchbook brought Joséphine's thoughts back to the runway. A tall man with brown hair came out, modeling a suit. He walked straight down the runway, seemingly oblivious to the crowds at his feet. It was Luca! He strode along, his enigmatic face seemingly unconnected to the rest of his body. *Maybe modeling is what gives him that aura of mystery,* thought Joséphine.

When the show was over, the models came out to wave good-bye. They gathered around Gaultier, who was bowing with his hand on his heart. The atmosphere onstage was festive and relaxed. Luca was standing just a few feet away. Jo reached out and called his name.

"You know him?" Hortense asked.

"Yes, I do. Luca! Luca!" Jo called. He turned to her, and their eyes met, but he showed neither surprise nor pleasure at seeing her.

"Luca! That was wonderful! Bravo!"

He gave her a cold, distant look, the kind you might give a cloying admirer to keep them at a distance.

"Luca! It's me, Joséphine!"

He turned away and joined the rest of the models as they waved and headed backstage.

"He doesn't know you from Adam!" said Hortense.

"Of course he does. It's him!"

"You mean the Luca you went to the movies with?"

"Yes."

"He's totally hot!"

Joséphine sat back down, her feelings in a whirl.

"He didn't recognize me. He didn't *want* to recognize me."

"He probably just didn't expect to see you here, that's all. Put yourself in his place."

"But the other evening in Montpellier, he kissed me." Joséphine was so upset that she forgot she was talking to her daughter.

"Whoa! You, Mom? You've been kissing him?"

"That's all we did. After the conference he kissed me and said I was wonderful, that I made him feel calm, that he felt good around me . . ."

"You sure you haven't been working a little too hard?"

"No. It's him, it's Luca. The one who takes me to the movies. At the library, we have coffee together. He's writing a thesis about tears in the Middle Ages."

"You're losing it! Come back to earth. What would such a gorgeous hunk be doing with a woman like you? I mean, come on, Mom!"

Joséphine started picking at her nails. "That's what I keep asking myself. That's why when we were in Montpellier I didn't let it go any further. I was afraid I was too ugly."

"You turned him down?" exclaimed Hortense. "You've got to be kidding!"

Hortense was fanning herself with her sketchbook. Joséphine

remained slumped in her chair. Overhead, the ceiling lights were being turned off one by one.

"C'mon, let's go," said Hortense, tugging at her mother's sleeve. "Everyone's gone."

A buffet had been set up at the far end of a large red and gold lounge. Hortense suggested they get some orange juice or a glass of champagne.

"I think I want to go splash some water on my face," said Jo. "Let's meet in the lobby in fifteen minutes."

"Half an hour?"

"All right, half an hour, but no more. I need to get home."

"You're no fun at all! The one time we come out from under our rock—"

"Half an hour, Hortense, not a minute more."

Hortense shrugged and slunk off, muttering, "What a total drag!"

Joséphine found the bathroom, which turned out to be the most luxurious she'd ever seen. A small vestibule labeled "Powder Room" led to four pearl-gray doors with pink filigree trim. Jo pushed one at random and entered a round room, all marble. It had a deep sink, soft towels, a bottle of eau-de-toilette, bars of packaged soap, hand cream, and hairbrushes.

In the mirror, Joséphine looked haggard, and her lips were trembling. She filled the basin and plunged her face into the cold water. *Forget Luca*, she told herself. *Forget his I-don't-know-you look. If I hurt myself now, fill my lungs with air so that the pressure's enough to pop my eardrums, maybe the physical pain will replace the mental pain.*

It was what she used to do as a child. When she felt sad, she would hurt herself. She would lock herself in her room and pinch herself hard, or burn herself with matches, or jab a pencil point under her fingernail. She would then console herself. And it worked. In a cold fury, she would take out her notebooks and return to her schoolwork.

She would go join Hortense and stop thinking about Luca.

Jo plunged her face into the water again and held her breath as long as she could. Then she stayed under some more, gripping the edges of the sink. She began swallowing water, but kept her face down. Now blood was pounding in her ears, hammering at her temples.

When she yanked her head out of the sink, water splashed everywhere, drenching the immaculate white towels and the packages of soap. Jo was choking, suffocating, gasping for air. In the gilt mirror she saw the pale face of a drowned woman, and the memories suddenly came flooding in.

Daddy . . . Daddy's arms . . . Daddy yelling, "You're a criminal!" And Jo coughing up salt water and sobbing.

She shuddered as it all came back to her.

It was on the beach in the Landes that summer afternoon. She had gone swimming with her mother and sister. Her father didn't know how to swim, and stayed on the beach. Henriette dove into the surf with the girls. "Don't go out too far!" her father, Lucien, cried. "The currents are dangerous!"

Her mother was an excellent swimmer. When they were little, Iris and Jo would watch her in the water, mute with admiration. She had taught them how, and took them out in all kinds of weather. "There's nothing better than swimming to build character," she would say.

The sea was calm that day, and they were floating on their backs, kicking lazily. On the beach, Jo's father started waving his arms. Henriette looked at the shore. "We're being carried out," she said. "We better go back. Your father might be right; the sea can be dangerous here." They headed toward the shore, but the current started carrying them away. The wind had picked up, and threatening whitecaps appeared.

Iris started crying. "I can't do it, Mommy! I can't do it."

"Be quiet!" Henriette shouted through gritted teeth. "Stop crying! Crying won't help. Just swim!"

Joséphine could see fear on her mother's face.

The wind started to blow harder. Now they were struggling. The girls wrapped their arms around Henriette's neck. The waves were whipping them, the salt water stinging their eyes.

Suddenly Joséphine felt her mother shove her away. "Let go of me!" she shouted. Then she grabbed Iris and started swimming toward shore, holding the dazed girl under her arm. She swam sidestroke, head underwater except to breathe, kicking powerfully with her legs. Every stroke left Joséphine farther behind. Her mother didn't turn around.

Jo watched as Henriette fought to get through the surf line. She kept being knocked back, but was eventually able to drag her unconscious daughter ashore.

On the beach, her father was yelling now. Jo felt sad for him, and started swimming sidestroke like her mother, one hand out front reaching for the shore, ducking her head under with each kick. By the time she got to the surf line, the waves were bigger than ever, and she couldn't push through. Finally a wave lifted her up and slammed her down right in front of her father. He had waded in up to his waist, calling her name. He pulled her out of the waves and raced up the beach, carrying her. He was screaming, "You're a criminal! A criminal!"

She couldn't remember what happened next.

And no one ever spoke about it again.

Joséphine looked at the drowned woman in the gilt mirror.

What are you so scared of? she asked her reflection. *You should have died that day, but you got through it. A hand reached out and set you back on dry land. So don't be afraid. You're not alone.*

And she suddenly knew it was true; she wasn't alone.

Joséphine dried her face, fixed her hair, and powdered her nose.

A girl was waiting for her out in the lobby. Her own daughter, her love.

Ever since that day in the Landes, Jo had worked, and worked hard. She had thrown herself into her studies and built herself a life. Another wave had swept Antoine away, but she'd survived. And there would be more waves, some that would carry her off, some that would bring her back. *That's life*, she told her reflection. *Waves and more waves.*

Joséphine looked at the woman in the mirror and smiled. Then she took a deep breath and went out to find Hortense.

It was Sunday evening, and their flight back to Paris had just taken off from JFK. Philippe looked at his wife, stretched out on the seat next to his. They had hardly spoken since the gala dinner at the Waldorf-Astoria that ended the New York Film Festival.

With her eyes closed, Iris looked like any other elegant woman in first class, comfortably settled under her blanket. But Philippe knew Iris wasn't asleep. She was probably going over the events of the previous night.

I know everything, Iris, he wanted to tell her. *I know, because I arranged it all.*

In the limo that had taken them into Manhattan from Kennedy two days earlier, Iris had held his hand and chattered like a little girl: "How bright the weather is, for November . . . Look at that billboard! . . . What a funny-looking house!"

At the Waldorf, she grabbed the Arts section of the *Times*, which duly noted Gabor Minar's arrival in New York. "The only thing the great European director lacks," said the article, "is a contract with a major American studio. That may not be long in coming, because Minar is rumored to be meeting with a certain well-known producer." Other papers—the *Wall Street Journal*, the *New York Post*—had similar articles. Iris read them from beginning to end, barely looking up to answer Philippe's questions.

"Which movies do you want to see?" he asked, studying the festival program.

"You choose. I trust you," she replied with a distracted smile.

Gabor was supposed to speak after the screening of his film, but when the lights came on, one of the organizers announced that the director wouldn't be there after all. A murmur of disappointment ran through the audience. Turns out Gabor had spent the night partying in a Harlem jazz club.

"You can never count on Minar," said one disgruntled producer. "You have to cater to his every whim."

"Maybe that's why he makes such powerful movies," another remarked.

At breakfast the next day, Gabor's no-show was on everybody's lips. That afternoon Philippe and Iris went to see more films. Iris fidgeted in her seat, and sat up every time a latecomer came in. Philippe could feel her body tense with expectation.

Gabor was the guest of honor at the gala dinner that night, and Iris lost herself in anxious preparations. This dress or that? These shoes or those? Which of these jewels, if any? She finally settled on a violet taffeta evening gown that accentuated her eyes, long neck, and graceful posture. To Philippe, she looked like a sinuous jungle vine. Iris hummed to herself as she left their suite and ran to the elevator, the folds of her dress flapping behind her.

When Gabor entered the ballroom, everybody stood and applauded, their resentment forgotten. Suddenly, everyone was praising his movie: *magnificent, sublime, compelling, unnerving!* He strode in, surrounded by his actors. A disheveled giant, he was wearing a pair of old jeans, a leather jacket, and motorcycle boots, his ever-present wool cap set firmly on his head. He bowed with a smile. When he removed his cap, his matted hair sprang free, and he patted it into place.

He crossed the room to the table where Philippe and Iris were sitting with Gabor's actors, and took his seat. Iris was on the edge of her chair, her neck arched, her gaze bent toward him like a bow. One by one, Gabor acknowledged each guest at the table with a nod. When he came to Iris, he looked hard at her for a few seconds as she leaned toward him, trembling. The other guests exchanged surprised glances.

"Irish! Irish!" he suddenly shouted. "Irish! You here! Unbelievable! Such a long time!"

She stood up, beaming with joy, and he took her in his arms.

Everybody watched Gabor Minar kissing Iris Dupin. In his arms, she accepted the room's silent homage as if she belonged to him. The world had been righted, the past repaired. She was gazing at him in a way that Philippe would never forget. It was the look of a woman finally coming home, home to her man. Iris's great blue eyes devoured him; her hands fit naturally into his.

Then Gabor loosened his bear hug, and introduced a slender blonde in a colorful gypsy skirt—a shy beauty standing in the shadow of a giant.

Gabor put his arm around the smiling woman's shoulder and said, "This is Elisa, my wife."

Iris's eyes widened in astonishment.

"You're . . . *married*?" she blurted, unable to keep a tremor from her voice.

He laughed.

"Yes, and I have three kids!"

Then Gabor released Iris the way you might put down a valuable object you'd been admiring, and seated his wife next to him. Other people came over to say hello, and Gabor stood and hugged each of them with the same enthusiastic warmth. "Hey, Jack!" "Hi, Terry!" "Hey, Roberta!" He would take them in his arms, practically lifting them off the ground, momentarily making each one feel as if he or she were the most important person on earth. Then he would turn and introduce his wife.

Iris sat down. She didn't say another word for the rest of the evening.

And now she was sleeping—or pretending to—in the first-class Air France cabin. *It's going to be a rough homecoming for her*, thought Philippe. *But a whole new chapter for me.*

John Goodfellow had been masterful in setting everything up. He had patiently tracked Minar's wanderings and finally got confirmation that the director would be at the Waldorf-Astoria dinner. Stage-managing the encounter between Gabor and Iris had taken two years and three previous failures, at Cannes, Deauville, and Los Angeles. Through others, Goodfellow promised Gabor and his producer a meeting at the Waldorf with the head of a major American studio. Then, to persuade the L. A. honcho to come to New York, he dangled the possibility of Gabor Minar directing the studio's next picture. He arranged to have these fictions quietly passed along by carefully chosen intermediaries. But the whole scheme would have collapsed if the wayward director had failed to show up.

The morning after the gala, Philippe and Goodfellow met in a quiet café on Lexington Avenue near Forty-eighth Street.

"You did a great job, Johnny!"

"Thanks, Philippe. It took some doing. I've never seen a man who was so hard to keep track of, and I've been doing this for a while, as you know."

Goodfellow ordered orange juice and coffee, then glanced around and lowered his voice.

"His wife is quite a beauty, isn't she? But she looks exhausted. She'd like them to settle down somewhere. She's a smart woman, and has him figured out. Knows how he operates, and stays in his shadow. Never a photo of her or their kids in the press. Hardly anyone knows he's married. And behind Minar's bohemian facade you'll find a faithful husband. He's completely absorbed in his work, doesn't screw around. Oh, maybe the odd bit of crumpet—you know, a quickie with a script or makeup girl—but nothing to hurt his relationship with his wife. Deeply respects her. Loves her. She's his alter ego." Goodfellow chuckled. "It might surprise you, but I think the fellow's a romantic."

He paused. "So, Philippe, do you have any more work for me?"

"Sorry, John, but no. I have only one wife. And I'm not sure for how much longer."

They both laughed.

"How did she take it?"

"Total silence. No reaction. She hasn't said a word since last night."

"This whole thing has been awfully hard on you, hasn't it?"

"You have no idea what it's like to be in some sort of weird threesome—and with a ghost, to boot! Iris idealized him so much! Minar was perfect: handsome, intelligent, famous, engaging, fascinating . . ."

"And a slob. He really should clean himself up a little."

"Oh, that's just the English gentleman in you, holding your nose. Minar is too busy communing with his soul to pick up the dry cleaning!"

"I've enjoyed working with you, Philippe. I'd be very sorry if this were good-bye."

"Whenever you're in Paris, let me know, and I'll treat you to the best lunch in town. I mean it."

"I know. You're a man of your word."

"Thanks, Johnny."

They finished their breakfast talking about movies and about Goodfellow's wife, Doris, who complained that she and the kids never saw him. Then they shook hands and parted. Watching Goodfellow walk away, Philippe felt a twinge of regret. He would miss their meetings at Roissy; they had a slightly clandestine feeling that he enjoyed.

On the plane, Iris stirred in her sleep and muttered something Philippe didn't catch. There was just one last lie, one final illusion, for him to deal with: *A Most Humble Queen*. He now knew that Joséphine had written it, and not Iris.

Before flying to New York, Philippe had phoned Joséphine to see if she could translate another contract. She'd turned him down gently.

"I have to get back to my research dossier," she said.

"Your what?"

"My postdoc scholarship work. You know, for my professorship."

"What do you mean, you have to 'get back' to it? Had you put it aside?"

Joséphine paused before answering.

"I have to watch what I say with you, don't I, Philippe? Are you this tough on everyone?"

"Only with people I love, Jo."

An embarrassed silence followed. To Philippe, Joséphine's shy awkwardness had become a grace. He missed her. Sometimes he would dial her number, let the phone ring once, and hang up.

Philippe looked at the beautiful woman asleep beside him. His relationship with Iris was going to end soon, and he would have to handle that very carefully. He didn't want to lose his son to her.

"You never cease to amaze me!" exclaimed Shirley. "You stick your head in a sink, and your whole life flashes before your eyes! Just like that, with the touch of a magical lav!"

"I swear that's how it happened. Well, to be perfectly honest, it's happened before. Little bits would come back to me like pieces from a puzzle, but the central meaning was always missing."

"That mother of yours, what a bitch!"

"I don't care. I survived."

"Yes, but at what cost?"

"I'm so much stronger now, I can let all that go. It's a gift from heaven, you know."

"Stop talking to me about heaven with that beatific look on your face!"

"I'm sure a guardian angel watches over me."

"And what has your guardian angel been up to these past few years? Sewing new wings?"

"He taught me patience and endurance. He gave me the courage to write a book, and gave me the money from it. Now I don't have to worry about the day-to-day. You don't need money, by any chance? Because I'm going to become very rich, and I don't plan on being stingy."

"Don't worry, I'm loaded."

Shirley restlessly crossed and uncrossed her legs. The two women were at the hairdresser's, getting their highlights done again. With silver foil pleats all over their heads, they looked like Christmas trees.

"What about the stars—do you still talk to them?"

"I speak directly to God when I speak to them. When I have a problem, I pray and ask him to help me, and he does. He always answers me."

"Jo, you're going a little overboard there. Luca gives you the cold shoulder, you lose your mind, you stick your head in a sink, and you come out cured of an ancient trauma. Are you getting yourself mixed up with Saint Bernadette?"

"Here's another way of looking at it: Luca gives me the cold shoulder, I think I'm going to die, I relive being abandoned as a child, and I put the pieces together."

"Have you heard from Antoine?"

"He e-mails the girls. Always tells them the same old crocodile stories. At least he's getting paid and is repaying the loan. Antoine doesn't live his life, he dreams it."

"He's going to hit a wall one of these days."

"I don't wish that on him. Anyway, Mylène will be there to help him."

They were about to begin singing Mylène's praises when it was time to take out their silver foils.

Joséphine insisted on paying. Shirley refused. They quarreled at the register, much to Denise's amusement. Jo won.

The two women walked down the street, admiring their reflections in the store windows.

"Do you remember, a year ago, when you dragged me kicking and screaming to have my highlights done for the first time? And we were mugged on this very street."

"I came to your rescue!"

"And I was amazed at your strength. Shirley, please tell me your secret. I can't stop thinking about it."

"Just ask God. He'll tell you."

"Don't you go making fun of God! Just tell me, please. I tell you things, I trust you all the time, but you don't say a thing."

Shirley turned around and gave Joséphine a serious look.

"It's not just about me, Jo. I'd be putting others at risk. And when I say risk, I mean great, earthshaking danger."

"I've known you for eight years, Shirley. No one's ever put a knife to my throat for information about you."

"That's true."

"So?"

"No. Please don't insist."

They walked along in silence. Joséphine slipped her arm under Shirley's and leaned against her friend's shoulder.

"Why did you tell me that you were rich, earlier?"

"Did I say that?"

"Yes. I said I'd help you out if you ever needed it, and you said you were loaded."

"See how tricky words are? Once you get close to someone, you let yourself go. Anyway, you'll discover the truth all on your own someday—probably in some fancy washbasin!"

They burst out laughing.

Sitting on the doorstep in front of Shirley's apartment was a man dressed all in black. He saw them coming but didn't stand up.

"Oh my God!" Shirley whispered in dismay. "Just act natural and smile. You can speak to me, he doesn't understand French. Can Gary stay with you tonight?"

"No problem."

"Can you also watch out for him, and make sure he doesn't come to my flat, but goes straight to your place? This bloke mustn't know that Gary is living with me. He thinks he's in boarding school."

"Okay."

Shirley went up to the man, who was still sitting, and as casually as possible said, "Hi, Jack. Why don't you come in?"

Later, when Jo mentioned the man in black, Gary immediately got the picture.

"I have my backpack, so I can go straight to school tomorrow. Tell Mum not to worry."

Zoé was intrigued and asked questions during dinner. She'd come home before Gary and Hortense and had glimpsed the man in black sitting by the front door.

"Is that man your dad?"

"Zoé, be quiet!" Jo snapped.

Zoé nibbled at a bite of gratin Dauphinois and set her fork down, looking sad.

"I really miss Daddy. I liked it better when he was here. It's no fun without him around."

"You're such a drag, Zoé!" said Hortense.

"I'm always afraid he'll get eaten by the crocodiles."

"They didn't eat you last summer, did they?"

"No, but I was very careful."

"Well, Dad is being really careful, too."

"Sometimes he's absentminded. And he spends a lot of time staring into their eyes. He says he's teaching himself to read their minds."

"You don't know what you're talking about!"

Hortense asked Gary if he wanted to earn some pocket money modeling for Dior.

"They're looking for tall, romantic-looking teens to model their new collection, and Iris mentioned you. Remember when we went to see her at Studio Pin-up? She thought you were very handsome."

"I'm not sure it's my thing. I want to be the guy who takes the pictures."

"We can go back, if you want. I'll ask her."

With dinner over, Joséphine cleared, Gary loaded the

dishwasher, and Hortense wiped the table. Zoé just stood there with tears in her eyes, murmuring, "I want my Daddy."

Joséphine took her in her arms and carried her to bed, pretending to complain about how heavy she was, what a big girl she was, how she was so beautiful that she felt she was carrying a star in her arms. Zoé rubbed her eyes.

"Do you really think I'm beautiful, Mommy?"

"Of course, my love. Sometimes I look at you and I wonder, 'Who is this beautiful girl who's living right here in my very own house?' "

"As beautiful as Hortense?"

"As beautiful as Hortense. As elegant and irresistible as Hortense. The only difference is that she knows it, and you don't."

"It's hard to be little when you have a big sister." Zoé sighed, turned her head away, and closed her eyes.

Late the next morning Shirley knocked on Josephine's door.

"I finally got him to leave. It wasn't easy, but he's gone. I told him he couldn't come here anymore, that there was an agent living in the building undercover."

"And he believed you?"

"I think so." Shirley paused. "I made a big decision last night, Jo. I'm going to get out of here. It's the end of November; he won't be back right away, but I have to leave. I'm going to go hide out in Mustique."

"Mustique? The billionaire island? Mick Jagger's place?"

"Yes. I have a house there. He won't come."

"A house? That's . . . You mean you're going to move away? You're going to leave me?"

"You wanted to move too, remember."

"Hortense did. Not me."

"I know what! We'll all go to Mustique for the Christmas hols, and then I'll stay on. Gary will go back with you so he can finish his school year and pass his *baccalauréat* exam. It would be stupid for him to interrupt his studies so close to the end. Can you keep him for me?"

"I'd do anything for you, but please tell me what's going on!"

"I'll tell you on Mustique, at Christmas."

"You're not in danger, are you?"

Shirley smiled faintly.

"For now, no. Everything's fine."

Marcel rubbed his hands in glee. Everything was going according to plan. He'd expanded his empire by buying out Zang Brothers, a move that left his European competitors in the dust. He'd played his hand well. He'd also found a scheme to squeeze Henriette out of his life, and had rented a big apartment for Josiane and Marcel Junior. It was in a beautiful concierge building right next to his office. The apartment had high ceilings, Versailles-style parquet floors, and fancy fireplaces. The crème de la crème lived there: barons and baronesses, a prime minister, an eminent scholar, an important businessman's mistress.

Marcel was sure Josiane would come back! In the mornings, when he got to the office, he would climb the steps slowly, on tiptoe. Before going through the door he first closed his eyes and told himself that his little turtledove would be there, with her big tummy and her shock of blond hair, sitting at her desk, the telephone wedged against her neck.

And I won't say a thing, he thought. *I'll just hand her the keys, and she can go to the apartment and wait for me there in bed. And we'll christen the place in style.*

As it turned out, Marcel didn't have to wait that long. He came to the office one morning, and there was a very pregnant Josiane, sitting at her desk.

"Hi, Marcel. How are you?"

"You're here?" he stammered. "Is it really you?"

"The Virgin Mary in person, with a little tadpole all cozy in my tummy."

He fell to her feet, put his head on her knees. "Oh, sweetie-pie! If you only knew!"

"Actually, I do know. I met Chaval at the bar at Chez George."

She told him the whole story: flashing the platinum card all over town, hiding out at the George V, spending a month and a half ordering the most expensive dishes on the menu, the big, soft bed, the carpet so thick she didn't need to wear slippers.

"Luxury's nice, Marcel, but after a while you get tired of it. And when Chaval told me all about your big score and the situation with the Toothpick, I finally understood. You love me, and you're building an empire for Junior. I knew in a heartbeat that I was going back to you."

"Oh, sweetie-pie! It's felt so long! You have no idea."

Marcel stood up, dug around in his pocket, and dangled the keys to the new apartment in front of her.

"It's ours. It's all decorated, ready to go. All that's missing are the curtains in the bedroom."

Josiane grabbed them.

"What beautiful keys! Nice and heavy. The keys to paradise! So where's our little love nest?"

"Right next door. That way I won't have to walk very far to get into your pants and watch over the little one's progress."

He put his hand on Josiane's stomach, and his eyes filled with tears.

"Is he already moving?"

"Like a breakaway cyclist in the Tour de France."

"Can I talk to him?"

"Absolutely! But introduce yourself first. I was pretty pissed off for a while, and I didn't talk about you very much."

To her belly, Marcel said, "It's me, Junior. It's Daddy."

Jo had been working in a new library for some time now. It made her life more complicated, but she didn't risk running into Luca there. That was worth changing buses twice, and getting home later.

Jo was standing in the 174 bus, with a baby stroller jabbed into her stomach and an African woman in a *boubou* stepping on her feet, when her cell phone rang. She rummaged in her bag and found it.

"Joséphine? It's Luca."

She was speechless.

"Joséphine, are you there?"

"Yes," she mumbled.

"It's me, Luca. Where are you?"

"On the one-seventy-four bus."

"I need to talk to you."

"I don't think that's a particularly—"

"Please. Get off at the next stop. I'll meet you."

"But the thing is—"

"There's something really important I need to tell you. I'll explain. What's the name of the stop?"

"Henri-Barbusse."

"I'll be there," he said, and hung up.

Joséphine was dumbstruck. This was the first time she'd heard Luca speak in such a commanding tone. But she wasn't sure she wanted to see him again.

They met at the bus stop. Luca took her by the arm and firmly steered her to the nearest café. He took off his duffel coat and ordered two coffees.

When the waiter was gone, he steepled his fingers and spoke in a hoarse voice.

"Joséphine, if I said, 'Sweet Jesus, good Jesus, even as I desire you, even as I beg you with all of my soul, give me your holy and chaste love, let it fill me, hold me, take my entire being,' what would you say?"

"That you're quoting Jean de Fécamp."

"And how many people know who Jean de Fécamp is, other than you, me, and a few religious nuts?"

Joséphine gestured to indicate that she didn't know.

Luca's face was pale, his eyes bright. He irritably brushed a lock of hair away from his forehead.

"And do you know where I read Jean de Fécamp's prayer recently?"

"No idea."

"In Iris Dupin's book, *A Most Humble Queen*. Do you know Iris Dupin?"

"Sure, she's my sister."

"I thought as much."

He slammed his hand on the table, making the ashtray jump.

"There's no way your sister could have come up with that on her own!"

"I loaned her my notes for her book."

"Oh, did you really?" Luca looked exasperated. "Joséphine, do you remember a conversation you and I had about Saint Benedict and his penitential grace, which allowed him to shed tears daily and freely?"

"Yes, I do."

"Well, in *A Most Humble Queen*, the author repeats a story about Saint Benedict's mattress catching fire while he was praying, and how he put out the fire with his tears."

"You can find that story in lots of old books, Luca."

"No, you can't find it in old books. And do you know why? Because I made it up! It was a story I made up just for you. You seemed so scholarly, I wanted to see if I could fool you. And now I find it in a novel—*your* novel, Joséphine! Along with a couple of other passages that your sister couldn't possibly have found in a library because they came from up here." Luca tapped his temple with his finger. "That's how I figured out that you must have written the book."

Luca was squirming in his chair, fiddling with his shirtsleeves and licking his lips.

"You seem really upset about this, Luca."

"Damn right I'm upset! Guess what: I really liked you. For once, I'd met a woman who was sensitive and sweet. For once I didn't see that question in a woman's eyes, 'When are we going to bed?' I loved your shyness, your awkwardness, the way you were so formal with me, giving me only your cheek to kiss. I wasn't exactly delighted that you turned me down in Montpellier, but almost."

Luca was getting worked up. His eyes were flashing, and he was waving his arms around. He's definitely an Italian, thought Joséphine.

"I thought I'd finally met an intelligent, good-looking, thoughtful woman. And when you disappeared and I was missing you, I pick up *your* novel and read it, and there you are! I see and hear you on every page. The same restraint, the same modesty. I can even tell who inspired one of the characters. I wouldn't be a little like Thibaut the Troubadour, by any chance?"

Joséphine lowered her eyes and blushed.

"He's very attractive, so thank you. Seeing the number of pages you devote to him, I must have been in your good graces at the time."

He paused.

"I probably shouldn't say this, Joséphine, but you made me so happy, I was floating on a cloud."

"Then why did you ignore me when we saw each other at the

Jean-Paul Gaultier show? Why didn't you answer when I called out to you?"

"What are you talking about?"

"At the Intercontinental Hotel the other day. On the runway, when you looked so coldly at me. I was so hurt, I almost died!"

Joséphine could feel herself tearing up. Luca was staring at her, perplexed.

"Jean-Paul Gaultier?" he muttered. "The Intercontinental?"

Suddenly he sat bolt upright. "Vittorio! That was Vittorio you saw, not me!"

"Who's Vittorio?"

"He's my brother, my twin brother. He's a fashion model. He's the one you saw."

"A twin brother?"

"Yeah. We're almost identical, at least physically, because I get the feeling that psychologically, Vittorio's like your sister Iris. He uses me. I'm always running around after him, cleaning up his messes. He once got busted for cocaine possession, and I had to bail him out. He'll call me up from some bar, drunk out of his mind, and want me to come pick him up. Soon he'll be too old for modeling. He hasn't saved any money, and he thinks I'll take care of him. But I don't have any money either. You were smart to turn me down. I'm no prize!"

Joséphine stared at him. A twin brother! Then, as the silence between them grew longer and heavier, she mustered her courage.

"I turned you down for just one reason," she said. "Because you're so handsome, and I'm so plain. I shouldn't be telling you this, but since we're baring our souls—"

"You don't think you're good-looking?"

Joséphine shrugged shyly.

"I've been taking care of myself. I'm improving."

He reached out and stroked her cheek. Then he leaned across the table and gently kissed her.

Leaning close, he whispered, "If you only knew how happy I was to meet you! To talk to you, to walk with you, to take you to the movies. And you never asked me for anything, never pressured me in any way. I felt I was reinventing the whole concept of romance."

"Because women throw themselves at you, do they?" Joséphine asked, smiling.

"They're always in a hurry, they're eager . . . And then there's always Vittorio in the background."

"Do they mistake you for him?"

"All the time. And when I tell them I'm his twin, they ask, 'What's your brother like? Can you introduce me? Do you think I could be a model, too?' But you don't know a thing about that world, Joséphine. It's like you're from another planet. A wonderful apparition."

"Like Saint Bernadette of Lourdes?"

He smiled and kissed her again.

PART V

♦   ♦   ♦

Chapter 18

♦ ♦ ♦

"You know how I was telling you that life is like a dance partner, and that if you just relax and let go, you'll find yourself waltzing?" Joséphine asked. "Well, Luca came back to me."

The two women were lying by the pool at Shirley's place in Mustique, a strikingly modern house overlooking the Caribbean. The living room had white sofas, white rugs, and low coffee tables with magazines and photography books. Abstract paintings hung on the walls. Quiet, refined luxury. *My apartment would fit into any one of these rooms*, Joséphine thought that morning, when she climbed out of a bed with satin sheets and walked into the light-filled dining room for breakfast.

"You'll wind up convincing me, Jo," said Shirley, who was dangling a hand in the blue water of the pool. "Soon I'll be talking to the stars, too."

It was early, and the children were still asleep: Hortense, Zoé, Gary, and Alexandre, whom Joséphine had brought along as well. When Iris returned from New York she seemed disillusioned and bitter, and spent whole days locked in her study. Joséphine didn't know what happened in New York, and she didn't pry. And when Philippe asked if she could take Alex for the Christmas holidays, she agreed without questioning him. She felt it was none of her business. Iris had distanced herself, and Jo had distanced herself in turn.

Jo now glanced at the huge bay window above the terrace where they were sitting.

"Having all this, how could you stand living in Courbevoie, Shirley?"

"I was happy there. It was a change, a new life. I'm used to changing lives. I've had so many of them."

She leaned back and closed her eyes, and Joséphine fell silent. She was dying of curiosity, but she knew that Shirley would only talk when she felt like it.

The days went by, light and gay. Zoé and Alexandre spent all their time in the pool or the sea, turning into small golden fishes. Hortense worked on her tan poolside, leafing through luxury magazines. Joséphine found a box of birth control pills in her daughter's things while looking for an aspirin, but said nothing. She didn't want any more confrontations. Hortense wasn't being hostile to her anymore, but she wasn't exactly cuddly, either.

They celebrated Christmas out on the terrace under a warm, starry night. Shirley had put a present by each plate. Joséphine got a Cartier bracelet, as did Hortense and Zoé. Alexandre and Gary were given brand-new computers.

"This way," said Shirley, "you can send me photos and e-mail when we're apart."

Gary gave his mom a big kiss, and she stroked his hair.

There was a party at a house down the road, and Gary and Hortense asked if they could go. After a glance at Joséphine, Shirley said yes, and the two teens left after the cake. Zoé took a piece of it to bed with her, soon followed by Alexandre.

Shirley brought out a bottle of champagne and suggested they go down to the private beach below the house. They settled into hammocks and gazed up at the stars. Champagne flute in hand, Shirley covered her feet with her pareo and started to talk.

"Do you know Queen Victoria's story, Jo?"

"Sure. Queen of England, empress of India, grandmother of Europe, with children and grandchildren on every throne. She reigned for fifty years."

"The very one." Shirley paused. "Then you also may know that Victoria had two great loves in her life: Prince Albert, whom everybody knows about, and John Brown."

"Who was that?"

"Her Scottish gamekeeper. Victoria adored Albert, who died in December 1861 after twenty-one years of marriage. She was forty-two, the mother of nine children, the youngest of whom was four. She was also a grandmother; her oldest daughter's son Wilhelm would become kaiser of Germany.

"Victoria hated being a queen, though she played the part to perfection. She was a short, stocky woman with a mean streak, and after Albert's death, she found herself very alone. Albert had always been at her side to advise her, help her, even reprimand her at times. She didn't know how to live on her own. Fortunately, John Brown was there, loyal and attentive. Soon Victoria couldn't manage without him. He went everywhere with her. He watched over her, took care of her, even saved her from an attempt on her life.

"Their friendship soon became a scandal. People took to calling her 'Mrs. Brown.' She gave Brown a title, and bought him houses emblazoned with the royal coat of arms. She publicly called him 'the greatest treasure of my heart.' Notes written to him turned up that she'd signed 'I can't live without you. Your loving one.' People were horrified."

"You make it sound like Princess Di!" Joséphine exclaimed. She had stopped her hammock rocking so as not to miss a word.

"When Brown died in 1883, Victoria was as heartbroken as she'd been when Albert died. She had his room kept exactly as it had been, with his big kilt spread out on an armchair, and a fresh flower put on his pillow every day. She wrote a two-hundred-page book about him, and it was only with great effort that she was persuaded not to publish it. More than three hundred highly compromising letters from Victoria to Brown turned up in an attic recently. They were discreetly bought—and burned. Victoria's personal diary was entirely rewritten."

"I didn't know anything about this!"

"That's not surprising. There's the official story and the private truth. The great and good of this world are people just like us—weak, vulnerable, and most of all, very lonely."

"Even queens," Joséphine murmured.

"Especially queens."

They poured themselves a last glass of champagne.

"You've probably guessed I'm not telling you all this as a history lesson," said Shirley.

"You'll laugh, but I was just thinking about Albert of Monaco and his illegitimate son."

"I'm not going to laugh at all, Jo. I'm an illegitimate daughter."

"My God! Whose?"

"A queen's. A wonderful queen who had a beautiful love affair with her high chamberlain. That was my father. He was Scottish, too, but his name wasn't John Brown; it was Patrick. And unlike Brown, he was very discreet. No one ever knew. When he died two years ago, the queen kept up appearances. For a long time she seemed sad and distracted, but no one ever knew why."

"I remember how subdued you were when you came back from that vacation two years ago."

"It all started in late 1967. The queen found out she was pregnant, and even though she was past forty, she decided to keep the baby—me. She's a very determined woman. She loved my father, loved his gentle, attentive presence. He treated her like a woman and respected her as his queen. She was also an excellent rider, and you know that women who ride develop strong stomach muscles. Three weeks before giving birth, my mother had tea with General de Gaulle at the Elysée. From the photos, no one could tell she was about to have a baby!

"I was born in Buckingham Palace late one night. My father had his own mother come to assist in the birth, and she took me away that night. A year later, he introduced me to the palace, explaining that I was his daughter and that he was bringing me up on his own. I was happy there. And to tell you the truth, when Dad told me everything on my seventh birthday, I wasn't surprised. My mother's behavior in public and private showed how much she loved me.

"I was in the charge of a governess, Miss Barton. I loved her, but I played a million horrid pranks on her. It was when I turned fifteen that things got complicated. I started kissing boys, drinking in pubs, sneaking out at night. One morning my father said he was sending me to a posh boarding school in Scotland. I didn't understand why he was sending me away, and I resented it.

"I became a real rebel overnight. I started sleeping with every boy I met, taking drugs, even shoplifting. At twenty-one, I found myself pregnant by a fellow student. He was very handsome and charming, but when I told him he was going to be a father, he pretty much said, 'That's your problem, dear.'

"Gary's birth was a real wake-up call. For the first time in my life I was responsible for someone. I asked Dad to bring me back to London, and he found me a flat there. And then one day I went to the palace to introduce little Gary. My mother was both concerned and moved. She was angry at me for misbehaving, and upset to see me with Gary in tow. She asked me why I'd done this. I told her that I couldn't bear being sent away from her. The separation had been too hard. That's when she came up with the idea of hiring me as a bodyguard and passing me off as one of her servants."

"So that's why I saw you on television!"

"That's right. I learned self-defense and combat skills, and became a martial arts champion. It all would have worked out perfectly if I hadn't met that man."

"You mean the guy in black I saw waiting on your doorstep?"

"Yes. I fell madly in love with him, and one night I told him my secret. That was the start of all my problems. He's a terrible man, Jo, but I find him incredibly attractive physically. That's a part of me I'm not proud of. When we're apart, I can resist him. But when he's right there . . .

"Very soon, he started blackmailing me, threatening to tell the press everything. Those were the Diana years, the scandalous years, the *annus horribilis*, remember? I warned Dad, he told my mother, and they did what every royal court does when they want to hush something up: they bought the man off. That's when I moved to France. I spread out a map of Paris, took a pin, and closed my eyes. It came down on Courbevoie. Gary and I go to England during the holidays, and I'm assigned to the queen or a member of the royal family, undercover. That's where those photos of Gary with William and Harry came from."

Shirley paused.

"So now you have the whole story, pretty much."

"And Gary knows all this?"

"Yes. I did what my father did. When Gary turned seven, I told him the truth. It forced him to grow up, and it's created a strong bond between us."

"What about the man in black? Won't he keep following you?"

"When he showed up in France, I alerted MI6 and the royal secret services, and they put the screws to him. But I've decided to make a fresh start. That's why I can tell you all this. His coming to Courbevoie was the last straw. I decided I wouldn't let him terrorize me any longer. When he left my flat early that morning, I felt disgusted. Disgusted and ashamed at letting myself be manipulated all those years. Now the services will keep him away from me."

Shirley looked at the sky for a moment, then continued.

"You can send me Gary here for the holidays—and the girls too, if they want. Then in June, when Gary's in Courbevoie studying for the *baccalauréat*, I'd like to come stay with you, to be near him. Would that be okay?"

Joséphine felt so shaken by Shirley's story, it took a while before she could answer. When she did, she kept her tone light.

"Sure," she said. "You'll be a big improvement over Christine Barthillet!"

Iris stared out her bedroom window. She hated January. She hated February too, and the cold drizzle of March and April. In May her pollen allergy kicked in, and June was too hot. She hated her bedroom furniture. She wasn't looking well. Her closet was full of clothes, but she didn't have a thing to wear. Christmas had been grim. *What an awful holiday*, she thought, leaning her forehead against the glass. *Just Philippe and me sitting silently in front of the living room fireplace.*

They never spoke about New York.

They were avoiding one another. Philippe went out a lot. He might come home at 7:00 p.m., but only to spend time with Alexandre, then go out again when Alex got ready for bed. Iris didn't ask where he was going. *Philippe is living his life and I'm leading mine*, she thought. *It's always been that way, so why worry?*

She tried to put Gabor out of her mind, but every time she thought about him, something ripped at her heart.

Worse, Iris's fifteen minutes of fame were winding down. After the frenzy of the first three months, the media had moved on to other topics. She wasn't as much in demand anymore. Iris looked at her date book. *Oh, yes, here's something: a photo shoot for Gala next Tuesday. I wonder how I should dress? I bet Hortense will have some ideas.*

She turned on the TV and caught an evening talk show she'd once appeared on. A young writer was discussing his new novel, and Iris felt a pang of jealousy. The host—Iris couldn't remember her name—was saying how much she'd loved the book and its clean style: subject, verb, object. Short, fast sentences.

"That's not surprising," said the novelist. "I write so many text messages."

Iris fell back on her bed, feeling depressed. *My book isn't written like a text message. My book is real literature. What do I have in common with that nitwit?* She began to pace around her room. She had to come up with an idea.

"You aren't looking your best these days," Bérengère said at lunch the next day.

"I need to get back to my writing, and the idea terrifies me."

"Well, you've created a tough act to follow. Pulling that off a second time must not be so simple!"

"Thanks for the encouragement," snapped Iris. "I should have lunch with you more often. It does wonders for my morale."

"Listen, for the past three months you were all anyone ever talked about. You were everywhere. So it's normal to feel a bit low at the idea of shutting yourself away again."

"I want it to go on and on."

"But it has! When we walked into the restaurant just now I heard people whispering, 'That's Iris Dupin! You know, the one who wrote that novel.' "

"Yeah, but that'll stop."

"No, it won't. You'll write another one."

"It's hard. And it takes so much time."

"Well, it's either that, or do something a little crazy, like hook up with some cute young guy. Look at Demi Moore. She hardly makes movies anymore, but people still talk about her because of her young boyfriend."

"I don't know any guys like that. Alexandre's friends are too young. And there's Philippe, let's not forget!"

When their meals arrived, Iris looked at her plate in disgust.

"Eat!" said Bérengère. "You're going to end up anorexic."

"It's better for television! The camera adds twenty pounds, so it helps to be thin."

"Iris, listen to me. You'll drive yourself crazy obsessing about all that. Go back to writing. That's the best thing to do, if you ask me."

Bérengère is right, thought Iris. *I'm going to have to work on Joséphine. She's balking at the idea of writing a second book. Goes*

*all stiff when I mention it. Next Saturday I'll drive out to her place
and we'll talk. And then I'll take Hortense shopping.*

"No, Iris! Don't keep insisting. I'm not doing it again."

The two sisters were in the Courbevoie kitchen, and Joséphine was making dinner. With Gary added to the ranks, she felt
as if she were feeding an army.

"I don't get it, Jo. We've already done the hard part. We've
made ourselves a place in the sun, and you're giving it up."

"I want to write for myself."

"For yourself? You won't sell a single copy!"

"Thanks a lot!"

"I'm sorry, that's not what I mean. You just won't sell nearly
as many. Do you know what the *Humble Queen* sales are? I'm
talking real numbers, not the bullshit figures they print on the
advertising inserts."

"I have no idea."

"A hundred and fifty thousand copies in three months! And
it's still selling. And you want to stop that?"

"I just can't do it, Iris. It's made me feel dirty, like having sex
with some stranger in a dark alley."

"Do you know how much this little business is going to
earn you?"

"Sure, fifty thousand euros."

"You're way off the mark. Ten times that!"

"Oh my God!" Joséphine gasped, covering her mouth with
her hand. "What am I going to do with it?"

"Whatever you like. I don't care."

"What about taxes? Who's going to pay taxes on that much money?"

"It'll just get slipped into Philippe's return. He won't even notice!"

"Oh, no, I can't do that."

"Yes, you can. And you will, because we have a deal, and you're going to stick to it. There's no way Philippe can find out about this. He and I aren't getting along, so this really isn't the moment to tell him the whole story. Think about me, Joséphine, I'm begging you. Do you want me to get down on my knees?"

Joséphine shrugged.

"Cric and Croc clobbered the big Cruc who—"

"Forget it, Iris. The answer is no."

"Just one book, Jo, and after that I'll figure it out on my own. I'll learn to write. I'll see how you do it, I'll work with you. It'll only take you—what? Six months of your life?"

"Iris: no!"

"You're so ungrateful! I didn't keep a penny for myself, I gave it all to you. It's completely changed your life. *You've* completely changed."

"Oh, so you noticed that, too?"

Hortense stuck her head in the kitchen door. "Are you ready to go, Aunt Iris? I still have homework to do tonight. I don't want to get back too late."

Iris looked at Joséphine one last time, her hands pressed together in fervent prayer, but Jo firmly shook her head.

♦ ♦ ♦

"Are you and Mom having an argument?" asked Hortense, as she fastened her seat belt.

"I asked her to help me with my next book, but she said no." Suddenly Iris had an idea.

"Do you think you could persuade her? She loves you so much. If you ask, maybe she'll change her mind."

"Okay. I'll talk to her about it tonight."

Hortense made sure her seat belt wasn't wrinkling her brand-new Equipment shirt and turned back to Iris.

"Seems to me she ought to help you. I mean, after everything you've always done for her and for us."

Iris assumed a piteous expression. "You know, the more you help people, the less grateful they are."

"So where are we going shopping?"

"*Gala* is taking pictures of me next Tuesday, and I want to look disheveled, classy, and chic."

Hortense thought for a moment.

"Let's go to Galeries Lafayette. They have a whole floor devoted to new designers. I go there a lot. Can I come watch the photo shoot? You never know, I might hook up with some fashion editors."

"No problem."

"And bring Gary? That way, we can take his scooter."

"Sure. I'll give your names to the studio."

When Hortense got home that evening, she was laden with bags of clothes Iris had bought her as thanks for devoting the afternoon to her.

"Mom, why won't you help Iris with her book? She's done so much for us these past few years."

"That's none of your business, Hortense. It's between me and your aunt."

"But Mom, for once you can do something to help her!"

"Hortense, honey, as I said, it's none of your business. And now it's dinnertime! Call Gary and Zoé, please."

They didn't speak further about it that evening, and headed for their respective bedrooms after dinner.

Hortense had been surprised by her mother's firm tone. *That's something new*, she thought as she got undressed. She was hanging up the clothes her aunt had bought when her cell phone rang. She sprawled languidly on the bed and answered in English, which immediately alerted Zoé that something was up.

"Who was that?" Zoé asked after the call. "An Englishman?"

"You'll never guess!" replied Hortense, stretching on the bed with a graceful languor.

"If you tell me, I'll tell you an incredible secret! A real grown-up secret!"

Hortense glanced at her sister. Zoé looked serious, her eyes full of the importance of her revelation.

"That was Mick Jagger. I met him in Mustique, and we became . . . friendly."

"But he's so old and skinny! And he has big lips."

"Well, I think he's attractive. Very attractive, in fact!"

"What about the other guy, the one who always calls when I'm asleep?"

"You mean old Chaval? I dumped him. He was crying on my lap and drooling all over the place. The king of pathetic."

"Wow!" said Zoé admiringly. "That was fast!"

"You can't waste any time in life. Gotta go for what you want. So, what's your secret?"

Hortense was smirking. Whatever her sister's secret was, it couldn't possibly measure up to knowing Mick Jagger.

"I know why Mom doesn't want to help Aunt Iris write the book."

Saying this made Zoé feel very important, and she wanted to make the suspense last.

"How do you know that?"

With her sister looking at her with so much eagerness, Zoé couldn't hold it in any longer. She told Hortense the story of how she and Alexandre had been hiding in the armoire, and what they overheard.

"Uncle Philippe was telling some man that Mommy wrote the book."

"So that's why Iris is pressuring her. She doesn't just want Mom to help, she wants her to write the whole book!"

" 'Cause she never wrote the first one. Mommy wrote it. She's the best, you know, the way-best!"

"Now I get it. Thanks, Zoé-cannoli."

Zoé felt a wave of joy. Her adored older sister had called her "Zoé-cannoli," which didn't happen very often. She climbed into bed, smiling.

"I like it when you're like this with me," she said. "G'night, Hortense."

"Nighty-night."

Lying in her own bed, Hortense reflected how interesting life was becoming. Mick Jagger was phoning, her aunt was helpless without her, money would be pouring in . . . At the end of the year she'd take the *baccalauréat*, but she needed to pass with honors if she wanted to get into one of the top design schools in Paris or London. Learn and be successful; don't depend on anyone else; charm men to get ahead; have money. Life was simple when you followed the right rules.

Mom's going to earn lots of money, she thought, *but only if she owns the rights to the book. I'll have to make sure she didn't get taken for a ride! How can I do that? Who can I turn to for advice?*

She would figure something out.

Hortense shifted into her favorite position for going to sleep: on her back, arms at her sides, and legs together like a mermaid's tail—or a crocodile. She'd always liked crocodiles. They didn't scare her. She thought about her father. How life had changed since he left! *Poor Daddy . . .* she thought as she closed her eyes. Then she caught herself. *No, I can't waste my time pitying him. He'll find his own way.*

Philippe was surprised when Joséphine walked into his office. It wasn't just that she had a tan, had lost weight, and looked younger. There was something else. She no longer slouched along staring at the ground, as if apologizing for existing. She strode into the office, gave him a quick kiss, and sat down.

"There's something I need to tell you, Philippe."

He gave her a sly smile. "Are you in love, Joséphine?"

Flustered by the question, she nodded. "Is it that obvious?"

"It's written all over your face, in the way you walk, the way you sat down just now. Do I know him?"

"No."

They sat in silence for a moment, and Philippe caught a look of turmoil in Joséphine's eyes that surprised him. It eased the unexpected pang he'd felt at her news.

She took a deep breath and began. "You're not going to like what I have to tell you, and I absolutely don't want you to think that I wish Iris any harm."

She hesitated again, and Philippe wondered if she would have the courage to look him in the eye and tell him the truth about the book.

"Let me help you, Jo," he said kindly. "Iris didn't write *A Most Humble Queen*. You did."

Joséphine's jaw dropped in astonishment. "You knew?"

"I had my suspicions from the start, and they've only gotten stronger. . . . Would you like a glass of water?"

Her throat suddenly dry, Jo nodded.

Philippe asked for some water and coffee to be sent in, then told his story.

"It happened more than fifteen years ago, when I was a young lawyer. I'd practiced in France for a few years, and was doing an internship with Dorman and Connelly in New York, in their intellectual property division. Feeling pretty full of myself, as you can imagine.

"One day I got a call from a studio executive who had a problem that involved a young Frenchwoman. As he told it, a group of film students in their final year at Columbia had written a screenplay together. It won a faculty award as the year's most promising student work, and was later directed and shot by a certain Gabor Minar. The movie went on the festival circuit and won some prizes. As it happens, Iris was a student in the same group as Minar, and had participated in writing it.

"So far, so good. But then things started to go wrong.

"Iris reedited the screenplay, turned it into a full-length script, and presented it to a Hollywood studio as her own work. They loved the story and promptly offered her a contract as a screenwriter, for lots of money. This was big news, and it was all over the industry press."

"Yes, I remember," said Joséphine. "Mother was thrilled."

"And for good reason! Everything would have been fine except that one of the other students in the group heard about it. She got hold of a copy of Iris's screenplay and compared it to the group's original. She showed the studio that Iris had plagiarized it—that she was a thief. So they called my firm.

"The case intrigued me, and I went to work on it. When I met your sister, I fell in love with her, and moved heaven and earth to get her out of the jam. We hushed up the mess, and neither Minar nor any of the other students ever found out. The student who'd blown the whistle agreed to keep quiet in exchange for a wad of cash. I'd recently handled a couple of big cases and had plenty of money, so I paid her off myself."

"Because you were in love with Iris."

"Passionately." Philippe smiled ruefully. "Iris agreed to the settlement, but she was very ashamed at being caught cheating.

Your sister is a frustrated artist, and that's the worst thing in the world. So when I heard she was writing a book about the twelfth century, I knew we were going to have more problems. How did it even come about?"

Joséphine explained about Iris meeting the publisher, boasting about writing a book, and getting trapped in her lie.

"I was having money problems at the time," she said, "and I'd always wanted to write, so I agreed to the scheme. Now Iris is begging me to write another book, and I don't want to."

They looked at each other in silence. Philippe toyed with his silver pen, bouncing it on the desk over and over.

"And there's another problem."

"What is it, Jo?"

"I don't want you to pay the taxes on the *Humble Queen* royalties. Iris says I'm going to earn a lot of money. She also says that you can afford to pay the taxes, that you wouldn't notice. I can't let you do that."

He smiled at her affectionately. "That's a decent thought, and I respect you for it. But what choice do we have? If the publisher writes you a check for the royalties, word will get out, and soon everyone will know you wrote the book. Iris couldn't survive the public humiliation, believe me. She might do something very foolish."

"You really think so?"

He nodded. "I'm sure you don't want that, do you?"

"No, of course not. She's my sister. I'm grateful to her. Without her, I would never have written anything. The experience has changed me. I want to do more writing, but for my own enjoyment. If I'm successful, fine. If not, no big deal."

"You're a hard worker, Jo. Who said that genius is ninety percent sweat and ten percent talent? Iris refuses to face reality, whether it involves the book, her child, or her marriage."

He told her about the New York trip and Iris's encounter with Gabor Minar, as well as her stubborn silence since their return.

"That's a whole other story that doesn't concern you. But I don't think this is a good time to tell the world that you actually wrote the book. The rights have been sold in some thirty countries, and there's talk of a movie deal with a well-known director. Can you imagine what a scandal that would cause?"

Joséphine nodded. Philippe had stopped bouncing his pen.

"In that case, let me at least give you a big present," she said. "Take me to a gallery that has a painting or a piece of art you want, and I'll buy it for you."

"That would be very kind. Do you like art?"

"I'm more of a history and literature person. But I can learn."

He smiled, and she came around the desk to give him a kiss good-bye.

At the last minute he turned his head, and their lips unexpectedly met. Jo pulled gently back, but stroked his hair affectionately. He took her wrist and kissed it.

"I'll always be there for you, Jo, always."

"I know," she murmured. "Thank you."

Oh my God! Jo thought once she was out in the street. *Life is going to get very complicated if things like this keep happening to me!*

Feeling elated, she hailed a cab to go home.

Chapter 19

♦ ♦ ♦

The *Gala* photo shoot was wrapping up. Iris sat perched on a large white cube on a sheet of white seamless paper that ran up the brick wall of the studio. She was wearing a low-cut pink jacket with satin lapels and three enormous rose-shaped buttons. A wide-brimmed pink hat hid her short hair and brought out the blue of her eyes

"You look beautiful, Iris!" exclaimed the fashion editor.

"Thanks, Capucine, but let's not exaggerate."

"I'm serious. And I love your combining the Armani jacket and torn jeans with the big rubber boots. Very original."

"That was my niece's idea. Come introduce yourself, Hortense!"

Hortense stepped into the light and came over to meet the editor.

"Hello, Mademoiselle Cartier. I'm Hortense Cortès."

"Are you interested in fashion?"

"Yes, very much."

"Would you like to come to other shoots?"

"I'd love to!"

"Give me your cell phone number, and I'll call you."

"Can I have yours, too, in case you lose mine?"

Capucine looked at Hortense, amused by her nerve.

"Why not? You'll go far!"

The photographer had finished his pictures. But before he packed up his gear, Iris asked if he would take some shots of her with Hortense.

Hortense came over, and they posed together.

"How about Gary too?" asked Hortense.

"Sure," said Capucine. "Come on out, Gary!"

When he appeared, she gave a low whistle. "Well, aren't you the handsome one! Would you be willing to pose for us?"

"Thanks, but I'm not interested. I'd rather be taking the pictures."

After the shoot, Iris invited everyone over to the Hotel Raphael for a drink.

"I love the bar there," she said. "Are you kids joining us?"

Hortense glanced at her watch and said that they couldn't stay long. They had to get back to Courbevoie.

They walked over to the Raphael together. Capucine leaned close to the photographer and whispered, "Keep your camera handy. We've got to get some photos of the boy. He's so gorgeous, it makes my teeth hurt."

At the bar, Iris ordered a bottle of champagne. Gary and Hortense had Cokes. The photographer and the editor had a glass of champagne each, and Iris finished off the bottle. Soon she was talking and laughing loudly, swinging her legs, and jingling her bracelets.

At one point, she grabbed Gary by the neck and pulled him onto her. They almost toppled over, but he caught her in his arms. Everyone laughed, and the photographer snapped some shots.

"This is so much fun!" cried Iris, draining her glass.

Hortense stared at her aunt in embarrassment. She gave Gary a let's-get-out-of-here! look, and he got the message.

"We have to go," he said, standing up. "Joséphine is expecting us, and I don't want her to worry."

Out in the street, Gary ran his fingers through his hair. He looked uncomfortable.

"Holy cow, what was with your aunt tonight? She had her hands all over me!"

"She was drunk. Forget about it."

They got on the scooter and headed home.

For the first time in her life, Hortense felt something like pity. She was ashamed of Iris. *Mom would never have done that,* she couldn't help thinking. *She wrote the book all by herself, but she doesn't boast or make a spectacle of herself. I just wish she were tougher, and wouldn't get screwed out of her royalties.*

Suddenly Hortense had an idea. A brilliant one, if she did say so herself.

Three weeks later, Henriette was at the beauty parlor, waiting for her weekly peel and massage. Spotting Iris's name in a magazine cover line, she found a two-page spread about her.

The article headline read, "The Author of *A Most Humble Queen* in the Arms of Her Page." The subhead: "At forty-six, Iris Dupin goes out with a boy of seventeen, beating Demi Moore's record." A series of photos showed Iris leaning against a handsome teenager's chest, with her head thrown back and her eyes closed.

Henriette snapped the magazine shut and hurried out of the salon. Gilles the chauffeur wasn't there, so she dialed his cell and ordered him to come pick her up. She had barely put her phone away when she spotted a newsstand display rack given over entirely to a big photograph of Iris in the arms of her young lover.

When the car arrived, Henriette jumped into the backseat before Gilles could even open the door for her. She felt faint.

"Did you see your daughter, madame?" he asked with a big smile. "Her face is all over Paris. You must be so proud!"

"Gilles, not another word about that, or I'm going to be sick!"

She could feel a migraine coming on. Back at her building, she avoided the concierge's eye and hurried up to her apartment.

Joséphine had gone out to buy bread, and used her moment of freedom to phone Luca. The children were taking up all her time, and she and Luca could only see each other during the afternoon, when the girls were in school. He lived in a studio apartment in Asnières, on the top floor of a new building with a terrace and a view of Paris. Joséphine had stopped going to the library; she now met Luca at his apartment.

"I've been thinking of you," she said very quietly.

"Where are you?"

"Buying bread, as usual. Gary ate two whole baguettes when he got home from school."

"Tomorrow I'll serve you tea and cookies. Do you like cookies?"

At that pleasant thought, Joséphine closed her eyes, but was snapped out of her daydream when the *boulangère* asked her to take her bread and move aside so other customers could have their turn.

"I can't wait to be with you," she said, stepping outside. "Do you realize my days have become my nights lately?"

"So I'm both the sun and the moon? You flatter me!"

Joséphine smiled. Then her eyes lit on the photo of Iris and Gary on the newsstand rack.

"Oh my God, Luca! You're not going to believe what I'm looking at!"

"Let me guess," he said, laughing.

"Oh, no! This isn't at all funny. I'll call you back."

She quickly bought a copy of the paper, and read it in her building stairway.

Philippe had gone to pick Alexandre up from school. Every Monday, he got out at 6:30 p.m. after his extra English class.

"I understand everything, Dad! Absolutely everything."

Their new ritual was to walk home together, speaking English. *Children like regular routines*, Philippe thought. *They're* *more conservative than adult*s. Holding Alexandre's hand, he felt deeply happy, and he walked slowly to make the trip last.

Alex was saying how he'd scored two goals in soccer when Philippe noticed the photo of Iris on the front page of a tabloid at his usual newsstand. He quickly led them on a detour so Alex wouldn't see it. When they got to their apartment door, he slapped his forehead.

"I'm such an idiot. I forgot to buy *Le Monde*. Go on in, son, I'll be back in a minute."

He went out to buy the tabloid and read it as he climbed the stairs. He stuffed it into his coat pocket, thinking hard.

Hortense and Zoé were walking back from school together. This only happened once a week, and Zoé used the time to perfect the detached and haughty look her sister used to turn men on. It didn't come naturally to Zoé, but Hortense was working hard to teach her.

"It's the key to success, Zoé-cannoli. C'mon, try!"

Zoé felt she'd become more important in her sister's eyes since she'd revealed The Big Secret. Hortense was being nicer to her, and less nasty at home. *Almost not nasty at all*, mused Zoé as she squared her shoulders the way Hortense told her to.

That's when they spotted the photo of Aunt Iris on the newsstand tabloid, with an inset photo of Gary and Hortense. They stopped in their tracks.

"We're going to pretend we didn't see a thing," Hortense declared. "We're staying out of this."

"But we'll come back and buy it when no one's looking, right?"

"No. I already know what's in it."

"Oh, please, Hortense!"

"We're staying out of it, Zoé. I mean it."

Zoé walked by the newsstand without a sideways glance.

Feeling a little embarrassed, Iris decided to lie low for a while. *Did I go too far, sending the photos to the newspaper anonymously?* She thought it would be funny, that it would stir things up a little and get her back in circulation. But her mother's reaction made it clear that she now had a scandal on her hands.

Iris, Philippe, and Alexandre were having dinner together, but Alex was the only one talking. He was saying he'd scored three soccer goals in a row.

"Before, you said two goals. You shouldn't tell lies, Alex."

"Two or three. I can't remember exactly, Dad."

At the end of the meal, Philippe folded his napkin and said, "I think I'll take Alexandre to London for a few days, to visit my parents. He hasn't seen them in a while, and it's almost winter break. I'll call the school to let them know."

"Are you coming with us, Mom?"

"No," he said quickly. "Your mother's very busy right now."

"Is it still the book?" Alexandre asked, sighing. "I'm sick of that book."

Iris nodded and turned her head. She had tears in her eyes.

Gary asked if he could have the last piece of baguette, and Joséphine resignedly handed it to him. The two girls watched in silence as he mopped up the ratatouille on his plate.

"Why are you all looking so gloomy?" he asked. "Is it because of the pictures in the paper?"

They looked at one another in relief. So he knew!

"It's no big deal," he said. "They'll talk about it for a week or two and then it'll go away. Can I have some more cheese?"

"But your mother . . ."

"Mum? She would probably punch Iris's lights out for doing that. But she's not here, and she isn't gonna find out."

"How do you know?"

"I'm pretty sure they don't read that tabloid crap in Mustique. Plus, hey, my stud factor is really going to shoot up! All the girls will want to go out with me! I'll be the star of the school, at least for a few days."

"Is that all this means to you, Gary?" Jo asked, dumbfounded.

"Hey, you should have seen the British press in the days of Diana. It was pretty terrible, but it eventually died down. Can I finish the Camembert? And is that all the bread?"

Defeated, Joséphine nodded.

As she had hoped, the photos put Iris back in the media spotlight, if only briefly.

"I don't understand this flurry of attention," she wondered out loud on a popular talk show. "I mean, if a forty-year-old man goes out with a twenty-year-old, it doesn't exactly make headlines. I'm for equal rights for men and women—on all fronts."

Sales of *A Most Humble Queen* started to climb again. Women copied Iris's beauty secrets, and men sucked in their stomachs when they saw her. She was asked to host an evening radio talk show, but declined, saying she wanted to devote herself heart and soul to literature.

Seven thousand miles from the brouhaha in Paris, Antoine was sitting on the veranda of his house in Kenya. He was miserable that he hadn't been able to bring the girls down for winter break. They didn't come at Christmas, either. Jo asked if she could take them to a friend's house in Mustique, and the girls were so excited about going to the Caribbean that he had to say yes. His and Mylène's Christmas was makeshift and sad. Unable to find a turkey at the Malindi market, they cooked wapiti, and ate it in silence. Mylène gave him a diving watch. He didn't have a gift for her. She didn't say anything. They went to bed early.

For Antoine, things were now going really badly.

A particularly aggressive crocodile killed Pong's pet Bambi one day as he was happily waddling along the edge of the swamp. Pong and Ming were devastated.

Mylène, on the other hand, was fine. Her little business was booming, and her partnership with Mr. Wei was taking on new dimensions.

"Leave those dirty beasts and come to China with me," she whispered to Antoine one evening as they climbed under the mosquito netting on their bed.

But leaving would be admitting that the crocodiles had won, and Antoine refused to let that happen. He would walk away from those dirty beasts with his head high. He wanted to have the last word.

Meanwhile, he was spending more and more time with them, especially in the evening. During the day he exhausted himself at work, but after dinner, he would leave Mylène to her spreadsheets and order books and go walking along the swamp.

The idea of going to China for Mylène's cosmetics business didn't appeal to him. It meant a new struggle, and for what? He didn't have the energy to fight anymore.

"But I'll do all the work," said Mylène. "You can keep the books and take it easy."

She just doesn't feel like going alone, Antoine thought. *So now I'm nothing but her boy toy.*

He had started drinking again, while staring at the yellow eyes in the darkness. He imagined he could feel the sarcasm in the crocodiles' gaze. *We kicked your ass*, they seemed to be saying. *Look what you've turned into: a loser. You drink on the sly, you don't want to fuck your girlfriend, you eat wapiti at Christmas. We could rip you to shreds if we felt like it.*

"You filthy bastards!" he growled. "I'll kill you all!"

Antoine missed Joséphine. He missed the girls. When he leaned against the door to his office, it reminded him of the doorway in his old kitchen. Just rubbing his shoulder against the wood took him back to Courbevoie.

Life was so sweet back in Courbevoie, he thought. Courbevoie. Those magic syllables, Cour-be-voie. They set his mind wandering, the way Ouagadougou, Zanzibar, Cap-Vert, or Esperanza once did. To return to Courbevoie. After all, he'd only been gone for two years . . .

A few weeks later, Antoine called Joséphine late at night, and was surprised to get her answering machine. He looked at his watch; it was 1:00 a.m. in France. He hung up without leaving a message. When he called again the next morning, he asked to speak to the girls. She reminded him that they were away on vacation.

"They went to Shirley's house in Mustique."

"Weren't you home last night, Jo? I called, and no one answered."

There was silence on the other end of the line.

"Are you seeing someone?"

"Yes."

"Are you in love?"

"Yes."

"Well, good for you."

There was another silence, longer this time.

"It was bound to happen," said Antoine.

"I didn't go looking for it. I didn't think I would ever interest anyone again."

"But Jo, you're a wonderful person."

"You never used to tell me that."

"'We only recognize happiness by the sound it makes when it leaves.' Who said that, Jo?"

"Jacques Prévert, I think. How are you?"

"Oh, overwhelmed with work, but I'm fine. I'm going to finish paying off the bank loan and I'll send you some money for the girls. Business is much better. I've hit my stride again."

"I'm happy for you."

"Take good care of yourself, Jo."

"You, too, Antoine. I'll tell the girls to call you when they get back."

He hung up, and wiped his sweaty brow. He found a fresh bottle of whiskey on a shelf and polished it off.

Chapter 20

♦ ♦ ♦

*J*osiane felt the first contraction on May 6, at around six in the morning. Remembering her birthing class, she kept track of the time between each contraction. She woke Marcel at seven.

"Marcel, I think it's happening. Junior is coming!"

He sat up like a punch-drunk boxer and muttered, "He's coming? Are you sure, sweetie-pie? Oh my God, he's coming!"

He stumbled out of bed, tripped on the quilt, spilled a cup of water reaching for his glasses, swore, sat back down, swore again, and turned to her, completely at a loss.

"Take it easy, Marcel! Everything's ready to go. I'm going to get dressed. You take that suitcase over there, next to the cupboard. Get the car, and I'll be right down."

"No! No way are you going downstairs by yourself. I'm coming with you."

He jumped in the shower, splashed himself with aftershave, brushed his teeth, and combed the tufts of hair around his bald scalp. Then he stopped dead, unable to choose between two blue shirts, one plain and one striped.

"I have to look my best, honeybunch! I have to look my very best!"

Josiane looked at him affectionately and chose a shirt at random.

"You're right! That one's brighter, more youthful. And a tie, a tie! I want to greet him in style!"

"You don't need a tie."

"Oh, yes, I do."

He came out holding three neckties. Josiane again picked one at random, and again Marcel approved.

"I don't know how you can stay so calm. Don't forget to time the contractions!"

"Are you done in the bathroom?"

"Yes. I'll go get the car and come back up for you. Don't go anywhere, okay? Promise?"

Marcel left, came back because he'd forgotten the keys, left again, and came back again: he couldn't remember where he'd parked the car. Josiane calmed him down and told him where the car was. He went out again, but this time walked into the kitchen by mistake.

She burst out laughing, and he turned around, visibly upset.

"Don't make fun of me, sweetie-pie! I've been waiting for this day for thirty years. I'm not sure I'm able to drive."

In the taxi, Marcel kept giving the driver instructions. The amused cabbie, who had eight children of his own, watched the father-to-be in his rearview mirror. On the backseat, Marcel was clutching Josiane, his arms around her like a second seat belt.

"Are you okay, sweetie-pie? Are you okay?" He was mopping his brow and panting like a puppy.

When they arrived at the clinic Marcel gave the driver a hundred-euro bill, and the man grumbled that he didn't have any change.

"I don't want change! It's for you. My son's first cab ride!"

"Hey, I'll give you my number, and you call me whenever your son feels like going somewhere."

The baby let out his first cry at half past twelve. The new father almost fainted, and had to be led out of the delivery room. Josiane held her breath as they put her wet, sticky son on her belly.

"He's so beautiful! Look how big he is! And strong! Have you ever seen such a beautiful baby?"

"Never," replied the doctor.

Marcel recovered enough to come back to cut the umbilical cord and give his son his first bath. He was crying so hard he couldn't hold the child and wipe his eyes at the same time, but he wouldn't give him to anyone else.

"It's me, baby. It's Daddy! Do you recognize me? See, sweetie-pie? He recognizes my voice. He turned his head toward me, and he stopped squirming. My son! My boy! Wait till you see the life we've got in store for you, your mother and I. A life fit for a prince! You'll have to work, too, because here on earth, if you don't bust your butt, you don't get anywhere. But don't worry! I'll show you how. Just wait and see."

"This son of yours has his work cut out for him," the obstetrician said with a smile. "What are you going to call him?"

"Marcel!" he practically shouted. "Marcel Grobz, like me."

Mother and child were taken upstairs to the luxury recovery suite that Marcel had booked. Now he didn't want to leave.

"You're sure they're not going to switch him on us?"

"Of course not!" said Josiane. "He's wearing his bracelet. Besides, he's the spitting image of you."

Marcel strutted proudly back over to the little bassinette.

"You have to go register him at city hall, and I need to rest," she said. "I'm a bit tired."

"Oh, so sorry, honeybunch. It's just hard for me to leave. I'm scared I'll never see him again."

Marcel took some pictures of his handsome new son, now bathed and clean, sleeping in a white onesie. Then he left, bumping into the door on the way out.

Josiane started to sob with happiness. She cried for a long time. Then she got up, took baby Marcel in her arms, and fell asleep with him snuggled against her.

Ginette organized a party for Marcel at Casamia, and the staff gathered for a buffet under the wisteria vines, which she'd decorated with little blue bows.

As the proud papa stood drinking champagne, his cell phone rang.

"Sweetie-pie?" he cried.

But it wasn't sweetie-pie, it was Henriette. She was at the bank, checking her accounts and being updated by her financial adviser, Madame Lelong.

"There's something I don't understand, Marcel. We seem to have two separate accounts. There must be a mistake!"

"No, dear, there's no mistake. We have separate accounts now, and separate lives too. My son was born last night. His name's Marcel. Eight and a half pounds, twenty-one and a half inches—a giant!"

There was a long silence. In the same curt tone, Henriette finally said that she would call him back. She couldn't talk in front of Madame Lelong.

Marcel rubbed his hands in delight.

"Call back anytime, dear Henriette, and I'll give you the surprise I have in store for you!"

René and Ginette looked at him with relief. At long last, Marcel was deposing the tyrant.

Like all small-minded and malicious people, Henriette was con- stitutionally unable to abandon her preconceived ideas, or to hold herself responsible for her own unhappiness. She preferred to blame other people.

That day was no exception. She quickly wrapped up matters with Madame Lelong and left the bank. Gilles was waiting with the sedan's door open, but she dismissed him, telling him to wait. She had an errand to run that didn't require the car.

Henriette started walking around the block to clear her mind. She had to think, to regroup. She was so used to having Marcel under her thumb that she had signed papers during the Zang Brothers acquisition without really paying attention. *That was a big mistake*, she thought as she strode along, her knees clicking like knitting needles. *I have to change my tactics.*

But a little farther along she stopped, struck by a horrifying thought: she was now dependent on Marcel! She would have to swallow her pride and keep thoughts of revenge in check. Separate accounts . . . Her savings gone . . . What would be left for her?

She stumbled into a portico and dialed his number.

"Is it Natasha? Did that slut bear you a child?"

"Wrong again!" chortled Marcel. "It's Josiane Lambert, the mother of my child—and my future wife."

"You're sixty-six years old. You're being a damned fool!"

"Nothing's foolish when you're in love, dear."

"Love! The woman's just after your money and you call it love."

"Ah, now you're being vulgar, Henriette! But you don't have to worry about money. I won't leave you naked on the street to fend for yourself. You can have our apartment, and I'll send you a stipend every month, enough to live comfortably for the rest of your days."

"A stipend! You know where you can stuff your stipend! I have a right to half your assets, Marcel!"

"Correction: you *had* the right. But not anymore. Remember all those papers you signed? If you'd bothered reading them, you would have realized you were formally stepping down as CEO and ceding me your stock in the company. You're out of my life, Henriette. Your signature is worth zilch now. You can go sign rolls of toilet paper, for all I care."

"You have no right to speak to me this way!"

"Why not? You spoke to me this way for years. Today, my dear, I'm the bluebird of happiness. You should take advantage of it, because tomorrow I may turn vicious."

Then, like all small-minded and malicious people, Henriette had a last small-minded and malicious thought.

"What about Gilles and the car?" she barked. "Can I keep them?"

"I'm afraid not. First, because Gilles can't stand you, and second, because I will need him to drive my queen and my little prince around. I have a son, Henriette! A son, and a woman who loves me. I've started my life over. It took me a long time to shake off your yoke, but I've done it. I hear from Gilles that you've been walking around the block, spinning like a top. So keep walking. When you're exhausted and you've emptied your sack of venom, you can go home and contemplate your fate."

"You're drunk, Marcel! You've been drinking!"

"Yes, I have. I've been celebrating ever since my son was born this morning. But my head is clear. You can hire all the lawyers in the world, and you'll still be fucked!"

Henriette hung up in outrage, only to see Gilles drive off around the corner, abandoning her to her new solitude.

"What are you thinking about, Jo?"

"That I've been with you every afternoon for almost six months."

"Does that seem like a long time?"

"Like the blink of an eye."

She moved closer to Luca, who was propped up on one elbow and was running a finger over her naked shoulder. She brushed a lock of hair out of his eyes and kissed him.

"I'm going to have to go," she said with a sigh. "I wish I could stay forever."

Everything happens so quickly, she thought while she was driving home. The kids were back from Mustique, brown as berries. And Gary had been right: nobody talked about the tabloid article. Life goes on.

A few weeks later, Joséphine went to have lunch with Iris. Philippe and Alexandre were in London, where they went more and more often. Was Philippe thinking of moving there? Jo had no idea. They didn't speak much anymore, didn't see each other. *That's just as well,* she told herself each time she found herself thinking about him.

Carmen served the sisters lunch in Iris's study.

"Why did you do it, Iris? What was the point?"

"It was just for fun. I wanted people to be talking about me again. And instead, I blew it! Philippe is avoiding me, and I had to tell Alexandre that it was just a stupid joke. He was so disgusted, I couldn't look him in the eye."

"You're the one who sent the photos, right?"

"Yes."

What's the use of talking about all this? Iris thought wearily. *Why go over it again? I messed up, and I got caught. Life was easy, and I shouldn't have tried for more. I would roll the dice, and the dice were always hot. Then they suddenly went cold.*

Iris shivered and sank deeper into her big sofa.

She looked over at Joséphine, at her serious expression. *She's figured it out. I don't know how she does it. My little sister is all grown up.*

"Didn't it occur to you that it would hurt the people around you?"

God, that sounds nasty, thought Iris. *Why use such dreadful words? Wasn't boredom enough of an excuse?* She looked at her sister again. *Jo was born with so much less than me, and yet she seems to be getting on just fine.*

"Even Hortense has stopped coming over," said Iris. "And we used to get along so well. She must be sick of me, too."

"She's studying for her *bac*, Iris. She's working like a dog, trying for honors. There's a design school in London she wants to go to next year."

"So she really does want to work? I thought she was saying that for show."

"Hortense has changed a lot, you know. She doesn't blow me off like she used to. She's gotten softer."

"How about you, Joséphine? How are you doing? I don't see much of you anymore, either."

"I'm working. We're all working. The atmosphere is very studious at my house."

Joséphine giggled mischievously, and her smile widened into a grin. She radiated the ease of a cheerful, contented woman, and Iris would have given anything to be in her sister's shoes.

For a moment she almost asked, "How do you do it, Jo?" but she held her tongue. She didn't want to know.

Chapter 21

♦ ♦ ♦

𝒥oséphine parked in front of her building and unloaded the groceries she'd picked up before going to Luca's. There was plenty of time to get dinner ready. Gary, Hortense, and Zoé wouldn't be home for at least an hour. She took the elevator up. On the landing she found the hall light and turned it on.

A familiar-looking woman was waiting for her. As Jo struggled to remember who she was, the red triangle suddenly came to her. It was Mylène! The manicurist from the salon, the woman who had run off with her husband. To Jo, it felt as if a century had passed since then.

"Mylène?" she asked hesitantly. "Is that you?"

She nodded and grabbed the bags slipping from Joséphine's grasp as she fumbled for her keys. The two women sat down together at the kitchen table.

"It's about Antoine, isn't it? Did something happen to him?"

Mylène nodded, and her shoulders began to shake. Joséphine took her hands, and Mylène burst into tears, sobbing on Jo's shoulder. Joséphine rocked her for a long time.

"He's dead, isn't he?"

Through her tears, Mylène managed to say yes, and Joséphine held her tighter. She couldn't imagine Antoine dead. She started to cry as well, and the two of them hugged each other, weeping.

After a while, Joséphine sat up and wiped her eyes.

"How did it happen?"

Mylène told her about everything: the farm, the crocodiles, Mr. Wei, Pong, Ming, Bambi. How the work got harder and harder. The crocodiles refused to reproduce. They attacked anyone who came near them. The Chinese workers went on strike and started stealing chickens.

"Meanwhile Antoine was drifting away," she said. "He was there, but not there. At night he would go talk to the crocodiles. Every evening he'd say that: 'I'm going to talk to the crocs. I have to make them listen!' As if they could listen! One evening he was walking by the swamp as usual, and he waded into the water. Pong had shown him that if you kept very still, you could get right next to the crocodiles and not get bitten. But they ate him alive!"

Mylène burst into tears again.

"There was almost nothing left of him," she said, pulling a tissue from her purse. "They just found his shoes and the diving watch I gave him for Christmas."

Joséphine straightened. "We can't let the girls know, Mylène. Hortense has her *bac* in a week, and Zoé is so sensitive. I'll tell them soon, just not right now. He'd stopped writing, and he never called anymore, so they won't expect news of him right away."

And then it all came back to her: the day they met, so many years ago.

The first time Joséphine saw Antoine, it was on the street. He was holding a map of Paris and looked lost. Taking him for a foreigner, she screwed up her courage and walked over to him. Very slowly, she asked, "Can I help you?"

He answered in perfect French. "I have an important business meeting and I can't find the address. I'm worried about being late."

He showed her the address, which was on avenue de Friedland.

"That's not very far. I'll take you there."

It was a beautiful day, the first day of summer. She had just passed her teaching qualification exam in literature. She was wearing a light summer dress and was out for a stroll.

She led him to a large polished wood door on avenue de Friedland.

He was sweating. He wiped his face and asked, "Do I look all right?"

She laughed and said: "You look great."

The man thanked her, looking a bit sheepish—a look Joséphine would long remember. Then he said his name was Antoine, and suggested they meet for a drink after his appointment. "If it goes well, we'll celebrate my new job. If not, you can console me." The invitation felt a little clumsy, but she accepted.

That was a good deed, she'd thought to herself. *I was of some use today. Poor man, he looked so uncomfortable, like a little boy. Maybe that's why I didn't get all tongue-tied with him.*

To kill time while she was waiting, she went for a walk on the Champs-Elysées, bought an ice cream cone and some lipstick. She met him back at the same door. But the man who came out was now dashing and self-confident, almost imperious.

Had she idealized him while she was waiting, or did she misperceive him the first time? Later, she would wonder if her feelings for a person depended on the way she perceived them. Where do feelings come from? she wondered. From a brief, variable impression? From a shifting point of view that's then replaced by an illusion that you project onto the other person?

There won't be any more shifts now, she thought. *Antoine is dead, and the image I'll keep of him is of an unfocused but gentle and lovable man.*

"What are you planning to do now?" she asked Mylène.

"I'm not sure. I may go to China. I don't know if the girls told you, but I started a business there. I could earn good money."

Mylène's eyes had brightened. You could tell she was thinking about her projects, her orders, her future earnings.

"In any case, I don't have a choice, because I'm broke. I gave Antoine all my savings." Then she quickly added, "Oh, I'm not asking you for anything! I wouldn't want you to think this was why I came."

When Mylène mentioned money, Joséphine had recoiled slightly. But she looked so sweet and upset that Jo felt guilty about her reaction, and tried to make up for it.

"My stepfather, Marcel Grobz, does business in China. He might be able to give you some advice."

Mylène blushed.

"I already used his name to find a lawyer once," she admitted.

She was quiet for a moment, fiddling with the handle of her purse. "But it's true that it would help me if I could see him."

Joséphine wrote down Marcel's address and telephone number. "You can tell him I sent you, and that—"

She was interrupted by a clatter in the stairway and the sound of a door being thrown open. Zoé came running in, red-faced and out of breath, but stopped short when she saw Mylène.

"Where's Daddy?" she asked her. "Isn't he with you?"

Zoé went over to Joséphine and put her arm around her waist.

"Mylène was just telling me that Daddy has gone off to scout locations farther inland. He wants to expand his crocodile pens. That's why you haven't heard from him in a while."

"Didn't he take his computer with him?" she asked suspiciously.

"A computer in the jungle?" exclaimed Mylène. "What an idea, Zoé! Aren't you going to give me a kiss?"

Zoé hesitated. After a glance at her mother, she gave Mylène a cautious peck on the cheek.

When Hortense arrived, she was as surprised and wary as her sister.

They're taking my side, Joséphine was pleased to realize. *Not a very admirable thought, but comforting just the same.* She repeated to Hortense what she had told Zoé, with Mylène nodding approvingly.

But Hortense didn't seem convinced. She went to her room, opened her books and notebooks, and started to do her homework. But something in the house felt out of whack. *What the heck was Mylène doing in the kitchen with Mom, and the two of them looking upset and teary? Something's happened to Dad, and Mom isn't telling me.*

She stuck her head out into the hallway and called her mother. Joséphine came to her room.

"Something's happened to Dad, and you won't say what it is."

"Listen, baby—"

"I'm not a baby anymore, Mom. I'm not Zoé. I'd rather know."

She said this so coldly, with such determination, that Joséphine wanted to hug her to prepare her for the news. But Hortense jerked free.

"Stop beating around the bush. He's dead, is that it?"

"Hortense, how can you say that?"

"Because it's true, isn't it?"

Hortense was holding her arms rigidly by her sides, and looked at her mother with unconcealed hostility.

"Yes, he's dead," Jo said. "He was eaten by a crocodile."

"He's dead," Hortense repeated. "He's dead."

Joséphine tried to come close again, to put her arm around her shoulder, but Hortense shoved her away so roughly that Joséphine fell onto the bed.

"Don't touch me!" she screamed. "I can't stand you, Mom. You're driving me crazy! You're just, you're just . . ."

She sighed in exasperation. Head down, Joséphine waited.

Hortense plopped down on the bed next to her, but far enough away so they didn't touch.

"When Dad was out of work and hanging around the house, you put on your fake composure, you did your sweet, reassuring routine, to make us think that everything was fine, that Dad was doing a 'job search.' Nothing to worry about, right?"

"And you blame me for that?"

"I blame you for being so damned clueless. You just don't get it. You go on the balcony and talk to the stars like some sort of moron. You think I never heard you, babbling away? I felt like pushing you right off the damned balcony. I used to feel sorry for you and hate you at the same time."

Joséphine waited in silence.

"You were getting uglier and flabbier by the day, whereas Dad at least tried to keep going. He would shower and shave, and put on his nice suits. It wasn't surprising that he turned to Mylène. She made him feel like a man, at least.

"And those lectures you used to give about money and life values. They made me want to puke! When Dad left, you'd practically forgotten how to drive a car. You spent whole evenings balancing your checkbook, counting your pennies. We only survived because Uncle Philippe has money and connections. If he hadn't been there, where would we be now? Tell me that!"

"There's more to life than money, Hortense, but you're too young to realize it."

"I loved Dad so much. He was the one who taught me to stand up straight, to be pretty and different. He took me clothes shopping in Paris, and afterward, we'd drink champagne in fancy bars and listen to jazz. With him I was unique and beautiful. And he gave me something else, a kind of strength he didn't even have. I know he was weak, but to me, he was magical!"

She was sitting up at the edge of the bed. Joséphine kept her distance, allowing Hortense to let out her sorrow however she chose to phrase it.

Suddenly she turned and looked her mother right in the eye.

"But I'll tell you one thing: we're never going to live the way we did when Dad was out of work. I won't do it, you hear? I don't want to go through that ever again! Was he giving you money?"

"Oh, you know—"

"Was he giving you money, yes or no?"

"No."

"So we're able to get by on our own?"

"Yes."

Provided Mom gets the royalties, thought Hortense.

"Zoé mustn't know, that's for sure," she said. "Zoé isn't like me. She needs to have it broken to her gently. I'll leave that to you. That's your department."

She stayed silent for a long time, wrapped up in her sadness and anger.

After waiting a while, Joséphine said, "We'll tell her gradually, and take as much time as it takes. She'll learn to live without him."

"We were already living without him," replied Hortense, abruptly standing up. "Well, that's that. And now I have a *bac* to study for."

Jo left and went into the kitchen, where Mylène, Gary, and Zoé were waiting.

"Mommy, can Mylène stay and have dinner with us?" asked Zoé. "Say yes, Mommy!"

"That's sweet of you, Zoé, but I think I'd better go back to the hotel," said Mylène, kissing her hair. "We're all pretty tired, and I have a long day tomorrow."

She thanked Joséphine and said good-bye, saddened by the thought that she would probably never see them again.

Chapter 22

♦ ♦ ♦

*I*n early June, Hortense and Gary endured their week of *baccalauréat* exams.

Joséphine got up early to make them breakfast. She offered to give them a lift, but Hortense said no, that it would sap her morale.

Hortense came home feeling satisfied at the end of the first and second days, and got through the week without getting too stressed. Gary was more low-key, and didn't act especially worried. They would have to wait until July 4 to find out how they'd done.

Shirley didn't come over to Paris to keep Gary company after all. She had decided to settle in London, and was looking for an apartment. But she called every night, and Gary went to join her as soon as the exams were over.

Zoé graduated to the next grade with honors, as did Alexandre. Philippe took them horseback riding in Evian. He saw Joséphine at the train station the day they left, and kissed her hand. "Forget me not," he murmured. She felt a terrific urge to kiss him.

♦ ♦ ♦

Zoé quit asking for news of her father.

Hortense phoned Capucine, the fashion editor at *Gala,* and landed a three-week internship as an accessory consultant for photo shoots. She left for work every morning, griping about how long it took her to get there by public transportation.

"Shirley isn't here in Courbevoie anymore," she said. "When are we going to move into Paris?"

In fact, Joséphine had been looking at apartments in Neuilly, just across the Seine. It was close, so Zoé wouldn't lose touch with her Courbevoie friends, and Hortense declared that Neuilly suited her perfectly. "It has trees, a Metro, and bus lines, and nicely dressed people with good manners. I won't feel like I'm living on an Indian reservation anymore."

Hortense asked whether they could get the TV out of storage now that exams were over. She wanted to watch the fashion shows on cable. Joséphine signed up for the stations that she wanted, happy to see her daughter moving on.

One Sunday in the middle of June, Joséphine was alone in the house. Hortense was out, but had told her to watch Channel 3 that night, because she might catch a glimpse of her. "Don't miss it, because I won't be on for long."

Around 11:30, Jo was listening for the kids in the stairwell and absentmindedly channel surfing, but regularly switching back to Channel 3 to look for a shot of Hortense. Luca had offered to keep her company, but she turned him down. She didn't want her daughters to see her with the man she was sleeping with. She wasn't ready to combine her life with Luca with her life with the girls.

Jo flipped back to Channel 3, and suddenly there was Hortense, being interviewed. She looked very attractive and relaxed. Made up and with her hair done, she seemed older, more mature. *My God, what a natural she is!* thought Jo admiringly. *She looks like Scarlett Johansson!*

The show host introduced her, told the audience how old she was, and said that she had just taken the *baccalauréat*.

"So how did the exams go?"

"Pretty well, I think," Hortense said, her eyes shining.

"What do you plan to do next?"

Hortense said how badly she wanted to break into the tight-knit fashion world, that she was leaving for design school in London in October but would be thrilled if some Paris designer wanted to offer her a summer internship.

The host interrupted. "But that's not the only reason you've come on the show, is it?"

Joséphine recognized him. He was the same man who had hacked Iris's hair off. Suddenly, she had a sinking feeling she knew what was coming.

"No, it isn't. I'm here to say something about a book," Hortense said, speaking very clearly. "A book that's been a big success recently: *A Most Humble Queen*."

"And you claim that this book wasn't written by its presumed author, your aunt Iris Dupin, but by your mother, Joséphine Cortès."

"That's right. And I brought you the proof: my mom's computer, which has all of her rough drafts."

So that's why I couldn't find my laptop this morning! thought

Joséphine. She had searched for it everywhere, and figured she must have left it at Luca's apartment.

"We had a specialist examine the computer before the broadcast," the host said. "And he confirmed that the computer indeed contains different versions of the manuscript of *A Most Humble Queen*. He also confirmed that the computer belongs to your mother, Joséphine Cortès, a scholar at the Centre National de la Recherche Scientifique."

"She's a specialist in the twelfth century, which is exactly when the novel is set," Hortense said.

"And just to be clear, you're saying that the novel was written not by your aunt, Iris Dupin, but by your mother, Joséphine Cortès?"

"That's right," said Hortense firmly.

"You realize that this is going to cause a major scandal?"

"Yes, I do."

"Yet you're willing to risk ruining your aunt's life."

"Yes."

Hortense was perfectly calm, and it wasn't an act. She looked right into the camera and answered each question without hesitating or becoming flustered.

"I have to ask: Why are you doing this?"

"Because my mom is raising my sister and me on her own. She works really hard, and we don't have a lot of money. I don't want the royalties from the book to go to someone else."

"You're doing this for the money?"

"I'm speaking out mainly for justice for my mother. The money is nice, but it's secondary. My aunt came up with the book idea for fun, and I'm sure she didn't expect it to be such a big success. But I think it's right to render unto Caesar what is Caesar's."

"You've talked about *A Most Humble Queen*'s success. Can you give us some figures?"

"Sure. The book has sold five hundred thousand copies so far. I hear it's being translated in forty-six countries. And Martin Scorsese has optioned the film rights."

"Hortense, you've brought a lawyer with you, Lionel Gaspard, who represents a number of show-business stars, including Mick Jagger. Maître Gaspard, can you tell us what might happen in this kind of situation?"

The lawyer launched into a long discussion of plagiarism, ghostwriting, the trials he knew about, the parties he had represented. Hortense listened, sitting very straight and looking into the camera. She was wearing a green Lacoste shirt that brought out the color of her eyes and the copper tones of her long hair. Joséphine couldn't help but notice the shirt's insignia: a crocodile.

When Gaspard was finished, the interviewer turned back to Hortense, who talked about her mother's brilliant work at the CNRS, her research on the twelfth century, and a personality trait that drove her crazy: her shyness and excessive modesty.

"You know, when you're a kid—and I was a kid until not that long ago—you need to admire your parents, to think that they're the best and the strongest. Parents are your fortress against the world. But I never felt like my mom was tough enough. I thought people would always walk all over her. I revealed a secret today, but I only revealed it to protect my mother."

The studio audience burst into applause.

Joséphine sat rooted to the couch, thinking, *So now the whole world knows!* She was shattered, but also relieved. She was going to get her life back. She wouldn't have to lie, or hide. She'd be able to write under her own name. That was scary too, because now she didn't have any excuse for not trying!

Joséphine had written down a quote from Seneca when she started her graduate studies: *It's not because things are hard that we don't dare; it's because we don't dare that they're hard.* Back then, it was to give herself courage. And now, she was going to dare. Thanks to Hortense.

My daughter, who has no use for love, tenderness, or generosity— my daughter, who faces life with a knife between her teeth—just gave me a gift no one has ever given me before: she looked at me and said, "Go ahead, take your name back! You can do it!" Maybe she does love me, in her own way. Who knows?

Joséphine pushed open the glass door to the balcony and leaned on the railing next to the dead plants. She'd forgotten to throw away the pots. *They're all that's left of Antoine,* she thought, touching them. *And I let them die.*

Glancing up, she saw that the stars were out. She thought of her father and started speaking aloud to him.

"She doesn't know, Daddy. She's so young, she doesn't know anything about life. She thinks she does, she judges everything, judges me . . . At her age, that's natural. She would rather have had Iris for a mother! She doesn't see the love and tenderness I've showered on her from the day she was born. She just doesn't see it.

"Hortense thinks money is everything. But money wasn't the reason I was there when she came home from school to make her a snack, or dinner, or lay out her clothes for the next day. Money doesn't buy that, love does. Please make her understand that, Daddy. Bring my little girl back to me. I love her so much! I'd give everything just to hear her say, 'Mom, I love you.' "

Joséphine paused and put her face in her hands. She prayed with all her might that the stars would hear her, that the little star at the end of the Big Dipper would twinkle.

Just then, Joséphine felt something lightly touch her shoulder—probably the wind, or a leaf falling from the balcony above. She turned around.

It was Hortense. Jo hadn't heard her come out. Joséphine smiled sheepishly, like someone caught doing penance.

"I was looking at your father's plants," she said. "They've been dead for ages. I just forgot to take care of them."

"It's okay, Mom," Hortense said gently. "Don't feel bad."

She helped her mother to her feet. "Come on. You're tired, and so am I. I didn't realize how tiring it would be to say the things I said tonight. You heard them, didn't you?"

Joséphine nodded. "You stood up for me tonight, Hortense. You fought for me. I'm so happy, you can't imagine!"

They were back in the living room, and Jo was feeling chilled and a little shaky. "I don't think I'll be able to sleep tonight," she said. "I'm too excited. Want to have some coffee?"

"Mom! That's just going to keep us awake!"

"I'm already awake, Hortense. You woke me up! You woke me up! I'm sorry, I'm repeating myself—"

Hortense took her mother's hand. "So, do you know what your next book will be about?"

A PENGUIN READERS GUIDE TO

THE YELLOW EYES
OF CROCODILES

Katherine Pancol

An Introduction to
The Yellow Eyes of Crocodiles

Katherine Pancol's delicious novel begins as middle-aged medieval scholar Joséphine Cortès learns that her perpetually unemployed husband, Antoine, is leaving her for a woman named Mylène, a manicurist at a local salon. Even worse, the two plan to run off to Kenya to start a crocodile farm. Frustrated and unsure of herself, Jo must now find a way to support her two daughters—confident, beautiful teenager Hortense and shy, sweet preteen Zoé—while maintaining their suburban middle class way of life. Maybe Jo's nasty mother, a social climber who mocked Antoine and his checkered employment history, was right all along.

Meanwhile, on the right side of the Seine, Jo's sister, Iris, seems to have it all: beauty, enormous wealth, a successful lawyer

3

husband, and a chic Parisian lifestyle. But Iris is struggling with the choices she has made in her life, too. A former film student at Columbia University, she regrets leaving America and her now-famous director ex-boyfriend behind for gossipy, leisurely lunches and endless shopping trips. While seated with a renowned publisher at a dinner party, Iris reveals that she's writing a book—a romance novel set in the Middle Ages—and he immediately asks to see it. The only problem, of course, is that no such book exists and everything she's told him is based on her sister Jo's research.

So, Iris hatches a plan that is seemingly simple and beneficial for everyone: Jo will write the novel and pocket the book advance and any royalties—but the story will be published under Iris's name and she'll take all the credit. Desperate for a new income stream, Jo agrees, ignoring nagging warnings from her conscience and her liberated friend Shirley, who seems to have some secrets of her own. As Jo races toward her deadline, she discovers a newfound love of writing, begins a flirtation with a handsome man she meets in the library, and feels her life changing in ways she hadn't expected. But when the book becomes a runaway bestseller, she begins to wonder who really got the better end of the deal. . . .

International bestselling author Katherine Pancol has created the ultimate entertainment. Told through alternating points of view, this rollicking story features a vividly drawn cast of characters, sharp pacing, and an unsparing eye for comic detail. Fun, contemporary, and irresistibly French, *The Yellow Eyes of Crocodiles* is sure to appeal to readers looking for a smart, guilt-free indulgence.

About Katherine Pancol

Katherine Pancol is one of France's best-known contemporary authors. *The Yellow Eyes of Crocodiles* won the Prix de Maison de la Presse for best novel of the year and has sold 2.4 million copies in thirty languages. Pancol was born in Morocco, grew up in France, taught school in Switzerland, and worked as a journalist at *Paris-Match* and the French *Cosmopolitan*. She lived in New York from 1980 to 1990 and currently resides in Paris.

A Conversation with Katherine Pancol

The title of your book refers to Antoine's new life and livelihood in Africa, but it also seems to work as a metaphor of sorts. What does it mean to you?

One morning when I was in New York I read an article in *The New York Times* about a man who went off to raise crocodiles because he was sure he would make a fortune. He was like a Forty-Niner during the Gold Rush. As it happens, raising crocodiles can be very profitable, because every part of the animal can be used, from its hide to its blood and claws. Antoine thinks he'll make a fortune and realize his dream of becoming a rich, powerful businessman. In fact, the opposite happens. He winds up bankrupt and despairing, tracked by the crocodiles who watch him at night, waiting to get close enough to devour him. The crocodiles' yellow eyes shining in the darkness represent the appeal of riches, the glittering gold that leads men to their doom—and women, too.

I think the story illustrates the situation modern people are in. They're dealing with their bosses, bankers, creditors, and sometimes their partners, while being tracked by "crocodiles" who have just one thing in mind: swallowing them whole.

Joséphine is a medieval history scholar. Why did you choose this particular time period as her area of interest, and what inspired the story of Florine specifically as the subject of Jo's novel?

I always begin my novels with a bare-bones story and a few little details, which then grow like a snowball. Here is how *Crocodiles* got started: I own a small seaside house in Normandy, and I love to go swimming early in the morning when there's nobody else around. The beach isn't "a" beach anymore, but "my" beach. One day I met a woman on "my" beach, and was very upset. Who did she think she was, daring to come on my beach? But we swam and talked, and then started to have coffee together after swimming, and we became friends. It turns out she worked as a high-level university researcher. These eminent professors can spend their lives studying very, very specific times and topics in French and world history.

This woman was an expert on the periodicals that itinerant peddlers sold to girls in the eighteenth-century French countryside. I was fascinated, and I asked her hundreds of questions, sensing that I might have the beginning of a story. I also learned that this woman had two daughters; one of whom was very nice, and the other of whom was hateful and mean to her.

So for *Crocodiles*, I stole her job, her daughters, and the kind of sweetness and passivity she had about her. But I decided that Joséphine's period would be the twelfth century, because it isn't studied much in French schools (we usually start around the fourteenth century), and I figured I would learn a lot of history I didn't know. I love learning new stuff. I feel unhappy if I don't learn something new every day.

Like your character Iris, you studied film writing at Columbia University. How has this experience informed your writing style?

Being at Columbia in the 1980s was the icing on the cake, because by then I had already been working on writing. I read a lot as a girl, all sorts of books. I would go to the library and read authors in alphabetical order. I must've read Dostoevsky when I was twelve! We didn't have a television, so in the evening I would read, and I majored in comparative literature, studying all the great French, American, Russian, and German writers. I became a journalist, first for *Paris-Match*, and then for the French *Cosmopolitan*. There I met a terrific woman named Juliette Boisriveaud, who taught me how to write. She must have felt I had talent, and she got me to "deliver" my words.

I published my first novel, *Moi d'abord*, in 1979. It was a huge success in France, selling more than 300,000 copies. This allowed me to go live in New York, and thanks to a friend, I was able to audit creative writing classes at Columbia. What a joy that was! Talking about narrative structure, the rhythm of paragraphs, building the intensity of a plot. It was a pleasure spending two years around people who were as passionate about writing as I was. I had a wonderful time, and I came away with that classic piece of advice, "Show, don't tell." Don't write, "It was snowing." Instead, show the footsteps in the snow, the crunch of snow under your boots, how wet gloves feel or smell.

All of the characters in this book seem to be experiencing what Americans call a "midlife crisis." What makes midlife such a challenging period, and how, in your opinion, can we manage it more gracefully?

There is a moment in *Crocodiles* when Joséphine says that you can't always avoid making the big choices in life. You have to decide, not let somebody else do it for you. Who am I? What do I want to do? Where is my place in the world? Why am I afraid? Am I responsible for what happens to me? Etc. At some point, you have to answer those questions. Face life without cheating. If you don't, if you lie to yourself, you can find yourself facing failure, illness, divorce, or unemployment. In other words, life has made the decision for you. It's saying, "You don't want to choose how to live? I'll force you to." And that's what makes a novel: the confrontation between life and you, the moment you are facing yourself and you have to take your life in hand, or it will escape you. It's a very dramatic moment. But life is generous; it gives you time, doesn't hit you all at once. It usually gives you several chances to change and grow. But if you run away each time, it will come crashing down on you. And that's often what's called a midlife crisis.

Among the themes you explore is the notion that it's never too late to reinvent yourself, or even to get to know yourself. Can you talk about this idea and how it came to be part of the novel?

I think life is like a dance partner—sometimes it sweeps us off in a glittering waltz, and our head spins with happiness. Sometimes it steps on our toes and causes us pain. You have to accept every part of the dance. Not just hold on to the moments of happiness but also take advantage of the times when nothing is working to ask yourself what you can learn from them. And while you're learning, you reinvent your life, you begin it anew. There's no particular age to start again. The main thing is to stay alive, really alive. To learn, to challenge yourself, to move ahead. Not to sit on the sidewalk feeling sorry for yourself, but get up and move on. To waltz with life!

The Yellow Eyes of Crocodiles features multiple interwoven narratives. What was your process for creating and juggling the storylines?

E. M. Forster says that a novel's action has to come from inside the characters and their psychology, and not be imposed from the outside. That's why you have to spend time working on your characters. You must know everything about them, including details that you won't use but are part of the person's dynamic and add to the richness of the plot. Before I start writing, I spend a lot of time with my characters, like a theater director rehearsing every scene. The characters become so intense and alive that when they step onstage I hear a voice in my head yelling, "Action!" And then I watch and follow them. All I have to do is write.

As you alternate points of view, even the most flawed characters here are given a chance to tell their story, and the reader is able to identify with their insecurities and disappointments. Which characters surprised you along the way?

They all surprised me! Even if I know many things about them, when they step onstage, they can always slip away and go off in some direction I hadn't expected. It's like raising children. You think you've given them the best of everything, and nourished them with beautiful things and beautiful values. And then they can go off the rails completely, or else they do things that are so wonderful you couldn't have imagined them! When I start a novel, my characters are all very well behaved, and they do what I tell them. By the time I reach the end, I'm struggling to chase after them to wrap up the plot, and they're running off in every direction.

Iris is concerned that the book Joséphine has written is "women's fiction." How do you feel about this genre and how would you categorize your own writing?

I find that kind of question very hard to answer. I write, I'm happy when I find just the right word; I tell stories, and I tell myself stories. I don't know who will read them and, to be honest, that's not my concern. I know that women tend to buy novels, but that's all. Having said that, I get lots of e-mails from men who write me after reading books they borrowed from their wives!

There are two sequels to The Yellow Eyes of Crocodiles. *What is it about these characters that keeps you coming back to them?*

It's their fault! They just won't go away! Usually when I finish a novel the characters disappear once I write "The End." But when I finished *Crocodiles*, I realized they weren't leaving. They were staying in my life. I thought about them all the time. I would wonder what they were doing, who they were becoming. So I wrote *La valse lente des tortues* (*The Slow Waltz of the Turtles*) in 2008. And when that was finished, they came tiptoeing back again, and I got the idea for the first scene of *Les écureuils de Central Park sont tristes le lundi* (*The Central Park Squirrels Are Sad on Monday*) in 2010. So we're off again!

QUESTIONS FOR DISCUSSION

1. Why do you think Joséphine reacts the way she does when Antoine leaves her? What are her coping strategies?

2. In the wake of her parents' divorce and their new lifestyles, Hortense is not particularly nice to her mother. Do you think Hortense's behavior ultimately helps or hurts Joséphine?

3. Iris and Joséphine are near opposites. What do these sisters secretly think of each other and what do they—or could they—learn from each other?

4. Love and money are intertwined throughout this book. From what you've seen of these characters, how can money buoy or damage a relationship?

5. How does Antoine's experience in Africa change him? Do you think this change is a positive one, and why or why not?

6. History repeats itself in Iris and Joséphine's family. What patterns do you notice running among the generations?

7. While this novel is clearly set in France, its themes are not unique to its setting. In what ways is the story culturally specific and in what ways is it universal?

8. Over time, all of the marriages in this book have soured. How might any or all of them be salvaged, or were they doomed from the beginning?

9. As the rift in their marriage widens, Iris and Philippe begin to suspect each other of dishonesty. Were you surprised by what the two learned about their suspicions?

10. How has Joséphine's life been transformed by the experience of becoming an author? What do you imagine comes next for her?

To access Penguin Readers Guides online,
visit the Penguin Group (USA) Web site at www.penguin.com.